A Conversation on Health and Healing

Centenary Year of Medical Education 1918-2018
Christian Medical College, Vellore

A Conversation on Health and Healing

Centenary Year of Medical Education 1918-2018
Christian Medical College, Vellore

Editors
D. K. Sahu
Arul Dhas T

2019

A Conversation on Health and Healing: Centenary Year of Medical Education 1918-2018: Christian Medical College, Vellore — jointly published by the Rev. Dr. Ashish Amos of the Indian Society for Promoting Christian Knowledge (ISPCK), Post Box 1585, Kashmere Gate, Delhi-110006 and Christian Medical College (CMC), Vellore–632004

© Christian Medical College, Vellore, 2019

ISBN: 978-93-88945-24-0

Laser typeset by

ISPCK, Post Box 1585, 1654, Madarsa Road, Kashmere Gate, Delhi-110006
• *Tel:* 23866323

e-mail: ashish@ispck.org.in • ella@ispck.org.in
website: www.ispck.org.in

Contents

Foreword 1
   Anna B Pulimood   ...   *ix*

Foreword 2
   J. V. Peter   ...   *xi*

Editorial
   D. K. Sahu and Arul Dhas T   ...   *xiii*

Keynote Address
"Waiting for God: Towards a Theology of Health and Wholeness"
   Nicholas John Wood   ...   1

A Response to the Keynote Address by Professor Nicholas John Wood
"Waiting for God: Towards a Theology of Health and Wholeness:
   Joseph George   ...   28

Part-1
Reconceptualization of Healing Ministry

Minority Within Minority
'If we Talk the Talk, we have to Walk the Walk'
   Dhirendra Sahu   ...   47

'I was Stranger':
Towards a Theology of Hospitality
   Samuel Richmond Saxena   ...   58

Understanding of Health and Healing in Religious Context of India
   Ravi Tiwari   ...   75

Disruptive Agenda and the Kingdom of God
Reflections on John Chapter 9
  Jayakumar Christian   ...   82

Suffering, Healing and Meaning of Life
  Joshua Kalapati   ...   90

Part-2
Healing Ministry as a Vocation

A Personal Search for Deeper Meaning
  John Oommen   ...   103

Healing and Wholeness
  Sunil Chandy   ...   111

Healing-My Passion and Vocation!
  Selva Titus Chacko   ...   119

Lessons from Jesus' Ministry of Healing
  Sara Bhattacharji   ...   127

An Expected Career and an Unexpected Vocation
  Ruby Nakka   ...   134

Vocation: An Allied Health Scientist's Perspective
  Hima   ...   141

Part-3
Healing Ministry and Counselling

Possibilities of Pastoral Care and Counselling
  B.J. Prashantham   ...   155

Not Cured But Healed
  Stanley C. Macaden   ...   161

Mission of God and Pastoral Counselling
  Richard Howell   ...   170

Theology of Healing
  M J Paul   ...   180

A Theology of Health
  John Swinton   ...   186

Mission of God and Pastoral Counselling
  Edison Samraj   ...   192

Listening to One Body, Many Parts and Myriad Stories
  Reena George   ...   198

Healing: A Pastoro-Praxis Reading
  R. Christopher Rajkumar   ...   206

Part-4
Identity and Accountability in Healing Ministry

Identity, Credibility, Responsibility
  Anna B Pulimood   ...   213

Towards a Renewal in the Ministry of Healing
  Valson Thampu   ...   223

Identity-Credibility-Accountability
  Joyce Ponnaiya   ...   242

Accountability and Christian Healthcare
  Hugh Skeil   ...   246

Part-5
Patient Perspectives about Healing

A Patient's Understanding of Healing
  Usha Jesudason   ...   261

My Journey from Brokenness towards Healing
  Anthony Samy   ...   267

From 'Take up your Bed and Walk' to 'My Grace is Sufficient for You'
  Reema Samuel   ...   272

The Care-Giver's Cross
  Bibhudutta Sahu   ...   277

Part-6
Pastoral Care and Healing Ministry

Biblical Interpretation in Healing Ministry
  Arul Dhas T   ...   291

"To Serve: A Counter Pedagogy of 'To Be Served"
  Deepak Gnana Prakash   ...   298

Spiritual Care Through Healing Communities
  Finney Alexander   ...   305

Ministry to the Dying
  Samson Varghese   ...   315

Being and Becoming a Community of God's People
  Sunny Philip   ...   320

Inclusive Hospitality of God's Kingdom
  Joseph Devaraj D   ...   330

Part-7
Conversation

Conversation   ...   339

A Centenary Thanksgiving Sermon
  Nicholas John Wood   ...   352

Contributors   ...   359

Foreword 1

The centenary year of the Christian Medical College, Vellore was a time for thanking God for his countless blessings and faithfulness to us over the past 100 years. It was also a time for us to renew our commitment to the vision of our founder and review the implications of being involved in 'building the kingdom of God' in our lives and our work for the institution today.

The challenges we are facing due to enforced changes in our admission processes, the rapid expansion of our health care services and widening outreach programs all called for a fresh look at our identity, credibility and accountability. The widening gap between the 'haves' and 'have nots' of our country and the continued marginalization of a large proportion of our population in terms of affordability and accessibility to health care are important reasons for reviewing our understanding of the practice of medicine as a vocation rather than a profession, and the role of the healing ministry of the church in the world today.

I would like to thank Bishop Dr. D.K. Sahu and Rev. Arul Dhas for editing the volume as well as organizing this colloquium with the cooperation of the department of CMC chaplaincy and friends. Their contributions have been immense, and I am sure that the publication of the keynote address, articles and discussion of this colloquium will constitute an important resource for our institution and others in the healing ministry in the decades to come.

Dr. Anna B Pulimood
Principal, CMC Vellore

Foreword 2

The Centenary year of Medical Education in 2018 was a time of celebration and thanksgiving for God's continued guidance and faithfulness to our institution and for enabling us to be a co-worker to build the Kingdom of God. The Colloquium that was organized as part of the Centenary events reaffirmed the vision and commitment passed on through the generations 'to serve and not to be served.' The theme, 'Theology of Health and Healing' enabled us to focus on and initiate conversations on the expectations of the Christian community to deliver healthcare in the context of it becoming commercialized.

It was a privilege for Christian Medical College, Vellore to host this event in December 2018. I am very happy to note that the Colloquium provided a platform for discussion on several aspects of health and healing with inputs from experts in the field of Health and Pastoral Counselling.

I wish to thank Bishop D.K. Sahu and Rev. Dr. Arul Dhas who were the driving force behind this event. I also want to congratulate them for taking the initiative to bring out this publication that collates all the presentations and discussions during the Colloquium. I am confident that this would be a source of inspiration and guide for the healing ministry of the Church.

Dr. J.V. Peter
Director, CMC
Vellore

Editorial

Celebrating one hundred years of Medical Education is a momentous milestone in the life of any Institution but we are not talking about just any Institution. We are talking about the Christian Medical College, Vellore. A Colloquium on the theme 'Theology of Health and Healing was held as part of centenary celebration on 8th and 9th December 2018. It was a Colloquium of conversations in different clusters consisting of fifteen interventions by selected medical doctors, nurses, theologians, educationists, and church leaders presenting ideas to initiate conversation. The Keynote address, given by a Theologian-Pastor-Hospital Chaplain from the University of Oxford, the response to the Keynote address and a Bible study set the tone of the conversation among seventy participants. The participants also had access to the extracts of the articles written by authors who could not attend the Colloquium.

Conversations and friendships are absolutely central in a journey as they serve as significant indicators pointing towards the change and challenges. The many layers of conversations may be called a process of reception, absorbing renewed lives and changed relationships. It intends to be highly particular, sometimes ad-hoc and accidental, lived and living human contexts of commitment. The conversations could be viewed from a perspective of Hospitality. 'Hospitality' may sound alarming as the healthcare providers are incorporating best practices from the hospitality industry to create hospitality-based environments for their patients, accounting for both patient well-being and revenue consideration. But CMC Vellore can explore the same with a deeper theological understanding of Health and Healing, Pain and Suffering, Governance, Management, Patient Care and not the least by the pastoral care.

God became flesh and dwelt among us. He communicated and worked through the life, death and resurrection of Jesus of Nazareth. Theology reflects on this story of healing and we must tell and act out this story. We can only learn to live in heaven in the presence of our creator only when we learn to live on earth here and now, inhabiting the space in which God has placed each one of us with a vocation.

The publication contains the keynote address, response to the keynote address, addresses in different clusters including articles written for each cluster, the conversations during the Colloquium and the centenary thanksgiving sermon preached on 9th December 2018 in the Ida Scudder Auditorium. The centenary volume by the Christian Medical College Vellore is an offering for a larger audience of our alumnus, medical, nursing, allied health fraternity, friends and well-wishers. The story of Thomas Jackson, a professor of divinity in Glasgow is interesting. On his retirement, this elderly divine purposed to accomplish his lifetime dream: to write his greatest work of theology. When Jackson died after four years of labour, it was only this single sentence that was found left behind: "Theology is everything, and everything is theology". This is a simple thesis-yet so profound. A Myopic attitude to theology ends in not being able to see the forest for the trees.

Lastly, a charitable organization is a complex affair like an automobile; it needs a broad highway to run on. It cannot penetrate the little paths; those are for men and women to walk through, with open eyes and hearts full of comprehension. It is often these little bypaths that you can find 'Aunt Ida' on now. Can we find 'Aunt Ida' now in the little bi-paths of India?

Bishop D.K. Sahu

Arul Dhas T

Keynote Address

"Waiting for God: Towards a Theology of Health and Wholeness"[1]

Nicholas John Wood

These theological reflections on health and healing are rooted in my experiences as a pastor and as a teacher, and as someone who has had the privilege of learning something of our diverse human experience in various roles: as a high school teacher, as a church minister, as a university tutor, and for three years as a Chaplain in the Nuffield Orthopaedic Hospital in Oxford. For those three years I interacted not only with the patients who were my prime concern, but also with clinical and nursing staff, with administrators and with domestic staff, and of course with the systems without which no hospital can function, but which can occasionally seem to inhibit our work as much as they facilitate it. I come as a Christian, but also as a Westerner and in particular from Britain, and I am very aware of the ambiguities of the legacy of Britain's colonial history, especially here in India. So, I come in humility, to listen and to learn, as well as to speak. Above all, what I share here, I share as a fellow human being, with all my limitations, but also as one who shares in that faith in Christ which inspires so many of us to work in the various professions and occupations represented in this centenary colloquium.

In reflecting together on this centennial of medical education at CMC Vellore, we cannot but be conscious of the legacy of Dr Ida Scudder, that determined and inspirational pioneer of medical education, especially for women, to whose vision and wisdom we are all profoundly indebted. In 2018 we commemorate the centenary of medical education at CMC, starting with the Licentiate in Medical Practice for women, which subsequently developed into the full degree programme in 1942, and which from 1947 also included men alongside the women students. Today we are not only beneficiaries of that original vision, but also those who have been entrusted to carry that vision into the future, a future which God graciously invites his people to co-create with him.

The English word "hospital" comes from the Latin *hospes*, signifying a stranger or foreigner, hence a guest. Another noun derived from this root, *hospitium*, came to signify hospitality, that is, the relation between guest and host: in other words the *hospitalero* (Spanish), the one who offers hospitality, friendliness, and a generous reception. *Hospes* is thus the root for the English words host, hostel, hotel, hospitality, and of course hospital and hospice. What then is a hospital but a place where the patient, the 'guest', who is sometimes perhaps the client, or indeed the 'customer', can receive a welcome which contributes to their sense of well-being, wholeness, health; or in Biblical terms *Shalom*. Another way to put this would be to suggest that a hospital is a location for Salvation.

Salvation in Christian thought is a far more comprehensive term than is often realized. It concerns the whole person and every aspect of life. One of the lessons which I learned from Bishop Lesslie Newbigin[2] is that salvation is not, in the first instance, a question about what happens to an individual when they die; rather, biblically, it is about the fulfilment of God's purpose for the universe God has created. This is not to say that salvation is not profoundly personal, but to recognize that it is never narrowly individualistic.

Already, at the start of Jesus' ministry, Mark's Gospel reports that the Kingdom is "at hand"(Mark 1:15); in other words the day of salvation has dawned and the experience of redemption and renewal is real for the people whom Jesus encountered in the Palestine of his day. For many of them the salvation that they experienced in their encounter with Jesus of Nazareth came in the form of the healing of their physical, psychological and spiritual ailments. But the New Testament Greek verb *sozo*, refers not only to healing in the sense of 'curing', but also encompasses a wider sense of health and wholeness, that is Salvation. For the Gospel writers Jesus is the origin of salvation, both in the narrower meaning of healing, and in the broader sense of wholeness, *shalom*. Therefore, as a Christian institution, through your ministry of hospitality, in which you serve rather than are served, I would argue that you share not only in the healing work of Christ but in his gift of salvation to the world. But I would further suggest that much of this work involves waiting, sometimes patiently, and more often perhaps impatiently, for the fulfilment of God's purpose, not just in us but also through us; which is to recognize that for all the gifts, skills, expertise and experience that we bring, in the end our work is God's work, and such work inevitably means that we must wait on and for God.

Medicine in the last century – progress and problems

An anniversary is a good time to look back and reflect on the journey on which we and others have come; to give thanks for all that has been accomplished in the fulfilment of Dr Scudder's vision, but also, as in this colloquium, to reflect on the way forward. As we are all aware the vision afforded by hindsight is always 20/20! Looking to the future things often become a little less clear and we do well to pause and consider our next steps. The statistics of your work for the last year make astonishing reading; over 100,000 inpatients treated from all over India and approaching 10,000 patients from other countries. A typical day at CMC Vellore includes the treatment of over 9,000 outpatients and some 2,000 inpatients; you carry out 185 surgical procedures; 2,405 radiological tests, and attend the birth of 55 babies.[3] All this is accomplished by your dedicated staff of clinicians, nurses, domestic staff, administrators, engineers, pharmacists, social workers, teachers and librarians, and not forgetting the chaplains; some 9,500 staff in all, working together under the motto of CMC, "Not to be ministered unto, but to minister", or, as more recent translations of Mark 10.45 would render it, "not to be served, but to serve."

This is remarkable work and its amazing range could scarcely have been imagined by that handful of dedicated staff who opened that single-bedded clinic under Dr Scudder's leadership, a century ago. The progress which these statistics reveal reflects the wider progress of medicine itself over the last century, and many of you gathered here today are better placed than I am to consider its implications. Over this century we might note the development, and now widespread use, of antibiotics since the discovery of Penicillin in 1928, just ten years after the work began here; the incredible developments in transplant and key-hole surgical techniques; the outreach work into the more rural areas to offer preventative care, and CMC's groundbreaking advances in the treatment of Leprosy through the renowned Dr Paul Brand in the 1950s and 60s. Or we might mention the outstanding work of Dr Mary Verghese, and her pioneering work in the surgery of the hand despite herself being confined to a wheelchair following a motoring accident. And the list could go on and on. All this and more is surely to be not just acknowledged but celebrated.

However, as many of you will be well aware, the development of modern medicine is not without controversy. Modern medicine comes at a cost, not simply in terms of finance, time and many other resources, but also brings probing questions about its ethos and its ethics. The British theologian, Stephen Pattison, who has himself served both as a hospital chaplain and as an administrator with a regional community health council, notes that medicine is not merely a personal experience, nor just a scientific paradigm, but a social and political phenomenon: "There is a socio-political context for all kinds of healing, even the healing of Jesus."[4] Indeed, we must remember that, "the whole way that illness is perceived and dealt with in particular societies is heavily dependent on the wider social and political order".[5] Pattison outlines a number of ways in which the inevitably ambiguous experiences of illness and healing have been understood. These include:

1. The (bio)medical model, which focuses on the processes of the body (somatic); he notes that, at least in the West, this tends to be individualistic, with a focus on 'cure'. With the result that it can sometimes be (overly) aggressive in addressing the perceived disorder/s.[6]

2. The psychological model, which recognizes the psychosomatic complex of human experience, and the place which life events, emotions and character play in our experience and response to illness. Such psychological insights "complement and broaden those of the medical model".[7]

3. Epidemiological approaches recognize the ways in which diseases affect whole populations, and notices the various ways in which (especially) poverty and other social factors affect the incidence of disease. "While the ultimate locus of pathology may be the suffering individual, there are all sorts of wider factors which bear upon whether such an individual becomes ill or not and what happens to her once she is ill."[8]

4. Sociological analyses have distinguished between *disease*, that is, the objective symptoms of pathological abnormality; *illness*, which is the subjective experience of disease; and *sickness* which is the socially sanctioned role in response to the above. We should note then that what is considered to be 'sickness', "varies from society to society, from time to time and from place to place ... The identification of sickness is ... heavily contextual."[9]

5. Anthropological approaches situate illness within particular cultures or sub-cultures, which may focus on teleological questions (why?) rather than causal ones (how?) and suggest queries as to whether illness is mainly perceived to be exogenous (from outside) or endogenous (from within); [10] with the result that we may recognize

that our practice is also culturally located: "Western biomedicine, with its scientific language and its focus on individual pathology, fits in with a generally secular view of the universe and a strong emphasis on the supreme importance of the individual as the basic unit of social discourse."[11]

Whatever model, or combination of models, we may use in analyzing the experience of illness and healing for both individuals and society, for Christian practitioners, there are also pressing ethical and theological questions, often framed in terms of what theologians call *theodicy*, that is, 'the vindication of God in the face of evil and suffering'. In other words, the question of why 'bad things happen to good people',[12] and why a good God would allow such things in a world he has created.

The American theological ethicist Stanley Hauerwas argues that the question of theodicy is posed in new ways in our post-Enlightenment world, and this is of course the context in which contemporary medical practice has developed. Hauerwas cites the work of Daniel Callahan, an American Catholic philosopher and social commentator. In *Setting Limits: Medical Goals in an Aging Society* (New York 1987) Callahan asserts that, "Medicine is perhaps the last and purest bastion of our Enlightenment dreams, tying together reason, science and the dream of unlimited human possibilities ... Nature, including the body, is seen as infinitely manipulable and plastic to human contrivance." Such individualistically located medicine agrees Hauerwas "is a potent engine of endless, never-satisfied progress."[13] The issue of sickness and health is of course potent in every age, but it is especially pressing in a post-Enlightenment world since serious illness threatens the radical autonomy of the individual on which the Enlightenment worldview is based.[14] But Hauerwas is also clear that the issue for Christians is not simply that of theodicy, but the broader question of: "how the God in which we ought to believe, should make a difference to the way in which we understand the nature and function of medicine". Especially as Christians, we must ask why we place what Hauerwas calls a "desperate faith in medicine".[15]

Such 'faith in medicine', was famously and fundamentally challenged during the 1970s by the radical Catholic priest and cultural critic, Ivan Illich (1926-2002), in his polemic against modern Western medicine, *Medical Nemesis*.[16] In this work Illich argued that in the last century, what he termed 'the medicalization' of so many of the vagaries of life, including sickness and death, frequently caused more harm than good, and made many people effectively permanent patients. He marshalled a body of statistics to show the shocking extent of post-operative side-effects and drug-induced illness in advanced industrial society. He introduced to a wider public the notion of *iatrogenic* disease. The term *iatrogenesis* (Greek) means 'brought forth by a healer'. According to a recent article in the *Lancet*, it is estimated that 142,000 people died in 2013 from the adverse effects of medical treatment, an increase of 51 percent from approximately 94,000 people in 1990.[17]

Illich claimed that: "The study of the evolution of disease patterns provides evidence that during the last century doctors have affected epidemics no more profoundly than did priests during earlier times. Epidemics came and went, imprecated by both but touched by neither. They are not modified any more decisively by the rituals performed in medical clinics than by those customary at religious shrines."[18] Illich is clear that the evident improvements in public health in the West are due mainly to other factors such as improved nutrition, better sanitation, advances in hygiene and the development of vaccination – a relatively inexpensive and less invasive technique, together with the widespread use of antibiotics. He does concede that:

> "Some modern techniques, often developed with the help of doctors, and optimally effective when they become part of the culture and environment or when they are applied independently of professional delivery, have also effected changes in general health, but to a lesser degree. Among these can be included contraception, smallpox vaccination of infants, and such nonmedical health measures as the treatment of water and sewage, the use of soap and scissors by midwives, and some antibacterial and insecticidal procedures. The importance of many of these practices was first recognized and stated by doctors – often courageous dissidents who suffered for their recommendations – but this does not consign soap,

pincers, vaccination needles, delousing preparations, or condoms to the category of "medical equipment."[19]

Illich's polemical tone unsurprisingly met with a defensive and often dismissive response from the medical professionals of his day, but in recent years his thought has been revisited. For example, Dr Seamus O'Mahony, Consultant Gastrologist at Cork University Hospital in Ireland, suggests that, "A new generation has been influenced by Illich's ideas" and "a growing resistance is developing within medicine" to the trends identified and anticipated by Illich.[20] These movements include the notion that "industrialisation and institutionalisation had robbed people of their freedom and handed over fundamental aspects of human life to professions and their institutions". Today some people, including some medical professionals, are more inclined to recognize that "modern medicine had hubristically taken on a mission to eradicate pain, sickness even death", when rather these should be understood as "eternal human realities, which we must learn to cope with; in fact coping with these verities is what it means to be 'healthy.'"[21] Illich prophetically anticipated the growth of and widespread concern over the influence of the pharmaceutical industry.[22] Dr Joanna Moncrieff, a practicing consultant psychiatrist in North East London, who teaches and researches at University College London, is also critical of the dependency of her field on pharmaceutical treatments. Moncrieff recalls that Illich's book "blew her away" as a medical student and comments that, "Re-reading it recently, I was struck by its originality, and audacity, as well as [its] continuing relevance ..." She suggests that his basic thesis, that "technological hubris has led us to forget the limits of the human condition" remains sound, and she concludes: "Medical miracles come at a cost – and that cost is dignity."[23]

Dr O' Mahony is inclined to argue that while Illich's diagnosis was "astute," "his prescriptions were risible."[24] But he acknowledges that, in line with Illich's predictions, "Healthcare makes up 10% on the entire global economy." Similarly, O' Mahony recognizes that in the intervening period, at least in the West, death has moved from the home to the hospital, "And hospitals have become a dustbin for all sorts of societal problems, not just dying"; although, he also argues that contrary to Illich's assumptions, these developments were certainly not sought by the medical profession. Indeed many within the medical profession "view with alarm the direction that modern healthcare has taken."[25] These social, cultural, and indeed medical, critiques are echoed in some of the recent theological discussions to which we now turn.

Theological responses

In his already-mentioned volume, *Alive and Kicking*, Stephen Pattison notes that, "Illness and healing are central to human existence ... a theology which cannot speak to the issues raised by disease and suffering could well seem a theology not worth having."[26] But there is little agreement, suggests Pattison, in either in the religious or the medical worlds, in fundamental areas such as the nature of disease or its treatment: "What exactly is the relationship between institutional healing practices and ideologies, and isolated healers or healing communities?"[27] Christian responses must take account not only of the various explanations of disease within the medical and other professions, but also be alert to the diversity of illness and the enormous range of experience among patients. This is also true when reflecting on the causes of illness and the values reflected in our responses. Pattison comments: "Questions about whether disorder should be regarded as a manifestation of personal evil forces, as a result of personal responsibility for immoral behaviour, or as a result of the randomness of the universe, are to some extent questions of values and morality."[28] These, and even wider responses and explanations, are not necessarily mutually exclusive.

Stanley Hauerwas would go further. Christians are those who have been incorporated into a community of meaning through which we read the world 'in Christ'. But all too often "we turn the Christian faith into a system of beliefs that can be ... universally known *without the conversion of being incorporated within a specific community of people.* In effect it is to underwrite the Enlightenment assumption that we are most fully ourselves when we are free of all traditions and communities other than those we have chosen from the position of complete autonomy."[29] Or as another recent writer has put it, "The tragedy of our impatient generation is that we live as functional atheists, blind and deaf to the loving entreaties of ... God who waits eternally for our embrace."[30] Hauerwas contends that "The true god has been driven from the world – or at best has been made a transcendent watchdog, a bureaucratic manager – by the assumption that we must control our existence by acquiring the power to eradicate from our lives anything that threatens our autonomy as individuals."[31] The experience of "sickness challenges our most cherished presumption that we are, or at least can be, in control of our existence."[32]

Pattison agrees that, at least in the West, "the vast majority of contemporary Christians respond to illness and healing in ways that are probably indistinguishable from those of their non-Christian neighbours," observing that, "resort to sacraments, prayer, or any other distinctively 'religious' healing method will ... usually be very much an accompaniment, a second thought, or, indeed, a last hope."[33] Hauerwas suggests that in this way people in the West effectively reject the insights and experiences, the story, of the Christian faith community; we assume that, "we do not need a community capable caring for the ill; all we need is an instrumental rationality made powerful by technological sophistication." But Hauerwas is anxious that such an ideology, "requires that we interpret all illness as pointless. By 'pointless' I mean that it can play no role in helping us live our lives well. Illness is an absurdity in a history formed by the commitment to overcome all evils that potentially we can control."[34] According to Hauerwas, the outcome of this way of thinking is that: "physicians lose their freedom to care for the sick because they are now judged by the predictability of their performance; physicians must now provide a 'cure' based on the assumption that what is 'wrong' ... can be traced to specific 'causes'. The patient becomes a consumer ..."[35]

Interestingly this theological analysis is mirrored by Dr Joanna Moncrieff out of her own experience as a medical practitioner. Moncrieff argues that, "Medicine is no longer confined to the alleviation of suffering, but now involves a life-time of scrutiny, with checks and screenings from cradle to grave. Then when you get really sick, it unleashes relentless efforts to identify, remove or neutralize that part of your body that is malfunctioning. These efforts are concentrated in the last few months of life in a heroic battle to defy the inevitable." But this is part of a wider social phenomenon: "The problem with medicine," says Moncrieff, "is not just its relation with the individual body, however. It is also the premise that we can, and should, do all we can to fight and delay death. Medicine has created a myth that we can heal everything, given enough time and money." In an echo of Illich's critique she concludes that, "The wishful thinking that medicine has come to embody, obscures the limitations of the human condition, leaving people less aware of their own nature. This denial of our frailty and mortality reduces our ability to withstand the inevitable tragedy of life."[36]

Pattison suggests that in the face of all this, Christian responses to illness and healing are all too often narrow, uncritical and anachronistic. Moreover, "the practice of distinctively 'religious' healing methods, insofar as it [appears] to be the manipulation of the supernatural for the benefit of suffering humanity ... may be an obstacle to a more complex, more difficult and more authentic witness to healing" ... "truly religious responses are those which are sensitive to God's ongoing work in the whole of creation and through all people."[37] Such an approach, which recognizes ambiguity and appreciates nuance, is also echoed by Hauerwas. Despite the various attempts of philosophers and theologians, "what we must admit when we are confronted with ... suffering and death ... is that there is no 'explanation.'" In many ways neither creation nor suffering, have a 'point', but rather "both remind us that our existence makes sense *only insofar as we are able to place it in a narrative.*"[38] What the Christian community can offer is therefore a story in which we can locate our experience and offer some possibility of purpose, or what theologians and philosophers might call a *telos*.

Those religious communities who try to pretend that 'God is in his heaven and all is well with the world', are not only *deluding* themselves, but actually *colluding* in the avoidance of those realities we are called to confront. By contrast, Hauerwas asserts that:

> "Our willingness to expose our pain is the means God gives us to help to identify and respond to evil and injustice. For creation is not as it ought to be. The lament is the cry of protest schooled by our faith in a God who would have us serve the world by exposing its false comforts and deceptions ... one of the profoundest forms of faithlessness is the unwillingness to acknowledge our inexplicable suffering and pain."[39]

Especially must we refrain from pious platitudes in the face of manifest pain, recognizing for example: "for a child to die of disease seems to serve no purpose. It is a blackness before which we can only stand mute."[40] Of course it remains true that as Christians we can choose to offer even our unexplained and apparently undeserved suffering to God as "part of the telos of our service to one another in and outside of the Christian community", but "while it is perfectly appropriate for us to discover the suffering we experience in illness to have a telos in our service to one another in faith, it is not appropriate for us to try to force that account on another."[41]

According to Hauerwas (with reference especially to the West), "Our medicine ... reflects the way we think about death. There are very few things on which we as a society agree, but almost everyone agrees that death is a very unfortunate aspect of the human condition which should be avoided at all costs. We have no communal sense of a good death ..."[42] but rather, "we conspire to hide our deaths from ourselves and from one another, calling our conspiracy 'respect for the individual."[43] Echoing Moncrieff's medical analysis, Hauerwas asserts that modern Western medicine is all too often part of this conspiracy, going to elaborate lengths to keep us alive, because "cure not care has become medicine's primary purpose."[44] Hauerwas argues that, "If medicine is to serve our needs rather than determine our needs, then we must recover a sense of how even our illnesses fit within an ongoing narrative. The crucial question is what that narrative is to be, so that we can learn to live with our illnesses without giving them false meaning."[45] Again echoing Moncrieff's critique, Hauerwas notes that "aggressive medicine in the face of terminal illness can be the result of pressure exerted by the patient's family, but it can also be the result of our society's inability to place death in a morally intelligible narrative." He concludes: "our medical technologies have outrun the spiritual resources of our society, which lacks all sense of how life might properly end."[46] (It is worth noting that the literal meaning of the Greek *telos*, is of course the 'end'.) What then are the spiritual and theological resources which the Christian community might bring as sustaining our practice of health and healing? I suggest that we may find them in rearticulating the Christian story: by locating our medical practice as Christians within the narrative of salvation, and at the same time developing the spiritual practice of waiting.

Locating our work 1: The story of salvation

As we noticed at the outset of this discussion, it is important to recognize that the Christian doctrine of salvation is a far more comprehensive term than is often realized. It concerns the whole person and every aspect of life. In the language of Bishop Newbigin already alluded to, salvation is not, in the first instance, a question about what happens to me when I die; rather it is about the fulfilment of God's purpose for the universe he has created.[47] Although the language of salvation in the Hebrew Scriptures can be used of human figures who bring deliverance to the people, salvation is pre-eminently associated with God, who is frequently characterized as 'Saviour.' While Moses, David and Cyrus in their turn may be *instruments* of salvation, it is always God himself who is the *agent*. Only God is sufficient to accomplish salvation in his own strength; while even the greatest human leaders must rely on the strength of others, ultimately of God himself. This is why, for the most part, the Old Testament knows no other Saviour than God (so for example, Isaiah 43:10-11).

The paradigmatic experience of salvation for Israel is of course the Exodus and it is this experience of deliverance from the confines of slavery into the broad potential of the Promised Land, which has shaped Israel's understanding of God. This salvation from slavery was such a transforming experience that it continues to dominate Jewish self-understanding 3,000 years after the event. We should note that this was not simply an event on the spiritual plane but actual physical deliverance from a concrete experience of oppression, slavery and potential extinction. Throughout the Hebrew Scriptures the salvation envisaged is of a similarly tangible nature, actual deliverance from situations of real peril: sickness, tyranny, the danger of death, humiliation and extinction. Many of the psalms are a series of pleas for God to act, to save the king or his people, or else they form a litany of praise for the experience of personal salvation in a variety of circumstances. Slavery or exile is not a situation that many of us experience, so what might salvation mean for us? [48] Although we may not share the experience of the Hebrew slaves in Egypt, we are part of this common human predicament, a slavery to sin, which Paul captures so vividly in Romans chapter 7. At least part of our experience of this 'fallenness' and brokenness of the world is focused in our experience of ill-health and disease. Not only as individuals, but as communities and as societies, we are not at ease with ourselves or with each other. It is this 'dis-ease' which God is constantly working to heal and to restore, in the Exodus, through the prophets, above all in the story of Jesus' life, death and resurrection.

For the New Testament, the ministry of Jesus becomes God's supreme act of salvation for the world. The name Jesus itself provides a link, for the Aramaic *Yeshua* (Hebrew: *Joshua)* means "God saves." In Christ's ministry the kingdom is "at hand," the day of salvation has dawned, and the experience of redemption and renewal is real for many of the people whom Jesus encountered in the Palestine of his day. We have already noted that the Greek verb "sozo" covers both healing in the sense of curing as well as in the sense of health, wholeness and salvation. Interestingly, Lesslie Newbigin points out that this has links to the Sanskrit:

> "The Greek word which we translate as 'save' means to make whole. It comes from the same root as the Sanskrit *Sarva*. It means 'wholeness'. It means the healing of that which is wounded, the mending of that which is broken, the setting free of that which is bound."[49]

Hauerwas suggests that "any account of salvation includes questions of our health, but that does not mean that medicine can or ever should become the agent of salvation."[50] But perhaps like Cyrus or David or Moses medicine can and indeed does serve as an *instrument* of salvation? Moreover, I would argue that every such *personal experience* of healing or renewal carries within its implications for the corporate and the systematic, as well as pointers to *cosmic redemption*. This theme, which begins to find expression in the later prophets, comes to ultimate articulation in the New Testament understanding of the salvation of God as a 'new creation': the new heaven and the new earth of Revelation, for which the whole cosmos yearns in the evocative imagery of Romans chapter 8.

So: in scripture salvation always has this personal dimension, but it is never just individualistic. A common feature of God's saving activity in both Old and New Testaments is the formation of a covenant community. Indeed all the biblical metaphors of salvation refer to being brought from lostness or isolation into the new community which God is creating (e.g. 1 Peter 2:9-10). The salvation experience, while personal, is expressed in New Testament terms which are corporate: the New Israel, Kingdom of God, Body of Christ, The Elect, Church, communion, fellowship. The disciples of Jesus, the people of the new covenant, are called to continue his work and bear witness to the salvation which God has made freely available to all people in Christ.

As my Oxford colleague Paul Fiddes has argued[51] in many ways the experience of salvation must always be a *contemporary* experience, for it is the renewing of relationship between God and humanity in the here and now. It depends upon the past event of Calvary, but its current outworking must always be handled in the present tense. The Church has a vital role here, both as the model of the new community which God is bringing into being, and as the people who bear witness to the story of the cross and resurrection of Christ. This is central to the understanding of New beginning in his characteristic account of the church in which "the congregation is the hermeneutic of the Gospel." [52] This insight is also core to the position of Stanley Hauerwas: "God has entrusted his presence to a historic and contingent community that must be renewed generation after generation. The story is not merely told but embodied in a people's habits that form and are formed in worship, governance and morality."[53] By contrast, what the modern industrial West lacks "is the wisdom and skills of a community constituted by a truthful narrative that can comprehend such deaths without denying their pointlessness."

Even though it may be true that "… we have no theodicy that can soften the pain of our death and the death of our children … [yet] we believe that we share a common story which makes it possible for us to be with one another especially as we die."[54] Interestingly, Joanna Moncrieff argues that we should follow Illich's lead and organize society "around the needs of people to live meaningful lives, and not around production and consumption for its own sake", fostering not only autonomy and self-reliance, "but also [to] recognize the necessity of inter-dependence and mutual support."[55] What the Church can offer is a location in which meaning is created and lived out in communities of critical encouragement.

However, we must always remember that there is a future, eschatological, dimension to the experience of Salvation. It is a process in which we are caught up, but it is not yet finally complete. This is true on the personal level as we can be only too well aware, but it is also true on the other levels of intermediate and cosmic structures as well. God's covenant people are called to engage in a process that challenges the individual on a personal level, but also engages with the intermediate structures of human life and society, as well as being engaged in the cosmic struggle with spiritual realities of which most of us are scarcely aware.

As the South African missiologist David Bosch put it, the Church is "the sign, sacrament and instrument"[56] of God's saving mission to the world, and I would argue that the medicine practiced through CMC Vellore, in this illustrious centre of Christian care, shares these same qualities. In various ways we can all be the signs, sacraments and instruments of God's salvation; but only when all of God's creation has been fully redeemed at the end of all things, will God's purpose in creation and salvation be accomplished.

We must therefore learn to speak of salvation in three tenses, past, present and future, and in three dimensions, personal, structural and universal. Through God's saving activity in the past, in the life of Israel and supremely in the life, death and resurrection of Jesus, God has revealed Godself as the One who has the power to save. By God's continuing work in the present, through the power of the Holy Spirit in the world and in the witness of the community of the people of God (a people who don't simply tell the story but live it out in their experience), God reveals Godself as the one who is still the Saviour. And at the end, when all is brought to completion in Christ, God will reveal Godself as the one whose saving purpose can never be thwarted. But in the meantime:

> "Christians are called, in the power of God's Spirit, to live in the tension 'between the times' and to wait in hope for the final consummation of all things in Christ. This strong narrative of 'God's time' casts waiting as a 'necessary bridge between the temporal and the eternal', with patience as an indispensable virtue for the realization of God's ultimate purposes."[57]

Thus a key feature of Christian spiritual practice is waiting: waiting on God and waiting for God.

Locating our work 2: The practice of waiting

W.H Vanstone (1923-99) was a British Anglican priest who wrote a number of influential spiritual classics, notably the award-winning *Love's Endeavour, Love's Expense* (1977), and *The Stature of Waiting* (1982). Vanstone refused a number of academic appointments and spent all his life in pastoral ministry, although he did spend some time studying under the German-American theologian Paul Tillich in New York. Thus Vanstone offers the discussion of *The Stature of Waiting* as an exercise in the Tillichian method of 'correlation',[58] an approach that correlates insights from Christian revelation with the issues raised by existential, psychological, and philosophical analysis. He proposes that while Judas Iscariot has traditionally been portrayed as the ultimate symbol of betrayal, in fact the Greek word used to describe Judas as the 'Betrayer' is *paradidomai,* or 'to hand over.' He explores the way this plays out in the passion narratives of especially the gospels of Mark and John, and draws attention to the fact that after this pivotal moment of 'handing over', all the verbs in relation to Jesus are in the passive rather than the active mood. In other words Jesus, who has up until this moment been the centre of activity, now becomes the recipient of the actions of others. For example: he is abandoned by his disciples; he is tried by the various authorities; he is punished, and ultimately he is executed. All these things are done to him and Jesus simply, openly, passively, receives the actions of these others. They form his 'passion' narrative:

> "What happens in both Mark and John when Jesus is handed over is not that He passes from success to failure, from gain to loss or from pleasure to pain: it is that He passes from doing to receiving what others do, from working to waiting, from the role of subject to that of object and, in a proper sense of the phrase, from action to passion."[59]

The point Vanstone underlines is that this transition, and this new phase of Jesus' being – as one who waits and as one who is 'patient' – lies at the very heart of the Christian story of salvation. There is something profoundly redemptive in this being patient, in this waiting on and for God. In the central section of his book Vanstone explores some contemporary experiences of moving from action to passion, including the role of hospital patient, and considers in what sense this too may be seen as redemptive: "A person who becomes a patient enters into passion; he becomes one who is done to, is treated: he becomes the object of the decisions and care and treatment of others."[60]

What is more, suggests Vanstone,

"In the world of today the status or condition of patient is not confined to passing periods of illness and a brief phase of final infirmity: it seems to be experienced in ever new areas of life and to occupy an ever-increasing proportion of life ... the status of patient is becoming ever more widespread and familiar in our [Western] world."[61]

For example, such feelings of dependency and powerlessness often felt by a hospital patient may also be evoked by the experiences of retirement or unemployment. Even if the economic imbalance, which often flows from either of those states, is reduced or overcome, nevertheless: "the distinction will remain between those who are providing for themselves and those who are provided for, between those who achieve the wherewithal to live and those who receive it."[62] Vanstone observes that analogous attitudes are seen in our experiences of and attitudes towards old age and disability. In fact all these are instances that in the modern western world: "In our public attitudes we locate the value of life exclusively in those areas where, actually or allegedly, we are free from external dependence and are exercising our own initiative and creating our own achievement."[63] In other words we continue to cling to the Enlightenment value of individual autonomy.

But Vanstone argues that our passivity, our waiting, our patience, are no less valuable than our action: "the variety of man's potential passibility seems no less remarkable than the variety of his potential activity ... Human dignity seems – to put it crudely – 'to have another leg to stand on' in the manifold and various possibility of man ... and if the first gives to man a unique status and dignity in the world, so also does the second."[64] In general, suggests Vanstone, the popular imagination of the Western Christian world, "discerns nothing in God: no dependence, no waiting, no exposure, nothing of passion or possibility; nothing of the status of patient. And therefore, when these conditions appear in the life of human beings they must appear fundamentally 'ungodlike'; and therefore again they must appear alien to the proper status of man and unworthy of his unique dignity."[65] But in the passion story, in Mark but especially in John – with its distinctive note of the glorification of Christ through his passion – Vanstone persuasively argues that we see a redefinition of the notion of divine, and therefore also of human, dignity: "It is as Jesus is handed over, as He enters into passion, that the ultimate dimension of the divine glory becomes manifest in Him and evident to men (sic)."[66]

Although Judas is the instrument of this handing over, Jesus was fully aware that in living his life in the way that he did, and in his commitment to his Father's Kingdom, in many ways he made this action inevitable, so that Paul can say that in reality Jesus 'handed Himself over' (Eph. 5:2) or even that 'God handed Him over'. So, Christians can say: "Jesus, in handing Himself over, in passing of His own will from action to passion, enacts and discloses that which, at the deepest level, is distinctive of divinity, distinctive of God. He discloses the God Who Himself, of His own will, is handed over to pass from action to passion."[67]

It is in this willingness to wait that God reveals a fundamental characteristic which is in fact love: "The glory of that waiting figure in Gethsemane is not wholly strange and unfamiliar to us ... [it] is the glory of that not wholly unfamiliar activity which always, in the end, destines itself to waiting – the activity of loving."[68] Similarly, another Oxford colleague, the Revd Dr Margaret Whipp, until recently lead Chaplain at the Oxford University Hospital Trust, and formerly a Consultant Oncologist in the north of England, draws on another aspect of the gospel story, the Annunciation, to underline that: "socially, theologically and bodily, the enactment of Christian patience is a matter of learning to bear with life, and with one another, in graceful and whole-souled love."[69]

In fact, suggests Vanstone, "... any kind of waiting presupposes some kind or degree of caring"; for "a person who views the world with indifference rarely finds himself waiting. Conversely a person to whom many things matter will often find himself waiting. The experience of waiting is the experience of the world as in some sense mattering, of being of some kind of importance."[70] Vanstone offers examples drawn from a range of human experience which might include the naturalist, the scientist or the inventor; the actor, performer or artist, such that, "Their waiting, their final dependence on an outcome which is beyond their control, is, one might say, part and parcel of the adventure of creativity, which is as worthy of the image which man bears, as is the adventure of love."[71] But how far can we say that such creative, or perhaps even 'active', waiting in the passion of Christ is of the same order as that of the involuntary, passive, waiting of the hospital patient? In reality very few experiences are entirely without choice or volition, but even in our cognizance of need and dependency, important things are revealed:

> "Through our awareness of needs we become exposed to powers and qualities in the world which otherwise perhaps would pass unrecognized. We become more aware of what the world is, of the heights and depths of existence ... [it] generates a sharper sensitivity or a wider receptivity which is not wholly unlike the sensitivity or receptivity of the lover or the artist."[72]

Vanstone's point is that in this waiting we encounter that God who, "creating the world in the activity of love, destines Himself to wait upon the world and gives to the world power of meaning to Himself." So it is that "when man waits upon the world ... God also waits; and it is in waiting that He invests the world with the possibility and power of meaning."[73] Equally, Margaret Whipp writes that:

> "On every page of the scriptures, we ... meet the same patient Lover of souls who yearns and pleads, who seduces and suffers, who rages and ravishes, who labours and cries out, who whispers and agonizes, who burns and bleeds, for Love of the poor human creatures he is drawingto himself. This is the God who, from everlasting to everlasting, is waiting still for us."[74]

The image of God which is found both in humanity's capacity for creative and loving activity, and for creative and loving waiting, is also to be found "in the various and commonplace forms of waiting which are 'imposed' upon us by our awareness of our various and commonplace needs."[75] Of course we must acknowledge that some forms of waiting may be uncomfortable or even disagreeable, but, even where that is the case, "from the Christian viewpoint, it is never a *degraded* condition, [it is not] a condition of *diminished* human dignity."[76] So humanity "must not see it as degrading that he should wait upon the world, be helped, be provided for, be dependent; for as such he is, by God's gift, what God Himself makes Himself to be."[77] Thus, concludes Vanstone, "as he waits in the future, increasingly dependent on systems and machines … on medical support and social provision, he will in no sense be deprived of his high calling … whenever he so stands man will be a figure of unique and almost unbelievable dignity."[78]

Sustaining our work through the life of the people of God

As we reflect together on this centenary of medical education at CMC Vellore, as we remember all the lives which have been touched through the caring ministry of hospitality exercised by generations of staff through the decades, and as we look also to the future, I suggest we need to read all this not simply through the lens of modern medical practice, excellent and professional though that is, but in the context of our Christian narrative. We locate our work and our calling in the greater story of God's saving mission to the world, focused in the life, death and resurrection of Jesus Christ. We sustain our work through the spiritual discipline of waiting on and for God; and we nurture all this by sharing in the community of the Church which continues to embody Christ's ministry and mission in our own day. In doing so we recognize that it is God alone and not we ourselves, who will determine the final outcome. Thus in one sense we live, as Stanley Hauerwas put it, 'out of control':

> "… 'living out of control' is important in that it suggests that Christians base their lives on the knowledge that God has redeemed his creation

through the work of Jesus of Nazareth. We thus live out of control in the sense that we must assume God will use our faithfulness to make his kingdom a reality in the world."[79]

It is not that we cease to work with all the insights and skills and expertise that modern medicine affords, but we acknowledge that none of this is done "under the illusion of omnipotence."[80] Rather we appreciate that both the life of Church and our medical practices are instruments in the hands of God to bring about the fulfillment of God's purposes in creation and Salvation. But we must recognize further that we live 'between the times' and that therefore we find ways to nourish our life and our practice as we wait patiently for God's final purpose to be accomplished. Living in this way requires stamina and the resources both of Spirit and community we find within Christ's people. As we work at the limits of our skills and expertise, our patience is constantly tested:

> "Yet the fact that medicine through the agency of physicians does not and cannot always "cure" in no way qualifies the commitment of the physician. At least it does not do so if we remember that the physician's basic pledge is not to cure, but to care through being present to the one in pain. Yet it is not easy to carry out that commitment on a day-to-day, year-to-year basis. For none of us has the resource to see too much pain without that pain's hardening us. Without such a hardening, something we sometimes call by the name of professional distance, we fear we will lose the ability to feel at all."[81]

What the Church offers to such a practice of medicine is a community which embodies in its very life God's sustaining presence in the world: "medicine needs the church not to supply a foundation for its moral commitments, but rather as a resource of the habits and practices necessary to sustain the care of those in pain over the long haul."[82] Margaret Whipp, drawing on her long experience as both pastor and physician, notes that:

> "The empathy and the willingness to draw alongside another person in their suffering is a wonderful expression of human solidarity. At a deeper level, it also reflects the truth of God's intimate involvement in our human afflictions, which was embodied to the uttermost in the sufferings of

Christ, and in the consolation that still sustains us through the ongoing ministry of the Holy Spirit, the Comforter (John 14.16)."[83]

Such solidarity is expressed through presence and through prayer. Prayer "which is an act of steadfast waiting on God."[84] Prayer such as this "is not a supplement to the insufficiency of our medical knowledge and practice; nor is it some divine insurance policy that our medical skill will work; rather, our prayer is the means that we have to make God present whether our medical skill is successful or not. So understood, the issue is not whether medical care and prayer are antithetical, but how medical care can ever be sustained without the necessity of continued prayer."[85]

Only in this way can we continue 'not to be served, but to serve', walking together towards that coming fulfilment of God's purpose of salvation, of healing and wholeness, for us and for the whole cosmos; created and redeemed in self-giving Love.

Endnotes

[1] I am grateful to the Principal, Dr Anna Pulimood, and to my long-standing friend and colleague, Bishop Dhirendra Sahu, and to the Chaplain, the Revd Arul Dhas, for the kind invitation to share in this Colloquium, reflecting together on a "Theology of Hospitality: A Conversation on Health and Healing". I am deeply honoured to be asked to give this keynote address, and I want to underline at the outset that I do so in the spirit of the colloquium, that is, as but one contributor to the conversation.

[2] Formerly the CSI Bishop of Madras, I came to know Bishop New begin when I was a doctoral student, following his return to the UK in 1974.

[3] http://www.cmch-vellore.edu/sites/common/Facts%20&%20Figures%202017%20-%202018.pdf accessed 25 November 2018.

[4] S. Pattison (1989) *Alive and Kicking: Towards a Practical Theology of Illness and Healing*, SCM Press London, 13.

[5] Pattison, 19.

[6] Pattison, 24.

[7] Pattison, 26.

[8] Pattison, 28.

[9] Pattison, 29f.

[10] Pattison, 32f.

[11] Pattison, 34.

[12] The title of a well-known book by Rabbi Harold Kushner: *When Bad Things Happen to Good People*, Random House, New York (1981).

[13] S. Hauerwas, (1990) *Naming the Silences: God, Medicine and the Problem of Suffering*, T & T Clark London, pp106f (citing Callahan, 60f).

[14] S. Hauerwas, (1990) 49-51.

[15] Hauerwas, (1990) 36f.

[16] I. Illich, (1976) *Medical Nemesis: The Expropriation of Health*, Random House, New York.

[17] GBD 2013 Mortality and Causes of Death, Collaborators (17 December 2014). "Global, regional, and national age-sex specific all-cause and cause-specific mortality for 240 causes of death, 1990-2013: a systematic analysis for the Global Burden of Disease Study 2013". *Lancet. 385* (9963): 117–71.

[18] Illich, 5.

[19] Illich, 6.

[20] S. O'Mahony, (2016) *Medical Nemesis 40 years on: the enduring legacy of Ivan Illich*, Journal Royal College Phys Edin: 46, 134-9.

[21] O'Mahony, 135.

[22] O'Mahony, 136.

[23] J. Moncrieff, (2016) *Limits to Medicine: Re-visiting Ivan Illich*, joannamoncrieff.com/2016/04/18 (accessed 4 Nov 18).

[24] O'Mahony, 136.

[25] O'Mahony, 138.

[26] Pattison, 7.

[27] Pattison, 9.

[28] Pattison, 13.

[29] Hauerwas, (1990) p53 my emphasis.

[30] Margaret Whipp (2017) *The Grace of Waiting* Canterbury Press Norwich, 97.

[31] Hauerwas, (1990) 59f.

[32] Hauerwas, (1990) 62.

[33] Pattison, 49.

[34] Hauerwas, (1990) 62f.

[35] Hauerwas, (1990) 63f.

[36] Moncrieff, ibid.

[37] Pattison, 73.

[38] Hauerwas, (1990) 78f my emphasis.

[39] Hauerwas, (1990) 82f.

[40] Hauerwas, (1990) 86.

[41] Hauerwas, (1990) 89.

[42] Hauerwas, (1990) 99.

[43] Hauerwas, (1990) 101.

[44] Ibid.

[45] Hauerwas, (1990) 108.

[46] Hauerwas, (1990) 122f.

[47] L. Newbigin, (1956) *Sin and Salvation*, SCM Press London, 15.

[48] This is not to deny the continuing experience of forms of slavery of many people in the modern world, but to recognise that from the Western perspective from which I am writing it is often a hidden reality, and especially overlooked within many Christian communities.

[49] Newbigin, (1956) 15.

[50] S. Hauerwas, (2001) "Salvation and Health: Why Medicine needs the Church (1985)" in *The Hauerwas Reader* ed J. Berkman and M. Cartwright, Duke University Press.

[51] P. Fiddes, (1989) *Past Event and Present Salvation*, DLT London.

[52] L. Newbigin (1989) *The Gospel in a Pluralist Society*, SPCK London, chapter 18.

[53] S. Hauerwas, (2001) *The Servant Community: Christian Social Ethics (1983)* op.cit.

[54] Hauerwas, (1990), 148.

[55] Moncrieff ibid.

[56] D. Bosch, (1990) *Transforming Mission*, Orbis Maryknoll New York, 374.

[57] Whipp, 18f.

[58] W. H. Vanstone (1982), *The Stature of Waiting*, Darton, Longman &Todd, London – preface.

[59] Vanstone, 31.

[60] Vanstone, 35.

[61] Vanstone, 36.

[62] Vanstone, 39.

[63] Vanstone, 44.

[64] Vanstone, 60.

[65] Vanstone, 65.

[66] Vanstone, 75.

[67] Vanstone, 89.

[68] Vanstone, 99.

[69] Whipp, 23.

[70] Vanstone, 102f.

[71] Vanstone, 105.

72 Vanstone, 107.

73 Vanstone, 108f.

74 Whipp, 97.

75 Vanstone, 109.

76 Ibid, my emphasis.

77 Vanstone, 112.

78 Vanstone, 115.

79 Hauerwas, (2001) *The Servant Community (1983)* op. cit. 381.

80 Ibid.

81 Hauerwas, (2001) *Salvation and Health (1985)* op. cit. 551.

82 Ibid, 553.

83 Whipp, 48.

84 Ibid.

85 Hauerwas, ibid, 554.

A Response to the Keynote Address by Professor Nicholas John Wood

"Waiting for God: Towards a Theology of Health and Wholeness"

Joseph George

It is a well prepared paper by the keynote speaker. The paper not only highlights some of the current key and critical issues in illness and healing but also the dilemma that the faith community (CMC) encounters in terms of understanding their theology of health and healing as God-given mission and the call to act as God's agents of wholeness and salvation that comes through the Lord Jesus Christ.

Professor Nicholas Wood began with a brief history of the CMC, Vellore, highlighting the progress of this well acclaimed, respected, and trusted institution with its excellence in medical education and providing health care (patient care) during the last century. I join the keynote speaker, and all of us gathered here, to thank God for letting CMC grow over the last century to become what she is today. This was possible with generations of caring and teaching professionals and the students who had shown extra-ordinary commitment for God and a deep sense of love for the suffering humanity. I concur with Professor Wood that in all these achievements "involves waiting, sometimes patiently, and more often perhaps impatiently, for the fulfillment of God's purpose" by being a caring committed professional medical community (p.2). It is in this context one could make sense of the NT understanding of shalom implying – healing and wholeness.

Let me begin with a personal note before I make my response to Professor Wood. As a child growing up in a small village in Kerala (50 years ago), I often heard people talking about going to Vellore whenever they encountered critical illness and needs special medical attention. After my theological education I served on the faculty of a theological college in Mokokchung, Nagaland, for ten years (1982-1992) where I heard similar expressions in the midst of critical illness making reference to CMC, Vellore. During my travel this morning I told someone that I am travelling to CMC, Vellore, and the first query was "what is wrong with you"? Even though every city in India has multi-facility hospitals with modern technology and advanced level specialized care, the name of CMC, Vellore, is close to millions of people in this country. During my B. D. studies I had written a research paper on the 'medical missions' in India with special reference to CMC, Vellore, which made me understand the struggles during the initial years and its various stages of development. I can only say that I join each one gathered here to praise God for making what CMC is today. It is God's doing, and we celebrate. In the past and in the present I can see how the CMC community walked and worked with absolute faith in God's providence and the as per the direction of the Holy Spirit. With this personal note let me share my response to Professor Wood.

I am impressed with this august gathering this evening. I do agree with the Professor that the colloquium as a space for listening to the richness of this diverse group and responding in such a way that enhances mutual edification and personal and communal transformation. The professionals in medical education and patient care, social workers within the hospital system and with community outreach programmes, pastoral counselling experts, leaders of the church and Christian institutions, and those involved in the Chaplaincy work are gathered here for mutual edification. This meeting provides us space for asking questions and finding answers not only about what happens within the CMC community but also from a larger framework, which includes our own identity as a Christian Institution in this country. I am worried we need to worry about our own identity and freedom to practice in the years to come.[1]

The keynote address has four sections, and a detailed conclusion, highlighting issues and concerns about the theology of health, illness, healing, and the questions and concerns about the ethics and ethos of the use of advanced medical technology and the pharmaceutical industry with their promise of prolonged life. The budget of the cosmetic industry is another major issue that the community faces today. The advertisement says 'look healthier and younger' using this product. This is a big enticing trap for the modern urban community across the globe. This is the same with health care practices across the globe. India has major problems in providing health care for the socially and economically disadvantaged along with those who can pay for the health care package.

Medicine in the last century – progress and problems
The probing questions and ethos of contemporary medical practice indicate the inevitable ambiguities in understanding health, illness, and the goals of the Christian Hospital ministry in brining God's cure, healing, wholeness, and wellbeing - Shalom. Based on Stephen Pattison, Professor Wood examines a number of models with regard to understanding and healing.[2]

The biomedical model with its emphasis on the curing of the bodily symptoms tends to be highly individualistic and aggressive in addressing the disorders. With this tendency, person seeking medical help and the health providers negate the value of life and worth of living when the ideal is only extending the death – not facing suffering and death. It is common trend that bodies are kept on the life supporting systems, only to prolong death. This has been brought into discussion by the speaker elsewhere in this paper. It is important to note that the medical model has its own limitations (Pattison, p.24), though this is the fundamental mode of understanding illness and treatment across the globe, including India.

The psychological model comes with its emphasis on the psychosomatic complexity on mind, body, and emotions; and even the spiritual. The personal qualities and displayed character is directly impacted by life experiences and events. The psychological theories across various schools provide ample information today on the psychological processing with illness and healing which is complementing the medical model.

The Epidemiological approaches analyze various diseases affecting the whole population and its link with socio-cultural factors, such as poverty, unhygienic living conditions, and various forms of discriminations. In this context, I want to add, that Pattison laments about the marked inequality across various social classes in Britain (Pattison, p.27). This is also the case in India where the inequality remains between those who can pay for the essential medical services and those who cannot. What is more problematic in India is the frequent epidemics with which people at the margins suffer greatly. For example, the recent spread of Nipa virus in Kerala that caused many deaths and affected many with health concerns.

The anthropological approaches focus on the cultures and subcultures asking the 'why' question rather than the 'how' question. This would mean that each culture and subcultures have their own mode of understanding health, illness and healing. I do agree that none of these models are perfect but they all come with some epistemological insights and directions.

Looking from an Indian context one can see deficiencies in each system and none can claim superiority over the other. Each system can help and complement the others. In this sense may I also suggest the use of Alternative Medical practices which are employed across the globe. The Indian health care systems, apart from the Allopath, have worldwide acceptance as their process and procedures are mostly non-intrusive and less worrisome. The world community looks upon India for the alternative medical practices, such as, Ayurveda, Unani, Siddha, Yoga, Homeopathy, and Yoga.

Realizing the importance of these ancient medical practices, its efficacy for presenting holistic health, and the demands from across the globe, the Indian government has taken steps to strengthen these practices by creating a separate department, known as Ministry of AYUSH, which was inaugurated on the 9th November, 2014. "With an increase in lifestyle-related disorders there is a worldwide resurgence of interest in holistic systems of health care, particularly with respect to the prevention and management of chronic, non-communicable and systemic diseases. It is increasingly understood that no single health care system can provide satisfactory answers to all he health needs of modern society." (AYUSH, www.ayush.gov.in, accessed on 4th December 2018).

What is more important for us in this colloquium is locating the presence of God in the midst of suffering. The question of theodicy comes, but with no answers. In Job's suffering his friends came to be with him. They sat in silence. His suffering was great. They waited in silence. (Job 2:11-13). How can a perfect, loving, righteous, all powerful and ever present God allow the evil and suffering is an age-old question but with no answers. What we need today is finding answers for the suffering humanity around us.

Professionally trained and practicing health professional versus the charismatic leaders and miracle worker who easily manipulate the vulnerable suffering persons and their families.

The Christian mission hospitals that are closed over the decades for multiple reasons is another major concern. The admission process at CMC was hampered by forces that one cannot explain in spite of her record of transparency and excellence in medical education. The CMC, Vellore, is not competing with any of the emerging high-tech hospitals but they are competing. How do we maintain the standard of care when things are tough on the caring community?

Modern medicine comes at a cost, not simply in terms of finance, time and many other resources, but also brings probing questions about its ethos and its ethics. The British theologian, Stephen Pattison, who has himself served both as a hospital chaplain and as an administrator with a regional community health council, notes that medicine is a not merely a personal experience, nor just a scientific paradigm, but a social and political phenomenon: "There is a socio-political context for all kinds of healing, even the healing of Jesus."[3] Indeed, we must remember that, "the whole way that illness is perceived and dealt with in particular societies is heavily dependent on the wider social and political order".[4]

I am convinced that deliberate and conscious effort to reduce the 'aggressive medicine' that treats only my body. The treatment models, following the model exemplified by Jesus of Nazareth, also must address the whole person, family, and community that help them to experience the salvation of God and healing in its full sense.

Theological responses

In this section Professor Wood successfully highlights the dilemma between 'faith in God' versus 'faith in Medicine'. The social, cultural, theological, and medical critiques have raised pertinent and critical questions on the ethics and morals of the high-tech medical practices today which primarily focus on the body, and very little on the mental, emotional, and spiritual side of the bigger problem.

Based on Stephen Pattison, Dr. Wood asserts that illness and healing are central to human existence and a theology of healing must address the issues raised by the disease and suffering. I am delighted that a strong critique on contemporary medicine is presented with the help

of insights from Stanley Hauerwas, Johanna Moncrieff, and Stephen
Pattison. In this context Professor Wood laments on the 'manipulation
of the supernatural' for the suffering humanity while conveniently
ignoring suffering and death as realities in the plan of God.

The contemporary medical technologies have overturned the
community and spiritual resources of our society, laments the speaker.
Religious, theological, and spiritual issues are drastically declined in the
face of modern medicine (p.9). This desperate faith in the medicine
reduces the process of God in his creation – with all God's creations
– when they are well and when they are sick and ill. I would add that
the meaning and purpose of life must be found in God and God alone,
as health, salvation, and wellbeing comes from God.

As Dr. Wood depends much on Pattison's *Alive and Kicking* (1989),
much of his insights are based on the 30 years old reflections. Hence,
the presenter has done very little with the issues of medical practice
post-globalization across the globe. India has seen mushrooming of
multi-specialty high-tech hospitals in all major and minor cities in
India, promising professional medical care and cure from all ailments.
There are many issues and concerns arising from the post-globalization
era that needs our immediate attention which are not part of the paper
presented. The care versus cure dilemma; cure versus healing; healing at
what cost; extending life versus extending death; body on the machine
versus death as God's end for humanity; quality of life and wellbeing
narratives; faith healers versus faith in healing; miracle workers versus
doctors working hard day and night; and the right to die are a few of
such recent discussions.

Another significant contribution in the discussion of Christian faith
and medicine today is from Abigal Rian Evans, Associate Professor
of Practical Theology at the Princeton Theological Seminary, who
advocates for a return to faith and religious resources in the process of
healing ministry. She calls for redeeming the medicine from the market
place.[5] For Evans, healing is more than treating diseases; health care is

more than a commodity; she advocates for a direct role of the church in health delivery system which is accessible for all.

In all these the art of the spiritual practice of 'Waiting on God' is lost and the 'desperate faith in medicine' is all the more significant for the contemporary communities.

It is not easy to have clear and concrete theological articulations on illness and healing. I am of the opinion that the CMC Mission statement carries its theology. Life is from God; healing and health from God; the ministry of healing is being part of that God's mission of salvation and healing; the call is to become servant-leaders, following Jesus of Nazareth, to help with ushering values of the Kingdom of God.

> "The primary concern of the Christian Medical College, Vellore is to develop through education and training, compassionate, professionally excellent, ethically sound individuals who will go out as servant-leaders of health teams and healing communities. Their service may be in promotive, preventive, curative, rehabilitative or palliative aspects of healthcare, in education or in research."[6]

As a pastoral counsellor listening to people of all faiths and no faiths, it is my conclusion too that we are chosen to do this privileged task of God's mission with all its challenges and pains and at the same time the joys too. There is a saying, ordinary people, extra-ordinary situations. It is in these extra-ordinary situations that God helps us to learn, un-learn, and re-learn about ourselves, others, and God's mission in the world.

Locating our work 1: The story of salvation
The story of Salvation in Christian Faith is fundamental in understanding God and God's activity in the world today. It concerns the whole person and everything about life. I agree with Professor Wood when he says salvation is not primary about what happens after one's death, but it is about fulfillment of God's purpose in the universe that God created. In the OT there are many agents of God's salvation at different times, but God is the source of salvation – which is life in God. The healing and health narrative (as well as suffering and death narrative) is located

in the salvation narratives. Life is from God; healing is from God; and wellbeing is from God.

I concur with the speaker that salvation of the people of Israel from the bondage in Egypt and the hope of the Promised Land is not merely about personal spiritual experience but it was saving them from the bondage – sickness, tyranny, death, humiliation, and even extinction. The faith community's experience with God is central in the exodus narrative. It makes sense when he says 'we are not at ease with ourselves or with one another' and that God constantly working with us to heal and to restore from this inner and relational brokenness (p.9).

Wood's statement that "Slavery or exile is not a situation that many of us experience, so what Salvation might mean for us? There is a reference to the socio-political-cultural context in with regard to understanding health, illness, and healing (p.3) and the related medical enterprises. It is a matter of great concern that many forms of slavery exist today across the globe.

Speaking from the Indian situation, I must argue that people continue to struggle with many kinds of enslavements in Urban and Rural India. This is true with other parts of the world too, in my opinion. The socially and economically disadvantaged peoples live without the basic necessities of life, leading to serious and critical health issues. For example, the slum dwellers in the major cities, families living in the marginalized communities without enough for their survival, women who suffer with negligence and exploitations, the homeless, orphans, underemployed, unemployed, financial debts among the urban community, poverty in the slums and villages, unorganized work force, people living at risk areas and many other similar issues. The tension between various religious groups and the destructive ways of the fanatic groups are also major concerns in India today.

I accept the position expressed by Professor Wood in the following statement and the quotation from Whipp. "We must there learn to speak of salvation in three tenses, past, present, and future, and in three dimensions, personal, structural, and universal.... God reveals himself as the one who is still the Saviour" (p.11).

> "Christians are called, in the power of God's Spirit, to live in the tension 'between the times' and to wait in hope for the final consummation of all things in Christ. This strong narrative of 'God's time' casts waiting as a 'necessary bridge between the temporal and the eternal', with patience as an indispensable virtue for the realization of God's ultimate purposes." (Whipp, p.18f).

The Salvation narrative, that includes healing and restoration, must be found not only in the personal domain but also the faith community. The structural and universal dimensions of salvation and healing cannot be overlooked in our times. It is in the context of the faith community that one seeks God's healing and wholeness.

This is an issue that medical professionals, mental health workers, pastors and counsellors encounter quite often without finding any satisfactory solutions. What is God's ultimate purpose at this point of time? Where is God's community? What is the role of the community of God in terms of facilitating salvation and fullness of life? I close this section with a quote from Benard Haring, a well known German Catholic theologian, who explicitly expressed the role of the faith community in God's plan of salvation and healing. In this context I must add God acts in the faith community for all God's dealings, including the ministry of healing the sick and the dying, which the CMC is entrusted with. He writes:

> "In order to be a healing force, a faith-community should be deeply rooted in knowledge of Jesus and in wholesome doctrine and invigorated by healthy and healing intercommunal relationships and practices, including keen appreciation of special charisms of healing. But the basic healing activity is continuous and patient reconciliation within the community and through the community to a larger context. A reconciled and reconciling community will be ever attentive to maintain committed solidarity for the healing of the sick and loving care."[7]

A number of presentations by the reputed Doctors in this colloquium have been noteworthy and enriching as they come with experiences of healing and salvation. What one needs today is a theology that can be formulated from the actual experiences. This explains the wider context of the healing narrative and understanding God today. I would like to quote Dr. John Oommen, a CMC alumnus, who said in this colloquium:

> "Our calling is to join God, to be co-workers with Him; to share the pain of people, in humility and love. And from that position, to treat, to cure, to rehabilitate, to prevent, to accompany, to heal – as the case may be. Our hospitals and clinics are points of concentration of pain, and therefore of God too – holy ground, and we are privileged to be part of the healing circle.[8]

Locating our work 2: The practice of waiting

This section on the 'practice of waiting' though appears extremely hopeful and positive, I am afraid, it is clinically and practically problematic. The presentation heavily relies on the philosophical principle of passivity-passion rhetoric based on W. H. Vanstone's insights. His explanation of the passion narrative based on Mark and John is interesting, but problematic proposition. What I am troubled here is the link between 'passivity and passion'. I am not sure whether it was a 'willing wait' at Gethsemane which is sign of love. Certainly there was 'waiting' for God. The other side of 'handing over' is the evil of Jesus' time and the suffering inflicted on him. I read great amount of suffering (physical and mental) during the passion narrative. It was very strange, unfamiliar, and cruel experience enforced on him by the forces of evil.

The feelings of 'dependency and powerlessness' are ever present in the hierarchal order of our society and they play vital roles in determining indices of health and pathology as well as the standard of care in a given socio-political context. This is also true at the hospital corridors and courtyards where hundreds wait in their desperation, helplessness, and abandoned state. At CMC they are homeless, powerless, and in total despair. In this context, I want to repeat your question: "But how far can we say that such creative, or perhaps active, waiting is the same order as that of the involuntary, passive, waiting of the hospital patient?"

Vanstone's point is that in this waiting we encounter that God who, "creating the world in the activity of love, destines Himself to wait upon the world and gives to the world power of meaning to Himself." (p.12). So it is that "when man waits upon the world … God also waits; and it is in waiting that He invests the world with the possibility and power of meaning. Equally, Margaret Whipp writes that:

> "On every page of the scriptures, we … meet the same patient Lover of souls who yearns and pleads, who seduces and suffers, who rages and ravishes, who labours and cries out, who whispers and agonizes, who burns and bleeds, for Love of the poor human creatures he is drawing to himself. This is the God who, from everlasting to everlasting, is waiting still for us." (Whipp, p.71).

The image of God which is found in humanity's capacity for creative and loving activity, and for creative and loving waiting, is also to be found "in the various and commonplace forms of waiting which are 'imposed' upon us by our awareness of our various and commonplace needs." Of course we must acknowledge that some forms of waiting may be uncomfortable or even disagreeable, but, even where that is the case, "from the Christian viewpoint, it is never a *degraded* condition, a condition of *diminished* human dignity." So "[Man] must not see it as degrading that he should wait upon the world, be helped, be provided for, be dependent; for as such he is, by God's gift, what God Himself makes Himself to be." Thus, concludes Vanstone, "as he waits in the future, increasingly dependent on systems and machines … on medical support and social provision, he will in no sense be deprived of his high calling … whenever he so stands man will be a figure of unique and almost unbelievable dignity."(Vanstone, p.75). What does this waiting means at CMC in the here and now? Let me share one of my direct experience.

Negotiating religious-sacramental space:

Waiting for the waiting God

In this section I like to present an incident, quite an ordinary one, yet it presents extraordinary examples for "Waiting for God". This is a unique experience in the hospital ministry with wider implications for religion, theology, psychology, psychotherapy, pastoral counselling, and chaplaincy.

This incident is my direct experience of being with a medical (healing) community. At the Christian Medical College & Hospital, Vellore, I had the privilege of ministering with passion week meditations with the team of Chaplains who conducted regular worship services at the in the College and in the Hospital Chapel. The Chapel is located at the Centre of the hospital complex and has easy access to the patients, their relatives, and the visitors. In a day or two I realized that a large number of people who attend the worship services and seek help from the Chaplaincy were from many faiths and religious traditions. The most challenging scene I observed began to challenge my own theological understanding of certain specific Christian themes, sacraments, and rituals.

On the Maundy Thursday worship, there were a large number of patients who were 'brought and lined up' for Holy Communion. During the meditation I focused on "Salvation and Healing of God" that comes to all people through Jesus Christ, the Lamb of God for humanity. As the Holy Communion began it was obvious that many were from other faith traditions but they all participated reverentially (some even extra-reverential in my opinion) in the communion. All came forward, kneeling down, and praying as they wait for the celebrant priest to reach them.

During the process I noticed a father and a young son about 6 years, appear to be from another faith tradition, who also came kneeling down. The Chaplain came to the father and served him the bread which he took in his hands, and waited for the Chaplain to serve his son who was the patient. But the Chaplain just touched the lad on the forehead, blessed him, and passed by. The father once again requested the celebrant in sign language (as if he was making a protest) to give the bread to his son also. But the officiating Chaplain, with disapproval, went on with his task. The father, who had the bread in his hands, closed his eyes, prayed, and reverentially gave it to his son, which the officiating priest did not notice. When his turn came for the wine, which was served in individual cups, the father tried hard to get one for his son also but the priest again blessed the child and waited till the father drank the wine. Hence, the son had the bread and the father the wine!

In a sharing session in the department the Chaplains explained the challenges of working in the Hospital setting with multi-faith and multi-ethnic communities as their target population, particularly in their struggles with sickness, pain, suffering, and death. The team of chaplains did not (and could not) adhere to a set of rules that guided the celebration of Holy Communion. It became obvious to me that in spite of well formulated theologies and written and unwritten codes, persons and communities are always in the process of seeking the presence of God that comes through various ritual actions, celebrations, and sacramental participation. When someone comes kneeling down with prayer, seeking the blessing from the Almighty, seeking the gracious presence of the Divine, and with a feeling of utmost dependence before God, who can stop them? This is waiting on God.

What is important here is the meaning of the event for that person and to the community. One might have noticed continuous prayers in the chapel, burning of the candles round the clock in front of the cross, seeking prayers from the chaplaincy department, spending time in the corridors and courtyards where they eat and sleep and eagerly waiting for healing for their dear ones. This is real waiting for God!

This event indicates how 'meaning-full' experiences are created as part of ministerial engagements, emerging from critical and utterly helpless situations. The event challenges us to discern and to engage with meaning-making experiences and encounters in the life of the faithful. It reveals to us an area of human experience that includes going beyond the boundaries seeking the divine. In this event there is no question of beginning with a theology of Eucharist, baptism or church administration, or any well-articulated theological treatise supporting or rejecting such a ministerial action. Rather, such 'meaningful' faith expressions and practices could be interpreted from the theme today, Waiting on God for healing and wholeness.

This encounter and further reflections helped me to think further on the sustaining God's work in our communities today which is the subheading for Professor Wood's conclusion.

Sustaining our work through the life of the people of God

In conclusion, based on the insights from Hauerwas and Whipp, Professor Wood stresses the need for sustained, committed, caring God's work in the community today. The service- providing community is called to live her life in solidarity with the suffering and the needy, as Jesus had done. This solidarity involves meeting them at their waiting points, listening with respect, and waiting on God to give our best to them. The help seeking ones are vulnerable mentally, emotionally, economically, socially, and spiritually. What they long for is God's healing (and curing) and salvation. It is in this context one understands the motto of the CMC, "not to be served, but to serve."

This work involves waiting, sometimes patiently and at other times impatiently, for God's healing and restoration. The CMC history shows she had waited on God, decades after decades, beginning with Ida Scudder, to be a blessing in this country. Let her continue to be a blessing for the communities today.

Endnotes

[1] The Amnesty International held a programme at the United Theological College, Bangalore, on 13th August 2016, following which the attack by the BJP-VHP-ABVP volunteers with some ransacking. The College was forced to close the main gate for more than 24 hours. The attack still continues with branding UTC as a anti-national and anti-patriotic organization and they demanded the closure of this 108 years old College.

[2] Stephen Pattison, *Alive and Kicking: Towards a Practical Theology of Illness and Healing* (London: SCM Press, 1989), 19ff.

[3] Pattison, *Alive and Kicking,* 15f.

[4] Pattison, *Alive and Kicking*, 23.

[5] Abigal Rian Evans, *Redeeming Marketplace Medicine: A Theology of Health Care*, Wipf & Stock Pub, 2008, 17ff.

[6] CMC official website.

[7] Benard Haring, *Healing and Revealing* (London: St. Pauls, 1984), 14f.

[8] John Oommen, "A Personal Search for Deeper Meaning in Medicine and Health Care: A Vocation in the Healing Ministry" (Paper at this Colloquium, 6).

PART-1
Reconceptualization
of Healing Ministry

Minority Within Minority

'If we Talk the Talk, we have to Walk the Walk'

Dhirendra Sahu

A humorous note on the Dietary Advice by Purushotam Das Tandon, the then Congress President as mentioned by Pauline is quite amusing as well as intriguing.

> "To live the God–ordained span of life, don't take cooked food; don't eat salt or sugar. Gandhiji said white sugar is white poison. Don't take milk, butter, ghee and honey, which are concentrated foods and not meant for man…" Nature has provided the natural mother's milk till the age of three or four. For an adult, milk is not meant at all. The same applies to the use of honey… Vaidyas recommend it invariably to their patients, but it is not human food, and is only meant for the bees that produce it. With the exception of man no other animal takes cooked food; therefore, I ask, why should cooked food be necessary for man?[1] (Query: No other animal grows food- why should man grow it?!)

There was no prophet to predict that 9th December, 1870, the day when baby Ida arrived, was to become Founder's and College Day for several hundred medical school graduates and friends half a century later.[2] Nobody also had ever thought that one morning in the fall of the Jubilee year of CMC, the students and practitioners of the indigenous system of medicine will try to force India to put all her medical eggs:

Homeopaths, Unanis, Ayurvedics, Quacks and Nature Cure advocates in one basket. The debate between Indian and Western perspectives on Medicine is an ongoing debate in the history of health care.

CMC is the first Women's Medical College anywhere which has been started by a woman, staffed by women and run for women only, till men knocked at the door so persistently that the door had to be opened as a co-educational College. Often the sequence has been the opposite in the West where many a time a Men's Medical College has had to open its door to women. But for this, Ida Scudder was accused of being disloyal by her few old friends on the American Committee.[3] Today CMC Vellore is 2700 bed teaching, referral and multi-specialty medical college, training 100 undergraduates and 178 post graduates every year and 9000 patients knocking the door of outpatient department every day.

The vision statement of CMC Vellore is to be a witness to the healing ministry of Christ through excellence in education, service and research which has remain undiluted because of the commitment to the cause by generation of faculty and staff of the institution. In 2018 CMC Vellore was the best Private Hospital in India as per the survey done.[4] The CMC students of medicine get almost a free education. In CMC, a MBBS student pays just Rs3000 per year tuition fee and a postgraduate Rs400 tuition fee per year. It has been since 1978 and fees have not been revised in the last 25years. It has created a social climate for medical education that benefits all people instead of a commercial climate where healthcare is becoming an industry for profit. A medical student who is a beneficiary of this low fee privilege realizes that some poor patient have a role to play in his education. He completes his education and begins his career with a deep sense of obligation to those unknown patients whose mite has been part of his resources

Formation of an identity

The actions we take, the people we spend time with and the principles we choose, define our identity. We should choose to construct an identity that signals to the world our vision and core values. Therefore, the issue is how we define our identity as a 'Minority Institution' in Indian scenario today if we have to 'walk the walk'. Kethoser (Aniu) Kevichusa, in his address to mark Naga Day ceremony 2018, interestingly divides people under three broad categories. He classifies people under 'idiot', 'tribal' and 'citizen' groups. He says these types are broadly differentiated by sociologists tracing back to founders of democracy in ancient Greece. Greeks believed the first kind of people is 'idiots'. They are not mentally deficient, but they are those who are totally self-centered. The 'idiots' always run for the private gains and personal interest. They have no public philosophy, no knowledge, no skill, no character and no virtue to contribute to the society. Such people always look out for personal pleasure and treasure. Tribal people follow tribalistic philosophy and such people are not able to think beyond the interest of their small tribe or group. For them, their primary religion is their tribe. They generally view everything from their own prism and interpret it in their own way. The third category is 'citizens'. Citizens are those who have the skills and knowledge to live respectable public lives, who know the value of common wealth as well as their rights and responsibilities towards the society. In other words, they help to form a civilized society.

"Governance" is the process of decision-making and the process by which decisions are implemented or not implemented! In simple terms, governance is the act of governing. This act is performed by a governing body, in our case the 'the Council'. Governance is the creation of policies that define the identity of an institution through debate and discussion. In our institution the Council members decide strategy/directions to propel the organization forward. Administration is concerned with the implementation of the decisions of governance. *One may say that Governance determines the "What?"-What the organization does and what it should become in the future. Management determines the "How?"-How the organization will reach those goals and aspirations.* Strategy is a long-term, forward looking approach to planning that must be guided by well defined policy through good governance to achieve the goal.

The identity of the Council is shaped by the identity of its fifty-two wide varieties of stakeholders who play or ought to play a decisive role in governance. In his autobiography called 'A Life and its Lessons', Samuel Paul, our former Vice-Chairman of the CMC Council and former director of the Indian Institute of Management, Ahmedabad narrates the story of CMC in one chapter. He cites that 'CMC has received numerous accolades and is widely perceived as a great success story'. The credit goes to generations of committed faculty and staff who have imbibed the story in their life and work. The oversight mechanism is a major contributor to its success and longevity, not the least CMC being a heath care provider. However, one longstanding constraint in the area of medical education is role of the regulatory body which the Council had never envisaged when on Ida Scudder's Jubilee celebration year the great announcement was made of full and unqualified affiliation with the Madras University.

CMC Vellore administrative model of healthcare where the CEO and top layers of administration are from the medical faculty with its home grown, in-house leaders goes against established healthcare management paradigms. Samuel makes a cautious observation "There is of course no guarantee that CMC's reputation and survival is assured forever just because it has outlived its first century. Failure to induct competent and experienced persons to guide and oversee non-medical management functions at senior levels is likely to hurt the institution's effectiveness and credibility."[5] In our journey from Chennai to Bangalore on road and over a cup of coffee in his home in Bangalore, he expressed many times that the line between governance and management is blurred in the Council. Interestingly, he also underlines 'the silence of good people', in particular the 'silence of the stakeholders' in the governance process in the Council may become a deterrent in the growth of an esteemed institution.

Institutions in general are facing crises of identity all over the world. Governance has come under scrutiny since the economic meltdown of 2008. The ethics of governance is in question. Christian institutions like

CMC need to be particularly conscious of the disruptive trends of the world. Honesty, ethics and transparency in governance must be kept above trivial concerns, and it is the Council's responsibility to insulate the institution from anything that could derail our vision and mission. The crucial question the Council must ask continuously is "Will we pass a test of credibility if done by an external Agency?" Samuel Paul's concern which comes as the worldview of a renowned management guru holds much water.

Redefining theology

Personal and Community aspects of religion and spirituality have been thriving often with the help of vigorous marketing or stage-managed spirituality. The commoditization of religion has generally been ambiguous. In the midst of immense changes, an attempt is made to discern what to welcome, what to reject, what to learn to live with and what to try to transform for the better. People directly involved with world's major religious traditions participate in conversation through understanding, values, virtues, convictions and practices that shape ordinary life. Theology in its broadest spectrum might be defined as thinking about the questions that arise precisely from ordinary living as well as from mysteries and to cope with the unanswered question of health and healing.

One could be to look at the' theology of Health and Healing' from a perspective of Hospitality but the term 'Hospitality' sounds alarming to some. The reason being the Healthcare providers are incorporating best practices from the hospitality industry to create hospitality based environments for their patients, accounting for both patient well-being and revenue consideration. But we can explore the same with a deeper theological understanding of Pain and Suffering, Health & Healing and Wholeness on the basis to reclaim the model of ministry of Jesus. In so doing, to rediscover a hospitable God, who not only welcomes all but expects to care for all.

Therefore one formative factor in re-defining a theology of health and healing could be through conversation. Conversation can be informal and spontaneous, disciplined or structured, but criterion of conversation should be 'Wisdom'. It is most inclusive to describe theology. In the words of David Ford:

> "Wisdom is perhaps the most comprehensive and least controversial term for what theology is about. Wisdom may embrace describing, understanding, explaining, knowing and deciding, not only regarding matters of empirical fact but also regarding values, norms, beliefs and shaping of lives, communities and institutions."[6]

Wisdom in Old Testament is identified with God. "All wisdom is from the Lord; she dwells with him forever" (Eccles 1:1). Intrinsic to the formation of a wise mind is habitual relationship with God as well as pursuit of wisdom wherever it is to be found. It is strongly self-critical in the book of Job. It is further specified in Christian thought "to see Jesus Christ crucified as the 'wisdom of God' (1 Cor. 1.24) is to find ourselves wrestling like Job. In Job 28 there are mining of analogy for searching for wisdom but it reveals that wisdom "is not found in the land of the living" (Job 28:13), but in the mind of God. Then the conclusion is that 'Truly, the fear of the Lord, that is wisdom; and to depart from evil is understanding" (Job 28:28). Our task is to discern the wisdom from the Bible and contribute to wise understanding and living before God today in the midst of multiple unanswered question of health and healing.

Mission vis-à-vis mission hospital

Mission(singular) refers to the *missio Dei* (God's mission) that is, God's self revelation as the One who loves the world, God's involvement in and with the world, the nature and activity of God, which embraces both the church and the world, and in which the church is privileged to participate. Missio Dei enunciates the Good news that God is a God for people. Missions, including medical mission (plural) refer to particular forms, related to specific times, places or needs and participation in the missio Dei.[7] The founder of the CMC even went further in saying 'we are not building a Hospital but the Kingdom of God'. If that is the paradigm of our mission, then it is pertinent to have introspection in our conversation.

Personally, my memory goes back forty-three years, when immediately after my ordination as a Presbyter of the Church of North India and marriage, we were posted to work as chaplain in the Mission Hospital and my wife was to teach in mission high school for the underprivileged in Kond hills of Odisha. I heard the story of the excellent medical service rendered by the mission hospital to the marginalized. The people used to call a micro form of CMC, not in terms of infrastructure or medical education but excellent dedicated service of Baptist Missionary Society missionaries. Now, when I had the opportunity to visit Kondhmal during the riot in 2008; I found the hospital a monument! It is not an isolated story but a story that finds space in every CMC council meeting.

The mission hospitals were set-up to deliver secondary healthcare with the support of various churches, denominations and movements to reach out to extremely marginalized regions of the country. Over time, due to various constrains most of them have been unable to sustain themselves. The Gospel is concerned with the sick person than with the particular sickness and that the sick person is part of an environment and a community which also stand in need of healing. The CMC Vellore came into being as a focus of two converging interests of functional and theological thinking. The theological concern was to seek new insights into the interconnections between the gospel, healing and the mission of the churches. Health is more than medicine. It is to do with the way we live and the way we die, the quality of life and death. It was well said during the Colloquium by Usha Jesudasan that 'one may be cured but not healed or may be healed but not cured'.

Minority within minority

The 'minority" "minority network" and "minority service" are the words in our admission process to defend our identity as 'minority'. The Oxford

Dictionary defines 'minority' as a smaller group representing "less than half of the whole or predominant population". The National Commission for Minorities Act, 1992 in the Section 2(c) of the act defined a minority as "a community notified as such by the Central government". Acting under the provision on October 23, 1993, the Central government notified the Muslim, Christians, Sikhs, Buddhist and Parsis (Zoroastrian) communities as minorities for the purpose of the Act.

Sponsorship of students by churches, denominations and healthcare linked organizations has been a CMC tradition and policy for nearly seventy years now. The idea was to create a model of human resources in medical care that would render service in the particular areas and people. The churches and healthcare related organizations serve through their hospitals. The fifty two stakeholders of CMC Vellore range from Eastern Orthodox Churches to the dioceses of the Church of South India, Church of North India, Lutherans, Baptists, Presbyterians, Evangelicals and Pentecostals. The students on completion of their study return to their respective regions to fulfill their service obligations. Some stay on and spend lifetime serving in remote areas. The practice ensures that mission hospitals and marginalized regions get a constant flow of well-trained young doctors.

'CMC developed a unique system of selection that evolved from the belief that practice of medicine is a calling, not a career. While merit is essential, that alone is not adequate. Merit by academic performance has to be complemented with a sense of mission and suitability to serve. Attitude along with aptitude is a non-negotiable prerequisite for the formation of a complete doctor.'[8] CMC's dual yardstick of 'merit and suitability' is not opposed to merit but to the notion of 'exclusivity of merit' as it goes beyond the numbers and ranking. However, with the introduction of NEET, the issue is how to adhere to this long cherished non-negotiable tradition of CMC. Sponsorship in CMC Vellore is a privilege of the church & organization in medical mission, long cherished and revered by the stakeholders. Legal battles are not only in place but also intriguing, costly and time consuming. Sometimes there is no light at the end of the tunnel except to make the journey in faith obeying the call to cast the net in the deep. The question often being asked by the judiciary is not that of the minority status of CMC as 'a Christian Institution' but claiming 'minority within minority' on multiple stakeholders' identities to claim a seat in the College to justify our minority status.

Ecumenical partnership

The modern ecumenical movement had its origin in the missionary movements at the end of nineteenth and beginning of twentieth century. The protestant churches began the conversation in missionary endeavor that resulted in the formation of the Church of South India and Church of North India. Perhaps the time has come to initiate a conversation among the stakeholders of all mission hospitals including CMC Vellore to envisage the medical mission of the churches not as denominational or organizational enterprise but united endeavor. The church has been fighting only for self-preservation as though that were an end in itself.

It is inspiring to remember that the missionaries those who came from overseas and initiated mission of the health care against all odds, were not the persons who had prior knowledge of the language and culture of the locals but gave their life time dedicated and committed service. There are number of CMC graduates who have also crossed the boundary of their own language bastion and region to give and are giving committed service for the marginalized in unreached areas.

The CMC Vellore Council has a unique role to play to develop a holistic and Christian understanding of 'Health and Healing' in a commercialized world. It should initiate a process to transcend the historic denominational and organizational boundaries of stakeholders. It is to reclaim the model of ministry of Jesus through innovative theological and biblical reflection and imaginative models of spiritual and medical formation. The challenge is and shall be how to construct an identity from 'minority within minority' to 'a minority' in the realm of God's kingdom. It is to proclaim God's love through a reconciled community that has internalized the power of the gospel. Therefore it is possible to develop a culture that could be really indigenous. It involves rethinking the medical vocation not as a profession to build a career or to serve only in a comfort zone but as a call by God to the ministry of health and healing like the specific calls to ministry in the church as people of God.

That would require a structured period of preparation by the churches and organizations, one year before NEET as well as formation during medical education in CMC. Nurturing young and bright minds for a vocation in health care is very crucial, that can rise above the mindset of so called 'bond period' as a fulfillment of service obligation. As a corollary to this the nature and composition of sponsorship meetings during the Council meetings every year will take a different paradigm and ethos. Perhaps it will not be that difficult to start re-thinking about the nature and role of 'sponsorship meeting' with the students twice in year during the Council meeting.

Peter Greer and Chris Horst share their journey of discovery as they address the pivotal question of 'Mission Drift'. They draw the attention to the fact that faith-based organizations inevitably drift from their founding mission. The cited stories in the book[9] is fascinating as well as alarming. Slowly and silently organizations routinely drift from their original purpose. It has happened repeatedly throughout history. They have said that Institutional drift is fundamentally unintended. But they give a call to institutional humility and accountability. The mandate of CMC Vellore is 'Not building a Medical College but the Kingdom of God. Celebrating 100 years of medical education 1918-2018 is a milestone of health and healing ministry of the church. However, there is a need to hear the prophetic voice. In the words quoted by Pauline: 'Organized welfare work is, of course necessary; but the gaps in it must be filled by personal services, performed with loving kindness. A charitable organization is a complex affair like an automobile; it needs a broad highway to run on. It cannot penetrate the little bypaths; those are for men and women to walk through, with open eyes and hearts full of comprehension. It is often these little bypaths that you can find 'Aunt Ida' now.[10]

Can we find 'Aunt Ida' now in the little bypaths of India today?

Endnotes

[1] Pauline Jeffrey, Ida S Scudder, Ida S Scudder of Vellore, Word of Christ, Chennai, India, 2014Ibid, 227.

[2] Ibid, 3.

[3] Ibid, 215.

[4] *The Week,* November 25, 2018, 84.

[5] Paul, Samuel, *A Life and Its Lessons,* Public Affair Centre, 2012, 255.

[6] Ford, F. David. Shaping Theology, Blackwell, 2007, 3.

[7] Bosch, David. The Transforming Mission, Orbis Books, 1997, 10.

[8] Chandy, Sunil, Christian Medical College, Vellore in: Nundy Samiran, Desiraju, Keshav & Nagral, Sanjay Eds. Healers or Predators? OUP, 2018, 577.

[9] Greer, Peter & Horst, Chris, Mission Drift, Bethany House Publication, 2014,

[10] Ibid, 249.

'I was Stranger': Towards a Theology of Hospitality

Samuel Richmond Saxena

In the winter of 1993 Professor Jürgen Moltmann a renowned *Hope Theologian* after finishing the lecture, asked one of his typical questions, both concrete and penetrating: "But can you embrace a *cetnik (terrorist)*?" They had been sowing desolation in Croatia, herding people into concentration camps, raping women, burning down churches, and destroying cities. After hearing this type of question in a class, Miroslav Volf grappled with various other questions that started to disturb him: Can I embrace a *nik—the* ultimate other, so to speak, the evil other? What would justify the embrace" Where would I draw the strength for it? What would it do to my identity as a human being and as a Croat? It took him a while to answer, though he immediately knew **"No, I cannot—but as a follower of Christ I think I should be able to."** The book written by him, *Exclusion and Embrace: A Theological Exploration of Identity, Otherness, and Reconciliation* is an excellent work in laying down the theology of reconciliation and embracing others in the midst of conflict and struggle.

Embracing others, identifying with others, treating others as equals, showing love to another person, offering hospitality or generosity is indeed a big challenge today in the midst of rising intolerance, violence, division, terrorism, rage, sectarianism, hatred etc. Whether reading the local newspaper or the global online news, whether watching the latest film or listening to the newest music, such issues seem to be omnipresent in one or the other form. What has Church to offer in such a situation? What is the responsibility of Christians who claim to be the followers of Christ? In what ways Christian theology in today's context may able to help in developing 'theology of hospitality' that may become a point of reference to the larger community?

In Judeo-Christian tradition, 'care and concern', 'hospitality', 'offering the best to others' and 'table-fellowships' were the key practices that made them different from the others. Even today, people from other faiths have great expectation from us. Whether we run schools, colleges, hospitals, homes, hotels, guest houses etc., hospitality, care for other and service for others are part and parcel of our Christian character. In fact the whole world looks at us as model in this regard and the Church should continue to retain its identity. This paper will make an attempt to know what 'Otherness' is, *secondly*, the experience of Christ as 'Other' as well as his concern for 'Others' and *thirdly*, in what ways the Biblical theology of hospitality for 'Strangers or Others' may offer hope to the world and *lastly* how the Church may equip herself towards her service to the humankind as part of the Kingdom principle.

Identifying others

"Otherness" as the difference is a reality; we do encounter people and their practices that are strange to us and it is a starting point for asking ourselves how we ought to behave toward people who differ from us. What is our responsibility toward them? The range of understanding 'stranger' or 'other' oscillates between the ancient notion of 'foreigner' (xenos) to the contemporary category of alien invader. Hence 'otherness' is always understood beyond the boundaries of national territory but in today's context it is right amongst us. Our behavior towards others has become a global concern which requires a fundamental restructuring of our value system with the help of Christian spirituality. In today's society, 'otherness' is determined within the dimension of identity which may be related to - language, ethnicity, faith, profession, caste, gender, disability, status etc. "One of the principal ways human beings choose to draw boundaries that secure their safety and identity" mentions Robert Schreiter, "by exclusion; placing beyond the boundary those who are not us/ who are 'them." Hence to label something or someone as "other" can be the first step in making them "other."[1] Much of the problem comes when "other" is neither recognized nor the differences have been properly respected. The Christian tradition places a strong emphasis on confronting and transforming the perception and experience of "otherness" In this strand of Christian thinking; the condition of being stranger and alien is a dimension of our unreconciled state.[2] Schreiter identified seven ways of "other-making":

1. We can *demonize* the other... considering other as wicked

2. We can, on the other hand, *romanticize* the other, treating the other as farsuperior to ourselves.

3. We can *colonize* the other, treating the other as inferior, worthy of pity or contempt...

4. We can *generalize* the other, treating the other as non-individual...

5. We can *trivialize* the other by ignoring what makes the other disturbingly different...

6. We can *homogenize* the other by claiming that there really is no difference. This is most in evidence in situations where two opposing groups are joined together forcibly...

7. We can *vaporize* the other... by refusing to acknowledge the presence of the other at all. This is often found in cases of racism, where the oppressed people's existence is not even acknowledged.[3]

For Miralsov Volf, in all wars, whether large or small, whether carried out on battlefields, city streets, living rooms, or faculty lounges, we come across the same basic exclusionary polarity; 'us against them,' 'their gain-our loss,' 'either us or them.' The stronger the conflict, the more the rich texture of the social world disappears and the severe exclusionary division emerges around which all thought and practice align itself.[4] Volf emphasizes, in order to erase conflict between the two parties there is a need for peace so that community may live in harmony. In view of this, the wall of hostility needs to be removed so that 'self' and 'other' may come together.[5] Overcoming the separation of self from other is at the heart of Christian reconciliation. Ian Barbour famous physicist writes, "We do not experience life as neatly divided into separate compartments; we experience it in wholeness and interconnectedness before we develop particular disciplines to study different aspects of it."[6]

Jesus: A stranger & a man for others

Matthew in chapter twenty five mentions that when Jesus Christ will return, it will be a time of *separation:* the wise will be separated from the foolish, the faithful servants from the unfaithful, the blessed (sheep) from the cursed (goats). The foolish and the unfaithful ones are those who lacked the gift of hospitality while the wise and the faithful ones are those who were able to fulfill the kingdom principles by taking care of the others. Interestingly, God's justice is determined by the treatment they offered to others. In this passage when Jesus mentions: 'I was hungry' 'I was thirsty' 'I was stranger' 'I was naked' 'I was sick' and 'I was in prison', He relates to the sufferings of common human beings.

When Jesus said, 'I was a stranger', He identifies himself to a particular group of individuals who are considered to be a foreigner or an outsider, neglected or even an enemy. Remarkably, Jesus is not considering 'strangers' as 'they' but he claims himself as a 'stranger' by becoming a stranger. In Jesus, God for our sake became hungry, thirsty, stranger, naked, sick and prisoner. Paradoxically, the one who claimed Himself to be:

- the Bread of Life (Jn. 6:35) – says I'm hungry (Mk. 11:12)
- the source of the Living Water (Jn. 7:37) – says I'm thirsty (Jn. 19:28)
- the Creator of Space and entire Cosmos (Gen. 1:1) – says I was a stranger (Lk. 2:7)

- wearing the garment was of splendor, majesty and light (Ps. 104:) – says I was naked (Jn. 19:23)

- Jehovah Rapha (Healer-Ex 15:26) – says I was sick (Isa. 53:4)

- The freedom of the prisoner (Luke 4:18) – says I was in prison (Mt. 27:35).

Our glorious King who is seated on the throne in heaven has already experienced the pain, suffering and agony of every human while he was on this earth as a man. Now the question arises, can God be said to suffer? If it is so then a point of contact is immediately established between God and the pain of the human world. God cannot then be thought of as being immune from the suffering of the creation. The suffering of God is the direct consequence of the divine *decision* to suffer, and the divine *willingness* to suffer. Hence the cross must be seen as an event between the Father and the Son, in which the Father suffers the death of his Son in order to redeem sinful humanity. It is only through the suffering through which one understands the pain of others and then responds with love and compassion. In *A Theology of the Pain of God* (1946), the Japanese writer KazohKitamori (1916–98) argued that the love of God for the whole creation was rooted in pain. "God is the wounded Lord, having pain in himself." God is able to give meaning and dignity to human suffering on account of the fact that he also is in pain, and suffers.[7]

According to the gospels, there are several other verses which bear witness that Jesus was considered a stranger by many people even by his own family members. The gospel of Saint Luke (2:7) records when Mary gave birth to Jesus, she laid him in a manger, and because there was no place for them in the inn (they were stranger). Further,we read how Joseph, Mary, and the child Jesus were forced to flee Bethlehem and went to Egypt as stranger because of Herod (Mt. 2:13-15).Jesus during his earthly ministry was with the people for three years but on the way to Emmaus, a strange question was asked by his disciple: '*Are you the only stranger in Jerusalem?*' (Lk. 14:18). The gospel of Saint John says, '*He was in the world, and the world came into being through*

*Him; **yet the world did not know him**. He came to his own home, and his own people received him not.'* At one point of time, he was thought as a *ghost* by his disciples (Mt. 14: 26). Simon the Pharisee failed to provide the required hospitality as per the custom which is counted as an insult to him. Shailendra Rodrigues writes, 'it was more a hostility than hospitality that Jesus experienced in Simon's house.'[8] In contrast to this, a woman honors Jesus by washing his feet by her tears. Why was he a stranger to own people? Or why he is still a stranger to many? Leonard Boff, defines a stranger as

> One who does not fit into a particular common criterion. Strangeness can be caused by someone's different behavior or by someone's belonging to a different ethnic background that is not present in a society or by someone who speaks a different language or by someone who presents different ideas or understandings of the world uncommon to a cultural group.[9]

Since Jesus came from heaven to earth, his thoughts, teachings, ideas, behavior, way of working were entirely based on Kingdom principles and appeared to others as strange. For example, traditionally Jews were taught to hate their enemy but Jesus says, 'Love your enemy.' There was no gap between his teaching and his actions.

The majority of theological works are made of words. But there is also a space for visual theology which exists in the form of icons, sculptures, and painting and they have their own mute eloquence, which bears witness to the curious texture of divine life. Such visual theology recurs in the painting of 'The Light of the World' by William Holman Hunt which hangs in the side Chapel of Keble's Chapel at Keble's College, Oxford. This painting is based on Revelation 3:20, where Jesus carrying a lantern, standing outside as stranger and knocking the door to get a place in our hearts. There is no handle on the door and hence it cannot be opened from outside. The rusty nails and hinges overgrown with ivy denote that the door has never been opened and that the figure of Christ is asking for permission to enter.

Even after the resurrection Jesus continues to be a stranger for many. Without inviting this stranger in our lives we cannot love others or give space to other strangers. In Matthew 25:31-36 when Jesus claims himself as a stranger, He invokes the Church to follow the acts of mercy. Christians are measured by the works of compassion that they receive from Christ so that they extend it other fellow beings. Christian theology has a pleasant task of offering genuine friendship of Christ in a fragmented world and one way of looking at this is to think of 'hospitality' as grace-driven.

Hospitality: A Biblical perspective

During a blistering hot day, a family was entertaining guests for dinner. When all were seated, the man of the house turned to his six-year-old son and asked him to say the blessing. "But daddy, I don't know what to say," he protested. "Oh, just say what you've heard me say," the mother chimed in. Obediently, he bowed his little head and said, "Oh, Lord, why did I invite these people here on a hot day like this!"

Looking for God in the people who come to us on our way is perhaps the key to practicing real Christian hospitality. How does hospitality proceed in an "age of terror and violence"? What happens to the concept of hospitality in an era where intolerance is rising, persecution among Christians is increasing, mannerism and courtesy are declining, minorities are under attack, insecurity among women and children etc. Hospitality, according to Bruce Malina, may be defined as the "process by means of which an outsider's status is changed from stranger to guest . . . [and] differs from entertaining family and friends."[10] It is a set of social instructions such as providing food and lodging which are to be applied to outsiders, such that potential enemies are transformed into allies, or outsiders into insiders. In Matthew 25:35, the Greek word for 'stranger' is *Xenos* which means "guest" and this guest may belong to another nation (foreigner), an unknown person or an alien, sojourner (pilgrim).

According to the Old Testament, a stranger was commonly understood as a foreigner settled among the covenant people, without Israelite citizenship, but subject to Israel's laws, and having a claim to kindness and justice.[11] The Israelites were commanded to extend generous hospitality to the stranger or sojourner in 'the Covenant code in Exodus (Exod. 22.21; 23.9), the priestly laws of Leviticus (Lev. 19.33-34), and the Deuteronomic law code (Deut. 16.14; 26.12).' Through these scriptures one may deduce that hospitality was an important custom throughout a significant portion of ancient Israel's history. Apart from the kind reception of a stranger or traveler in Jewish hospitality, the Jewish host was primarily expected to provide both provisions and protection.[12] In Jewish sources, we find the claim that whoever supports the poor, needy or stranger is as if they support the Lord. "What you give to My people you give to Me." Prophet Isaiah challenges people: *Is it not to share your bread with the hungry, and bring the homeless poor into your house; when you see the naked, to cover them, and not to hide yourself from your own kin?* (58:7).

The patriarchs considered their personal wealth as a gift from God and a sign of his favour and blessing. At the same time, however, such God-given wealth was also regarded as something to be shared with others, notably within the family and the tribe, but also by extending hospitality to the visitor and the stranger.[13] John Koenig contends that Jewish hospitality grew out of 'Bedouin traditions having to do with a resident's obligation to nourish and protect travelers who find themselves in hostile environments.'[14] Even today a traditional greeting to the guests among the Bedouin people of the Middle East is "You are among your family."[15] There is an ancient legend that Abraham invited into his tent a man, who at meal time gave no thanks to God for his mercy. Where upon the patriarch drove him forth into the desert unfed and unsheltered. But in the night God touched Abraham and awoke him, saying to him, "Where is the stranger?" Abraham said, "When he did not fear you, nor thank you, I drove him forth." God rebuked him, saying, "Who made you his judge: I have borne with him all these years. Could you not bear with him one night? Have you learned nothing from my mercy to you?"[16]

In the OT we find Abraham, Lot, Laban, Job, the Shunammite woman and others practicing hospitality. They opened the doors to the travelers so that strangers do not have to lodge in the streets (Job 31:32). In Gen 18:1ff. Abraham *rushes* out of his tent to greet three strangers who approach him–**in the heat of the day.** Abraham then *offers* them a little water so they can wash their own feet and rest under the tree shade. Abraham also *instructs* Sarah to make bread cakes using three measures of fine flour, *selects* a tender and good calf from the herd, has a servant *prepare* the calf, and *provides* curds and milk for his guests. When a feast is set before them, these unknown visitors reveal God's promise concerning the son to be born of Abraham. Once the men have eaten and refreshed themselves, they vow to return again to Abraham's house (18:10, 14). This story of Abraham functioned as the ideal picture of hospitality in the OT.

In the New Testament, Jesus himself says, *'Truly I tell you, whatever you did for one of the least of these brothers and sisters of mine, you did for me'* (Matt. 25:40). Further the writer of the Hebrews urges Christians to take hospitality seriously: *'Do not neglect to show hospitality to strangers, for by doing that some have entertained angels without knowing it' (Heb.13:2).* In Luke 10:25-37, the stranger was stripped, beaten and dumped by the robbers and was lying half-dead on the roadside. The priest and the Levite (Jews) who were considered to be the agents of hospitality and were taught from the beginning how to take care of the strangers, simply passed by on the other side. But a Samaritan while travelling **came near** him; and when he **saw him,** he was **moved with pity, bandaged his wounds,** having **poured oil and wine** on them. Then he put **him on his own animal, admitted him** in the infirmary, and took **care of him** probably whole night and next day **he** gave two denarii to the innkeeper, and said, *'Take care of him; and when* **I come back,** *I will* **repay you whatever more you spend.'** Here Samaritan was not only proved to be a true neighbour but also by his behaviour he lays down a perfect example before the Priest and the Levi with regard to our treatment to 'strangers' Hence, the Good Samaritan stands for all ages as an example of Christian hospitality.

A joyful **welcome** of Jesus and his disciples by Mary, Martha, and Lazarus at Bethany is recorded by John in chapter 12:1-11. Probably, because of their loving attitude, Bethany became a prominent station for Jesus during his visit. They **served him** as well as to his disciples with delicious food and **Mary wiped Jesus' feet** with an expensive perfume. It is said that Spikenard was a fragrant herb obtained from the roots of a plant grown in the Himalayas. From Himalayas, it came to Palestine and that must have added more value to the product. In this act of hospitality, they gave their best to Jesus. Ironically, Judas Iscariot showed his displeasure over the use of an expensive perfume for Jesus. Henry Drummond says: the most obvious lesson in Christ's teaching is that there is no happiness in having or getting anything, but only in giving. When Christ visits our home what best we may give to him? Later the apostles urged the Church to "follow after hospitality," As mentioned in Romans 12:13, hospitality literally means '**love of strangers**' and Christians are expected to '**offer hospitality without grudging**,' (1 Pet. 4:9) even bishops must be a "lover of hospitality" (Titus 1:8, cf. 1 Tim. 3:2). The practice of early Christians was in accord with these precepts. They had all things in common, and their hospitality was a characteristic of their belief.[17]

Hospitality in the early Christianity

Hospitality is the relationship between the guest and the host, or the act of practice of being hospitable. In Latin, there is the word *hostis*, which means stranger. From that, we get *hospitem*, Latin for guest or host. From these roots, we get English words such as hospital, host, hostel, hotel, hospitality. Hospitals were originally hospices[18] for the reception of pilgrims. *Hospitallers* were those whose duty was to provide *hospitum* (not just providing lodging but to do with care-giving and healing) for pilgrims. Hospitality was what you expected to get in a hospital. Thus hospitality means '*friendly reception*', generous treatment of guests or stranger etc.[19] Giving hospitality to others is a gift of the Holy Spirit where a person (host) opts to become uncomfortable in order to give comfort to the other (guest). St. John Chrysostom once said, 'the bee is more honored than other animals, not because she labors, but because she labors for others.' Apart from the practice of asceticism, prayer life and learning from the scripture, hospitality, health care system, medical healing also stands among the defining characteristics of Christian monasticism. For Monks offering hospitality was not just fulfilling the law of love but to receive Christ by welcoming and serving the strangers. The guest becomes a point of contact between the community and the wider society in the life of the monastery. The guest wing was the part within the structure of the community. The guest-master was an official appointed by the abbot to take charge of monastic hospitality and becomes the first contact between the guest and the monastic community. The constitution of an English Benedictine Monastery outlined specifically the role and responsibilities of the monks towards their guests. Interestingly, on the desk in each guestroom is a printed information sheet, which begins with a quotation from Chapter 53 of the Rule of St Benedict: "Let all guests be received in the Person of Christ, so that he will say to us: 'I was a stranger and you received me.'" The information sheet continues: "We welcome you to this place of prayer, whoever you are. You represent Christ coming to our community as our guest and as a pilgrim," and goes on to offer some practical information. The command *'not to forget to entertain strangers, for by so doing some people have entertained angels without knowing it'* (Hebrews 13:2) had a significant influence on monastic hospitality. In offering hospitality, the monks offer themselves as servants, and in showing love for their fellow being, the community also shows love for God. A Benedictine of St. John's Abbey in the American-Cassinese Congregation writes:

> At the last judgment, Jesus will reveal to everyone the mystery of this hospitality. Through and in the visitor, Christ himself is welcomed or sent away, recognized or unrecognized, just as when he came unto his own people.[20]

Celtic Christians were commonly famous for their hospitality and they drew inspiration from Desert Fathers and Mothers in this regard. Once a brother visited a solitary hermit and apologized for making him break his rule of fasting and silence. The Solitary replied, 'My rule is to receive you with hospitality and to send you away in peace.' Brigid, the fifth-century Irish saint, was famed for her hospitality. It was said that Brigid divided her dairy churning into twelve in honor of the apostles, and the thirteenth in honor of Christ; this was reserved for the poor and for guests. That tradition has been maintained in her native Ireland and is reflected in this Irish grace: *"Bless, O Lord, this food we are about to eat, and if there be any poor creature hungry or thirsty walking along the road, send them into us that we can share the food with them, just as you share your gifts with us all."*[21] According to Ray Simpson there are certain principles of hospitality one may learn from Celtic Church. For Celtic Christians:

- Hospitality means offering a generous heart to each person we meet.
- Hospitality means creating a welcoming home.
- Hospitality means giving time and encouragement to neighbours.
- Hospitality means welcoming all God's creatures.[22]

Simpson, beautifully writes, 'Hospitality is a way of life that is due for a comeback. It is the smile that greets friend and stranger. It is the warm embrace, and the welcome of each person as a gift from God, from the new baby in the mother's womb, to the old person nearing their end. Hospitality is the creation of a space in which the other person may feel secure, at ease with himself or herself; it is the encouragement of their gifts and the affirming of their person.'[23]

God is our ultimate cosmic host

A certain minister preached one day on Heaven. The next morning he was met by one of his wealthy members, who said: "Pastor, you preached a good sermon about Heaven. You told me all about Heaven, but you did not tell me where Heaven is." "Ah," said the pastor, "I'm glad of the opportunity this morning. I have just come from the hill yonder. In that cottage there is a member of your church who is extremely poor; she is sick and in bed with fever. If you will go and take her a good supply of provisions and say, "My sister. I have brought these nice provisions in the name of our Lord and Saviour," if you ask for a Bible and read Psalm 23, and then get down on your knees and pray, if you don't see Heaven, before you get all through, I'll pay the bill." The next morning he said: **"Pastor, I saw Heaven, and I spent fifteen minutes in Heaven, as certainly as you are listening."**

Every culture in the world holds up some standard of hospitality as a basis for civilized behavior and every institution has some set norms but practicing hospitality according to the Bible is one of the major principles of the Kingdom of God and we learn from God the Father, God the Son and God the Holy Spirit. Triune God is the ultimate cosmic Host. As a Host, he provides a space for us within the family of trinity by creating us in his own image and likeness. The creation story in Genesis 1 mentions how God creates orderly universe out of chaos. As an act of hospitality, he still brings order to our day to day chaotic lives by sustaining us, nurturing us, protecting us, providing and caring for us. God the Father as a Host invites us to be the partakers in his kingdom through his Son our Lord and Saviour Jesus Christ. The invitation is for everyone especially for those who are heavy laden. Heavy laden are those who are rejected, neglected, oppressed, depressed, suffering with all types of diseases, abandoned, broken hearted, crushed in spirit, poor, victim of injustices. In his hospitality we find ultimate rest and peace.

King David in Psalm 23 portrays God as the perfect model for hospitality. As a Host he makes his guests comfortable on the green pastures, quenches their thirst, gives rest to the weary soul, prepares a table, anoints the head with oil, and shows every kindness so that the guest's cup runs over. The psalmist sees the Lord himself as Host and his hospitality exceeds all others.

Although in the state of being stranger Jesus also became the host for those who were considered 'others' by the Jews. Jesus broke all the religious and social barriers by extending love and compassion to others. He goes to the well and asks for water from a Samaritan (Jn 4), He heals the servant of the Gentile officer (Mt. 8:5-13), He casts out the demon from the daughter of a woman who was a Gentile, of Syrophoenician origin. He shared the table with the tax collectors who were considered sinners by the Pharisee.

In God, hostile humanity finding space into divine communion is a model for how human beings should relate to the other. Volf mentions four steps from exclusion to embrace i.e. 'repentance' 'forgiveness' 'making space in oneself for the other' and 'healing of memory.'[24] For him, the mutual self-giving love in the Trinity (the doctrine of God), the outstretched arms of Christ on the cross for the 'godless' (the doctrine of Christ) and the open arms of the father receiving the prodigal (the doctrine of salvation) are the important metaphors of 'embrace' to bring together.[25] The embrace requires full reconciliation and it cannot take place until the truth has been said and justice is done. Thus the practice of embrace is accompanied by the struggle against deception, injustice, and violence. He suggests that the very idea of forgiveness implies an affirmation of justice. Every act of forgiveness draws attention to justice precisely by offering to forego its claims and providing a framework in which the quest for justice can be fruitfully pursued. For Volf 'forgiveness creates space.'[26]

Forgiveness is the boundary between exclusion and embrace. It heals the wound that the power-act of exclusion have inflicted and breaks down the dividing wall of hostility. Yes it leaves a distance between people, an empty space of neutrality, that allows them either to go their separate ways in what is sometimes called 'peace' or to fall into each other's arm and restore broken communion.[27]

Even after 2000 years the Host still stands outside as a stranger waiting eagerly for his entry in the hearts of many. Jesus said, "*Anyone who loves me will obey my teaching, my Father will love them, and we will come to them and **make our home (indwelling with the believers)** with them*" (John 14:23). One cannot be a good host unless he or she invites the cosmic Host to dwell and reign in their respective lives. Hospitality requires conversation, encounter, eye contact and attentive listening. It begins by giving space to the other. As the children of God we are expected to love and embrace others. Whether we are medical doctors, nurses, engineers, theologians, scientists, artists, writers we are called to help and care for others especially at the time of the need. In whatever capacity we are, we need to be attentive and responsible towards our work so that we may not hurt someone. Usually we grapple with a question: What is the summum bonum—the supreme good? According to medieval philosophy 'Summum bonum' was considered as 'righteous living' or 'life led in communion with God.' But Paul says, "The greatest of these is love." It is only through the love of God we are able to love others and carry out our responsibilities because the true love is not envious, nor boastful or arrogant or rude or is not easily puffed up. As dedicated servants of God we are ought to reflect Christ's behavior through our lives. So for the church today: to participate in the mission of the triune God in the world is to be willing to have our eyes opened by the Spirit of God so that we may see others "as brothers and sisters created by the same God and living as mutual guests in the same house provided by the same divine host."[28]

It was because of the gift of hospitality the stranger, Dr. Ida Sophia Scudder became the host and started serving the people of India. Started with roadside dispensary to the present structure, Christian Medical College Vellore even after 100 years continues to be the centre for excellence in the medical education. It is an epitome of hospitality through its selfless service, care and concern for the poor, sick and the marginalized. It is a matter of great joy and thanksgiving that CMC seeks to be a witness to the healing ministry of Christ, through excellence in education, service and research by partnering with the universal Church. Our aim is that "the whole created order may be reconciled to God through Christ" (Colossians 1:20). We seek to live as one Christian community so "that the world may believe" (John 17:21) that we are one. The goal of the Way of Life is to develop a disciplined spirituality centered on hospitality that will make us effective in our witness to Christ in the world.

Endnotes

[1] Robert J. Schreiter, *Reconciliation: Mission and Ministry in a Changing Social Order,* The Boston Theological Institute Series 3 (Maryknoll, NY: Orbis Books; and Cambridge, MA: Boston Theological Institute, 1992), 52.

[2] Jay T. Rock, No Longer Strangers or Aliens: 'Otherness' as a Binding to Be Loosed in Christian Tradition in Journal of Ecumenical Studies, 52 no 1 Winter 2017, 113-119.

[3] Robert J. Schreiter, 52-53.

[4] Mirosalv Volf, *Exclusion and Embrace: A Theological Exploration of Identity, Otherness, and Reconciliation.* (Nashville: Abingdon Press, 1996), 99.

[5] Mirosalv Volf, 110.

[6] Alister E. McGrath, *Science & Religion: A New Introduction* (Oxford: Blackwell Pub, 2010), 47.

[7] Alister McGrath, *Christian Theology: An Introduction* (Oxford: Blackwell, 1994), 218.

[8] Shailendra Rodrigues, *Hospitality: A Key to Eternity* (Mumbai: St. Pauls, 2018), 33.

[9] Leonard Boff, *Virtues: For another Possible World Trans. Alexandre Guileherme* (Eugene: Oregon, Cascade Books, 2011),. 68.

[10] Joshua W. Jipp, *Divine Visitations and Hospitality to Strangers in Luke-Acts: An interpretation of the Malta Episode in Acts 28:1-10* (Boston: Brill, 2013) cited in Bruce J. Malina, "the received View and what it Cannot do: III John and hospitality," *Semeia* 35 (1986): 171–189.

[11] Exo. 12:49; Lev. 24:22; 25:6; Deut. 1:16; 24:17,18,19; 10:18,19; 26:11.

[12] Andrew E. Arterbury, *Entertaining Angels Early Christian Hospitality in Its Mediterranean Setting* (Sheffield: Sheffield Phoenix Press, 2005), 57.

[13] Jack Mahoney, Theology, Wealth and Social Justice' in *Peter Byrne and Leslie Houlden* Companion Encyclopedia of Theology, *760.*

[14] John Koenig, 'Hospitality', in *Anchor Bible Dictionary*, Volume III, 299.

[15] 'Hospitality' in R. F. Youngblood, Nelson's new Illustrated Bible Dictionary. Rev. ed. of: Nelson's Illustrated Bible dictionary.; Includes index. T. Nelson: Nashville, 1995 [DVD].

[16] 7700 illustration.

[17] W. Smith, Smith's *Bible Dictionary.* (Thomas Nelson: Nashville, 1997).

[18] A home providing care for the sick or terminally ill.

[19] M. Mani Chako, 'Hospitality as a Relevant Missiological Paradigm for our Times: A Subaltern Perspective' in Ravi Tiwari &Bibhudutta Sahu *Sound of Silence: A Festschrift in honour of Bishop Dhirendra Kumar Sahu at his Shashti-Purti* (New Delhi: ISPCK), 41.

[20] Richard D. G. Irvine, 'The Experience of Ethnographic Fieldwork in an English Benedictine Monastery: Or, Not Playing at Being a Monk' in FIR 5.2 (2010) 225-227.

[21] Ray Simpson, *Celtic Christianity: Deep Roots for a Modern Faith* (Vestal: UK, Anamchara Books, 2014), 113-119.

[22] The hospitality of Iona was always one of its greatest features, not only to human beings, but even to birds and beasts. In the time of Columba, a crane—driven off course by fierce winds was found lying exhausted on the beach. Columba asked a monk to tenderly take the bird to a hut, and to nurse and feed it for three days. After the crane flew off gratefully, Columba said to the monk: "God bless you, my son, because you have well looked after our pilgrim guest." Adamnan, Llanerch.1988 cited in Ray Simpson, *Celtic Christianity: Deep Roots for a Modern Faith* (Vestal: UK, Anamchara Books, 2014), 118.

[23] Ibid, 120.

[24] Mirosalv Volf, 110.

[25] Mirosalv Volf, *Exclusion and Embrace*, 100.

[26] Ibid, 125.

[27] Ibid., 126.

[28] Amy G. Oden (ed), *And You Welcomed Me: A Sourcebook on Hospitality in Early Christianity* (Nashville: Abingdon Press, 2001), 27.

Understanding of Health and Healing in Religious Context of India

Ravi Tiwari

Preliminary Remarks

I understand that most of the patients, coming to Christian clinics and hospitals, for treatment, belong to religions other than Christianity. I have been teaching religions, like my father, to theological students, all through my life, and would like to reflect the general topic, related to Hinduism in the umbrellic term, in my present article; Hinduism is referred as the source of all Indic religions

Hinduism, therefore, is not a religion, but a league of religions, signifying that every religious tradition, with its philosophies, theologies, liturgies, rituals, superstitions, practices etc., can be accepted in its broadest possible accommodative umbrella; it accommodates almost all religious that have origins in Indian sub-continent- Indigenous, Aryan, Buddhist, Jain, and later off-shoot, Sikhism. Furthermore, it is, as Supreme Court of India also recognized, a way of life, and a way of thinking. Religion, for the Hindus, symbolizes the association of man with the Divine. The sole objective of religion, for Hindus, as with the adherents of other religions too, is to make its followers realize the 'Truth' (Sans. *sat*), in addition to restoring health and sickness which mortal human often face. It is in the broader context, and in general terms, we will be dealing with this religious phenomenon "Hinduism" in this paper.

Psycho-somatic understanding of Human in Indian religious traditions:

Bulk of religio-philosophical literatures, in Indic religions, are numerous where human existence is propounded and discussed, though recognized ones are the Vedas, the Upanishads and the Bhagvad Gita. The basic concepts that are related to human existence and destiny, discussed there are:

- Atman (Soul/Spirit) is the eternal and core principle which is the cementing force of five elements, Panch-tattva/Panch Mahabhuta) - Prithivi (Earth, Matter), Vyayu (air, breath), Aakash (Space), Jala (Water), and Agni (Fire), of Nature (Prakriti). For them, every human individual, like Spinoza, is a microcosm of nature and therefore contains all five elements, that dissolve at the time of his death.

- Moksha/Mukti is the release or liberation/salvation, which is the ultimate aim or goal of life of all human beings

- Dharma, is the cosmic force that regulates human destiny. It is a complex concept, meaning of which differs according to the context such as religion, social order, law, duty or righteousness.

- Karma implies a principle and refers to all the actions of the individuals that results with certain consequences ultimately shaping one's destiny, present and past. It is also related to Paapa (bad karma/sin), and Punya (good karma). Concept of sin, in Hinduism is not ontological, as in Semitic religions, but consequential of bad karma, which can be removed by religious/moral/ethical/medical remedies/prescriptions/penance.[1] Illness, disease, physical and mental sufferings/disorders are considered to be caused by bad karma.

- There are various theological-theistic and atheistic, and philosophical theories that are propounded in Hindu Scriptures and philosophical treatises, in an attempt to explain the origin of human, but none can be considered to be satisfactory. Theory of Maya (ignorance/lack of true knowledge/illusion), however, is the most popular and accepted way of looking at human existence among the Hindu populace. It is important to make an attempt to understand this world-view of an individual Hindu patient in his/her healing/counseling-process.

Understanding Healing: Healing is a course of action of the restitution of health to an unbalanced, diseased or injured physical human organism/soul. Healing is correlated with themes of wholeness, narrative, and spirituality. Spiritual healing leads to the maintenance of health, emphasizing meditation, specific movements of the body (Yoga) so that the health of the individual is restored to its normal and wholesome state of Being. Modern medicine claims to restore the physical health of the individuals but does not heal in the complete sense of the word. Unfortunately, the role of the physicians has now been transferred from being the healer to the curer of the disease. Thus, religion has to step-in and has taken up a massive foothold in the field of providing wholesome healing to its followers. The Hindu religion as a whole consists of large amount of measures by which a person receives wholesome healing., not from physical suffering alone. Healing needs to take place in all the three dimension of human existence- physical, mental and psychological. A patient of Indic religious tradition expects his healer to be physician/surgeon, counsellor and pastoral rolled into one. Ancients pray for the wholesome healing for one and all in the prayers, often recited by the pious Indian: 'May all become happy; May none fall ill; May all see auspiciousness everywhere; May none ever feel sorrow; Om Shaantih Shaantih Shaantih'.[2]

Tradition of practical ways of healing has an ancient one, and has been naturalistic in nature where the plants and botanical products were used as the chief ingredients of medical remedies for physical and health problems. Vedas are the primary sources of information about the healing practices in the subcontinent, the common diseases, their causes and remedies too. It also gives some glimpses into the non-Aryan healing practices as well. One may not surprise to find an additional source of healing very early in the sub-continent as spiritual healing became one of the accepted forms of treatment in restoring the health of an individual.

Incidentally, tradition of systematized healing system in Indic religious traditions is known as Ayurveda (Sacred Knowledge/science of growth of body), and is considered to be highly esteemed - the fifth Veda.

Healing–Body, Mind and Spirit: An individual, in Indic religious traditions, is a body-mind-spirit complex, therefore healing tradition has given importance to spiritual consciousness, relaxation of mind, and curing of physical ailments/disorders in a complementary way; all treated as a combined whole for its proper and consonant functioning. In the process of diagnosis, understanding of body and mind is one of the crucial factors that is considered while examining a patient. His/her diet and emotional conditions are taken into account which are used in prescribing medicinal remedies. Medicinal plants that are 'natural antibiotics' are used as vital healing agents to restore the bodily disorders. The Indic healing traditions generally pay attention towards strengthening the immune system and the homeostatic mechanism of our body. Apart from medicinal plants, ayurvedic physicians use elixirs (*arks* (tinctures/solutions), metal preparations (*bhasma*) and herbs (*jadi-buti*) to treat infirmity while the Siddhas/jadi-buti walas use only herbs to treat illness.

Yoga: One of the novel innovations in the process of healing in Indic tradition is the practice of Yoga. It, in fact, is considered to be a part of healing, along with the development of spirituality through meditation. It is a philosophy of the ancient and is considered as a practice of well-being of the individuals. By doing Yoga, one can control the mind. The mind is the ultimate source from where concentration emanates. Therefore, the ability to focus and discipline the mind is the work of the yoga. Yoga may not cure an individual from any kind of diseases (for example AIDS) but it can give strength to the individual and heal his mind to bear with the consequences. There are different types of yoga, among them three are well-known: (a) Hatha Yoga is slow-paced, gentle, and focused on breathing and meditation. It relieves stress and improves breathing along with physical exercise; (b) Raj Yoga is an inclusive of all yoga and emphasizes on meditation and self-realization as well as gradual evolution of the consciousness, and (c) Tantra Yoga aims at expanding consciousness. It promotes a one-pointedness and centeredness that helps us to free the consciousness from any kind of limitations. Concept of wholesome healing (of body, mind and soul), through the process of Yoga, in the Indic religious traditions is succinctly summarized by Sri Krishna in the Bhagvad Gita[3] where Lord Krishna is believed to be the Yajna, Shraddha, ausadham, mantra, ajam or ghee, ahavaniyas (fire); all these concepts laid down in the Gita act as a source of healing to all its readers in their crisis period. It calls for abandonment of worldly ties for the sake of self-realization. People in their time of deluge of physical, mental and spiritual miseries refer to these words of the Gita, which thereby provides them with a strong mind and makes them able to face the odds in life.

Patients in India: Indian patient is a complex entity; (s)he is the product of his/her socio-religious environment. Much sensitivity is required, on the part of the team of healers, in treating them. Invariably, most of the patients have a simple answer for their physical ailments, as that of all other existential problems and situation -Karma. They have committed something awfully wrong- ethically, morally and spiritually, that resulted into such situation in life. They have various examples and illustrations from various scriptures (Puranas and Epics) to convince themselves or others.

Causation, relation between cause and effect, is one of the important concepts that the human mind ever discovered, and applied in solving most of his/her intellectual, theoretical and existential problems. Ancient medical professionals have been greatly helped by the application of this principle in developing their science in the service of human kind. Theoretical application of the same, in the context of Indian philosophical-theological thinking, developed into a static dogmatic universal principle, Doctrine of Karma, from which all human situations, physical, mental, spiritual, could be explained.[4] This principle still has an over-powering influence over the rational thinking of Indian patients. Gautam Buddha was one of the first who tried to draw back to the rational explanation of human situation, as far back in the sixth century BCE, but not with much success; so is the case with the contemporary medical professionals. Moral predicament of the patient gives rise to a sense of guilt; over-indulgence raises stress, strain, anxiety, fatigues and physical ailments. Patient, thus, analyzes/ accepts his/her own situation from the world-view he/she has created from their understanding and application of the doctrine of Karma. This doctrine has to be reinterpreted, by the involved healers, for the sake of their patients' wholesome healing.

Some patients do have a sense of sin, associated with their sickness, ascribed to doctrine of Karma.[5] Vaishnavite-tradition often elaborates the 'karma' of previous or present births resulting into various kind of diseases - leprosy, epilepsy, skin-diseases, jaundice, blindness etc., and resulting into some forms of existence in the present and future life.[6] Health Minister of Assam once quoted Bhagavad-Gita to prove his contention that sin causes cancer to the dismay of many, though he was echoing the general perception of the Hindus towards life-threatening diseases.[7] Some Christian theologians do subscribe to the suggestion that this association of Karma to sin is akin to Christian doctrine of Sin.[8]

Indian patients do have some idea of sin, to which they associate their physical diseases. In the Rigveda, Soma and Rudra are prayed for medicines for the cures of diseases caused by their sinful actions.[9] *Papam* is ascribed to 'sinful actions' in Bhagvad Gita,[10] as such, it has an ethical-moral implication rather than religious. Apart of medicine, patients do accept the efficacy of prayer, *japa* (recitation), blessings, *puja* (worship) and charity in the process of healing. Many have argued that the counseling/psychotherapeutic model available in Bhagavad-Gita may be helpful in treating patients with strong belief in the Doctrine of Karam/sin as propounded in the Indian religious traditions.[11] One may, however, have to apply his/her own discretion, in choosing one among different approaches available, in counselling the patients in such cases.

Indic religions have a very high esteem for the medical professionals and practitioners. Dhanvantari ascribed to bring the medical sciences to mankind in the form of Ayurveda (science of long/healthy life) is revered as god from ancient of days. Medical practitioners, therefore, are greatly revered, almost as a representative of God, sometimes god himself. This faith of the innocent masses in the healing touch, and power, of medical practitioners need not be betrayed, though superstitions associated with the faith needs to be avoided.

Endnotes

[1] Curiously enough, John talks about the cause-effect relationship (Law of karma) with reference to a blind by birth of a person Jesus healed (Jn. 9); see also, Job 4:8; Prov 22:8).

[2] Source and reference are varied and are not ascribed to any one Upanishad though used in many liturgies and rituals.

[3] 9:16: 'I am ritual action (krit), I am sacrifice (yajna), I am the ancestral oblation (swadha), I am the (medicinal herb (aushadham), I am the (sacred) hymn Mantra), I am melted butter (ajyam), I am the fire (agni) and I am the offering (hutam).' (tran. S. Radhakishna).

[4] Cf. Brihadaranyaka Upanishad 3.2.13:'Truly, one becomes good through good *deeds*, and evil through evil *deeds*'; also4.4.5-6. *Mahabharata, xii.291.22:* As a man himself sows, so he himself reaps; no man inherits the good or evil act of another man. The fruit is of the same quality as the action.

[5] Cf. Bhagwadgita 3.13; also 3.37.

[6] Cf. Garuda Purana, ch.5 (http://www.sacred-texts.com/hin/gpu/gpu07.htm)

[7] Cf. https://theprint.in/talk-point/karma-himanta-biswa-sarma-cancer-comment/17856/

[8] Meadow, Mary Jo, *Christian Insight Meditation.* Wisdom Publications Inc. p. 199. Some Indian Christian do equate *karma* with Sin or Maya. Cf. Robin Boyd, *An Introduction to Indian Christin Theology*, New Delhi: ISPCK, 1989, p. 244.

[9] Cf. RV. VI.74.3

[10] Cf. Bhagvad Gita 18.66

[11] See, M. S. Reddy, Psychotherapy - Insights from Bhagavad Gita, in Indian Journal of Psychol Medicine. 2012 Jan-Mar; 34(1): 100–104. (https://www.ncbi.nlm.nih.gov/pmc/articles/PMC3361835/)

Disruptive Agenda and the Kingdom of God

Reflections on John Chapter 9

Jayakumar Christian

A few years ago, I was visiting a family in Aizawl whose four year old daughter Anu[1] had been diagnosed as HIV positive. Her mother had just returned from Anu's school with her report card. It was obvious that she was proud of her daughter's performance in singing, dancing, games and so on. I then asked the mother what her dream was for Anu. She stopped for a while and with a deep sense of pain, replied, 'what dream can I have for Anu? I cannot afford to dream dreams for Anu.'

When the right to dream is robbed due to a personal health condition, socio-political-religious systems or the abuse of power, oppression and marginalisation, is birthed. The church is called to 'be present' precisely in those margins to challenge the seeming inevitability of the situation (a lie) and communicate that the last word belongs to our living God. By her presence in the margins, the Church serves as a signpost to God's eternal purposes – the Kingdom of God.

I would like to propose and explore the theme that the Church is called to provide not only par excellence healing ministries, but to do so 'with a deliberate bias' for those who cannot afford to dream dreams. A significant aspect of the church's healing ministry, especially in a highly stratified society as ours, are the 'margins' of our society. The healing ministry of the church which began as movements, have become institutions requiring significant energy merely to sustain the machinery. Our healing ministries must cause ripples resulting in the transformation of a whole nation.

Healing ministry especially among those who are hurting and neglected is not merely an accident of compassionate vocation or a brilliant pursuit of career. It is designed to be an intentional prophetic presence among the most vulnerable and hurting. Dr. Ida Scudder's ministry calls for a redefinition of the healing ministry as demanding investment of life, healing of relationships and challenging evil in the system – so relevant, even today.

Jesus' encounter with the blind man in John chapter 9 provides a classic frame for developing a theology of healing that will trigger a movement in the nations – a disruptive, prophetic presence serving as a sign post for the Kingdom of God. In this paper we will explore five critical themes for constructing a theology of healing.

Jesus' encounter (John 9:1-41)

The encounter (v1) with the blind man seems so much like 'business as usual' for Jesus - very much like an average day in an institution like CMC. I was particularly intrigued by the anonymity of the 'blind person' and the attention that John the gospel writer provides for this particular encounter – it must be of great value in the Kingdom, demanding greater attention. The act of healing itself seems so mundane and routine – Jesus spat on the ground, made mud with saliva and anointed the man's eyes with the mud, sent him to wash in the pool of Siloam- he went, he washed and came back seeing.

But the disruptions this simple act of healing caused were enormous. It upset the disciples' theology, the security of power of the religious leaders, fanned the fears of his parents, disturbed the curious neighbours and transformed the blind man. Could 'disruption' of the status-quo of society be the pattern for the healing agenda of the Church? Could it be that every 'anonymous' patient who walks through the portals of the Church and her institutions is a potential candidate for God to trigger a movement of transformation of our nation.

Disruptive healing

- **Disturb the theologically complacent (v1-3)**

  Very interestingly the first ones to notice the blind man were the disciples. They had the categories all ready to analyse the 'unfortunate state' of the blind man – 'did the blind man sin or his parents sin?' Many of our philosophical and faith leaders (of various faiths, including the church) often provide well thought through frames to explain the unfortunate experiences, oppression and marginality of the underprivileged sections of our society. Many of these explanations are birthed out of academic & theological interest, with no sense of pain in the discourse.

  But Jesus very interestingly provides a 'third view' on the blind man's unfortunate state. Jesus points out the reason could be 'that the works of God might be displayed' (v3). Later in verse 39, Jesus suggests it was 'for judgment I came into this world' that those who claim to see are 'really the blind,' requiring healing.

  The people of God are called to challenge status quo by challenging categories used by society to define reality and reinforce status quo. We seek to challenge meanings ascribed to reality. We challenge the questions that the world uses to reinforce structures of suffering, oppression and marginalisation. Because of our intimacy with a living personal God, the people of God are called to offer a 'third perspective' that points towards God. We offer a third perspective that demands our intimacy with this living, loving God and knowledge of His word.

  Does the Church in India today have a credible third perspective to offer? or have we been co-opted by the powers and succumbed to the pressures to survive. The healing of our nation is dependent on our offering of a third perspective. The stakes are high. It is beyond healing. It is about the transformation of a nation.

- **Sensitizing the complacent neighbors (v8-12)**

Even as we study the narrative John offers of Jesus' encounter with this anonymous blind man, we see that the neighbours are shocked and surprised. They were not even sure if it is the same person. He was probably part of the natural scenario on the streets – a beggar whose name we need not know. He did not even merit a second glance, but suddenly he is part of the headlines. The neighbours were probably indifferent to the daily experience of this beggar.

Not so for Jesus. The beggar was too important to be ignored. The healing of the blind beggar, disturbed the otherwise complacent neighbours. The healing stoked their curiosity. Suddenly, the blind beggar was headlines.

Walking with Jesus, the Church is in the business of changing the headlines in a subversive manner. We are called to draw the attention of the complacent middle class to the suffering, oppressed and marginalised millions. In our country we have this strange phenomenon, where a minority middle class and rich can afford to live comfortable lives serviced by the majority of millions living on the margins and still ignore them. We have become a society which can exclude the majority with a deep sense of impunity. Could it be because of our flawed world view?

Is it not incumbent on the Church and her healing ministries to challenge this complacent world view? Our religious systems have probably many explanations for the suffering around us. Can CMC offer an alternate worldview? The Church's healing ministries which have such close and credible engagement with suffering must be the most appropriate instrument our God uses to offer a counter narrative on suffering. Could CMC be that prophetic voice that will challenge our nation's complacent worldview towards suffering, oppression and marginalisation?

- **Challenging power definitions (v13-41)**

  The blind beggar's explanation 'I was blind now I see' (v25) was not enough for the insecure Pharisees. They wanted to get into the details – who healed you, what do you think about him and so on... To complicate it, Jesus healed the man born blind on the wrong day, at the wrong time. We in India know the sacredness of the right time, very well.

  For the Pharisees, the healing of the man born blind was a major threat to their power positions. Religion was a source of power, often reinforced by politics and economics. The healing challenged their popular perceptions of god, holiness, prophet, law and other such religious practices & beliefs. Finally out of exasperation the Pharisees ask the man born blind "you were born in utter sin, and would you teach us? (v34)." They then used their power to excommunicate him - twice marginalised.

  Suffering, oppression, and marginalisation are the pillars on which our power edifices flourish. The healing ministries of the Church must not only heal the person but also transform the 'world of our patients' – the world that flourishes on the suffering of the millions.

  Unfortunately the Church in India today and her institutions have become par excellent in 'playing power' – excelling in the world's understanding of power. The people of God who worship a crucified saviour know the power of powerlessness. We are called not to excel in playing power, but called to redefine power. India is deprived of a credible alternative which the church alone can provide, for we know the power of the cross and the resurrection that followed.

  Could CMC be that institution of the church which is in the forefront of redefining power, for you have this unique privilege of being in the midst of suffering, tears and brokenness? Can the church in India (re)learn about power, from the healing ministries of the church? Can we together challenge India's understanding of power as peddled by religious institutions, political leaders, and the economically powerful? Could the healing of the man born blind – the anonymous patient - trigger a movement of transformation of the nation, at a critical time such as this?

- **Embracing a fearful family (v18-23)**
  John, the gospel writer very interestingly, in the midst of this intense power and high level religious conversation, draws our attention to the parents. The parents lived in fear. They were fearful of a society who 'did not believe' (v18) and the Pharisees (religious leaders) who had the power to excommunicate them (v22). As parents they could not disown their son, even if he was a blind beggar all his life (almost). We see these parents in fear. The choices before them all sounded terminal.

  In today's socio-political-religious world 'fear' is a powerful instrument used by those in power. Any sign of non-compliance to 'their view of reality' could mean near death and in many cases death itself. Those loved ones around the suffering, oppressed and marginalised, live in this state of perpetual fear and slow death.

  Could the Church and her healing ministries embrace those who live in fear – provide a caring community for them? Can care be a political instrument that challenges those who flourish by perpetuating fear; for Dr. Ida Scudder, it did. Jesus did that to the blind man who was excommunicated – 'when he heard they had cast him out, he found him (v35).' Can the people of God who do not live by fear but by the power of the Spirit, be that caring community for those who live in hurt and fear?

- **Changed narrative for a blind beggar (v8-38)**
  Even as we (re) read John's narrative we see an interesting progression in the blind man's understanding of what happened to him and who this person who healed him was. It progressed from 'I do not know' to 'He is a prophet' to 'Lord I believe.' Jesus heals the blind man and allows him the joy of discovering who the healer was. We

see the blind man who was healed answering the many questions from a community that did not recognize Jesus and in fact did everything to discredit Jesus. At one point the blind man had the audacity to ask the powerful priests 'if they wanted to know Jesus' (v27) - politically wrong question. But in his simplicity he spoke of his own desire to know this healer. So much so, when Jesus met him the second time, and asked 'do you know the healer' his spontaneous response was 'who is he sir, that I may believe in him (v36.) He seemed so ready.

The Church in India with its ministries of healing, must be that instrument that creates the desire to know the 'healer.' The mandate it seems was not just healing the blindness but the transformation of the whole person that included an encounter with the healer. Wholism (holism) is not merely about being multi-sectorally comprehensive; it is about radically transforming the person impacting their whole life. Do our ministries of healing raise the question 'who is he' and transform the whole person?

Can the Church in India offer a counter narrative to those who are abandoned to suffering, oppression and the margins of our society? Do we have an alternate that raises the question about the identity of the healer and transforms the whole person?

A prophetic agenda that disrupts.

The healing ministries of the church in India is an integral part of the mission of the whole Church and its prophetic ministries. We are called as the people of God for whom the Kingdom of God is a common mandate, to be present among the suffering, often the most vulnerable, oppressed and marginalised, to be a sign post to the Kingdom of God. We are called to be that radical community which,

I.   disturbs the theologically complacent in our various religious traditions.

II. challenges the complacent neigbours who are often numb to the realities of suffering.

III. challenges the power structures of the socio-political-economic–religious powers.

IV. cares for those who experience slow death due to fear

V.   transforms the marginalised.

The healing ministries of the church in India are called to be a prophetic community, that triggers movements patterned after the Kingdom of God.

Endnotes

[1] Not her real name.

Suffering, Healing and Meaning of Life

Joshua Kalapati

Today we face two different, though not inconsistent, foundational definitions of health: First, "Health is a state of complete physical, mental and social well-being and not merely the absence of disease or injury" (Preamble to WHO Constitution 1948). Second, "Health is the absence of disease, and diseases are states that interfere with species-typical natural functions."[1]

In our Christian perspective, our starting point, however, is God and his creation. Any *theology of health and healing* should be based on these core beliefs: a)God is the creator of all life (Gen 1:1); b) God created them as man and woman in his own image (Gen 1:27); c) Humans are made to be the stewards of his creation (Gen 1:26); d) When sin entered into the world, it broke relationship between God and humans; through sin, came sickness and death into the world (Rom. 5:12); e) Our body is the temple of Holy Spirit (1 cor. 6:19); our mind needs to be renewed so that we may prove the perfect will of God (Rom. 12:1-2), and (f) Christ came into the world to restore this broken relationship and he promises to give abundant life to one and all (John 10:10). If there is one verse in the Bible that could sum up all *theology of health and healing*, it is what God has promised in Jeremiah 33:6 "I will heal my people and will let them enjoy abundant peace and security". I would like to discuss **SIX** different dimensions of pain, suffering and meaning of life, which are germane to any discussion on the Theology of healing:

Pain and suffering as Christian virtues: 'Suffering' and 'Healing' present a poignant paradox for Christian believers. Does God intend our bodies to silently bear suffering in moments of sickness or allow them to be healed through the instrument of medicine. Both the *theology of suffering* and *theology of healing* could be explained and sustained biblically. We see no inconsistency between these two, for we believe it is ultimately God's will that allows us to 'bear the thorn in our flesh', as Paul would narrate, or to get rid of it in his appointed time and way.

Theology of pain and unmerited (innocent) suffering is more fully articulated in Christianity than in any other religion. Today, we could notice two opposite attitudes to pain and suffering: We may experience and receive pain and suffering as a 'gift of God'[2], so that his greater purposes are realized, or we may conclude, quite helplessly, that religions could never offer a solution to the problem of innocent's suffering.[3]

The Bible makes it amply clear that suffering and sickness are not a result of sin (karma). Two passages related to Eliphaz (Job 4:7-9) and the blind man (John 9:3) provide a clear contrast. Eliphaz implied that Job was perhaps not innocent and that he was reaping what he sowed:

"Consider now: Who, being innocent, has ever perished? Where were the upright ever destroyed? As I have observed, those who plow evil and those who sow trouble reap it. At the breath of God they perish; at the blast of his anger they are no more."

This fatalistic view was clearly rejected by God when he vindicated Job, and charged his friends. In the New Testament passage, cited above, we understand that sickness was not a result of sin of parents or the individual sufferer, but healing was meant to for bringing glory to God.

Why does God allow suffering in a believer's life?

Although this is an increasing complex and difficult question, the Bible provides several dimensions of suffering, and how it is connected to the redemptive plans of God. At the outset, let us be clear that every believer should be prepared for both highs and lows in life. In an important passage (2 Cor. 12:1-10), Paul narrates how he beholds a glorious vision of heaven, and yet little later admits that he was given a thorn in the flesh. Even as he pleaded with God for the thorn to be removed, the answer he received was: "My grace is sufficient for you, for my power is made perfect in weakness." Therefore a true believer would never surprised by sickness or suffering. We do not discern the voice of God or his presence in moments of pleasure, but pain is the 'megaphone of God,'[4] which reminds of our mortality and vulnerability in this world.

Secondly, Pain and Suffering are ways to reveal one's true self. Trials are a test of faith; they produce perseverance and maturity (James 1:2-4; 12); Also, pain could be understood as a gift of God, and it has a redemptive value.[5] This positive understanding of pain and loss is reflected in the lives of countless believers. When a preacher told Fanny Crosby that it was a great pity that God did not give her sight, she replied: "Because when I get to heaven, the first face that shall ever gladden my sight will be that of my Savior." She firmly believed in what St. Paul wrote in 2 Cor. 4:17 "For our light and momentary afflictions are achieving for us an eternal glory that far outweigh them all".

Thirdly, it is such a sobering thought that we have a *Suffering God*, the *Crucified Christ*. Many contemporary theologies are centred on this notion of the suffering servant: 'Theology of Hope'[6]; 'Theology of the Disabled'[7]; 'Theology of AIDS'[8];'Theology of the Cross'[9], to name a few. It is inevitable that every decade throws up deadly diseases, which may be a result of our promiscuous life styles or ill-effects of globalization or natural calamities or man-made disasters. But, when Christ asked us to take his yoke upon us, he precisely meant to say that he is always there with us to bear our burdens, just as it requires two oxen to carry the yoke.

A theology of health and healing

In Christian perspective, biology is inalienably related to spirituality. Each organ of the body is designed with a purpose, and 'we are fearfully and wonderfully made' (Ps. 139:14).Such a bio-spiritual perspective can radically shape and affect our approaches to health and healing process.

One disturbing development in the recent decades is, what is called, 'biological reductionism'. Both religions and ethics are sought to be reduced to biology, and human values are interpreted as mere natural, sociobiological appendage. E.O. Wilson, the well-known exponent of Sociobiology declares, "The time has come for ethics to be removed temporarily from the hands of philosophers and biologicized.[10] Michael Ruse is more explicit when he said, "Morality is a biological adaptation no less than are hands and feet and teeth.[11] One of the penetrative critics of these views is Holmes Rolston III, who illustrates several dangerous contradictions in these approaches.[12] Although Darwinian biologists such as Richard Dawkins tries to explain moral, altruistic behavior in terms of cultural 'memes', their arguments are far from convincing.[13]

We are whole beings, not perfect beings

God wants us to be whole beings, not perfect beings: Perfectionism has external standards, is unrealistic, unattainable, and costly; By contrast, wholeness is based on individual's self-worth, recognition of his/her self as a holistic personality. Physical health and productivity should produce deeper gratitude and worship, not self-reliance and pride in productivity. Sickness need not be an end for me, but a beginning of a new life and new confidence. Paul boasts of his weakness.(2 Cor. 12:9). Lord Jesus gave the command to his disciples--"Go and Heal every disease and sickness" (Matt 10:1).

It is also pertinent to realize that healing, as explained by Jesus, is connected to *Faith*: *Jesus said to her, "Daughter, your faith has healed you. Go in peace and be freed from your suffering."(Mark 5:34)*. At the same time, the Lord also said that "It is not the healthy who need a doctor, but the sick (Luke. 5:31). Faith heals some times, or many times, and yet there are times, when diseases require the doctor's care and attention.

We also realize that there is a close link between 'confession' and 'wholeness', the idea which inspired *Confession Therapy/Integrity Therapy*(Hobart Mowrer). Honesty, openness, restitution and willingness to help others are keystones in Dr. Mowrer's therapy, which also has a Biblical basis: James 5:16: "Confess your faults one to another." Also, "He that covers his sins shall not prosper; but whoso confesses and forsakes them shall have mercy.(Proverbs 28:13). The Lord also warns that our gifts offered with a guilty conscience would never be acceptable to him: "Therefore if you are offering your gift to the altar and there remember that your brother has something against you; leave your gift there in front of the altar. First, go and be reconciled to your brother, and then come and offer your gift." (Matt. 5:23-24). This is why, Counselling, especially Christian, occupies such an important place in contemporary times—Counselling in families, educational institutions, hospitals, and in larger societies. If only, we are honest to each other, listen to each other, confess to each other, share with each other, most of the maladies in our societies will disappear.

Yet another perplexing dimension of healing is that of 'miracles'. Supernatural miracles lie at the centre of every religion, including Christianity. There are many attempts in contemporary times, to explain them away or to deconstruct them to render them as natural phenomena or as myths. Aren't miracles (healing) contrary to the laws of nature, and in turn to science? Responding to this pertinent question, St. Augustine of Hippo, makes a profound observation: "Miracles are not contrary to nature, but only contrary to what we know of nature."[14]

In similar vein, 'Particle Physicist' and theologian John Polking horne argues that an apparently simple event like boiling water, where a small quantity of liquid changes into a large quantity of steam would seem miraculous to someone who had not seen it every day. God, thus, cannot control things on the macroscopic scale by acting microscopically on each elementary particle in the universe, but that he can act within the framework of "pure spirit". As the complex nonlinear systems of life oscillate back and forth trying to decide which strange attractor to move towards, God intervenes gently in the direction that moves the system where he wishes it to go.[15]

Lastly, there is another important distinction believers should make viz. that of visible and invisible healing. Any presupposition of the existence of an Almighty God enables us to believe that there is a divine, unknown and unknowable realm in which God acts, and which may be taken for granted by us as every day, routine. Divine appointments and divine intervention—are unseen realities in a believer's life.[16]

Meaning and purpose of life

Meaning of life is intimately with connected with the goal and purpose of life.[17] The question, "How is Christian worldview different from others?" is a very important question. We derive joy in serving and loving others because of the command of our Lord: *Love The Neighbour as Thyself.* Jesus taught us that if we aim to find our life, we must lose it (Matt. 10:39). This means the focus of our life should not be on ourselves, but on others. The reason we serve others is to point them to our loving God and share the knowledge of him preserved in his Word.

Also, meaning of life is connected with the source of life, which is clearly revealed in the Scripture. The book *Ecclesiastes* teaches that life under sun is meaningless, everything is in vain, but if we look beyond sun, everything looks meaningful. This is also the teaching of Jesus Christ when he said, *Seek ye first the kingdom of God and His righteousness and all these things shall be added unto you.*

If one loses sense of hope and purpose in life, he loses direction and destiny of life. Every thinking person, reasons Ravi Zacharias, should ask FOUR fundamental questions: How did I come into Being (origin)?; 2. What brings life Meaning (meaning)?; 3. How do I know right from wrong (morality); and 4. Where am I headed after I die (destiny)?

Service and Sacrificial life enables us to find true meaning of life. eg. missionaries in India, who labored for centuries to lay the foundations of Christianity in India. They expected nothing in return except to share the gospel through service and sacrifice. Their lives are profound examples of 'purpose-driven' lives, and lives well-lived.

Treatment vs enhancement: Are there limits to healthcare? Should it focus only on therapy and treatment, or also on 'human enhancement'?-- are some of the serious questions confronting us today. The case of Mr. *N.R.* a 23 year old techie, who underwent 'height enhancement surgery' in a corporate hospital in Hyderabad in April 2016, perfectly mirrors the obsession of rich humans, especially youngsters, craving for 'perfect bodies'. He was already fairly tall, didn't inform his parents, and spent nearly four lakhs of hard earned money on this surgery. Even after six months, he is barely able to walk, nor does the corporate hospital seem very much concerned about this tragedy. This episode, and countless others around the world, raises several questions and dilemmas on 'human enhancement'.

What are the proper limits to health care? What is 'personal identity'? Is enhancement necessarily dehumanizing? Does enhancement amount to cheating? Does enhancement compromise authenticity? Just like paralympics, should we also organize 'super olympics', where athletes compete with one another with their 'enhanced' gadgets?[18]

'Treatment vs Enhancement' is a dilemma which is confronting many a corporate hospital in India. If the person could afford to pay for his/her enhancement of body, do the corporate say yes or no? If so, on what grounds? Artificial Intelligence and fast-developing technological advances are already promising to create new world, where the distinction between what is natural and what is artificial is getting increasingly blurred. The number of bioethical dilemmas is on the increase day by day.

A distinct Christian worldview of science and technology is the need of the hour: Science and Technology could never be value-neutral. Every researcher brings in his/her 'personal knowledge', or 'tacit knowledge' or 'passion' to bear upon his academic work, including in scientific research.[19] Therefore, we as Christian professionals need not shy away from offering faith-based assessments of all scientific and technological developments. It is our considered view that the natural sciences should not be regarded as independent sources of authority, but as standing in a *hermeneutical relation* to the Scripture i.e. these will help us to understand and interpret the Scripture to our own contextual realities.[20]

Scientific developments and application of technology, while making our lives lot easier, are also posing several moral dilemmas to the academic fraternity, much more so to the Christian professionals today: Biotechnology, Cloning, Genetic Engineering, Abortions, Assisted Reproductive Technologies, and a host of other bioethical issues, which are growing by the day.

Can we evolve a distinct Christian worldview of science and technology, where resources are drawn from professionals from diverse academic backgrounds and expertise?

Partnering with secular, progressive and liberative voices: Today we cannot fight a lone battle against the several health-related evils, and de-humanizing influences in the contemporary world. There is a dire need to partner with the secular, progressive, liberative intellectuals and activists, *as long as their views are consistent with our core Biblical values.* There are many academicians who have offered radical insights on how we could have a broader scope and understanding of health and healthcare in India.

One such intellectual is Professor Amartya Sen, whose 'capabilities approach' can enrich our discourse on health and healthcare. For Sen, healthcare is not an isolated, individual issue, but is linked to the economic progress of the nation. Poverty and sickness are understood as factors of 'capability-deprivation'. 'Capability refers to the ability of a person to achieve a given functioning (doing or being)'. Huge social investments in education and healthcare could be critical for sustaining economic prosperity. Also, poverty and inequalities in the society need not prevent any government to enact 'universal health care (UHC).[21] Amartya Sen also challenges us to evolve mechanisms and standards to define as well as measure 'quality of life', which is directly linked to health and health care.[22] Healthcare is also being looked at as a Justice issue. As a document of WCC narrates, Health is a Justice-issue, a Peace-issue, an Integrity of Creation issue, and above all, a Spiritual issue.[23]

Issues such as pain, suffering and meaning of life are bound to surface, when we articulate any theology of health and healing. There are no easy answers to life's most profound existential questions. Life teaches us not only to confront these, but also explore solutions. Our academic responses to health and healthcare need to resonate more and more in the public sphere. Our concerns do not relate just to the Christian community alone, but to the entire humanity, wherever human rights are suppressed, and wherever abundant living is denied to individuals and communities. We find true meaning and purpose in life, only when we are connected with the divine destiny, and therefore St. Augustine said this beautiful prayer: *O Lord! You have made us for Yourself, and hearts are restless, until they can find rest in Thee.*

Endnotes

[1] Christopher Boorse, *Health as a Theoretical Concept*, 1977, cited in Neil Messer, *Flourishing: Health, Disease and Bioethics in Theological Perspective*, Wm Eerdmans, Cambridge, Michigan, 2013.

[2] Philip Yancey, *Where is God when it hurts?* Zondervan, 1977.

[3] Arun Shourie, *Does He know a mother's heart? How Suffering Refutes Religions*, 2011.

[4] "God whispers to us in our pleasures, speaks in our conscience, but shouts in our pain: it is His megaphone to rouse a deaf world." C.S. Lewis, *The Problem of Pain*, New York: HarperCollins, 1940, 91.

[5] Philip Yancey, *Where is God when it hurts?*, Zondervan, 1977.

[6] Jurgen Moltmann, *Theology of Hope*, Fortress Press, Harper Collins, 1967.

[7] Nancy Eiesland, *The Disabled God: toward A Liberatory Theology of Disability*, Abingdon Press, 1994.

[8] Donald E. Messer, *Breaking the Conspiracy of Silence: Christian Churches and the Global AIDS Crisis,* 2004.

[9] James H. Cone, *The Cross and the Lynching Tree*, Orbis books, 2011.

[10] Edward O. Wilson, *Sociobiology: The New Synthesis*, 1975, 3.

[11] "Evolutionary Theory and Christian Ethics: Are They in Harmony?" in Zygon, 29, 1994, 5-24.

[12] Holmes, Rolston III, *Genes, Genesis and God*, Cambridge University Press, 1999.

[13] See for example searching criticisms such as that of Alister McGrath found in his book, *Dawkins' God: Genes, Memes and Meaning of Life,* 2004.

[14] Augustine, *The City of God*, Book XXI, Chap. 8.

[15] Polkinghorne, J., "God's Action in the World", 1990 J.K. Russell Fellowship Lecture, and also his book, *Belief in God in the Age of Science*, New Haven and London: Yale University Press 1998. I had the great privilege of listening to a lecture delivered by this outstanding Christian scientist in Oxford University during the C.S. Lewis Summer workshop in 2003.

[16] See Larry Tomczak, *Divine Appointments: Igniting Your Passion to Fulfil Your Destiny*, 1998.

[17] Rick Warren, *The Purpose Driven Life: What On Earth Am I Here For?*, Zondervan, 2006.

[18] See the Stanford Encyclopedia online article on 'Human Enhancement', 2015.

[19] Michael Polanyi, *Personal Knowledge : Towards A Post- Critical Philosophy*, Routledge, 1958.

[20] Richard B Hays, *The Moral Vision of the New Testament: Community, Cross and the New Creation*, Edinburgh: T& T Clarke, 1997.

[21] See Amartya Sen and Jean Dreze, *An Uncertain Glory: India and Its Contradictions*, Princeton University Press, 2013.

[22] Amartya Sen and Martha Nussbaum (ed.) *The Quality of Life*, Oxford University Press, 1993.

[23] See *Healing and Wholeness: The Churches' Role in Health*, Document of The Christian Medical Commission (CMC), a sub-unit of the Unit on Justice and Service of the World Council of Churches (WCC), 1990.

PART-2
Healing Ministry as a Vocation

A Personal Search for Deeper Meaning

John Oommen

I am not a scholar or a theologian; a scientist or a professor. I am a part-time pilgrim on a journey, seeking truth and understanding in the midst of life and work; conscious of my fragility, fearfulness and sinfulness that both shackle and deepen the search. What I share in this paper therefore are imperfect and incomplete lessons learnt from interactions, conversations and reflections over the years. The holy grail of my pursuit is an understanding of the meaning and purpose of suffering and pain; life and death; health, healing and wholeness; of what some call the "Healing Ministry," while others call "Medical Missions." This is an ongoing life-long search and I draw on my growing up years on the CMC Vellore campus, as the son of the Chaplain; in a home that saw many passionate discussion on issues, which at that time flew over my childhood head, but later became the goal of my search. I would like to share some milestones or transformational events in this personal search, and some insights and reflections from this journey.

Milestones in a personal search

As a medical student in CMC in the early eighties, every Wednesday evening, we in the SCM visited patients with Spinal Cord Injuries in the Rehabilitation Institute. Patients asked us: Why me? What did I do to deserve this? Where was your God when I had my accident? We searched for insights, but they were inadequate. We had to find our own answers.

I would like to share with you five selected experiences of personal encounters over the last thirty years that have given me some light on this journey and cajole me into a new understanding of our mission in health care, centered around the idea of sharing the pain of people. While success and happiness are much sought after, it is pain that teaches us much. We are privileged in our lives as health professionals to encounter pain each day. All of technology and science is in the business of preventing and avoiding pain. But pain seeps through the cracks and gets to us willy-nilly. Let me share some incidents that changed my understanding and my life.

Rehab (1992-93)

After my MD in Community Medicine, I worked for a year in CMC's Dept of PMR and the Rehabilitation Institute, primarily to learn from Dr. Suranjan Bhattacharji, the then leader of the Rehab team. I got a ring-side view of some amazing work, and I want to share one incident with you that taught me so much, with apologies to Dr. Suranjan for sharing this without his permission.

There was a young girl, maybe 15 years old, admitted in Rehab with tetraplegia. Her parents were distraught as they wondered what her future would be. One day, they had a loud altercation with the physiotherapist. Much anger boiled up on both sides. The boss had to step in. I sat in on the meeting. Dr. Suranjan first listened to the parents of the patient as they poured out their anger and frustration. He listened, tears in his eyes, and then apologized sincerely to them. They cried for awhile, and left the room. Now the physiotherapist was very angry. He felt humiliated and unsupported in what he perceived as an unjust apology. I am so sorry, Dr. Suranjan said to him, that you have to go through this. The youngman cried, and left the room. And then Dr. Suranjan sat alone in that room and cried. I couldn't say a word. I suddenly got a glimpse of what rehabilitation truly meant. May be we could not give that young girl her mobility again. But we could share her pain. And together we could be healed. Rehabilitation was the process of accepting our weaknesses and strengths, and learning to build on what we have, to make up for what we don't; and this was true for the patient and the therapist, for you and for me. This is so true in Palliative Care too, as we seek to ease the way for the terminally ill, hold their hands, and share their pain. This is true too in work with HIV, in Oncology and Hematology. It is the foundational principle in Christian Nursing and in Christian Counseling. In Christian Health Care, we are called to share the pain of our patients; to get alongside and see the situation together; and to walk the journey to healing.

Runa's death (1996)

The year was 1996. I was now a community doctor, working with the people of 38 tribal villages in Bissam cuttack, in south Odisha. Each morning, our small team would set out, medicines and samosas in our backpacks, to visit our people and treat their illnesses. We had trained village health workers in each village. One of them, Runa Kolaka, was a really spunky young lady. She was pregnant for the first time. In my class on emergencies in labour and retained placentas, she asked me if it would happen to her, and if she would bleed and die. Would I be there to help, she asked. Have no fear, I replied, for I am here for you. But one terrible Tuesday morning she went into labour, weeks before her time, and her placenta was not expelled and she bled. She sent her husband to find me, but I was off in another village, on a mobile clinic. By the time I got the message and reached her village, she was gone; dead for more than seven hours. The baby still remained cord uncut, because she had told her village before she died, that Dr. Johnny would come. I sat there in that village, in the deep darkness of that night, crying my heart out as I cut the cord and held that baby. It shattered me, and changed my life in many ways. I asked myself, what use I was, if after an MBBS and MD from CMC Vellore, I could not even save the life of my health worker in labour. And as I searched and cried over the following weeks and months, it suddenly dawned on me that maybe this was my calling: to cry together with them; to share the pain of my people. And over time, they change, we change, situations change.

This became our approach to the practice of Community Health. There are so many issues in the community. You cannot play Dr. Fix-it. You really cannot change the world. You aren't meant to. The Christian approach to Community Health is to live with people; to cry and laugh and dream with the people; to get involved and become part of the community; to share their pains and their joys; and together to be transformed. Today, thanks in part to the lessons learnt from Runa's death, maternal deaths are relatively rare in our area; and infant mortality is less than 15 % of what it was then.

Lali's death (2007)

My sister, Lalitha, was a year older than me. In 2007, she was a senior clinical psychologist in NIMHANS, Bangalore. On the 16th of April, back home from duty, she suddenly stopped breathing. She was put on a ventilator in the ICU of the same hospital she worked in, and 36 days later, she died. As a family, this was a time of immense pain and spiritual learning. My father and I would sit together outside the ICU, reading and praying. The 6 patients in that ICU and their families spoke 3 different languages and belonged to 3 different religions. We prayed for each other and understood each other. And we became a community of pain. And as I searched for God, I suddenly found him; not on the other side handing out the pain and suffering; but on our side, on the seat next to me, sharing our pain, weeping with us. A broken and weeping God.

The Esther Paradox: Communal Riots in Odisha (2008)

In August-September 2008, our part of Odisha was wracked by communal riots, and for a change, we were the target. Churches were broken, homes burnt, Christians killed or impoverished as all they had was destroyed before their eyes. Our local Church was also vandalized, but we ourselves were safe in the hospital. A year later, we got together as the Christian Medical Association of India in Odisha, to reflect on what had happened and to seek God's guidance. We discovered that for some unknown reason, no Christian hospital had been touched by the riots. We called it our Esther Paradox. There we were, safe in our palaces of medicine while our people faced a pogrom of hate. And Uncle Mordecai was asking us "Who knows if you were brought to a position like this, for a time like this?" We did three days of deep study; of the Bible and of David Bosch. We asked ourselves what we were called to Be and called to do. And the answer that came to us, was that our calling was to Be God's People, and to Do his will; to listen to his music, and to dance to his tune ; to share the pain of the people of Odisha, in allhumility, and to respond as God would lead us. This was our mission.

The Sickle Cell Club: (2009)

Sickle Cell Anemia is a relatively common hemoglobinopathy in central India, a genetic disorder affecting mostly the Dalit and Adivasi communities. Those affected periodically have painful crises, often requiring hospitalization and blood transfusions and many suffer premature death. For us in CHB, SCA is a personal issue, as many of our staff and their children have Sickle Cell Trait or Disease. We as doctors are trained to provide treatment to people with SCA, but rarely do we appreciate the depth of the multi-dimensional pain involved. For one, there is the physical pain of frequent crises; and the cry of the child – Why me? Then there is the economic cost of treatment – life-long and draining. But only when we got up close did we realise there were other angles too. There is the guilt that parents feel when they find out that it was something in their genes passed on to their child that translated into this suffering. Health Education can have painful consequences. When the child realizes this too, it can be a very difficult confrontation for the family. There is also the factor of social discrimination. In rural India, we tend to marry within our communities. So any genetic disease tends to take on the social status of the community affected. Sickle Cell Anemia in our region is predominantly among the Dalit community and so the disease becomes marginalized, discriminated against and looked down on. Patients tell us stories of how badly they are treated in many hospitals.

In 2009, we in the Mitra team, asked ourselves how we should respond. A nurse, who herself had Sickle Cell Trait, wrote up a pamphlet from an Insider Perspective, to help families understand the problem. We got our Sicklers from the 50 Mitra villages together, along with their families and formed a Sickle Cell Club. Only people with homozygous SCA can join. They meet every 3 months, along with their families, to spend time together. They share their ups and downs; their challenges and achievements. The agenda includes blood tests, medications and updates. But most of all, they have a safe space where there are others who understand and share their pain. For nine years now, we have seen the difference this sharing of pain can make to the members.

Reflections of a medical pilgrim: The lessons from the journey

A. God is a healing God. I am the Lord that healeth thee, he says. Jesus in his ministry, uses healing as the proclamation of the Kingdom, the signs of God.

B. God's way of healing is through his participatory presence in situations of pain. Not by blitzing the problem away through remote control. But by involvement and engagement. Compassion means "to suffer with". Wherever there is pain, he is there, sharing the pain. A broken crucified God. The Suffering Servant in Isaiah, who takes on himself the pain and insult and injury. And by his stripes we are healed.

C. Mission is what God is doing in this world. Missio Dei. He calls us to get out of our churches and comfort zones, to join him, in the hustle and bustle of life, to be co-workers with him, in his ministry of healing.

D. The Jesus methodology as described so brilliantly by St Paul in Philippians 2:5–8 is our road map, a manual for incarnational mission. He does not consider equality with God something to be grasped or held on to, but empties himself, becomes a man, takes on the nature of a servant, and is obedient even unto death on the cross. And our attitude, says St Paul, should be like that of Jesus Christ.

E. Our calling is to share the pain of people; to cross the boundaries; to identify with; to share the pain in humility and vulnerability.

Our hospitals and clinics are platforms where people in pain stream in each day. They are not just broken down bodies for repair; or a lab for our scientific curiosity to be played out in. God is with the sick and the suffering. We are privileged to be allowed to participate with him. We should take off our mental chappals. God is here.

F. Healing is sacramental; health care is as holy as the breaking of the bread and the pouring of the wine. In touching those in pain, we touch God himself. This is the foot of the cross. Mother Teresa on a visit to CMC many years ago, spoke of one of her young sisters who described to her a dying man on the streets of Kolkata. He was covered with grime and infested with maggots, when brought in from the street. The young sister was carefully washing hisbody and removing the maggots, when the man quietly died. The mother asked her what she felt when this happened. And the young sister said she felt she was touching the body of Jesus.

Q.1 : What is God's dream or vision for us ?

Abundant life, as Jesus says in his statement of intent in John 10.10. God's verdict, in Genesis, on the original creation, prior to the fall, was that it was good, in all respects. Healing is restoration to the purpose of God.

Q.2 : Why is there so much pain and suffering in this world ?

I have not found a complete answer, but the reason includes the fall and corruption of the created order; God's provision of free will to man; the laws of nature. Sometimes, suffering is vicarious where one takes it on oneself for a higher cause. But this answer is incomplete, and the search continues – confident that even if I do not know, God does, and that is enough for me. I choose to trust.

Q.3 : Where is God, when people are in pain ?

I have found God is with them, sharing their pain – in the jeep with Graham Staines and his sons, burning with them. Pushing the wheelchair of Dr Mary Verghese. Holding us close and crying with us in our times of tragedy. He is with us, on our side – not the perpetrator, but the accompanier.

Q.4 : What then is our calling in the ministry of healing ?

Our calling is to join God, to be co-workers with him; to share the pain of people, in humility and love. And from that position, to treat, to cure, to rehabilitate, to prevent, to accompany, to heal – as the case may be. Our hospitals and clinics are points of concentration of pain, and therefore of God too – holy ground, and we are privileged to be part of the healing circle.

May I submit that our work in health care is far more than an occupation and a profession; and not to be reduced to a fishing net for unsuspecting souls in their time of vulnerability. It is our worship; a sacrament; holy ground. Can we engage with the poor, the needy, the disabled, the ones in pain? Meet God in them. Touch him. And offer our life and work, both individual and institutional, as a worship offering, to him. In Christian Health Care, we are part of something much bigger than we see or imagine. We see as if in a mirror. One day, we will see face to face. In our insecurity and fear, we clutch on to the tangibles, the visibles, the physical. May God give us the courage as individuals, institutions and as Church – to let go - and to find in him our meaning and purpose.

Healing and Wholeness

Sunil Chandy

Physical ill health has always been the prime constituency of healing. From the common man's perspective, it is largely physical illness that drives him to seek medical care. More recently though, wellness has broadened to include mental, emotional and social dimensions as well, driven by broad definitions of Health from the World Health Organization and other bodies. We live in a world where ill-health visibly transcends the physical realm into deeper layers of our existence. Today, the need for Healing transcends our bodies to the wider community we interact with, including our families, institutions, community, our nation and the world. Being of sound body, mind and soul definitely has a theological basis, as it was this status that God our creator wanted all his creation to bein.

Wholeness or Wholesomeness has been the central theme of the Judeo-Christian faith. In fact it pre-dates the "Christian" era from the time of Creation itself. God's emphasis on completeness and perfection to say that 'it was good' undergirds not only the seven days of Creation, but throughout the history of God's people as recorded in the Old-Testament. From the time this perfect world order went horribly wrong by a callous act of disobedience, it seems that God has been on a mission to set right the broken reeds of the God-human relationship. Restoration, reconciliation, recovery and renewal – all these have been strands of that cord called HEALING. Healing, more than an end, has been the means to an end – of restoration to the wholeness originally designed by God when he created Man.

The biblical journey towards wholeness has spanned several generations of people and is lined with different expressions of healing – repair of the brokenness in the garden of Eden, redemption of the people of Israel from Egypt, renewal of the testament of God from Moses to Jesus to the resurrection of Jesus, the Son of God. All these and more, are part of the continuing narrative scripted by God towards - making his creation complete. Is it over? Not close! God's mission to heal continues even today, through the self-inflicted imperfections brought on by human disobedience and misplaced intellect. Restoration of the imbalances of nature, asymmetry of knowledge, social dichotomies and biological ill-health are all still on God's radar screen towards healing human kind. It is towards this mission that God has chosen us to be instruments of healing, whether we are doctors, teachers, preachers or lay people.

I wish to allude to some specific biblical narratives which in my opinion help us understand healing in a broader sense. The garden of Eden, the Exodus from Egypt, Jesus and his ministry, the woman at Jacob's well are some of them. I am interpreting these narratives through the lens of a physician trying to derive their significance in our daily lives. These stories translate to three planes of existence – personal, community and spiritual. They interact closely enough with one another for different reactions to occur. Some happy, some sad, some of wellness, some of illness. More often than not there is turmoil, resulting in a constant need for healing.

The need for biological wellness will continue to dominate the mundane perception of Healing for some time to come. That's the reason why doctors and hospitals will continue to be in great demand in the foreseeable future. Much has been said about biological healing, and details on it are beyond the scope of this discussion. This is the business we all are in, as an institution. Science has helped greatly in unraveling the mysteries of the human being as an organism and we have successfully worked our way to conquer several diseases that disabled us. We stand on the threshold of several scientific breakthroughs that are predicted to change the language of Health care delivery completely. Technology, genomics and artificial intelligence are being proposed as the revolutionary tools of future medicine. Yet today, we are confronting the worst statistics of physical, mental, environmental and emotional diseases, both individually and combined. Where do we stand as an institution of healing in addressing the changing epidemiology of illness? Physical ill-health now appears as a multi-headed hydra interlaced with issues that arise from the broader impact of environment, community and workplace.

Aunt Ida's response that fateful night was a primary response to the needs of women and children. But it evolved into a journey with a larger purpose – that of healing a community of its vulnerabilities and empowering them into a state of dignified living. Her ultimate vision was even larger– to build the Kingdom of God. And what might that Kingdom sense be? It was and is a reiteration of the prayer we say every day, "Thy Kingdom come, on earth as it is in Heaven". The institution she helped build maintained the centrality of God's Kingdom on earth. There is a definite completeness in her vision statement – to serve, educate and research the truth of God's design. And that journey continues.

Healing, from a Biblical standpoint,can be viewed from different vantage points.

I.   Healing of the person

II. Healing of the community

III. Healing of our environment

Healing of the person

John Wesley, the founder of the Methodist Church wrote that man was created as "a well-working system." He said - "The perfect model or expression of health would be Adam before the Fall, a balanced, harmonious, human organism designed for immortality." When Eve bit the forbidden fruit in the garden of Eden, that perfect design was destroyed. That status of a sinless perfect world went awfully wrong and the essence of wholeness was shattered. The need for Healing started in the garden of Eden itself. It was not a physical ailment that day, but a situation of alienation that resulted in intense emotional stress, guilt and remorse induced by disobedience. There was shame and an immediate distancing between God and man. "Where are you" was God's first question, loaded with a sense of distancing, a disconnect in the relationship. "Who told you" signifies the entry of a third entity disrupting a harmonious bilateral relationship between God and humankind. A situation where God gifted humans with dominion over all things changed to one of hard work and toil becoming the way of life (Genesis 3:19). Pain and distress became a part of our earthly life. The whole saga pained God deeply, but instead of a terminal punitive response we see him engage in an act of empathy towards Adam and Eve. He instructed them on the ways to live and protected them from further harm and trouble. Adam and Eve left Eden hapless but not hopeless, assured of a way to live on God's earth. Though this brokenness, there was healing that arose from divine empathy and compassion. A way of life was restored.

The mission of Jesus is narrated in the Nazareth manifesto in Luke 4:18-19. Medical mission was an integral part of his mission for all practical purposes. His ministry revolved around healing 'diseases of every kind' (Mathew 4:24). He did that with fiery passion walking long distances, visiting homes, sitting by the sea-shore and climbing the hill side. He never said "No" to even the most unreasonable request for Healing. He walked the extra mile and talked about the need to be forgiven and made whole. This is the basis of our mission as well. Teach, Preach and Heal which relates to mind, body and soul respectively represents the message of Jesus towards making us complete, which became the principal mandates of the Christian church for 2000 years. Holistic healing is thus the highlight of Jesus' ministry, and ours. An example of healing beyond the physical is available in the parable of the

Good Samaritan. The Samaritan's response starts with an empathetic response of stepping aside from his destined path to enquire about the victim. He not only nurses his wounds, but transports him on his own animal, admits him to an inn, finances his care and promises to return to top up his after-care. What an example of walking the extra mile to make Healing complete. In the coming years, the need to lay emphasis on emotional, social and spiritual health alongside physical well being should become a greater part of our mission.

Healing of the community

God cares about his people as a community. The nation of Israel fell captive to Egypt. Slavery and indignity made the existence of God's people difficult. Enslaved by Pharaoh, their lives were an ignominy. They cried for healing and restoration. God responded by sending Moses as their redeemer. He led them out of Egypt and over a long and arduous journey that took forty years to complete. The entire saga is one of God's amazing engagement with his people through Moses. He labored with them through some very difficult experiences. God's perseverance stretches from ten plagues that weakened the stubborn Pharaoh, forming pillars and clouds of protection on the Israelite convoy, the splitting of the Red Sea, his tolerance of disobedience by the Israelites, provision of food and water in the most adverse circumstances to the entry into the Promised Land. There were several moments when the community rebelled but God continued to be caring enough to take them through to their destination.

In the New Testament (John Ch:4) we read of Jesus meeting a Samaritan woman at a well. There is no record of her being physically unwell. Jesus struck a conversation on 'the living water' which led to her discovery about herself, and the leading of an entire community in that Samaritan village to a revelation about many aspects of life. Jesus engaging with this Samaritan community is an example of the need to extend our healing initiatives beyond our patients to the communities they come from. It also highlights our mission to those who are seemingly ostracized by the prejudices of caste and beliefs. We are in the mission of healing and transforming communities through our thoughts, words and deeds.

Dr. Ida Scudder, our founder, has been a pioneer in the journey of healing communities. In her ministry, she catered not just to the physical health of needy women, but helped transform their status though education, training and livelihood. The social upliftment of the local community in Vellore by the impact of training and education over a century has been significant. The community in Vellore stands out as an empowered, educated and emancipated one. It may not be incorrect to say that CMC as an institution has transformed a socially impoverished community into a robust one. Healing has a social dimension which has been attended to through CMC's ministry. CMC has also created a diaspora of healers, chosen, trained and sent to the far ends of the nation to create similar communities. Several thousands have been restored to life; several families have been raised to living dignified lives in society. Empowerment though education and awareness has been a means to being Healed in totality. A visit to the colonies of our staff in Vellore will bear testimony to the upliftment CMC has induced through its mission. This must continue.

Healing of our environment

The connotation of the word 'environment' is broad here. It includes the ambience of our surroundings, our homes, our institutions and our workplaces. The inter-relatedness of our self with our surroundings cannot be ignored. How much does our environment help in our wellness? Going by the example that God himself set, the milieu we live in contributes immensely to our well-being. Eden, the designated home of Adam and Eve, was created to picture perfection. Situated at the confluence of four rivers with an abundance of food, flora and fauna, Eden provided the perfect environment for good health. Not only were these physical characteristics conducive to feeling healthy, but the entire experience was lifted up by the presence of God who would walk and talk with them daily. Eden represents our home where we can unwind from life and soak up the ambience of wholeness. Allow me to extend this ambience to our institutions. Though man-made, institutions represent the Eden of our professional lives. They are sanctuaries where we spend a good part of our day. They enhance our professional growth and provide the needed space for self-fulfillment. They must have all the needed elements of Eden- space, clean air, water, food, peace and tranquility. When the environment we live and work in becomes unhealthy, sickness follows. Today, in many large metros in India, air- pollution has become a major determinant of illness.

Our workplaces are part of our environment. The institutions we work in and for are crucial for our healthy existence as a healing community. World over, we are witnessing breakdown of institutions. Institutions that were formed on strong Christian foundations are undergoing major mission drifts. Many Christian institutions, especially in the east coast of the United States of America, have drifted away from their Christian moorings in favour of a secular philosophy. Modernism and intellectualism have replaced the essential principles of Christian thinking. This is beginning to be true of institutions in India as well. The slow but steady decline of mission hospitals is real. Of those who remain, few are robust enough to be watchtowers of healing in their regions. Beset by crises of leadership, governance, manpower and finances – these institutions are in need of healing.

Our workplaces require healing. If our institution needs to be the home to a healing God, its constituent departments and works stations must be sanctuaries of peace, friendship, companionship and love. The concerns of work-life balance, relationships and human resource management must be addressed with great caution. The community fabric, campus life, worship and informal interaction which our founder nurtured during her lifetime needs to be strengthened even more in these days when social media and gadgets are pushing us into isolation. Relationships outside the workplace have a positive influence on equations between people within the workplace. It is worth considering this dimension as an important factor in maintaining ourselves as a robust community in the mission of healing. Music and worship are two other things that bind us together by their ability to soothe, comfort and heal. Mother Teresa was asked by a journalist as to what gave her the strength to carry out the hard task she was doing. She replied saying that she and her co-missionaries would spend an hour each day at the feet of the Lord, recharging their batteries to keep going. Our task of being healers is just as tough. We need that constant renewal through personal and corporate interaction with God.

Institutions are not just brick and mortar. What makes an institution great is its culture and its ethos. That is determined by its unchanging core beliefs. CMC, grounded in the spirit of Christ, must stay rooted in this as it has done for the last hundred odd years. These beliefs remain the well-spring of all our resources. Our identity stems from this ethos, our uniqueness is rooted in it as well. When the winds of political change blow over us, it would require the label of Jesus Christ to be painted on our gates, much like God's people were asked to do at the Passover. Aunt Ida, in her personal diary (available in the archives) has expressed her concerns about the changing ethic of our times and advised us to stay committed to the call to be Healers *in the spirit of Christ*.

In recent times, CMC as an institution has faced unprecedented challenges. Changes arising from new statutes and political compulsions have challenged our mission and objectives. Our adaptations to these changes have helped us tide over the crisis temporarily. It surely has left us confused. It is in times like these that we need to reset our bearings to continue our journey.

At the threshold of a new century, it is appropriate that we are rethinking our role as a healing community. Through all our human imperfection, we can stay assured that our God who has led us thus far will continue this journey into the next hundred years. This he assures in Ephesians 3:20, " *now to Him who is able to do immeasurably more than all we ask or imagine, according to the power that is at work within us to Him be glory in the Church and in Christ Jesus, forever and ever, Amen.*"

Healing – My Passion and Vocation!

Selva Titus Chacko

I am humbled to share this platform with great people of God and share my thoughts on Healing – My Passion & Vocation. I am a pilgrim on a journey in search for truth, fragile and broken at many junctures. But God's faithfulness continues to hold me precious in his hands.

Our passion is our fuel. It keeps us going no matter how many challenges come our way. Vocation is a volatile act of an individual; personal desires take prominence here. Passion gives shape to the life of any individual. As a matter of fact, it is all about choices. You choose a vocation and pursue in that direction and enjoy what you do. Societal reformation and moral higher ground have shaped the vocation of many noble souls, in different parts of the world.

Our minds are afresh with the thoughts of Beethoven who was obsessed with music; the young missionary Jim Elliot was hell-bent on evangelizing the native Indians in Ecuador. And father of modern missionary movement William Carey, was quite serious about leaving the shores of England and coming to India. I am quite sure it is still fresh in our minds, the death of the Korean-American missionary John Chua, who lost his life in an attempt to reach the Sentinelese.

The pages of worldwide missions are replete with stories that clearly illustrate the ennobling involvement of men and women of God who brought in a sea-change in the healthcare scenario of people.

We do certain things out of compulsion, and we get involved in other work, when there is a necessity. In human life, we have to embark on certain other work that every human has to undertake or perform. But **a voluntary mission is solely because of inner compulsions and a nobler vision.** Down through the ages men and women of character chose to obey the beckoning of that still small voice.

God calls us to be witnesses in the entire world *(Acts 1:8)*. Being salt and light. *"For we are what He has made us, created in Christ Jesus for good works, which God prepared beforehand to be our way of life"* *(Ephesians 2:10).*

Healthcare professionals are in a privileged position for being indisputable during times of need, in a caring relationship.

The Nursing profession encompasses the care of individuals who need medical attention for a variety of reasons. Many are physical; some are psychosocial. No matter what the reason patient has sought care, the nurse has the duty to treat the whole patient. Nursing takes on a holistic view of people. The whole person, including the body, mind and spirit, must be provided care (McSherry, 2006). Gifted, called, blessed are terms a person is crowned with when he/she can touch a person of infirmity and the infirmity disappears.

Being a nurse, understanding the physiology, anatomy and biochemistry of the human body and its relationship with the disease process and healing or treatment or cure at a physical level is rewarding. But witnessing the lack of cure for most of the chronic and malignant disease processes has opened the understanding of the healing paradigm, which is very vital. **Healing is not just at the physical level, it happens when you have the ability to connect with God the creator.**

Nursing of the ancient days that motivated its pals with the spirit of compassion and caring has now evolved into professionalism that demands power, authority, status and appropriate compensation. As Christian nurses and health care professionals, it is high time that we relook at our ideals and understand our calling.

In Nursing as a vocation, the beauty of the intertwining of the human efforts with the Divine Grace is experienced. This cannot be felt by a person who has aimed to make money or achieve literary heights. This is filled with intolerable sacrifice, unwelcomed sarcasms and unyieldable lows but there's a halo of grace and peace that always surrounds your spirit, soul and body. This is the secret for a great healing ministry to be accomplished through a vocation called Nursing.

Here you don't talk about material benefits, popularity and a cozy lifestyle. A vocation is one that offers complete freedom and satisfaction! There are three things that we see, when we ponder over the idea of healing as a vocation – The Will of the individual, the Welfare of the society and the Wellness of the church.

The will of the individual

Nurses are healers because of the caring relationship that they make with the patients. Caring calls out for inner strengths.

T.S. Elliot describes the work of nursing in two dimensions: 'doing' and 'being'. All nurses understand the 'doing' dimension of nursing. So much of a nurse's preparation, socialization and role definition lie in what we do. The 'doing' skills and the technical accountabilities are that which keep nurses running and busy. This dimension of nursing work has clearly changed, grown and become more complex over time. 'Doing' is clearly more concrete, able to be measured and generally what has been perceived to be valued.

The 'being' dimension of the role of nurse is less about what nurses do and more about the how. Admittedly, this 'being' dimension is more difficult to describe, harder to measure and although valued by nurses and those patients who benefit from it, has not always been at the center of what is rewarded. 'Being' is what slows down the nurse so that space is created for an authentic, deep connection with the patient and healing. Embed in the 'being' dimension of the role lies the essence of nursing and it is here that the call to the profession is actualized.

Choosing healing as a vocation depends much more on the human will. The process of healing is intertwined with various kinds of setbacks, difficulties and even death. As such, the profession of healing looks very unattractive and cumbersome. You cannot get pass marks all the time. Since you deal with human lives, every step that you take towards healing is carefully gauged by the relatives and friends. And you are answerable to the hospital authorities and the society in general.

The will to serve and the desire to help, make healing a more desirable vocation. The Saint of Kolkata chose to do the role of a healer in that overcrowded metropolis. She cleaned the foul-smelling ulcers of the lepers and washed the dying bodies of the elderly. When somebody asked her about usefulness of her unheralded mission she curtly replied, "I dress the wounds, but God heals them". When you choose healing as a mission and vocation, your deeds become saintly and salutary. You get the inner peace that God is in your side and endorses all your efforts to heal the sick ones.

The welfare of the society
The last century A.D saw a deep slump in the healthcare setup, world over. Migration to cities became unabated, paving way for cramped clusters of immigrant laborers. Displaced people from neighboring nations added to the woes of decent housing and urban planning. The language cauldron brought its own problems and difficulties. All these factors, combined with insufficient monsoon, pushed the poor and the marginalized into a situation of unhealthy living. Hence, healthcare became a luxury for such hapless commoner in our country. Clinics sprang up in the dusty corners of cities such as Kolkata, Ahmedabad, Salem and Lucknow like mushrooms after a heavy shower. Run by quacks and cheap money makers, these clinics were in the business of fleecing the simple ones in the name of offering affordable medical care. News reports tell us about faulty injections, crude wayside dental extractions and death during delivery. When I step out to serve my country with my nursing knowledge, I become a crusader for better and affordable medical help. And thousands of men and women join in my mission

with a similar vision; my country gets more healthier and more vibrant. Because my resolve is purely voluntary and my commitment is quite sacred. Undeterred by the economic buoyancy and the endless publicity. As you choose the healthcare mission as your vocation, you contribute to the nation building and you help the national church to take stronger roots in the Indian soil. In the personal plane you get job satisfaction and a sense of patriotism. Nursing education from ancient times have been an outreach of the Christians. But now, institutions have sprung up everywhere, the core values and ethos are lost. So as Christian educators, we need to make that difference! Education paves way for a civilized society. Systematic education in relevant fields has been harbinger for sustained development in many a country. Hence, much care should be taken in identifying the topics/ subjects for education – what should be taught and what should be relegated.

The wellness of the Church

We live in an age where even Christian health care workers practice medicine for selfish ends. Sheer greed drives the Christian medical professionals to go for extra income, forgetting their noble calling and their glorious commitment. Health care in the present world is becoming commercialized–A business rather than a vocation or a calling. Patients are increasingly becoming customers rather than fellow human beings. Technology has simply become a tool to make health care workers life easier or to enhance income.

Jesus brought in the word-Holism. He addressed the alienation, fears, rejection and restored the total health of the person - spirit, soul and body. This is the idea that is ingrained in our nursing these days - Holistic nursing care. How foolish it is that we refuse to see God's wholeness in the richness of our own meagre achievements called technology! Taking a cue from the Master Healer, let us turn compassionate in meeting the health care needs of our fellow human beings. Let the church in India strive to produce missionary health care workers who prefer service over salary. Christian medical missions such as the Christian Medical College, Vellore and its mission network hospitals should impart

Christian values to every trainee in their training departments. The rationale here is, there are corporate hospitals in India where treatment is available only for those who can afford. Thus, the rich can afford to get the best form of services in these so-called medical megaliths. But where can the poor go for better medical treatment? They do not have much money. Mission hospitals should come forward to fill the gap. Trained and experienced health care workers e.g. nurses who love to serve the ailing mankind with devotion and compassion are the need of the hour. These dear ones have taken the nursing profession as a vocation, and not a career.

Nursing: An unpredicted switch, yet rewarding and satiating

A passion for healing requires our whole-hearted willingness and deepest values. From the first century AD, Christianity had a huge influence on nursing. The role of a nurse grew out of the Christian perspective of the human being created in the image of God and viewed as the "Temple of the Holy Spirit" as reflected in the scriptures in I Corinthians 6:19. In the early Christian church, caring for the sick was seen as a ministry to Christ, to an extent that everyone in the nursing profession was considered to be a Christian. By 1940, it was estimated that 90% of the nurses in India were Christians. The command of Jesus to 'Love thy neighbor as thyself' and the parable of the Good Samaritan had a significant impact on the development of the nursing profession in the early Christian era. Christianity introduced a new aspect of 'altruism', which was ascribed to be the highest possible motive of mankind. It taught that one's sincere love for God and a desire to be like 'Him' would be the chief motives for one's selfless and sacrificial service to mankind.

To me, nursing has been a sublime journey. I was born and brought up in a family from a different religion. But God chose me and called me for his mission. *"For I know the plans I have for you, declares the Lord, 'plans to prosper you not to harm you', plans to give you hope and future" (Jeremiah 29:11).* I called it an unpredicted switch, because being the best outgoing student in my Pre- University Course; I was offered a medical seat, at one of the premier Medical Institutions in our State.

But I decided to study in a Christian Institution that would nourish my hungry spirit. Never have I regretted my choice to follow him. I have been blessed and fortunate to have been mentored by Christian teachers like Miss A. Kuruvilla, Miss Anna Jacob, Miss Alice Jane David, Ms. Pauline King, Mrs. Violet Jeyachandran, Mrs. Accamma Chacko, Mrs. Achyamma John, Mrs. Saramma George, Mrs. Ann Sukumar, Mrs. Kasthuri Sundar Rao and many others along with great servants of God like Rev. A.C. Ommen, Bishop Dr. George Isaac, Miss Mary George and many caring friends here at CMC, who helped me place my trust in Jesus for my life. I joined as a young trained nurse at Christian Fellowship Hospital, Oddanchatram south of Tamil Nadu where I was trained and mentored by great Christian pioneers viz., Ms. Mariam K. Philip, Ms. A Cherian & Dr. A.K. Tharien. Both these great Christian nurse leaders held high ranks in the field of Nursing. Ms. Mariam Philip, was the Secretary of the Trained Nurses Association of India and Ms. A Cherian Nursing Advisor to the Government of India. Despite their expertise and professional stature, they were simple and humble; teachers with great character, holding strong Christian values and principles. Their lives and Dr. A.K Tharien's had a significant impact and if I am able to contribute in a small way to the profession today, it is because of their dedication, commitment and inspiration in me.

I obeyed God and he has honored me. I find it satisfying, helping patients find meaning in the creator. Not only patients but mentoring budding nurses in the Spirit of Christ has been quite cumbersome yet gratifying. And that in turn has brought inner healing and restoration within me. This choice may not be worthwhile in terms of luxury and economy, but definitely has helped me make an eternal bond with the maker. Having been an educator, care provider, mentor, manager, administrator and policy maker; these roles have packed my life with multiple opportunities for healing. In my journey of nursing, I have discovered the basis of healing. I urge each one of us to obey his calling and be diligent. Make that right choice that will shape your lives and touch other lives.

As we flip through the pages of Indian Christian medical records, we find tall and glittering personalities such as our founder Dr. Ida. S. Scudder, Dr. Paul Brand, Dr. Mary Varghese, Dr A K Tharien, Miss Pauline King and many others whom I have met and been inspired in my life time. These ennobling medical personnel chose Medicine/Nursing as a vocation. May be, they could not soar high in terms of economics and commerce. They were not popular in their times. They led a simple life and shunned a cozy and comfortable vocation. They were not appreciated both by their peers and their opponents. Truly speaking, many of them were ridiculed, criticized and spoken ill-off. In spite of the mounting opposition, these mission-minded warriors stood their ground, endured the ordeals and came out unscathed. *Isaiah*, the St. Paul of Old testament reminds us, *"Those who wait in the Lord will renew their strength; they shall mount up with wings like eagles; they shall run and not be weary; they shall walk and not faint"* (Is. 40:31) and St. Paul in New testament encourages us with these words, *"I can do all things through Christ who strengthens me" (Phil 4:13).*Mission is always a passion for those who set their minds on lofty ideals! Let us follow Jesus, whose clarion call is, *"Follow me, I will make you fishers of men" (Math 4:19).* I would call nurses as heaven appointed ambassadors of the Cross and divine wholeness. If you have heeded to the clear call of heaven, then you will heal with your looks, words, actions and nearness. Friends, on this occasion let us make a resolution to do our best in whatever we are called to do, measuring achievements not in terms of money earned, successes or failures, designations or titles, but in the **NUMBER OF LIVES WE HAVE TOUCHED**. This will be a fitting tribute to Aunt Ida as well in fulfilling her dream of *'Building the Kingdom of God'*. I conclude my words once again thanking Chaplaincy Department, CMC for giving me this unique opportunity and all of you for the patient hearing.

Lessons from Jesus' Ministry of Healing

Sara Bhattacharji

D uring his brief time as a wandering preacher and teacher, Jesus of Nazareth was also known as a healer. People with all kinds of diseases and illnesses flocked to him and we are told that he laid his hands on them and healed them (Luke 40:4). Jesus, apart from these mass 'camps' also performed individual acts of healing some of which are recorded in the gospels. The people who came to him for healing were a motley lot; men, women and children; the sickness acute like Peter's mother in law's, (Mark 1:30-31) or chronic like the paralysed man beside the pool. He also raised some people who were dead. Some came of their own accord, some with fear and trembling, some were brought by friends or family; some were just requests and the healing took place 'long distance' so to speak. And some were specially called out by Jesus like the man with the withered hand, and the bent over woman. In many instances he also gave strict instructions not to tell anyone. We are not given any names of the people who were healed, except for Bartimaeus, and the possessed man called 'Legion', though they have been identified in a variety of ways.

There were leprosy patients,(Matt 8:1-4; Mark 1:40-45; Luke 5:12-16; Luke 17:11-19) people with mental illness, (Mark 1:23-28; Mark 5:1-20) a paralysed man who had friends to care for him (Mark 2:1-12) and one who had no one to help (John 5:1-15). There were the blind, so many of them, (John 9:1-41; Matthew 9:27-31; Matthew 20:29-34;

Mark 8:22-26), the deaf and dumb (Mark 7:31-37, Mark 8:22-26, Mark 10: 46-52), a woman with a bent back (Luke 13:10-17) and one with a withered hand (Matthew 12:10-13) who were not even seeking to be healed. There was a woman with a bleeding disorder, so afraid and so stigmatised. (Luke 8:43-48; Matthew 9:18-26). There was the son of a nobleman (John 4:46-54) and the servant of the centurion (Matthew 8:5-13) who Jesus did not even see. There was blind Bartimaeus (Mark 10: 46-52) who was loud and insistent in his desire for healing. There was a boy with epilepsy and a distraught father, whom the disciples could not heal (Matthew 17:14-21). There was the daughter of the Syrophoenician woman who belonged to a different community, outside the traditional boundaries of the Jewish clan, whose mother's persistence led to healing and perhaps expanded Jesus' s horizons from narrow clan boundaries (Matthew 15:22-28). There were people he raised from the dead (Luke 7:11-18; Matthew 9: 18-26; John 11:1-46).

Jesus, it seems, always met those in need with welcome words and often we are told that he was 'moved with pity'. He put aside his own need for rest and responded to the great need that he saw. He felt for them, seemed to understand the way the disease had alienated them in myriad ways. He reached out to touch. He used mud, spit and pigs. And in many cases he gave them something to do to complete the process: 'go and show yourselves to the priest' or 'go and wash in the pool' or 'get up', or 'take your bed and walk'. Often he told them not to speak of what he had done, but sometimes he sought them out to encourage them to continue to live well. While he recognised that 'sin' alienated a person from God, he firmly negated the idea that sickness was a consequence of the person's or family's sin. He challenged the authority of existing societal and religious 'norms' calling for a radical rethinking of the meaning of health and what it means to be human.

And people reacted to the healing in different ways. Some came back to say thanks; some went away delighted in their healing, some talked about their healing, some got into trouble with the authorities and some followed him. Jesus probably did not see most of those he healed again. There were a few however, that he sought out for follow up. As with his preaching and teaching, for Jesus the ministry of healing was not an end in itself, but a means of making visible the love and grace of a creator, who wants the best for his creation.

What can we in the 21st century 'healing ministry', so vastly different from those far away days, learn from the 'Jesus Way'?

One common thread for me in all these acts is that Jesus was working for 'restoration'. This restoration was first of all physical. The blind saw, the deaf heard, the dumb spoke, the paralysed man got up and walked, the child with epilepsy had no more fits, the violent one with a mental illness was quiet and the dead came back to life.

But Jesus did not stop there. In many cases he made sure that those who were at the margins, excluded and stigmatised because of the illness, were restored to community. Some were asked to follow the rules of society, like the leprosy patients; some were publically affirmed for their faith, like the centurion, the woman with the haemorrhage; in some cases he affirmed the importance of friendship and relationship with each other. Some were called out for healing defying current religious law like the man with the withered hand or the woman with the bent back. In the case of the paralytic man who was brought to him by friends, and the one at the poolside, Jesus also restored their relationship with God, forgiving sin and exhorting them to 'sin no more'. In all this Jesus was risking his life because he was challenging current societal and common norms of his day.

The practice of medicine in the 21st century is vastly different from that in Jesus day. Advances in medical science and technology especially in the last 50 to 70 years have drastically changed the way modern Allopathic medicine is practiced. The early beginnings of care for the sick and destitute began as an off shoot of Christian caring ministry and the understanding of the early church about the ministry to the sick and dying. This ministry developed in time into the provision of institutional health care. As time went by and science, medical knowledge and practice grew more organised and governments took over this role in the west, the medical missionary movements that took the art and science of healing to many lands began. (That this movement by and large ignored the already present systems of healing in these places is another story).

With the development of 'Modern medicine' with its focus on technology and hospitals , the rise and fall of the primary health care movement, the commercialisation of medicine, and the decline of the Christian mission sector, there is a crisis of how the Christian healing ministry is perceived both from within the church and outside. World mission and health initiatives of the churches like the Christian Medical Commission of the World Council of Churches, which did a lot to promote the Christian understanding of health, healing and wholeness, have faded away. What is the relevance of the 'Jesus Way' for us today, whatever part of the healing ministry we are in?

I suggest that this means that we have to develop a great sensitivity to those in need. We have to be 'moved with pity' and practice compassion. Whatever our role in the technical aspects of medicine and care, we are called to reach out and touch the other, especially the ones who seem to be untouchable, discovering who they are in today's world. (In the 80's, it was the churches who first reached out with care to those with HIV/AIDS). We have to use innovatively what exists; be it mud, spit or pigs! We have to involve the ones who seek healing in the process of healing. We have to actively look out for the most vulnerable ones who may not come forward, and spot the ones who come with hesitation; responding with affirmation and gentleness. We need to bring in the wider community, affirming existing relationships, restoring where they are broken, including spiritual relationships. Sometimes we are also called to take risks, to take a stand that may not be popular.

Sickness and suffering are not easy to understand and there are no easy answers to question of why it happens. Thoughtful, constructive dialogue with patients, health care workers, lay people and theologians is vital for those involved in the healing ministry. And when cure is not possible or beyond us, we are called, I think, to restore life and affirm death by being the presence of God in loving support.

This is a tall order and we cannot do this alone. Jesus often withdrew, we are told, to gain strength from his father. And we too need to have times to renew our strength, asking for and receiving help from Jesus and our father. We also need to build our collective strength and community, learning to live in love and tolerance with one another, listening to each other in constructive dialogue, forging and building true community where each is affirmed and all are able to be whole.

I would like to share a couple of stories. The first one among so many from the time of working with volunteers in a Community Based Rehab project. The other is about a very brave friend who chose the path of accompaniment in a crisis.

In the community project, we trained volunteers who worked within their communities identifying people with various disabling conditions and addressing their felt needs. One of them found a young man who was born with mental impairment. Govindraj, by now 25 years old, was the classic 'village idiot' one reads about. He was soiled, smelly, had torn clothes and was the butt of jokes, shunned by all. Yet he went after people with a grin on his face, his teeth sticking out, drooling saliva, only to be met with insults, taunts and sometimes being pelted with stones. His family was ashamed of him and often beat him up for 'not listening' to what they told him to do. The volunteer and team outlined a possible strategy to deal with the situation. She spent some time speaking with the family, enlisting their co-operation. At first she worked alone, with great love and patience, and as they slowly saw the point of what she was doing, the family joined in with her. She would bathe him each morning, teach him to clean his teeth, put on a fresh set of clothes, teaching him to do this himself, and made sure that he was taken to the toilet every few hours. She got her own sons to befriend him and care for him. She pinned a handkerchief to his shirt so his spittle could be wiped off. And suddenly Govindraj the outcaste became a part of that community. He would be the first to come to the meetings of people with disability that she organised. Though his speech was restricted, he was happy to be in the group and to sing with the rest. The community, especially many of the young people began to see disablement through a different lens. Though he was never cured, I think that there was healing in the community and restoration of relationships. It was not easy and there were still times when people were exasperated with him, or people who saw him as a nuisance. But they were all together learning something about health, healing and wholeness.

My other story is from the time of the Ebola crisis that hit West Africa recently. The people in the Liberian mission hospitals called for help very early on in the epidemic from their mission partners in Europe. The call came to the director of a institute for infectious diseases and she felt that there really was so little that she could do from so far away and that this was a situation which called for her presence to be with the people who were in the midst of crisis. So, against all 'good sense' and the protests of family and colleagues, she went off, long before WHO and others appeared on the scene. What she did was first to acknowledge the pain, and grief. Then she set about working with the hospitals, teaching very simple, practical ways of good practice in dealing with the situation, like hand washing among many others. She was able to bring calm and some change to a desperate situation. What a risk she took for herself! But she passed this off cheerfully as something she just had to do because her faith told her at that point she could do no other. And in our ministry of healing sometimes we are called to this 'risky' involvement.

The Christian ministry of healing still has much to give to a world which is broken and in need of healing. Being professionally competent, technically the best, keeping up to date are all important and are surely a part of the Christian mandate of doing with your heart what your hand finds to do, but that is not unique. The mandate goes much further. It is this ministry of inclusion, of reconciliation, of compassion, of accompaniment, of seeking for the lost, building community in whatever we do, that is the challenge for us, whether we are in solo, group or institutional practice. In the Gospel of Luke (Luke 10: 1-23) we are told that Jesus sent out seventy two disciples in pairs before him with strict instructions, which are very enlightening for those of us who now work in the healing ministry. The workers are few said Jesus, but the harvest is plentiful. And he sent them out as 'sheep among wolves, with no purse or bag or sandals'. They were to go 'in peace'. but to 'shake the dust off their sandals' if they were not welcomed. And the disciples returned with joy because they were able to do so much and 'even the demons submit to us in your name'. And Jesus, we are told, responds in Joy, because he has seen Satan fall, but instructs them to rejoice not because of the power they have, but because their names are written in heaven'.

Today, the harvest is still plentiful, but the workers are few. Jesus calls us to go out with him to the highways and byways of life, in peace, not alone, but with others, relying on his strength and trusting that we will be looked after, finding healing and our common humanity; moving on if we are not wanted, leaving judgment to God, and continuing to build the Kingdom of God where all will one day be healed and whole.

An Expected Career and an Unexpected Vocation

Ruby Nakka

From the age of ten, I began to live in a Christian children's home. As long as I can remember, from my childhood, I wanted to be a doctor. It wasn't because I was academically superior but because, growing up, that is all I knew and also it made my parents very happy. As I grew older and began to internalize my poor academic caliber, I increasingly became fake which I refuse to acknowledge publicly. It all became evident when I wrote the entrance exam for MBBS three times in my state and didn't make it. Hence, I continued with my academics to pursue Bachelor of Science.

It was perhaps from my late teen years, I knew about CMC and Raya Vellore but I never attempted to write MBBS entrance exam here because all along until B. Sc, I studied in Telugu medium and I felt I wouldn't make it. After graduation in B. Sc, my future looked bleak as I didn't get into any higher studies so I pursued typing and shorthand. At the advice of one of my relative, I reluctantly applied to CMC to study Bachelor of Physiotherapy.

When I came for the entrance in 1986, there were 226 people competing for 10 seats in Scudder Hall. I could read the questions as I studied English as my third language but couldn't understand, so towards the end, I said a prayer and simply bubbled in all the answers at random. To my surprise, I was in, but I knew that I wouldn't clear the stage of interview because I never engaged in a meaningful English conversation till that point. In my interview room, there were four people - Dr. Suranjan Bhattacharji, Dr. David Rolston, Mr. John Samuel and Mr. Kerry Frey. I vividly remember the questions like it just happened yesterday. To speak about that day even after thirty two years, it gives me goose bumps and makes me emotional. Someone was speaking through me. My English was fluent like never before in that room. I couldn't speak as fluently, after I finished my interview. When I finished, I knew, I nailed it and I did. There began my journey in CMC – **An expected career in healthcare.** I was the recipient of CMC's full scholarship for the marginalized for all the three years of my education at CMC.

Each of these encounters, emboldened me to believe that I was the street-smart young man who knows to beat the odds rather than to acknowledge the divine intervention and get closer to God. I became proud and lived the best fake time of my life. But all of a sudden, it all unraveled and it was exposed on October 31st, 1987. I remember this day so vividly because it was my 22nd birthday. I was approached by my Pathology professor to ask if I had cheated on my class test. Without even thinking, I confessed my mistake. I was asked to meet the Head of the Department – Dr. C.J.G Chacko. I never met this man before so I was petrified of that thought but I had no other choice. When I walked in, I saw a mild-mannered gentleman in white clothes with thick spectacles. I was asked tough questions but I chose to remain quiet. My punishment was pronounced and I was asked to leave the room. To exit the room, I had to cross Dr. Chacko, and as I was leaving, I felt a hand grip on my wrist. I looked up to see Dr. Chacko holding my wrist and asking with a gentle voice "Son, can I pray for you"? With a trembling voice I said "Yes". Next, I heard the most passionate prayer anyone had ever said on my behalf till that point in my life. He chose to intercede with God to transform me and he pleaded with God to protect me. I could hear his pain to punish me for my transgression but could see his genuine love to see me become a better person. He made a live demonstration of a Bible verse James 3:20 that speaks of action that coupled with faith. After saying "Amen," I left the room quietly but filled with lot of emotions. When I reached my room in the Fitch Hostel, I broke down and I was on my knees not because I was caught but for God to have shown the genuine love and its impact. I made a decision on that day to live a new life. It was the beginning of my transformation.

My CMC bond was transferred from undivided Andhra Pradesh then to CMC and I was posted in Rehab Institute in 1990. I was living at the Mary Varghese Trust Home by paying Rs. 30/- monthly rent to Mrs. Koshy. Work at Rehab was physical and that became doubly hard during the summer months. One morning, as I was walking to work from Mary Vargheese Trust Home, I met Dr. Suranjan, who was also walking to Rehab, in front of the MHC main gate. I mentioned to him about the challenges of working in Rehab. He said something during that time of walking that I will always cherish. He reminded me of the Bible verse in Colossians 3:23 which reads "Whatever you do, work at it with all your heart, as though working for the Lord, not for human masters". I stopped complaining.

In 1992, I got a job in the US so I left CMC after two and a half years. I always knew that I will be back to India but didn't know when, where and why. Little did I know then of the life to come in the US. It was just too good to believe. I met my CMC classmate and got married a year later. I was living a typical so called 'American dream'. After eight years of our marriage, we adopted our two little girls in 2001 and 2004. Since then something began to stir in me. I could hear the knock on my heart to tell me to return to India. I resisted as much as I could as I couldn't reconcile of what I had then and what I would have in the future. But the knock gradually got louder and louder till it became a thud. I became completely disillusioned of not knowing what to do. I had everything that I wanted materially but I had very little peace. My family and I made a collective decision to relocate to India to work with the marginalized children and promote the message of adoption.

It was already 14 years when we relocated to Vellore in 2006 – that was the beginning of an unexpected vocation in the ministry of healing.

When we began the work, I couldn't forget the encounters that I had with Dr. Chacko and Dr. Suranjan. There began the foundation of our work – Don't preach but practice and practice the faith not for fame or name but the Glory of God. It was unreal that I was doing this work, so I decided to ask God why he chose a wretched person like me? I found his answer in John's Gospel 15:16 that said, "You did not choose me, but I chose you that you may bear fruit". Since then, I stopped asking God that question.

The more I began to involve myself with the children, the better I became as a human. Their vibrancy made me stronger and innocence and vulnerability made me softer. I began to see the sufferings of children. Along with physical sufferings, I had witnessed abuse, apathy, impact of parental alcoholism on children and abandonment of individuals who couldn't defend themselves. We try our best to provide a place that the children find it a refuge with unconditional love. We create an environment where they are accepted as they are and their rights are protected. Gradually, I began to witness something beautiful. Girls became stronger, confident and standing up not only for their own rights but also of others like their classmates and the Hope House sisters.

Little did I realize the impact of our actions till a young lady near Golden Temple of Vellore, was referred to us in 2012. Teachers of her school were deeply concerned of her prolonged and continuous absence from school so they sought the help of CHAD hospital's Social Worker. This young lady's mother was ill with no father figure in her life. When the Social Worker approached her, she was attending to her cattle in the nearby river bed. After several visits, this young lady agreed to study at the Hope House. She didn't like the restrictive environment to begin with, so she wanted to stay in the Hope House till she finishes 10th grade which she knew that she would fail.

When the 10th grade results were announced, to her amazement, she passed with good marks while many of her classmates back in the village failed and got married and some even started working in the construction industry. At that same time, our first batch of 12th graders got admission to College of Nursing in CMC. Her own results and the admission of her sisters to CMC began to stir bigger dreams in her. While studying 11th and 12th grade, she struggled with the decision whether to accept Christian faith. Our advice had always been to do what is acceptable to Christ.

She finished 12th grade in March of 2016 and went to her village for the Summer holidays. On April 5th, 2016, at about 5:00 PM, I received five missed calls from an unknown number. I returned the call to find this young lady answering and asking for my advice to help an incoherent elderly woman who seemed to have wandered off and reached her village. Living about 20 KM away, all that I could do was to provide phone advice which didn't seemed to have worked. During this entire duration, against the rebuke of her entire community and her own mother, she wouldn't let the elderly woman go anywhere but stay with her. As the dusk turned in to darkness, I was frantically working the phones to help her. At last, we found that she was a patient of Adukkamparai Government Medical College Hospital with mental illness and was wandering since 5:00 AM. Family came to the village and she was reunited.

She told me the next day why she did what she did. She said to the effect that she was cared and nurtured for, when she herself needed help and she knew what it meant to be vulnerable and be loved unconditionally. Soon after this experience, this young lady was convinced and her decision was made. On her own free will, she decided that she wanted to be a Christian. She was baptized. Today, she is one of the strongest witnesses for Christ in the final year of College of Nursing in CMC and dreams of working in a hospital in Bihar.

Career is something that we all make a choice to be in, but vocation is something that you're called to be in or called to be at. Looking back, growing up in a children's home, my admission to CMC along with the transformative experiences, adoption of my little girls and my stint in the US etc. and then being called to be in this field, I am humbled to know that God had planned everything meticulously for me to be in a vocation today than in a profession.

September of last year, Dr. P. Zachariah preached at the college chapel and I had the privilege to have read the script of his message. In that message he shared a beautiful story of a woman who chose a vocation above her career. Here it is in Dr. P. Zach's own words:

"But following a vocation in response to a vision has its costs. It calls for varying degrees of **self-denial**. This is my third foundational value of CMC. Let me illustrate it with the story of my predecessor in Physiology, Dr. Dorothy M. Jefferson. As a school teacher in Canada, she happened to hear the Vellore story and was moved by it. Eager to join this endeavour, she took up Medicine. But on graduation, she could not find a missionary body to sponsor her to Vellore. Undeterred, she came on her own. But when she arrived in Vellore, she was directed to the Physiology Department. Giving up her dreams of clinical work, she started teaching Physiology and devoted the rest of her time here to that vocation. She lived in the women's hostel where she was the hostel doctor. When she retired, there was no supporting body to look after her in retirement. She only received the meager benefits provided by CMC in those days, and that too only after eight years. She decided to take her household things from here and start a new working life in Canada. My last memory of her in Vellore was her boarding the train in Katpadi, with her old refrigerator secured with a rope. She made a living for herself in Canada teaching in a school of nursing, till she eventually succumbed to cancer."

In these last 13 years of our work among children, I have scores of stories to share about my vocation in the ministry of healing. In this work, I see little children who need healing mentally, socially, emotionally, and spiritually. As we march forward in this ministry, our daily reminder is this: "Be a reluctant preacher but be a willing practitioner of our faith" as it was taught to me by Dr. Chacko and Dr. Suranjan, more than 30 years ago. I was fortunate to have been a part of this Kingdom of God called CMC and I want to believe that the vocation that I am being placed in today is an expansion of his kingdom. Fruit of the labour that is stated in John 15:16 is what this young lady is yearning to go to Bihar to expand the Kingdom of God farther to the ends of the world. Thank you and God bless.

Vocation:
An Allied Health Scientist's Perspective

Hima

"And the light shineth in darkness;
and the darkness comprehended it not."

(John 1:5)

God chooses individuals, leads them through strange coincidences to Christian Medical College, then strategically places them to fulfil his purposes. Finding our vocation is a process compounded by difficulties faced at work. God seems to allow difficulties in our way, once the initial seeds of scripture have started taking root in our hearts. We tend to perceive this as unkind, but often it is at this point that we grow closer to God and the purposes he intended for us to fulfil. He equips us with the strength, knowledge and resources needed for the task to be accomplished. For our work to be in accordance with God's will, we need to develop a close relationship to God, by prayerfully dwelling on his word. This article explores the allied health perspective to healing ministry as a vocation. This article explores the allied health perspective to healing ministry as a vocation

Unbelievable!

"I was trying to catch the crippled man; did he run past this way?

He was rushing home to tell everyone, what Jesus did today.

And the mute man was telling me and the deaf girl, he's leaving to answer God's call.

It's hard to believe but if you don't trust me, go ask the blind man, he saw it all."

He saw it all, The Booth Brothers.

In a little town in south India, tucked between barren hills and a dry river, it is rumoured that miracles happen. People flock from all over world seeking healing, education, employment and research collaborations. Most witness surprises, some witness compassion, all witness miracles- events not explicable by natural or scientific laws. We who work at Christian Medical College, Vellore, use phrases such as "I never thought this would be possible," and "That was so amazing," on a daily basis. Yet we are moved not only by unexpected healing or success but also tears, pain, hardened hearts, loss and grief causing despair and bringing us to our knees. We witness miracles indeed.

You're still here!

For years I vowed to leave Christian Medical College, because of the 16:30 phenomenon.

As the hands of the clock pass 16:30, there is a hustle of activity in the buildings of Christian Medical College, Vellore. Employees bee line hurriedly towards the exit gate. They look catatonic, spent and preoccupied - devoid of signs of contentment or happiness. They get into autos 5 by 5, which ferry them away from the place they come back to everyday. It seems so futile and vain.

These are not individuals who save lives or cure diseases. They repeated several tasks innumerable times in the past 8 hours: Finding veins, drawing blood, labelling tubes; repeating the same instructions to patients; filing documents alphabetically or numerically, typing meaningless numbers into keyboards; trouble shooting various equipments, positioning patients for x rays; teaching exercises to people in pain; holding hands until tears stopped flowing; reassuring patients before procedures and many other tasks. Most of them go home to work their next job- the tasks vary in each life stage: cleaning the house, preparing food, meeting the needs of elderly, feeding children, teaching them etc. Few of them afford the luxury of household help. Holidays are encashed voluntarily for school fees or a new TV. Their life is work and work is their life. What would they say if you asked them if they thought their work was a profession or vocation?

I asked a few senior staff working in small positions in various departments, why they had stayed back at CMC. The reasons given were financial security, medical insurance, familiarity with the surroundings, educational support for children and having felt valued and supported. Culturally we are not tuned to thinking about higher purposes unless prompted to do so, but I know that each of them make a tremendous difference in the lives of the people they interact with. Strikingly, all of them started with their unique story on how they came to CMC. They came from various socio economic backgrounds, geographic locations, languages and cultures and chose to embrace a new language, a new cuisine, a new culture and a new way of living.

The unexpected ways in which they came to CMC, are too varied to be coincidental.

A patient became a caregiver.

One person came because their connecting train at Katpadi was 3 hours late.

A distant relative recommended CMC when all other options were exhausted and everything worked out fine.

Some thought they left for good and then found their way back.

Many stayed because they had to, as a bond obligation, and then didn't leave.

Others came for a year of experience and spent their life time here.

Some people joined CMC as a smart career choice, a stepping stone to higher education, and from a good reputation; then decided to stay.

Many of them hated hospitals and never thought they would work in one.

"I never thought I would stay on for so long", was a common exclamation.

Most students who join CMC testify feeling unworthy to have joined this prestigious institution, many have unique stories as well. Christian Medical College is a river, one that started way up the zenith of human faith, and has in the past 100 years crossed jagged peaks of opposition, mounts of discontent, rocks of rebellion and is yet flowing – as calm waters, ripples and waterfalls, making its way into a unknown future into a known great ocean. Some waters branch out to provide for the growth of the land in other geographic locations, little streams join into the main river to increase its volume. It then houses a variety of sea creatures, from dolphins to salmons and guppies.

How was your day?
"God does not give us everything we want, but He does fulfil His promises, leading us along the best and straightest path to Himself." – Dietrich Bonhoeffer.

CMC is not an easy place to work in for an Allied Health professional. In the hierarchy of medical professionalism, non medical staff will always be on the lower rungs. The work load and expectations are higher than in most other institutions. Like clinicians we juggle clinical work, student education and research, but have less flexible schedules. Intelligence and creativity are considered hindrances to work than assets, since those in charge seem to resent questioning by employees or suggestions for change. There is a constant struggle for rights to make independent decisions, space and recognition. Departments like mine that encourage professional independence are not the norm.

Many employees are embittered about a lack of opportunities to career enhancement, perceived injustice, pending promotions, disregard for seniority and preferential treatment among employees. Employees expressed discontent about administrators seeming unaware and unconcerned of the injustice at root levels. I am sure these problems are universal, and not unique to our institution.

Incentives to move to greener pastures are many. When contemporaries post happy pictures of themselves with the Eiffel tower, Statue of Liberty and holidays in the Maldives, it is easy to be discontent with the life you are leading. When opportunities beckon it is difficult to resist, rather, difficult to define reasons to not accept them. Some therapists who recently left the institution gave reasons such as huge financial benefits, a better life style, more opportunities for career advancement and education, peer pressure, and finally- feeling left behind, while classmates and colleagues had moved up the ladder. Choosing to stay in CMC requires you to define your calling and priorities; sometimes setting aside your personal dreams and ambitions.

What doesn't break me makes me- Are you sure?

"You become. It takes a long time. That's why it doesn't happen often to people who break easily, or have sharp edges, or who have to be carefully kept. Generally, by the time you are Real, most of your hair has been loved off, and your eyes drop out and you get loose in the joints and very shabby." ⊠ Margery Williams Bianco, The Velveteen Rabbit.

Students who join a health care profession need to develop a framework of caring within which they choose to operate. As they engage with patients and are confronted with moral and ethical dilemmas, they undergo a transformation in their sense of identity (1). On our first day as students, we were divided into groups of three, and were asked to perform 3 tasks with the help of others: Wear blindfolds, propel a wheelchair and use above knee callipers to walk a big route around the hospital. It was funny and embarrassing; intended to make us sensitive to difficulties of people with special needs, which is so vital in our profession. Later we made kheerabondas with wonderful older women in the Hansen's disease ward at CHAD.

We sat outside little huts enjoying the hospitality of the poor- eating hot dosa and chutney- during our Community postings. We learnt art and drawing from our beloved art instructor who taught us from his wheelchair. We learned empathy. We learned that many problems don't have solutions. We felt helpless against the magnitude of injustice and impact of disease. We also learned how privileged we were: we had never known hunger, or pain or need. We were supported by seniors and foster families through heart breaks and academic failures. Moreover we were enveloped in prayer, beginning at the start of everyday. The retreats helped us develop a closer relationship with God and with each other. For some of us, it was the first time that the Bible was taught to us in a deeper sense of meaning and understanding. Through it all, we became individuals who apart from sound academic knowledge and clinical skills, learned to give our best to those in need, without regard for class, creed or culture. But this was not the end.

Witnessing pain and suffering on a daily basis can have 2 outcomes: It either softens us or hardens us. It is said that "The same sun that melts wax hardens clay. The same sun melts the ice and dries out the moisture from the earth." Troubles can take us closer to God or far away from him (2). When God's word grows roots in your heart, you become mouldable. He prepares our hearts, so that we reach out to him in trouble and subject our will to his. It is never an easy choice and governed by willingness to look up to him in prayer. The Bible reassures us saying "He which hath begun a good work in you will perform it until the day of Jesus Christ." Philippians 1:6.

But oh! Why is there so much pain?

"How strangely sad is it, that we put the burden of our cumulative wishes on dying stars, how they carry the weight of it all so effortlessly." – To wish upon a star, Shlagha Borah.

Patients do not always discover healing- Some discover lasting suffering.

A parent said that having a child with Cerebral Palsy is worse than having cancer- while there is a visible outcome either good or bad in cancer, there is no visible end to disability, and the outcome is never healing.

An elderly couple sold all they had to afford an in vitro fertilisation treatment, now have a child who will need to be supported throughout life, with no means to support her.

An affluent couple lost one infant after the other- being a parent was the only thing they could not buy.

A child underwent surgery after surgery, each one promising a cure, but it never came.

Breaking bad news has always been my least favourite task. It do not dread the talk, but the emotional outbursts that follow. How do I answer all the questions that are asked?

Apart from the suffering of others, God uses personal suffering too.

Why else would God place people who lost significant loved ones, in departments that deal with people dying everyday? Or why would he place a person with failed infertility treatments in a place where babies are born? Why is a person struggling with his mental illness expected to help people suffering from similar difficulties? God seems to prefer narrow long winding paths to broad straight paths in his quest of shaping us for his purposes.

The age old question of "Why so much pain?" needs to be dealt with by each individual and has no consistent answer. In the face of intense suffering it is easy to doubt God's goodness. It forces you to make an ultimate decision. Does this good God so freely talked about really exist and do I believe in him. If he does, then my suffering and that of others has a meaning; if he doesn't all that I do is in vain. If I submit to him, I allow him complete control over my life, hold nothing back and trust him to use me mightily for his glory. This would mean that I let go of my self-conceived goals and dreams. If I decide not to submit to him, I may achieve all that I want to, and gain material benefits, but will walk life alone and will never find contentment. God seems to put a question back to us: "Are you willing to suffer for me?"

"Take my yoke upon you, and learn of me; for I am meek and lowly in heart: and ye shall find rest unto your souls. For my yoke is easy, and my burden is light." Luke10:29-30

ME serve others in spite of MY pain?

Do hardships make you a good health care professional, or do you become one in spite of them? An article that looked at the economics of vocation in the nursing profession, explains how increasing nurses' wages might reduce the quality of applicants, since the 'wrong sort' of people might be attracted into the profession. They conclude that in some professions, the attitude of that of a vocation comes from factors other than monetary gains (3).

I think of CMC as God's workshop- he has placed his tools carefully- each place chosen for maximum efficiency. There is so much work to be done! He gives special care to his raw materials. They are patients and students. He has a plan for each one of them. He uses his hands and his tools. Some projects take longer to complete; some material being pliable and easily moulded, while others are hardened and tough.

Tools are made with more thought and take longer. They come in intricate and fragile, plain and strong, or sharp and edgy forms- each one right for their special purposes. They need to be cut as diamonds, molten and poured into forms like iron, or welded under high temperatures as gold or silver. Occasionally they need sharpening.

My story is similar to that of many others. After a painful life experience few years back, I did all I could to leave CMC. I imagine God smiling to himself as he watched me impatiently knocking on doors which he had locked. He waited, as I banged, pushed, wedged and thrust myself on them- The doors wouldn't budge. He waited till the floor forced me to look up and submit to him- spent, tired and hopeless. Then he opened the Pandora box of dreams he had for me, and oh they were good! They included dreams long forgotten and wonderful. He also made me understand that I could do what I thought was impossible- to live with my thorn in the flesh. When painful experiences melt and shape you, you become better at comforting others. They are not big changes, but small ones.

Little words. Little smiles. Little actions.

It is as if your burdens ease others' pain, your scars help expose others brokenness, and your sadness soothes others' sorrow.

"He comforteth us in all our tribulation, that we may be able to comfort them which are in any trouble, by the comfort wherewith we ourselves are comforted of God." 2 Corinthians 1:4.

Yay, It's a Monday!
"All honest work is worthy of doing for the glory of God."- J I Packer

When sin entered the world, man's work changed from something that was good to something borne in pain. But by God's repelling sin on the cross, we have the freedom to make work good again. He allows us to choose the area we work in, as long as the work is honourable. There is no work more honourable than that of serving people in need and pain, we are privileged to do so. God uses us in ways that we cannot understand to fulfil his purposes.

God uses our strengths- our professional accomplishments and degrees- to lift us up amongst others. But he prefers using our weaknesses, so his glory is revealed. God puts me in situations that I am not qualified or trained to handle. The more afraid I am, the closer I cling to him because I know that I am safe and that he meets my needs.

At one time I was given a task in a research project, which was unrelated to my profession and seemingly of little use to patients. I was disheartened and wondered if I was wasting time, when I could be helping patients with real needs. God responded by showing me everyday of a week, how my work that seemed useless to me, was useful to him. He showed me how the normal infants I assessed, had parents in desperate need of encouragement, were at breaking points in their marriage, verged on making life decisions, or needed a listening ear. This made me trust God completely with my work schedule. When he takes control, my schedule is smooth. He so loves, that on days when I struggle with health issues, he interjects a break; on days when I'm distressed, he sends unexpected encouragement; on days when I am weary, He sends help.

In the process of God working through you, by being a source of healing, you are healed. You are healed in ways that you didn't realise you hurt. God's healing is not merely physical: it is social, emotional, spiritual. It is being filled in a way that you will never thirst again. It is being made whole.

You realise suddenly, you stopped living superficially. There is meaning in the little things you do- the conversations you have, the reports you write, the signatures you place, the smiles you spread. You stop being competitive or worrying about appearances. You have nothing to lose and only to gain- not because you will receive material or career benefits- but because life is full of the things you always wanted to do.

Give me another one, Lord.

"I press toward the mark for the prize of the high calling of God in Christ Jesus." Philippians 3:14

The river of CMC will keep flowing. It will harbour many species of animals. Some may go extinct- that is the course of nature and change is essential. But the substance that keeps the soil from eroding, and which nurtures the fishes and keeps the river from overflowing or turning poisonous- in spite of oil spills and drains- is prayer. The faithful and unchanging God, who heeds requests and doesn't cease knocking on hurting hearts, will lead us into a new future.

We do several tasks innumerable times for 8 hours every day. She gently finds the vein of the old man who looks anxious, holds his hand while drawing blood. He jokes about his own fears with the child, while labelling the tube. He gives the same instructions to patients, adding a joke here and there, hoping they understand broken language. She files documents alphabetically or numerically, and remembers everyone's birthday in her department. She makes murukku and adharasm for the doctors for Deepavali, knowing many of them could not spend it with their families. She types meaningless numbers into her keyboard, but notices her colleague crying. That conversation builds a friendship, which makes work easier and pleasant. He positions patients for X rays and always makes it a point to explain what was being done in a simple language. She does not stop with teaching exercises to people in pain, she asks about their family, what makes them happy and what worries them. It hurts him to hold hands until tears stopped flowing, so he prays while he listens. After explaining the diet changes made that day, she ends each bed side conversation saying, "We are only tools- healing is in God's hands."

We share pain. We save lives. We cure disease.

I thank all the innocent staff who shared their stories with me in the corridors, on the stairways or popped into my room, oblivious to the fact that their stories are written about. To the reader: All the examples are of real individuals, not fabricated. Names have been kept anonymous so that people can fearlessly continue to share their stories with me.

References

Clouder, L., 2005.Caring as a 'threshold concept': transforming students in higher education into health (care) professionals. Teaching in higher education, 10(4), 505-517.

Edward M. Bounds, Kris Valloton, *The essentials of Prayer,* Lulu.com, 2007, ISBN: 1424508002, 9781424508006

Heyes, A., 2005. The economics of vocation or 'why is a badly paid nurse a good nurse'?. Journal of health economics, 24(3), 561-569.

All Bible references are taken from the King James Version.

PART-3
Healing Ministry and Counselling

Possibilities of
Pastoral Care and Counselling

B.J. Prashantham

The beginning

Around the 148th birthday of the legendary founder of CMC Hospital, we are having this colloquium to celebrate the Centenary of this world famous Christian Medical College. The founder Ida Scudder was the Principal, Director and also the Chaplain of this place indicating that Pastoral Care and Counselling was an integral part of her work from the inception. While she focused on Bio spiritual aspects, her friend and Colleague Ms. Hancock focused on psycho- social aspects. Together they focused on Bio-psycho-social - spiritual aspects for a wholistic approach. Over the century there have been amazing number of worthy successors as Directors, Principals and Chaplaincy heads leading dedicated teams to achieve the objectives of the Christian medical college focusing on excellence in scientific medicine at affordable costs with special concern for the needy and in the spirit of Christ's Compassion. Scudder saw her mission as work in the kingdom of God not merely physical healing. Hence she put The Chapel in the centre of the hospital and College, powerfully giving asymbolic message more than words can convey. That Ida Scudder way back in the mid 1930s received the Kaiser-I- Hind award from the Viceroy of India at that time. It is equivalent to Bharat Ratna award today. This indicates the level of recognition she had for developing the CMC to which generations of patients from all over India and abroad have come and have been served to their deep satisfaction and hence earning their trust by more than seven generations of Doctors and other health professionals nearly 10000 of them now with 8500 out patients daily. That will be a major factor in the sustainability of this organisation. The first one bed dispensary in 1900 AD is now part of the Christian Counselling Centre. Therefore let me on behalf of CCC, a small sister organization which is proud to be associated with CMC in different ways for the past 48 years, bring warm congratulations for your support and yeomen service to humanity by possibly treating more than 500 million patients keeping in mind that the population of India at Independence was about 400 million people! May God bless you to reach new heights in the decades to come in meeting the health needs of our country not only by direct service but along with that, through training of doctors and other health professionals for mission hospitals. In order to do so in the future with zeal and fervour, it is critical to consider the possibilities in the context of the Pastoral Care and Counselling needs of several stakeholders namely, patients, attendants of patients- relatives or friends, students and spouses,staff and senior administrators as also well wishers and supporters of this great institution. This is a very big challenge.

Wonderful counsellor

I conclude with what I think is possible meaning of the term, 'wonderful Counsellor' given to Jesus, the good shepherd. Isaiah 9:6 (NIV) "For to us a child is born, to us a son is given, and the government will be on his shoulders. And he will be called Wonderful Counsellor, Mighty God, Everlasting Father, and Prince of Peace"

> They are the wonderful counsellor:
> A. Accepts people unconditionally
> B. Listens to people attentively
> C. Appreciates people genuinely
> D. Challenges people caringly and honestly.

If these competencies increase in all who work in Christian Hospitals all over India and become not only professional competencies, but also elements of one's life style then we can move into the next century with confidence and blessings of the wonderful counsellor. I will remain a prayer partner for CMC as I have been for more than 48 years as well as for the mission hospitals around the country. These are relevant for any institution for that matter.

Human's openness to the future

German Theologian Pannenberg said that one characteristic of God's highest creation namely the human being is continuous 'openness to the future'. This insatiable thirst leads humans to keep on expanding their horizons of reach and search to be good stewards of this planet. Scientific endeavors theologically are a fulfilment of the creation mandate to the humans by God which Christians need to continue to take seriously to be relevant. As the Orthodox theologian the late Metropolitan Mar Gregorious once said, "When we find how things work, that is science, when we experiment with how to work things, that is technology, when we use the findings for the good of God's creation, we use technology with the value of love". We know the difference in the effects of nuclear bombs and nuclear medicine, one for destruction and one for healing. Having been chairman of the Institutional review board (IRB) blue of CMC, I am amazed at the great quality of research and the commitment to adhere to robust scientific methodology as also high standards of ethics respecting the human rights of the subjects of research. This needs to continue to be nurtured and strengthened. Chaplains along with others scientists are involved in this committee. Since we do not know every things, research and openness to learning as a ministry is very important. It is the experience of Scientists and Pastors and Theologians that we do not know everything. Only God does. Hence we do our work with the humility that we do not know everything and answer to every question even as the following passage affirms:

> "1 Corinthians 13:8-12 "Love never fails. But where there are prophecies, they will cease; where there are tongues, they will be stilled; where there is knowledge, it will pass away. [9] **For we know in part** and we prophesy in part, [10] but when completeness comes, what is in part disappears. [11] When I was a child, I talked like a child; I thought like a child, I reasoned like a child.

When I became a man, I put the ways of childhood behind me. [12] *For now we see only a reflection as in a mirror; then we shall see face to face. Now I know in part; then I shall know fully, even as I am fully known."*

We can still commend people and their needs to the hands of a Loving God in the midst of mysteries and lack of full understanding and continue to research to find out more on an ongoing basis.

Students counselling needs

With so many students in more than thirty courses, apart from selecting them there is training , caring for them as Shepherds becomes a huge responsibility specially at critical times of homesickness, loneliness, times of anxiety. With deep understanding of their needs to care and to empower care through existing channels of foster parents and faculty support is continuously needed in these days of stress and challenge. Caring for the one out of hundred sheep as Christ taught would be critical. As we move into a digital era, the opportunities and challenges also multiply dramatically. In many colleges, addiction to internet, mobile phone, managing stress, time, priorities and to be prepared for the different world of mission hospitals with far less facilities can be a drastic transition. Orientation at the beginning, care in between and focus of preparing for the re-entry is a great responsibility and possibility. Taking success and failure gracefully, leaning life skills of communication, courtesy, managing conflicts, stress, spiritual growth etc. become again important. I know that a lot of good work goes on here. So there is need to be happy and pat ourselves and also look deeply into some of these needs and their implications which afford opportunity for growth.

Care and support to staff and families

Already many things are done through chaplains and developing HR initiatives by way of retreats, seminars, inputs, quality discussions. There can never be less need for more soft skills, and caring attitudes. This way the entire Hospital team will continue to be hospitable which is a characteristic of a Christian (Hebrews 13:2 and Luke 9-11). Among all groups the PG's who are married with small children seem to be in considerable stress. Continued encouragement and support from within and outside becomes vital to sustain. Many people in any society go to work as a job. Others go to work as a profession. For a place like Christian Hospitals you also continue to need those who see their work as a calling. This is where Pastoral Care and Counselling can motivate people to move from a perspective of Job to profession to a calling. That will ensure sustainability of the institutions into the new century. While it is true that even the disciples of Jesus were showing excessive spirit of competition making them wonder who is greater in the kingdom of God, Jesus confronted them about their preoccupation. For Jesus in the gospels, mere utterances of pious prayers or words was not equal to real spirituality. As one speaker at the teaching mission of CMC in the 70s said "stop being religious and start being open to the living God" is something for all hospitals staff and for that matter all Christian professionals to reflect upon. The historical roles of Pastoral Care and Counselling over the last 2000 years have been healing, sustaining, guiding, reconciling, nurturing and liberating combining the priestly, pastoral and prophetic dimensions of ministry.

Patients and relatives

When it comes to patient care I must say that the success of CMC is due to their amazing patient care specially the doctors even though they are hard to meet due to patient load and nurses, others and chaplains. My own students learn from the opportunities through chaplaincy at CMC. Relatives when cared for become more supportive of the patient whether they improve after struggle and anxiety, or struggle with conditions requiring various degrees of rehabilitation and become stronger and resilient, or face terminal illnesses leading to earlier death than normally expected with grace and go through a palliative phase. In these conditions of crisis, adjustment, loneliness, depression, optimism based on rationality as well as faith, resilience from perseverance, becoming wounded healers themselves, counselling plays a big role. The more this aspect continues to be increasingly used the better care that will be given in a holistic bio-psycho-social-spiritual ways and using relevant resources such as empathic presence, listening, responding, scriptures, prayers and social support along with professional care and self-regulation. These experiences can be continued in all Christian Hospitals and Christian Health practitioners in their ministries of Healing. The trainings available with Theological Colleges and other Chaplaincy departments and Counseling Centers can be used to strengthen personnel and their com

i. Hebrews 13:2 (NIV) "Do not forget to show hospitality to strangers, for by so doing some people have shown hospitality to angels without knowing it."

ii. Luke 9:11(NIV) but the crowds learned about it and followed him. He welcomed them and spoke to them about the kingdom of God, and healed those who needed healing.

Glad to note that several departments are additionally employing counsellors, some of whom are trained at The Christian Counseling centre.

References

Thomas, M. M. "Salvation and Humanization: A Crucial Issue in the Theology of Mission for India" in *International Review of mission; world Council of Churches*, Volume 60, Issue 237; January 1971 (Pages: 3-152).

Newbigin, Lesslie. *The Open Secret: An Introduction to the Theology of Mission* by Eerdmans: Later Printing Used edition (October 30, 1989).

Bonhoeffer, Dietrich, Simon and Schuster. *The Cost of Discipleship*. India, 3rd Edition, 1995.

Pannenberg, Wolfhart. *Human Nature, Election, and History*. 1977.

Chardin, Pierre Teilhard de. *The Divine Milieu*. November 6th, 2001 by Harper Perennial Modern Classics.

Nouwen, Henri J. M. *The Wounded Healer: Ministry in Contemporary Society*. Image Books; 1st edition (March 1979).

Henderson, Charles P. "Toward a Science Charged with Faith" Chapter 5 of *God and Science*.

Prashantham, B.J. *Indian case studies in therapeutic counselling*. 6th edition. Vellore: Christian Counselling Centre, 2006.

Not Cured But Healed

Stanley C. Macaden

A proper Christian understanding and practice of healing and health is essential for Christian health professionals and Christian patients alike. This is even more critical in situations of incurable illnesses with extreme suffering, leading on to death. It is therefore necessary for us to have some basic guidelines as explained in the Bible on the following matters.

Biblical insights

1. God is sovereign. He is in control of our lives and our world and universe. There are many verses in the Bible which proclaim God's sovereignty. Timothy 6:15: "God will bring this about in His own time. He is the blessed and only Sovereign, the King of kings, and the Lord of lords." Colossians 1:17: "He is before all things, and in him all things hold together." 1 Chronicles 29:11-12: "Yours, LORD, is the greatness and the power and the glory and the majesty and the splendor, for everything in heaven and earth is yours. Yours, LORD, is the kingdom; you are exalted as head over all. Wealth and honor come from you; you are the ruler of all things. In your hands are strength and power to exalt and give strength to all."

2. Salvation, healing, wholeness, deliverance, preservation, restoration, are all from a common Greek root word, *Soteria*.

3. Jehovah Rapha - The Lord Heals: (Exodus 15:22-26, Psalm 103:1-4, Isaiah 53:4-5, Deuteronomy 32:39, Psalm 147:3, Matthew 8:16-17). Salvation, healing and wholeness is God's mission. This includes physical healing of the body, mind and heart and spiritual healing of our soul and spirit.

4. Sin may be a cause for disease when we bring it on ourselves due to bad habits or wrong doing. However, God doesn't punish us with disease or disability because of our sin or the sin of our parents. He may use our disability for his works to be manifested. (John 9: 1-3)

5. Faith in Jesus does not mean freedom from suffering. In fact, Jesus says that in this world we will have tribulation. But he offers us peace and asks us to be of good cheer as he has overcome the world. (John 16:33). He promises that he will be with us in our suffering and that he will never leave us or forsake us.(Hebrews 13:5)

6. God always answers prayer. However, it may not be how and when we want it. His answer may be a yes or no or wait or here is something better. A cure may or may not happen, but what he promises is healing of our soul.

7. Fear of death and dying is universal and associated with much distress. This can be helped by building a relationship of trust by a caring team and explaining all queries and clarifying doubts. Encouragement from God's Word can do wonders in allaying fears. Perfect love casts out fear. (1 John 4:18). Helping them to experience the touch of Jesus can be transforming. Jesus is the victorious God who has conquered death and only he can abolish such fears.

8. Anxiety due to various concerns could be helped by facilitating the family to do something about the specific concern so that the person is reassured and has peace. Jesus tells us to cast all our care upon him for he cares for us (1 Peter 5:7). We must trust and obey.

9. No suffering is meaningless or without purpose. God allows suffering to refine us and use us to help others who are suffering. He allowed

his one and only Son to go through maximum total suffering to fulfill his plan of atonement for the sins of the world and our redemption.

10. Even when there is no physical cure, God's healing will enable the sufferer to transmute the suffering into glory. Many beautiful hymns were penned by people going through tremendous suffering. (Fanny Crosby, Horatio Spafford). Also, great Christian work have been accomplished in India and all over the world by many Missionaries who endured much hardship for the sake of the Gospel. All the early disciples, (except Judas and John) and the early Christians were persecuted and martyred for the sake of Christ's 'Good News' of healing and wholeness.

11. An important reason for spiritual distress is the need to be forgiven or to forgive. This is a great burden all of us carry through our lives. It robs us of peace and certain relief. Jesus encourages us to come to him with our burdens and he promises us rest. (Matthew 11.28)

12. For times of distress God has already provided us the comforter, the Holy Spirit. Physical comfort is what health care can provide by good relief of symptoms and excellent nursing and all other supportive care. However, 'anguish, the angina of the soul', needs the comfort from the Holy Spirit.

13. Dying with dignity is a term often used. Our dignity is inherent, and it is because God created us in his image. So, irrespective of a person's social standing or disfigurement due to disease, we must take care to respect their God given dignity. (Genesis 1:27)

14. Caring for people, especially those facing death, with love, compassion and competence must be the hallmark of every health care service. We are encouraged to be moved by God's love and compassion of Christ to care for the suffering. Jesus summarized the Law and the Prophets into two commandments of loving God with our total being and loving our neighbour as our self. (Matthew 22:36-40). St Paul also challenged our great works by calling us a 'sounding brass' if it is not motivated by God's love. (1 Corinthians 13)

15. Another governing principle is 'Sanctity of Life'. We cannot create life, and neither can we take life. So, Euthanasia or Physician Assisted Suicide is not an option for Christians. It is also illegal in our country as of now. A request for Euthanasia is often a cry for help which can be adequately met by compassionate and competent Palliative Care.

16. When death is inevitable, what we all want to see and hope for is a peaceful end. Jesus promises us his peace which the world cannot give. (John 14:27)

17. Total submission and surrender to God's will helps us to come to terms and acceptance of our situation. It replaces our struggle and distress with God's peace and strength to cope.

18. Man lives on hope. But can we die with hope? As a Christian we can die with hope as Jesus came that we may have life, life in all its fullness and abundance and eternal life with God. (John 10:10 and John 3:16). Jeremiah 29:11- "For I know the plans I have for you," declares the LORD, "plans to prosper you and not to harm you, plans to give you hope and a future. "There is surely a Future Hope for us and our Hope will not be cut off. (Proverbs 23:18)

The best and total solution to all the agonizing issues mentioned above is total trust in God and in obedience total submission to God's will. In Psalm 31 King David takes us through a whole list of distressing issues but finds his strength and hope by completely trusting in God and submitting to him. In Psalm 23, he ends with a tremendous attitude of peace in dwelling in the house of the Lord forever. In the garden of Gethsemane our Lord facing death cried out in deep anguish, asking the Father twice, to take away the cup of suffering, but always ended in obedience by saying "Thy will be done" (Matthew 26:36–46).

My personal journey and experience

I am sharing this to show how God has molded me, guided me and blessed me through various Christian health institutions, committed

Christian people, and my dear family including my Church family. I am grateful to God for all that has happened in my 72 years of life! Born into a Christian home to God fearing and honouring parents and growing, with two other siblings, guided by Christian values. At age 14, following confirmation classes and understanding the Creed, I made a profession of my faith of knowing Jesus as my personal Saviour, before the local congregation. Completed my schooling in Hindi medium and joined CMC for Medicine, in the most famous batch ever, of 1963! Acquired my degrees and my wife, my classmate Ragini before leaving Vellore. We worked in Jalna Mission Hospital under the guidance of my father Dr. Cecil (Susheel as known by the community). It was a great time of learning the practice of good medicine in a Christian environment and this built our confidence in handling all kinds of medical problems. It was also an opportunity to see fully committed Christian doctors at work and see the transformation in a small Christian community facilitated by a Godly mother. We as a family went through a period of severe distress due to Cancer killing our dear mother at a young age of 47. However, God in his mercy also provided our first born at that time, our son Santosh who was a great source of comfort and joy for my father and for all of us. After completion of our service obligation at Mission Hospital Jalna we returned to Calicut with my father. Ragini got a place for MD Microbiology with Dr. Jayram Panikkar and I had to go to UK as I didn't get a place for MD Medicine at CMC Vellore. This was a great disappointment for me at that time but looking back it has turned out to be a great blessing. The five years in UK granted me an opportunity to visit and spend time with the many missionaries who had lived and worked in Jalna. It gave me my MRCP and also enabled a small pension which I enjoy today. We returned to India and Bangalore in 1978, Ragini joined St John's Medical College and I joined Bangalore Baptist Hospital. Baptist Hospital enabled me to venture out and provide varied services such as Coronary care, Intensive Care, Endoscopy and Ultrasound. Baptist Hospital and the Koramangala Methodist Church have helped me in my Christian growth and maturity. For personal financial needs I resigned from BBH to do a three-year stint in Hail,

Saudi Arabia and this enabled me to build my home in Koramangala. I rejoined BBH in 1985 and worked there till my retirement in December 2008. In 1990 I was given the privilege to lead Baptist Hospital after a tripartite arrangement with CMC Vellore, The International Mission Board of the Southern Baptist Convention, USA and BBH. This was considered as a 'God ordained' arrangement which has continued till this day. BBH became a Unit of CMC Vellore and I served as Director till 2000. This major shift for me from clinical medicine to Hospital Administration was facilitated by the one-year Certificate course in Hospital administration at CMC Vellore before taking on this leadership responsibility. By God's guidance during my watch I embarked on Internalisation by staff, of the Vision and Mission of BBH, Christ centredness, team building and human resource development at all levels. I was able to facilitate all training programmes such as, Allied Health training programmes through CMAI, Doctors training through DNB programmes, Nursing School through CMAI and Chaplaincy training through CMAI and affiliated to Serampore University. The emphasis on wholistic care took concrete shape through initiation of a fully integrated Palliative care service in 1995. This was indeed a paradigm shift for me, for the better, making a huge difference in me. God has blessed this initiative and has enabled BBH to be a beacon of hope for people with life limiting illness. BBH by God's grace has withstood all the competition from many corporate hospitals springing up over the past 25 years. It is also rewarding to see more able leaderships down the line as a result of God's blessings on BBH and maintaining our prime ethos of Christ Centeredness.

A hospitable God

It is important for us to reflect on our health care service in the light of God's word. We must, to begin with, have the special experience of knowing Jesus as our personal Saviour. We will not be of much use to him if we do not have the indwelling Holy Spirit as a result of knowing the Saviour. Then we will realise that we are not just in a profession, but that we are called by God to serve him and his people.

Jesus is our role model and the Holy Spirit will enable us to emulate this great Physician. Everything depends on our attitude and Jesus has spelt out every aspect of our behaviour in his 'Sermon on the Mount'. The 'Beatitudes' in the beginning of the sermon on the mount are the crystallization of the whole Sermon. We are in a blessed state when we realize our need for God and to be in his Kingdom. We therefore mourn because of our destitute situation and the state of a lost and corrupt world. We become meek as our master healer. We then diligently seek God and his righteousness. We are then able to be merciful. Our state of blessedness continues in our striving to be pure in heart. Striving to serve God without being adulterated by World views and its values. We therefore work to be peace makers than being peace lovers and compromise to world views. Finally, our state of blessedness is in our standing up for Kingdom values whatever the price to pay for.

Thus, having aligned ourselves to Kingdom values we venture out to making this healing and state of blessedness available to others. Jesus in Mark 7:34 while healing the man who was deaf and dumb, puts his fingers in his ears and shouts "Ephphatha" meaning "be opened." C.S Lewis says "God, whispers to us in our pleasures, speaks in our conscience, but shouts in our pains: it is his megaphone to rouse a deaf world". The question is are we listening to the tremendous cry for help from people who are suffering especially due to a terminal illness and facing death? In India less than 3-5% can hope to get wholistic care through good and effective palliative care. Even in our Christian Health network only about 10% Mission Hospitals have a palliative care service. To improve this situation at least all our Mission Hospitals must have a palliative care service including home care so as to reach everyone in need.

Our Mission Hospitals have a great opportunity to bring people to Christ for his Healing. More people pass through our hospitals than our Churches. There are many who are seeking the Lord as they have faith in him. Like the healing miracle of the woman with bleeding (Luke 8: 43-48) Jesus is asking us "who touched me?" Are we just as unaware as the disciples and do not know? We must take effort to meet such silent seekers and take them to the Lord for his healing.

The Church community can be motivated and trained to be involved in caring as almost 70% of the needs of such people can be met by the community. We must strive to make our Church communities, healing communities and be the people God wants us to be. We need to ask the Lord to open our eyes to see the suffering around us, open our ears to hear the cries for help, open our hearts to feel the pain, open our minds to plan actions, open our hands to respond with love and compassion, open our feet to go the second mile. Christ's healing ministry involves sacrificial giving to provide wholistic care to achieve healing and wholeness in Jesus. There are good training programmes in palliative care for volunteers based on a WHO curriculum of 16 hours. On completion the volunteer will get a national level certificate by the Indian Association of Palliative Care and could help with confidence and understanding. These are opportunities which our Churches must use to equip the Church community in helping people and families going through a terminal illness and in bereavement support later for the family.

We need to reflect and ask ourselves, have we turned something good and glorious into an idol. Instead of lifting up Jesus, have we lifted up ourselves by idolising our knowledge, our position, our passion, our experience and praise of people. Have we eclipsed the glorious face of Jesus by coming in between? We are called to be salt and light to make a difference in this world. Salt acts by its presence not absence. We must be involved and our saltiness, as declared by Jesus in the beatitudes, must make the difference. Also, our lives, lived with high moral standards and with fear of the Lord, must shine to expel the darkness around and draw people to Jesus, the light of the world. As a Church community we need to repent and seek God's forgiveness and pray for healing of ourselves, the Church community and our Nation. (2 Chronicles 7:14)

The best thing we can give a dying person is Jesus and we can do it through our acts of wholistic care with love and compassion and by telling and making them aware of Jesus' finished work of grace on the cross for healing, wholeness and hope. This must be done sensitively and with permission of the person concerned. Having built a relationship of trust this permission is gladly given and then without hesitation, we must give freely what we ourselves have freely received.

References

The following is a list of authors and Godly people whose lives I have found helpful in my Christian understanding and practice of Healing and Health.

Dr. Ida S Scudder, Dr. William Osler, Dr. David Livingston, Martin Lloyd Jones, A.V Tozer, Dietrich Bonhoeffer, Charles Spurgeon, William Barclay, J.I Packer, John Stott, Max Lucado, John McArthur, Joni Erickson Tada, Ravi Zacharias, Philip Yancey, John Piper, Victor Frankel, William Carey, Amy Carmichael, Pandita Ramabai, Helen Keller, Corrie Ten Boom, Lee Strobel, J. Oswald Sanders, J.C Ryle.

Stories of famous Hymn writers: http://www.cgygfellowship.com/Topical/Hymns%20&%20Hymnists.pdf

Mission of God and Pastoral Counselling

Richard Howell

The one and only purpose God created us for is to love; for God is love (1 John 4:16). And the nature of God's love as holy is revealed in this that he sent his Son to be an atoning sacrifice for our sins (1 John 4:10). The nature of Triune God is holy love. And the Scriptures teach that the "love of God has been poured into our hearts by the Holy Spirit" (Romans 5:5). This enables and empowers us to participation in the Triune God's mission of the reconciliation of humanity and the healing of all creation.

The same Spirit of God who was instrumental in creation is also instrumental in re-creating and healing the world. To engage in mission of God is to relate human work to the goal of history, which will bring God, human beings, and nonhuman creation into the harmony of *shalom*. We need both justice and love in operation to create a human society. For with justice and love there is no *shalom* of the kingdom of God which Jesus proclaimed and inaugurated. Miroslav Volf comments, "Jesus' healing miracles are a sign of the inbreaking kingdom. As deeds done in the power of the Spirit, healings are not merely symbols of God's future rule, but are anticipatory realizations of God's present rule. They provide tangible testimony to the materiality of salvation. They demonstrate God's desire to bring integrity to the whole human being, including body, and to the whole of injured reality."[1] To engage in the ministry of health and healing in a hurting and fragmented world is a divine calling in which the Household of Christ is duty bound to engage. It is both "kingdom participation" and "Kingdom anticipation" which is its necessary consequence.

The context

In God's fallen world, history narrates a gory tale of pursuit and misuse of absolute power and control which dominates and decimates humans. The ruthless market economy celebrates accumulation of wealth as power, even by crushing its competitors, leaving behind a trail of causalities of crippled losers. Race-based narratives of social structures seem to suggest that consequent racial differences produce inherent superiority of a particular race. The advocates of patriarchy still perpetuates gender inequality as male is considered superior to the female gender. The discourse of casteism has exploited and divided humans for thousands of years in the categories of purity and pollution.

Daily we are confronted with children who self- abuse through self-harm behaviours, eating disorders, drug, alcohol abuse and rising suicide. We witness the harm inflicted on children through a range of violent acts and human trafficking. Families life also is in trouble with rising domestic violence and divorce rates. Every year millions of middle income group family's hit below poverty line specially in their old age as they are unable to keep with the rising medical costs.

Much of the emphasis in the 'spirit of the age' is on youthful vitality, physical perfection and denial of the ageing process. In a cultural milieu that prizes perfection over defects, fitness over frailty, youth over old age, we have generated 'a particular glorification of youthfulness and an irrational denial of the natural life processes of ageing and dying.

The ambassadors of reconciliation

It is in the context of seemingly hopeless scenario that God sends the community of Christ as ambassadors of reconciliation. The 5th chapter of 2 Corinthians offers a beautiful and radical vision: God's "new creation" in

Christ, and our becoming his ambassadors of reconciliation (vv. 17-21).

The Triune God is the source of reconciliation who has reconciled us to himself through Christ. The manner in which God made peace is far more radical than the diplomatic "peace treaty" signed between enemies when hostilities come to an end. The treaty God presented wasn't through a negotiated agreement or even a general pardon. God has brought a radical new thing in the world: God's "new creation". It's essential for us to be grateful for the enormity of the work of Christ that achieved our reconciliation.

The healing

God uses both miracles and medicines to heal. And faith in Christ empowers to cope with suffering, which helps to grow in godly character and righteousness. At the most recognisable level, Christian healing refers to cures done by God in the name of Christ and through the power of his Spirit. There are innumerable testimonies to healing and deliverance pointing to the power of God at work healing and restoring broken and wounded creation. However, faith healing represents only a segment of what Christians have experienced and meant by healing. Much more normally, Christian healing has involved relief of suffering and enriched capacity to deal with chronic ailments. Thus, many Christians still make pilgrims to visit healing shrines, apparently because such visits relieved suffering but did not produce a lasting cure.

Part of Christianity's appeal as a means of coping with suffering is the idea that suffering is not meaningless but part of a cosmic vision of redemption. Along with the actual healing that might be stimulated by faith in a higher power, this imputation of meaning to suffering has itself been a tonic. While the effectiveness of Christian practices as means to relief from suffering has contributed enormously to their popularity, the real genius of Christianity has been to embrace pain and disability and death and not to limit the meaning of health and healing to their expulsion. Thus, many Christians have accepted the onset or persistence of suffering as part of religious life, while also celebrating relief from suffering as a sign of the power and meaning of their faith. Beneath this apparent paradox, a fairly consistent tendency to experience suffering as a means of both self-understanding and communion with others has enabled many Christians to rest easier with pain and death, even as healing experiences have energized Christians, enabling some to defeat pain and death, at least temporarily.

Compassion of Jesus

In their attention to human suffering, many Christians have devoted themselves to caring for sick and dying people. Prompted by desire to emulate the compassion of Jesus and his healing ministry, Christians have launched countless agencies, institutions, and grassroots movements directed toward health care. In many of these efforts, Christianity and medicine have been deeply intertwined. Although sometimes competitive and even acrimonious, Christianity and medicine have often advanced together and depended on each other for support.

The mission of triune God

Trinity is not an esoteric piece of ancient dogma irrelevant to our daily experience. Trinitarian theology has a direct relationship to the topic of health and healing, because it is profoundly personal and deeply relational. One God in three persons, Father, Son and Holy Spirit, reveals to us the unique particularity of each person, inextricably bound to the other.

The belief in one Triune God revealed in Jesus Christ through the power of the Holy Spirit and testified to in Scripture is not predicated upon any human capacity or mode of thinking, but upon the initiative of God in making himself known to us and reconciling the world to himself. God is Triune both in his action and in his eternal divine or "inner" being". To deny this truth, as Gunton states it, "undermines our confidence in the gospel of Jesus Christ, the structures of creation, and 'the course of history'.[2] The Trinitarian theology emphasizes the profoundly interpersonal nature of Father, Son and Holy Spirit who invite us into the conversation and the rhythmic harmony of loving, reciprocal relationships, not for God's sake but for our own.

The trinitarian relationships reveal to us the meaning of unity in diversity; that each of us is uniquely irreplaceable and each of us reaches our potential not on our own but through our various relationships. We are whole persons only by being in a community of mutuality and interdependence; the foundation of this community is love. In this community our unique individuality is not subsumed; rather our humanity comes to full expression.

Loving relationship

In trinitarian personhood there is no hierarchy. The Spirit is not superior to the Son, the Son is not inferior to the Father, nor are the persons of the Trinity interchangeable. The Father is not the Spirit, nor can the Son be replaced by the Father. Each is unique and irreplaceable, but each cannot live apart from the others. The driving force of this relationship is love. The Father stoops down in love to envelop the whole creation into a personal relationship; through the humanity of the Son, God experiences our deepest wounds; and through the continued presence of the Spirit we become whole, and holy, persons. The unavoidable corollary is that we then reach out to others and respond to others in love, our humanity enriched by the humanity of others. 'At the deepest core of my being I need to be known and loved as I am.' Some in residential care may only experience the touch of another human in the feeding, showering or other caring activities, but never simply as an act of love.

Royal dignity of humanity

All human being irrespective of caste, gender, race or economic standing are created equal in the image and likeness of God (Genesis 1:27). And Jesus proclaimed with a call to repentance and belief in the gospel (Mark 1:15) welcomes those who believe as children of God having royal identity and dignity.

The Caste System of India is historically one of the main dimensions where people in India are socially differentiated through class, religion, region, tribe, gender, and language. Although this or other forms of differentiation exist in all human societies, it becomes a problem when one or more of these dimensions overlap each other and become the sole basis of systematic ranking and unequal access to valued resources like wealth, income, power and prestige. The Indian Caste System is considered a closed system of stratification, which means that a person's social status is obligated to which caste they were born into. There are limits on interaction and behavior with people from another social status. The caste system enforces the idea of purity and pollution as a means of exclusivism. Therefore, it is believed that the higher castes were purer and less polluted, while the lower castes were regarded as less pure and more polluted. Although discrimination on the basis of caste has been outlawed in India, it still exists in the community today. Is it also practiced in medical profession?

Interconnected whole

Each human person is viewed not as an amalgam of parts but as an interconnected whole. Each person is interconnected with every other person, none of us existing in isolation. Therefore, there our care falters when we divide a person into parts or when we separate them from their network of relations; more particularly when we separate ourselves as 'carers' from those who are 'in need of care'. As Henri Nouwen says:

> "As long as we continue to divide the world into the strong and the weak, the helpers and the helped, the givers and the receivers, the independent and the dependent, real care will not be possible, because then we keep broadening the dividing lines that caused the suffering of the elderly in the first place." (Nouwen and Gaffney 1976, p.153)

The various needs of individual persons (physical, mental, emotional, social, spiritual, etc.) can be perceived in separation of one from the other – as different 'bits' of each individual. Such separation is valuable only in that it helps to identify these different needs, one or other of which can easily be overlooked or neglected. Such rigid variegation however makes a travesty of individual personhood.

None can be addressed in separation or isolation from the others. This is true to ancient Hebrew thought in which body, mind, spirit are seen as interpenetrative of each other and not as separate parts of the one multifaceted person. It was Greek thought that created the separation of body, mind and soul that has tended to dominate medical practice and social care, as well as theology, through much of the history of the world and is still widely entrenched today.

In submitting to the holy god of autonomy, issues of relationships with others are ignored. When the emphasis is on interdependence rather than independence, freedom derives from shared goals and from helping each other achieve meaning as we age.

All in the mind?

On the other hand, the spirit of the age is characterised by a seductive invitation to well-being through independence, bodily perfection and agelessness. The pimple-free obsession of our youth has become the wrinkle-free obsession of old age. If this is not achieved, then we are encouraged, particularly by the media, to mend the flaws in our lives.

The language of the age is captured in the icons of 'drive-through surgery' or the quick fix. There is little place for words like faithfulness, commitment, interdependency, interrelationships, service, love, hope and long-term care. And yet long-term care will be required for many whose increased life expectancy may also include the processes of chronic disease. Aged care requires holistic loving, compassionate and faithful care to the end.

Dementia

With the increasing prevalence of dementia there are not many of us who will forever remain untouched in some way by this mysterious malady. Here also is a challenge to our language: 'He's lost the plot.'

'She's no longer the person I knew.' 'It's like a living death.' 'I couldn't bear to finish up like that!' What discourse is needed for engaging with those who are inarticulate or whose spoken words are unintelligible to the hearer? How do we describe our relationship with a person who appears unable to respond to us in any meaningful way?

Thinking seriously about the issue of dementia in relation to this discussion on ageing and well-being prompts further questions. What is the source of our humanity? Do we become less human if we are no longer able to remember our name? What is the source of our spirituality? What does it mean to be wholly human?

Assessing spiritual needs in the light of ultimate life meaning

The human spirit is nourished by and flourishes on hope. To find hope is one of the spiritual tasks of life. Hope for many is tied to seeing their children well established in adult life and their grandchildren doing well. The gospel of the resurrection gives hope of eternal life and hope to be reunited with our dear one who have gone to be with the Lord.

Assessing what lies at the core of one's life is important, both for people and for those who provide care. First, those who provide care must begin their care from a sense of self-awareness, so that they do not project their own beliefs and values onto another. It is only by being aware of one's own spirituality that one can meet others where they are. Second, what brings greatest meaning to each individual is the starting point for that person. For example, if the person has an image of a judgemental God, then guilt may be a central feature of their lives and they may not be able to see hope in their present situation. If the person has an image of a distant God or god who does not intervene in human events, that person will not see any possibility of help or strength from that source. On the other hand, if the individual has a relationship with a God they see as loving and close to them, this may provide a positive approach to well-being.

Response to ultimate meaning

People respond to what lies at the core of their being, what is most important in their lives. Some recent studies have shown for many, art, music or environment formed central sources of meaning. If the Triune God is central in providing vital meaning, then worship, prayer, reading of sacred scriptures, or meditation may be means of response. If loss of ultimate meaning was predominant for a person, then it may be hard for that person to find any response to meaning. This is a factor in grief and in depression.

Human beings are by nature meaning-makers in that they seek for meaning in the everyday situations in their lives. People use symbols and ritual to represent meaning. Good ritual connects deeply with the soul. It illuminates meaning for the individual and also represents shared meaning within a group of people. In Alzheimer's disease the use of symbol and ritual remain important because people who have cognitive disabilities are still able to respond to liturgy emotionally, and in this way, through Christian liturgy, they can still be part of the Body of Christ.

Let me close with a few incidents in the life of Stanley Jones. He reached a point in his missionary career where "the outer collapse took place because the inner experience could not sustain it". Stanley had a motto for his life, "I would not preach what I was not experiencing, so the outer and the inner collapse came together." He was sick and thought his mission work had come to an end. Stanley writes, "In that dark hour I was in the Central Methodist Church in Lucknow. The Rev. Tamil David was in charge of the evangelistic services. I was at the back of the church kneeling in prayer, not for myself but for others, when God said to me: 'Are you yourself ready for the work to which I have called you?' My reply: 'No, Lord, I'm done for. I've reached the end of my resources and I can't go on.' 'If you'll turn that problem over to me and not worry about it, I'll take care of it.' My eager reply: 'Lord, I close the bargain right here.' I arose from my knees knowing I was a well man. I walked home...I scarcely touched the earth as I walked along.

"Marble tablet was put up in the wall of this church with the inscription: 'Near this spot Stanley Jones knelt a physically broken man and arose a physically well man.' This tablet says, 'physically broken' and 'physically well', but this was more than a physical touch. It involved the total person. I was made well and whole – body mind, and spirit." (89-90). The mission continued.

Church in mission is well illustrated by Stanley, "I looked the face of the Son of Man and then looked into the faces of the sons of men, and I have spent my life trying to bring them together."[3]

Have we looked at the face of the Son of Man, Jesus Christ, are we proclaiming the gospel of the Kingdom of God in word and deed to see the faces of the sons and daughters of women and men become like the faces of the Son of Man? In doing so Christian community will become fragrance of Christ.

Endnotes

[1] Miroslav Volf, *Work in the Spirit,* (Oregon: Wipf and Stock Publishers, 2001, previously 1991). 104.

[2] Colin E. Gunton, *The Christian Faith: An Introduction to Christian Doctrine* (Oxford: Blackwell Publishers, 2002), 176,179.

[3] E. Stanley Jones, *A Song of Ascents,* (Abingdon. Nashville) 1968, 88-90 and v.

Theology of Healing

M J Paul

Jesus Christ dealt with societal tendency towards polarization by integrating the opposites. When we engage both, we can become better instruments of healing. The human mind tends to think in opposing polarities when faced with choices. This leads to much division in society and inequalities with regard to access to healthcare and allocation of resources. CMC practices 'the both- and' approach which illustrated the concept by caring for the less privileged but simultaneously providing specialized care that now extends from primary to quaternary focusing on all simultaneously. Jesus in his ministry chose to integrate the divisions that confronted him in many instances and showed us a non-judgmental way of dealing with the divisions we face in day to day life and gives us a practical theological basis for our philosophy of work in the institution. This concept may be interpreted in a way that encourages us to use our talents and privileges to help our less fortunate neighbors as Jesus enjoins us.

We look at some examples of integration that speak to us from the Gospel - Jesus performed his first miracle at his mother's request in a situation and time not in keeping with his primary mission. He gave up filial ties to focus on his mission forming a family of disciples and followers, yet made arrangements for the care of his mother from the cross. He catered to rich and poor alike. He catered to Jews and Gentiles; his message was mainly targeted at Jews but went out of his way to speak to the Samaritan community. He was critical of the Jewish clergy but spoke of obedience to authority. His focus was on another world – the kingdom inside even as we live in the world around us. Lived by both bread and word – spoke of spiritual matters, but fed the five thousand.

Current society and politics also tends to function by polarizing issues and does not spare the healthcare profession; we could take a leaf from Jesus' approach to live practically in personal and professional life building a harmonious society. "Thy kingdom come...on earth as in heaven."

How do we become effective healthcare workers in the work of the kingdom?

The worldly way in its fallen and lost state tries to polarize our lives and attitudes ... Sacred vs secular; Science vs religion; Conservative vs liberal; Words vs deeds; Faith vs works; Creation vs evolution; Socialism vs capitalism; Core values vs Change; Long term goals vs expeditious results; Cost vs Quality; Speed vs Safety; Volume vs Outcome; Eminence vs Evidence.

Our challenge is to integrate the polarities to manifest the kingdom of God. The integral approach allows both ends of the polarities to operate in the appropriate setting and the choice is made with love as the operating principle;the Golden rule (Mathew 12:7) is a guide for decision making. We struggle with our selfishness to make the loving choices and inner transformation is the key to change. God's grace gives us the capacity to transcend our limitations. Our rootedness in the spirit of God will help us in making the choice as the powerful forces of the world and ego buffet us about.

He gives us the Choice – God reaches out but allows us to decide our response. Depicted on the ceiling of the Sistine chapel, the creation story shows God reaching down from heaven coming close to Adam who is unaware of his presence and the fact that he only has to raise a finger to touch the hand of God who is always ready and waiting to enter our lives, should we become aware of his closeness. Allowing God's spirit to enter and transform us is the key to entering the kingdom and carrying out his will. Trying to do it on our own polarizes us and fills us with anxious striving.

The Lord's Prayer enjoins us to pray for the arrival of heaven on earth. Each time we help another selflessly and focus on the least of our brethren in doing his will, we bring heaven on earth. The 'both – and' philosophy – an integral approach in CMC's history; we were faced with a financial crisis in the seventies and advised to focus only on primary care. But we chose to integrate primary and specialized care and the rest is history. The loving contribution of many semi-saints among our staff who focused on developing infrastructure, resources and skilled staff to building teams while developing their own professional careers made CMC what it is.

The mission network and CMC have an organic integrated relationship built by over a century of attention to service and teaching. Mission doctors came in to develop the departments to create the teaching hospital; CMC trained and sent its doctors to the mission in reciprocation to act as a force multiplier in the mission network. In the current context, mission centers also need to develop centers of medical excellence in mission through relevant specialized services, while providing basic care to the unreached, to remain viable.

Jesus advised the rich man who sought eternal life in Mathew 19 to 'Sell all you have and give it to the poor' an invitation to sainthood. Only a saint can live happily in poverty and give till it hurts like St. Francis of Assisi and others of old and more recently Mother Teresa, Mohandas Gandhi, Martin Luther King and Nelson Mandela.

In a way, monastic life is a polarized approach because they have transcended the self and the world through separation. But it requires a saint to live in the material world and still remain detached in the mind; they can have tremendous impact but only a precious few can achieve that state while still living within society.

An integrated approach would be to focus ones efforts on helping others but at the same time not neglecting the needs of self and family. Semi-saints will make sure self and family are fed, clothed, sheltered and cared for, but they don't need to hoard, keep reserves of money or buy extra goods and houses which they will not need. God loves a cheerful giver; it is in giving that that semi-saints receive true happiness and joy. An integral question is what is the minimum need to keep body and mind happy? From a secular standpoint as well, surveys show that once basic needs are taken care of, earning and saving excess amounts will not increase happiness. An economic system that encourages overproduction and consumption so that what sells more wins in the market competition, engenders an antithetical attitude to semi-sainthood. Socialism or capitalism? It is not the system but the distortion of its original intent by our latent greed that makes it fail. An integral approach would use elements from both ideological systems to operate in an institutional or societal context by making the choices appropriate to the context.

Our Lord Jesus emphasized that the law was valid but not sufficient, as God wished the inner transformation to effect the outer manifestations mandated by law; else our devious hearts would circumvent its purposes. Jesus spoke of the law, that none of it would go away but be fulfilled by his new teaching. 'You have heard it said, but I say.... He brought in a new dimension - that of the inner life and the transformation required of those who follow him. He said in the sermon on the mount that showing external good works alone as the law commanded was not good enough, rather we must change our hearts and minds lest we become hypocritical.

We also need to integrate the scientific and humane aspects of ourpatient care. Much of our efforts focus on the medical aspects of our care; we also need to take the time to empathize with the patients to empower spiritual healing. The effect of empathy– sharing the spirit of love for our fellow human in suffering as an outflowing that we receive from God through our saviour would be felt as much as seen.

One common Indian expression used among the staff is that CMC is a pilgrim centre and we are the pujaris. As a surgeon I can sometimes feel the patients begin to heal even before the operation is done because of the faith that they are going to get well. This strong faith seen in many patients engendered by generations of committed staff of CMC is a powerful force. Empathy opens the window to the spirit in both healer and patient.

All trained healthcare workers will have to take leadership roles. Modern studies show that effective leadership involves self-awareness, self-regulation, empathy, social skills and enthusiasm/motivation. Enthusiasm = 'entheos' or 'God within' reflects the spiritual source for motivation that is inexhaustible as seen in saintly and semi-saintly examples. Not by our strength alone is the touchstone of our spiritual maturity.

The role of prayer – an integrated approach: Prayer changes things for us and us for things; prayer makes the choice for action clear when we open the door to God through prayer, the spirit gives us insights not otherwise possible. Jesus asked us to pray to the point, humbly, first making peace with our fellow men and with belief that what we were praying for would be received. Often our own doubts come in the way. In fervent prayer and belief God enables us to be the instrument of success. Each of us can recount how prayer opened up channels in our roles as learners, healers, teachers and administrators. Additionally the powerful reputation of hundreds of man-years of saintly and semi-saintly work at CMC creates a spiritual effect that opens up channels and changes people who deal with us in the present. We are gliding on the paths of saints.

Viktor Frankl wrote of his experience of torture and severe physical hardships in the Jewish camp, learning that the only thing we truly have control over is our reaction to any situation. We can choose to bear the hardship and not feel hatred, exemplified in Jesus response to the cross – 'Lord, forgive them for they know not what they do'. In the response to the Lord's call to sainthood in the Sermon on the Mount, by aiming for sainthood we can at least reach semi-sainthood – our hope for bringing the kingdom of heaven on this earth.

Our struggles will be – place of work, specialty, partner. Integrating patient care, teaching and research – will be the challenge and each of our journeys will be unique.

A Theology of Health

John Swinton

T he question of how Christians should understand health is complicated. The apparently obvious approach is simply to assume that health is the absence of illness. This makes the objective of healthcare fairly straight forward: To facilitate health by countering illness. But if we turn to Scripture, we find a different picture of health.

Concept of Shalom in the Old Testament

It is interesting to note that the Bible does not have a word for health understood simply as the absence of illness. The closest word is the Hebrew term shalom (Salôm) which occurs 250 time in the Old Testament. The basic meaning of the word shalom is 'peace'. However, the type of peace which is expressed in the concept of shalom is far wider than the absence of illness. The understanding of the word 'peace' expressed in the Old Testament's usage of the word shalom has specific theological meaning and intention. The root meaning of the word shalom is *wholeness, completeness* and *well-being.*[1] It does however have several secondary meanings, encompassing *health, security, friendship, prosperity, justice, righteousness and salvation,* all of which are necessary if wholeness, completeness and well-being are to come about.[2] The meaning of the word shalom, is thus seen, to express opposition to any disturbance in the well-being of a person, society or nation.[3] In the Old

Testament Yahweh himself is named as the source and giver of shalom. John Wilkinson observes that:

> One of the covenant names for God which Gideon used when he built his altar to the Lord at Oprah was Yahweh-shalom, the Lord is shalom. (Judges 6:24). It is he who offers his people a covenant of shalom, that is, a covenant which will secure shalom for them. (Numbers 25:12; Isaiah 54:10; Jeremiah 32:40; Ezekiel 34:25; 37:26, and Malachi 2:5) True shalom comes from God, for man finds his true wholeness and complete fulfilment only in God.[4]

Thus, shalom is found to be a gift given by God to his creation. As such it is a fundamentally holistic and relational concept. From the perspective of the Old Testament:

To experience shalom is to flourish in all one's relationships - with God, with one's fellow human beings, with the non-human creation, with oneself. Such 'flourishing' naturally presupposes peace in the usual sense, absence of hostility. But shalom goes beyond the absence of hostility, to fulfilment and enjoyment.[5] Shalom is therefore considerably more than the absence of conflict. It has in essence to do with the quality of a person's life and quality of their relationships with God, with one another, and with the rest of creation.

Central to the Hebrew Bible's understanding of shalom is the concept of *righteousness*. As Wilkinson explains in his discussion on the biblical understanding of health:

> "To be righteous in the Old Testament view is to conform to a norm, to be in right relationship. In the case of man, this norm is the character of God, and this relationship is to God and his will. Righteousness is fundamental to the Old Testament concept of health. A right relationship to God produces shalom (Isaiah 32:17). Righteousness and shalom flourish together (Psalm 72:7; 85:10; Isaiah 48:18; Malachi 2:6.)"[6]

Right relationship with God enables humanity to experience shalom, which encompasses both the wholeness and the holiness of human existence.

The creation narratives in the book of Genesis inform us that the natural state of the whole created order is harmony and peace: shalom.[7] However, although *justice, righteousness* and *peace* are all present in this original state, creation in its post-lapsarian state is found to be fragmented, scattered, disunited and without peace.[8] The cosmos currently exists in a state of dissonance and confusion. For the Old Testament prophets, the coming Messiah, the 'Prince of Peace' would be the one who would return God's shalom to his people. As Hoekendijk observes, for the Old Testament prophets:

> The Messiah is the prince of shalom (Is 9:6) he will be the shalom (Micah 5:5) he shall speak shalom to the heathen (Zechariah 9:10) He will realise the plans of shalom which the Lord has in mind for us to give as a future hope. (Jeremiah 29:11)[9] God's shalom is intended to be universal and everlasting, and the Messiah will be the bringer and founder of the kingdom of peace.

Concept of Shalom in the New Testament

In the New Testament, the messianic mission of Jesus is closely linked with the Old Testament understanding of God's Messiah as the bringer of shalom. Jesus, understood as the long awaited Messiah, was seen as the bearer and the sharer of God's eschatological shalom.[10] He is the chosen one whose primary mission is to restore the created order to its natural state; to turn the whole of creation from a state of Bedlam to shalom. Thus, in the same way as in the Old Testament, "Yahweh is Shalom"[11] so also in the New Testament the apostle Paul informs his readers that Jesus is Shalom. "For he himself is our peace, who has made the two one and has destroyed the barrier, the dividing wall of hostility"[12] From this it can be seen that shalom is not a distant utopian ideal. Shalom is a person. In John's gospel, Jesus promises that he will give his shalom, his peace, to all those who would follow him: "Peace I leave with you; my peace I give you. I do not give to you as the world gives. Do not let your hearts be troubled and do not be afraid."[13] Shalom is thus seen to be inextricably bound up with the nature and person of Jesus, and as such intricately connected with his work of restoration in its macro and micro dimensions. Shalom is not something which can be understood outside of its true context in Christ. It is not a political or ideological possibility. It is not a vision which inspires humanity to try harder. In fact, the empirical reality of the human condition would suggest that it is not even a sociological possibility. Shalom is a personal gift from a relational God to his fallen creation. It is a re-creative process that has been set in motion by the resurrected Christ. It is through entering into relationship with Christ that a person is enabled to experience shalom. It is in God's redemptive movement towards the world that the whole of creation is being reconciled and guided towards its true state of shalom.

This understanding has important implications for the life of the church. If the church is that community within which the first-fruits of restored humanity are in the process of being revealed; a body of forgiven sinners which has been brought into existence to participate in Christ's restorative actions-in-the-world, then the form of life which the church community manifests in its mission and ministry must reveal something of God's coming shalom. If the church is to participate authentically in Christ's work of restoring humanity (and creation) to its true state, then it must image God in its relationships with God, with one another and with the world.

Wuppertal neatly sums up the essence of what has been argued within this chapter when he observes that: this divinely wrought reality [God's gift of shalom] exercises a mighty influence in the present world, though it still waits its final fulfilment. Soteriologically, peace is grounded in God's work of redemption. Eschatologically it is a sign of God's new creation which has already begun. Teleologically it will be fully realised when the work of new creation is complete.[14]

As well as being an all-embracing eschatological concept, shalom also manifests itself in the micro-personal dimensions of human existence:

Shalom may be viewed as the integral experience of a person who is functioning as God intended, in consonant relationship with him, with others and with one's self. Shalom describes the experience of being harmoniously at peace within and without. It presents a picture of the person functioning as an integrated system in proper equilibrium. Because of the fall, human beings are unable to fully experience shalom, but to the extent that they are living consonantly with his design for human functions they experience higher degrees of it.[15]

The concept of shalom is therefore seen to be both a goal and a holistic process which is initiated and sustained by God as he seeks to deal with the relational alienation of creation through his ongoing movement within history, towards that goal. If we can begin to draw the argument into the area which is the primary focus of this course: health and healing, it becomes apparent that God's redemptive, eschatological movement towards shalom provides the context, the motivation and the goal of the church's health care ministry.

Endnotes

[1] John Wilkinson,. *Health & Healing* (Edinburg: The Handsell Press, 1980),.5.

[2] Ibid., 5.

[3] Sinclair B Fergusson & Wright, David. (Eds.) *New Dictionary of Theology* (England: Inter-Varsity Press, 1978), 777.

[4] Wilkinson, *Health & Healing*, 5.

[5] Wolterstorff in *Aitkinson and Field New Dictionary of Christian Ethics and Pastoral Theology*, 19–20.

[6] Wilkinson, *Health & Healing*, 6-7.

[7] Gen. 1:31,"God saw all that he had made, and it was very good. And there was evening, and there was morning–the sixth day."

[8] D. N Freedman, Ed. *The Anchor Bible Dictionary* Vol. 5: O–Sh. (New York: Doubleday, 1992), 207.

[9] J. C Hoekendijk. *The Church Inside Out. (London:* SCM Press, 1967), 19.

[10] John 14:27: "Peace I leave with you; my peace I give you. I do not give to you as the world gives. Do not let your hearts be troubled and do not be afraid." John 16:33: "I have told you these things, so that in me you may have peace. In this world you will have trouble. But take heart! I have overcome the world."

[11] Judges 6:24.

[12] Ephesians 2:14. It is interesting to note that a juxtaposition of these two passages strongly suggests an affirmation of Jesus' divine nature, and a consequent recognition of common purpose within the Trinity. This assertion that shalom is a common purpose of the Trinity becomes even more clear in the light of Galatians 5:22 where one finds Paul asserting that the Spirit also is the bearer and sharer of shalom.: "But the fruit of the Spirit is love, joy, peace, patience, kindness, goodness, faithfulness."

[13] John 14:27.

[14] V.R.B Wuppertal, *The New International Dictionary of New Testament Theology,* (U.K: The Paternoster Press Ltd, 1971), 781.

[15] Craig, Ellison and Smith, 'Towards an Integrative Measure of Health and Well Being.' *Journal of Psychology & Theology* Vol. 19: No 1. Spring 1991, 36.

Mission of God and Pastoral Counselling

Edison Samraj

I commend the vision of CMC in organizing a colloquium on Theology of Health & Healing. I am impressed by re-visiting some of the basics as part of the centenary celebration at CMC. The review of the foundational concepts will reinforce the most critical ideas that are essential for its effectiveness. I am expected to reflect over the theme: 'the Mission of God and Pastoral Counseling.' How do we consider Pastoral Counselling as the Mission of God in a health-care setting?

The mission of God

The mission of God is holistic and integrational. In simple terms, it is to make man whole—holistic from the point of bringing together the need to have a balance, a picture of the whole, and a commitment to bring harmony between the head, the heart and the hand. This holistic approach is essentially to make man whole. But wholeness is a journey that does not end. But how does it work? What are some of the principles that govern it? How do we begin pastoral counselling in the context of our post-modern world which has brought with it three major ideological underpinnings to nullify the very foundations of life? So it would be imperative to outline the context of our post- modern world so that we can address the problem at the root level. Today counselling has become sterile and ineffective because we have taken the neutral path. But the challenge is to use the integrated model to be effective.

Context of pastoral counselling

The Context of Pastoral Counselling is to be carefully assessed so our intervention will address the root of the problem. If you look at the world we live in, you will quickly observe there is a rejection of the logos, denial of the telos and the negation of the philos. Examining these three concerns will help us in positioning ourselves on the road to restoration. This will essentially play a critical role in addressing the needs of pastoral counselling.

"In a world where the logos (Word became flesh) is rejected as negotiable and more dangerously substituted for pluralism, In a world where philos (wisdom) is replaced with knowledge or information without a unifying factor, In a world where telos (purpose) is denied in the place of performance and productivity, how do we position ourselves as pastoral counsellors within the context of this rejection, denial and negation? It would be essential for us to establish the credentials and credibility of maintaining the logos as exclusive and integral to integration. Acts 4:12 categorically sustains the idea of exclusive status to Christ by which anyone can even obtain wholeness. This exclusive status and claim to trust is challenged by post modernity and more so by discrediting the claim of Christ who said, "I am the Way, the Truth and the Life."

More importantly, Indian sacred scripture has anticipated this Messiah (Logos) anonymously. So even within our cultural tradition, we have been anticipating him without naming him. Therefore, many have not taken him seriously. But if we do maintain that revelation is progressive, then the Hindu religious scripture can be forerunner in anticipating this Messiah for centuries without knowing that it was Christ that was referenced.

Seven imperatives for pastoral counselling in this post-modern world:

First imperative: significance of the logos

Understanding the significance of the logos as a critical factor is indispensable in integration—the single and exclusive and indispensable principle that cannot be negotiable. It has to be the point of departure in the quest for any pastoral approach in counselling. It has a transforming influence for integration. This has been diluted by post-modern thinking.

Second imperative: orientation of the mind to the basic concepts

Keeping the basics clear gives a point of reference to make the counselling with ease and strength to move on. Basic concepts such as faith, forgiveness, marriage, hope, if clearly explained and from Scripture, orients the mind to think differently and respond holistically. It is of critical importance that the mind has to be re-oriented to basic ideas that make healing work. So when explanations on basic concepts are outlined to those affected, it gives the person a sense of change in perspective so when the perspective itself is changed, then the way they look at their problem also changes. No amount of counselling helps when the basics are not clear. Only when the point of reference is carefully presented with non-negotiable base, then the patient begins to understand where they are in relationship to the problem, and they will respond to the overtures of the counsellor the plan of action to make their recovery process work. It would be almost sound like a readymade recipe for their restoration.

Third imperative: Using the mode of prayer for the patient

This helps the patient to understand not only the source of healing but also making him feel the need for link to the source of healing. Also, it allows the patient to have access to power that changes the colour of the soul. And therefore, it is also to comply with the Biblical passage recorded in Hebrews 4:16 "Let us then approach God's throne of grace with confidence, so that we may receive mercy and find grace to help us in our time of need."

Fourth imperative: Helping the person in discovering the true purpose of life
Explaining to the person to probe into his or her mind to discover the true purpose of life is essential in bringing excitement to life itself. It makes the person realize the reason for her or his existence and help them to look at their vocation as a way to abundant life. When this happens, the career becomes mission-centric and the total outlook radically changes the way they focus on everything.

Fifth imperative: Life of wisdom and understanding
Today's generation is smart, intelligent but not wise. When making major decisions, they act unwisely and also to some extent exhibit non-reflective status. So what gives them wisdom and how do we help them identify wisdom is the challenge of pastoral counselling. This is possible only when they understand the need for living a life of wisdom and understanding. And the Scripture necessitates the need for wisdom for living in Proverbs 3:5 and Proverbs 2. And it also offers to anybody who asks for it (James 1:5)

Sixth imperative: Presenting the Gospel of Jesus Christ
This raises the person's awareness of who God is and the nature and purpose of his existence. There is a radical perspective of life offered in every presentation of the Gospel. This is the missing link in pastoral counselling. People who are counsellors normally begin to advise patients from their point of view but what I have found in my years of experience is that when you introduce the power of the Gospel to people, they are necessarily equipped and empowered to handle the challenges of making the right choices and decisions. In other words, their whole outlook is transformed and radically changed. What makes that happen is the amazing quality of grace. Grace truly transforms the human soul. Power, money, knowledge does not make you eligible for Grace. Grace is a comprehensive gift that God gives to every soul that is lost and grace has the capacity to make us all sufficient in all things unto good words (2 Corinthians 9:8).

Seventh imperative: How to keep BQ central to managing the IQ (reason) and EQ (emotion)

We have the IQ test done to measure intelligence. EQ test is done to know your emotional quotient but no one does the BQ test. Why? The problem is this generation does not believe in anything so we must make the patients understand "reason" left to itself will become self-destructive. EQ without the framework of certain checks and balances would lead to emotional disaster. When BQ moderates the demands of reason and the expectations of the emotions, it is more holistic and integrated. The fastest way to manage rationality and emotions is to give the reigning power to BQ. So the best option is to help the person understand the power of how to use the belief of controlling *reason* and *emotion*. This will bring harmony, peace and well-being socially, physically, mentally and spiritually. This way the head, heart and the hand works in consonance with the Divine purpose.

A Post Script: 12-step program

No.	The Twelve Steps Adapted from the Twelve Steps of Alcoholics Anonymous	Biblical Comparisons (NIV)
1.	We admitted that we were powerless over our addictions, that our lives had become unmanageable.	I know that nothing good lives in me, that is in my sinful nature. For I have the desire to do what is good, but cannot carry it out. – Romans 7:18
2.	We came to believe that a power greater than ourselves could restore us to sanity.	So do not fear, for I am with you; do not be dismayed, for I am your God. I will strengthen you and help you; I will uphold you with my righteous right hand. – Isaiah 41:10
3.	We made a decision to turn our will and our lives over to the care of God as we understood him. "Jesus Christ is the Highest Power."	Then He said to them all, "If anyone would come after Me, he must deny himself and take up his cross daily and follow Me." – Luke 9:23
4.	We made a searching and fearless moral inventory of ourselves.	Let us examine our ways and test them, and let us return to the Lord.– Lamentations 3:40

5.	We admitted to God, to ourselves and to another human being the exact nature of our wrongs.	Therefore, confess your sins to each other and pray for each other so that you may be healed. The prayer of a righteous man is powerful and effective. – James 5:16
6.	We were entirely ready to have God remove all these defects of character.	If you are willing and obedient, you will eat the best from the land. - Isaiah 1:19
7.	We humbly asked him to remove all our shortcomings.	Humble yourselves before the Lord, and He shall lift you up. – James 4:10
8.	We made a list of all persons we had harmed and became willing to make amends to them all.	Leave your gift there in front of the altar. First go and be reconciled to your brother, then come and offer your gift. – Mathew 5:23
9.	We made direct amends to such people wherever possible, except when to do so would injure them of others.	Give and it will be given to you. A good measure pressed down, shaken together and running over, will be poured into your lap. For with the measure you use, it will be measured to you.- Luke 6:38
10.	We continued to take personal inventory and when we were wrong, promptly admitted it.	For by the grace given to me I say to every one of you: Do not think of yourself more highly than you ought, but rather think of yourself with sober judgment, in accordance with the measure of faith God has given you.- Romans 12:3
11.	We sought, through prayer and meditation to improve our conscious contact with God as we understood him, praying only for knowledge of his will for us and the power to carry that out.	May the words of my mouth and the meditation of my heart be pleasing in your sight, O Lord, my Rock and my Redeemer. – Psalm 19:14
12.	Having had a spiritual experience as the result of these steps, we tried to carry this message to others, and to practice these principles in all our affairs.	Brothers, if someone is caught in a sin, you who are spiritual should restore him gently. But watch yourself, or you also may be tempted. – Galatians 6:1

May you too experience life abundant as you walk this journey, joining David in his joyful declaration: "You have shown me the path of life." Psalms 16:11.

Listening to One Body,

Many Parts and Myriad Stories

Reena George

The microcosm of the human body, like the great rhythm of the universe, is silent, intricate, delicately balanced. Anatomy supports physiology as organs and tissues connect, communicate and nourish life. In illness, they speak through the patient's history. Even in this era of cutting-edge technology, the clinical history remains the foundation of patient care. In listening to anatomy speak, we understand how and where the body hurts. In health and infirmity, may we also marvel at the human form we touch and inhabit — so carefully and wonderfully made.

Anatomy

I confess that as a student I did not like the subject of anatomy. Mathematics called for logic, the languages inspired creativity, physiology offered an intriguing interplay of feedback cycles, but anatomy demanded that I laboriously read pages of dead, boring detail. It fogged my memory with long names swirling in fumes of formalin.

Before the days of integrated medical education, the first one and a half years of pre-clinical studies in Indian medical schools were completely separated from the clinical world. We lived far away from the hospital, but only a short walk from the dissection room. The dirty grey-brown tissues on the cadavers looked nothing like the colour diagrams in our atlas. Our seniors told us that the living body in the operation theatre looked very different. Since I did not have the qualities to be a surgeon, anatomy was only a subject to endure until my clinical years. Then I would search for a non-surgical discipline that seemed a natural home for my interests.

Clinical Anatomy

Radiation oncology was not a popular specialty in those days but it attracted me for many reasons. There was so much one could learn from a long relationship with patients and from ongoing discoveries in science. It offered physics and mathematics; psychology and statistics; medicine and surgery; pharmacology and pathology. It had clinical conundrums ranging from neurology to urology.

As a trainee radiation oncologist, I realized that anatomy mattered very much. Drawing upon our knowledge of surface anatomy, we would mark a field, paste radio-opaque metal markers, and take a plain x-ray. This "check film" became the litmus test of our radiotherapy planning skills. Had we correctly targeted the vertebra that had a painful deposit? We felt very happy if the check film occasionally showed we were 'spot on'.

The anatomy of Psalm 139

Although my own life has moved away from the precision of radiation oncology to the complex uncertainties of palliative care, anatomy still matters. It is a good friend now because it has remained true and steady. Its fundamentals have changed less than that of many of the other subjects that I studied in medical school. I am grateful to the teachers who enabled deep, long-term learning. But it is no longer the quick fix of check films that is rewarding. It is my wonder at the design and economy in the anatomy of the human body, where structure and location so logically and elegantly facilitate function and sustain life.[1]

I was wrong to think that anatomy was a dead, boring subject. I realize now that anatomy is alive because it speaks, as creatively as any rich language, not only through the history of my patient but also in the history of humankind. When my patient with lung cancer has recently become happy go lucky and expansive, my own heart sinks. It may not be because he has moved from grief to acceptance and positive thinking. Very often the imaging will show frontal lobe secondaries in the brain.

Senses

The body carefully shelters what is most vulnerable. The small, fragile pituitary that determines human size and virility is kept safe in the bony vault of the sphenoid. Close to it, in their own osseous bunkers, are the nerves of our major sense organs. The eyes are protected by two parents — tough bony brows and tender, sensitive eyelids. The eyes, the windows to the soul for the poet, are the peep-hole to the living body for the physician.

The ear pinna resembles the diaphragm of our stethoscope, wide open to receive sound waves. And like the instrument's rubber tubing, the middle ear shepherds the sound waves through a narrow path guiding them to audibility. The middle ear canal is far shorter than my stethoscope's tubing because it has the incus, malleus, and stapes to amplify the signals. These tiny ossicles with imperious names sit beneath the brain, deep inside a petrous submarine. Only the Eustachian periscope peeps into the nasopharynx. I remember an old man whose partial deafness and middle ear effusion was caused by an undetected, nasopharyngeal cancer blocking the Eustachian tube. It was only when the tumour grew to infiltrate the base of the skull and neuropathic pain demanded an investigation that the enemy was uncovered. No one had heeded what the secret agents in the middle ear had been whispering for months.

There is an economy, not only in structure and location but also in function. Air, before it reaches the lungs, wafts smells through the holes in the skull base to waiting olfactory nerves. Air also makes a little detour from the pharynx into the mouth so that the sweet, salt, sour, and bitter of our taste buds become a thousand flavours of the world's cuisines. A common cold reminds us that the tongue is not the only organ of taste.

Connections

The flexible neck allows us to look beyond the tunnel vision of our bone-sheltered eyes. The eyes, ears, and the nose are placed high to enable our human ancestors to look, listen, and breathe above the forest undergrowth.

The neck connects the processing engines within the abdomen and thorax to the outside world of food and air. Fleet-footed air speaks and sings its way through the flute of the larynx. With less delicacy, food pushes its way down the oesophagus. Bullied by the bolus, the oesophagus remains silent and hides behind the trachea. Very rarely does it speak up. We are worried when a patient with oesophageal cancer coughs on swallowing. "Drink a few sips of water," we say, and in the clinic, a trachea-oesophageal fistula may hoarsely announce its presence.

Spaces

Unlike most other parts of the body, the thorax and the abdomen can expand and contract. Both have to accommodate what enters from the outside, and so they have adapted to the needs of their residents. The latticed window of the thoracic cage allows both ventilation and protection. The lungs and the heart coordinate our gas supply. The body's biggest and busiest vascular channels run between them. In the body's economy, it is natural that these organs are in proximity. When things go wrong in the vital communication between the heart and the lung, the story of the pulmonary embolus can be breathlessly acute and scary.

I never understood the term "a potential space" throughout my pre-clinical studies. It sounded as mysterious and unreal as the wardrobe to Narnia. Finally, in my clinical years, I saw the potential space becoming oppressively real in a patient with a malignant pleural effusion. Left untreated, an ipsilateral tracheal shift is the next danger sign the lung has collapsed, after a knockout punch inflicted by just a few litres of pleural effusion.

A few litres of ascitic fluid do not tell such a violent story. The abdomen does not have ribs to constrain its expansion. Easy-going, it expands with a smiling umbilicus. This laxity enables it to make room for the growing foetus and to stock up food reserves.

Viscera

Within the abdomen, the more delicate vulnerable structures are housed with extra care. The vascular liver and spleen are protected in the basement of the bony thorax. In the sterile retroperitoneum, the kidneys lie not far from the major vessels whose blood they have to purify. Many of the chemicals that control the physiology of our inner world are produced by the adrenals that humbly wait upon the kidney. The adrenals determine life and death, hunger and thirst, love, fear, and happiness through electrolytes, hormones, and neurotransmitters. Yet, they remain content with a name subsidiary to the kidney. Perhaps they were labelled when we judged them by their position and not by their vital contribution. I think of the quiet, loyal workers who keep our busy hospitals running every day: the electricians, the cleaners, the plumbers.

The liver, the largest organ in the abdomen, is close enough to the upper gut to take over the portal circulation. It is as if the body has outsourced the processing of nutrient-laden blood to this factory of portal circulation. The liver adds chemical preservatives, conjugates, sorts, and stores after the pancreas has done the enzymatic slicing and chopping of food. It was in a patient with pancreatic cancer that I first realized how anatomy tells stories. It was a sad story of a tumour in the pancreas that had blocked the drainage of bile. The skin and urine were a deep yellow, as were the desperate, wide-open eyes of a young man who would not live to see his children grow up.

Anterior to the retroperitoneum, in the roomy abdominal cavity, many meters of intestines and miles of villi happily cohabit in a common dormitory. The near constant supply of food and drink keeps them in good spirits.

In good health, the peritoneum provides smooth, thick, waterproof insulation. The visceral peritoneum protects the abdominal cavity from the murky contents of the gut. A perforated bowel cancer changes the easy-going abdomen into a tense guarded structure that rebounds in pain. Cancer that seeds the peritoneum, more insidiously, sows discord within a once happy intraabdominal family. When cliques of matted omentum advance upon their woundedneighbour, even bowel resection surgery cannot bring catharsis and reconciliation. It is left to palliative care physicians to impose an uneasy curfew with medicines that numb the deep visceral pain caused by broken relationships.

Messengers

Pain is the most frequent spokesperson for anatomy in oncology. If a patient with breast cancer starts getting supra-scapular pain, I worry about recurrence near the deep brachial plexus, even if the chest wall is pristine. A patient may have multiple bone metastases, but when his deep tendon reflexes are brisk, we cannot ignore these hyperactive nerves — danger is near. The patient may soon become paralyzed.

Unlike most other cells in the body, the neurons travel far, communicate fast and shock us into attention. They are our high tension electric wires. Despite the speed with which our nerves convey orders, our responses are surprisingly accurate. This is partly because the brain has a detailed circuit diagram within the homunculus

Limbs

The brain gives much more to the hands than to the feet. In spite of such unfair treatment, the feet steadily carry our load, allowing freedom for our hands to learn new skills. The loyalty of the feet has, in turn, enabled them to grow – Relative to our size, our legs stronger, longer, and more independent thanthose of other species.

The big and the little toes are parallel to each other, but the thumb is placed almost perpendicular to the other fingers. This little difference has altered human history. Would we have ventured to plant seeds, light fires, cook food, sail ships, draw maps, teach children to write, administer injections, or write a book if we were created with thumbs that were parallel to the fingers?

Nurture

The brachial plexus that enabled all of these milestones in human history can be damaged by many cancers most notably the breast and the lung. Breast cancer is very versatile in the stories it can tell. Its metastases range from the eye to the ovary. Some breast cancers write long-running sagas. Every few years there is a distant site of relapse and therapy.

The breasts, we had learnt in anatomy, develop on the mammary line that extends from the armpit to the abdomen. Other mammals have many pairs breasts to feed multiple offspring. Only one pair remains in human beings. Before in-vitro fertilization and neonatology, twins sometimes survived, but triplets rarely did.

A woman's only pair of breasts is located closest to where the baby can hear his mother's heartbeat as he feeds, where her elbow can comfortably cradle him, where she can smile at him, sing to him. Most mammalian offspring are not carried with such tenderness. As infants, we had to be carried because we are born helpless. Unlike puppies, calves, or foals, the new-born human being cannot run or jump to claim nourishment. Even when we can physically stand on our own feet, we cannot manage to earn a livelihood for many years.

Perhaps it is such vulnerability that created human civilization. Babies needed parents for many years just to survive. And that dependence created families. For a decade or two children are given not only food, but love, knowledge, values, and laughter. Work and creativity, faith, and learning were shared and fostered across generations. One reason why the child is born almost prematurely helpless is because the head to body ratio is larger than in most animals. And before the head gets too big to escape the bony pelvis, the baby leaves the womb and moves into the care of its parents.

It seems unfair when the wombs that have been a safe home to many children are attacked by cervical cancer. The assailants come in different guises. Some invade \ with early bloodshed. The injury is worrying enough to bring the patient to the hospital. (Except when, as a doctor from Africa said, some simple postmenopausal women rejoice that their fertility has returned and keep waiting for the next pregnancy.) The bleeding cancers that do reach a radiotherapist are usually gratifying to treat. They often shrink quickly. Then there are obnoxious bullies who slowly torture before they kill. They gouge into the bladder or rectum, causing fistulae. Stigmatized by fetid smells, the patient, for no fault of her own, becomes the lonely pariah. Friends move away.

Broken and blessed

It took the mutilation and mystery of cancer to teach me the intricate composition of the human body. As clinicians, we witness the tentacles of cancer rip a finely balanced work of art into a tremulous jigsaw. The clinical history helps us to make sense of the jigsaw, to diagnose, to treat. But the history is also his story. And as the story is spoke and heard, a wounded person begins to make meaning, to embark on the long road to healing.

And some day, broken bodies and broken hearts may even be transformed to transcendent, translucent stained glass windows with the Master's touch.

References
Brand P and Yancey P. *Fearfully and Wonderfully Made*. Grand Rapids, Michigan: Zondervan Publishing House: 1980.

Adapted from
George RM, Mathew S. Anatomy Lessons. Christian Journal for Global Health. Nov 2017;
4(3). © George RM and Mathew S. This is an open-access article distributed under the terms of the Creative Commons Attribution License, which permits unrestricted use, distribution, and reproduction in any medium, provided the original author and source are properly cited. To view a copy of the license, visit http://creativecommons.org/licenses/by/4.0/

Healing:
A Pastoro-Praxis Reading

R. Christopher Rajkumar

P astoro-praxis approach to healing is a paradigm shift in the thought process to understand, practice and promote healing in our life (faith) journey as fellow humans. This presentation is not an attempt to initiate an academic discourse on the topic healing but to facilitate to look the healing spiritually, ministerially and diaconally with practical theological lenses. The aim is to deconstruct the popular views of the epistemologists, post-modernists and post-foundationalists on healing rather approaching through the socio-theological constructionalism where people and contexts are at the centre in this discourse.

Four contexts
Commonly, the academic fraternity approaches the issues to be read through four contextual views namely i. Post-modern or Liberal View, ii. Traditional / Cultural View, iii. Classical / Historical View and iv. Charismatic / Fundamentalists' View.

Theology of mission
The Bottom Line for Mission is nothing but to affirm, promote and defend the Gospel Value of Love, Justice and Peace

World view of healing

Healing is nothing but, a process **of** *‹becoming' well 'again' or healing is a process* **in which a** *bad situation* **or** *painful emotions ends* **or** *improves.* Healing is generally or popularly understood as Cure. It is the fact that there are two different schools of thought deal with these two areas such as Social Science and Medical Science respectively. It is unfortunate to note that, some of the popular faith movements including Christian faith misunderstood and mislead the public by holding healing crusades and performing physical 'cure'. Some of the faith or philosophical schools advocate for the healing of body and mind (heart and mind) through life style changes like yoga, meditation and diets and such.

Health and healing

a. God heals and desires our health and wholeness. But this does not mean that divine intervention is intended to provide bodily cures in every circumstances.

b. God does not always cure but heals through divine touch.

c. Fitness (Yoga) is a contemporary cult and it is a product / commodity of patriarchy and an idolatrous distortion of the 'Truth'.

d. 'Cult of normalcy': This internalised social thought prevails among the majority that define how those of us, who fall within the bell curve of ability as opposed to being labelled as people with disabilities and measured through the pro-creative potency, understand ourselves as "normal and healthy" human beings.

e. The 'ableism' and 'ablest' presumptions of the society undermines the God's interventions in the lives of the human society. But for sure ableism is counter to Yahweh's concern for the poor, the weak, and the marginalized. It also counters the upside-down world of Jesus as the face of the coming reign of God insists that the final banquet is attended by social outcasts, including "the poor, the crippled, the blind, and the lame."

Faith and healing

a. It is not wrong or a mistake to presume God will supernaturally intervene to heal or cure by the wonder-working power of his spirit! But it would also be wrong to think that if we live according to what we believe the covenant requirements are, we are guaranteed a healthy and long life.

b. Salvation is not necessarily to be understood through the fitness of body but through healing.

c. From that perspective the abled persons often presume that we know how to pray for others—for instance, that they want healing that make them normal just like us—rather than acknowledging the pertinent prayers of the people of the disabilities. This plays out most problematically when interacting with people with disabilities.

d. Religious belief in divine intervention does not depend on empirical evidence that faith healing achieves an evidence-based outcome. However, the emphasis is given on the touch of a divine energy than the physical touch of the religious leaders.

Theology and healing

a. We need to re-read the meaning of the 'people of God' and the 'body of Christ'! At the time of Pentecost, all flesh female and male, young and old, have-nots and haves, disabled and abled to be seen from the perspective that each flesh from the sight of the Spirit of God is whole and deserve salvation of God.

b. All should consider, including the sick and terminally ill and treat equally with prayer for their well-being of all – for all. Rejoice with each other, celebrate each other's lives with acceptance, laments, and grieves as God of the Bible exemplified.

c. Healing is Eschatological. It is not life after death but hope for the life on earth.

Healing and transformation

a. The Gospel of Christ transforms all lives by challenging and confronting the oppressive schools of thoughts and its practices by an individual and the society at large. The Gospel is not only transforming our minds but also hearts.

b. Hence, suffering and disability are not segregated from the Gospel that proclaims the reign of God, which is Just and Inclusive.

c. If we read the healing narratives in the Gospels in the New Testament, it facilitates the community to be part of God's inclusiveness by being with the healed individuals. Hence, the healing transforms the communities and societies at large not just limited with an individual themselves.

d. Accepting the physical status itself is a healing.

Pastoro-praxis reading of healing

a. Redemptive pastoral practices that embrace and await the full healing and wholeness promised by the gospel.

b. These can also be explicated in three interrelated domains: the interpersonal, the social/ecclesial, and the eschatological.

i.   Prayer for cure vs Prayer for healing.

ii. God heals the wounded psyche not necessarily cures the tormented parts in our physical bodies.

iii. Pastoral engagements should be sensitive in demeaning the ableists' presumptions.

Theological paradigm of mission

- Conventional to Covenantal.
- Great Commission to Great Commandment.
- Healing as a spirituality towards the community at large rather than a cure of an individual.
- Maintenance of Life and Witness to Towards Life and its Fullness.
- Proclaim to Practice - Doing the Gospel.
- Contexts from the Word rather than Word to the Contexts.

PART-4
Identity and Accountability
in Healing Ministry

Identity, Credibility, Responsibility

Anna B Pulimood

As Christians, the Christian Medical College at Vellore, our identity has always been linked to the first word in our name – Christian, identifying the kind of Medical College we are. We believe we have been called and given the responsibility to continue the healing ministry of Christ in our times. Our credibility is based on our being of the same mind as Christ - being his hands and feet and voice and making his love, care and concern known to all people, particularly the sick, through our words and actions.

The standards of Christ have always been our golden standard:

- Who healed all who came to him – rich and poor;

- Whose healing was always holistic – of the mind and body;

- Whose healing was always with great power - complete and linked to restoration to normalcy – Simon's mother-in- law got up from her bed immediately and proceeded to take care of her guests – the lame man was asked to pick up his bed and walk-

- Who worked long hours and in over-crowded places;

- Who passed on his healing ministry to his disciples and followers;

- Whose life of prayer and healing were closely intertwined and always demonstrated that healing came from God alone.

And though we are a far-cry from the ideals he set, we do see evidence of God at work here – in our work of healing, teaching and research – and in the life of our community. Our own experience and the witness of many who pass through here, encourages us to persist and continue our work for him, and in his name. And any success, any credit attributed to the work here, is for his glory.

Many of the patients who come to Vellore, even those from other faiths, give witness of the presence of God in our midst. Even earlier this week, one of the nurses who was looking after my mother in the hospital, told me that so many patients say that as they enter our campus, they feel the presence of God here. Many tell us that this is a pilgrimage centre. Not an easy identity to bear – to be loaded with such responsibility – but Christ has promised that his yoke is light and his burden easy to bear, and in faith we press on.... And continue to marvel at his provision and protection.

Among the many ways, the protecting hand of God here in Vellore has been the way our admission policies have uphold over the last many decades– admission policies that we feel are key to our success in training doctors relevant to the needs of the country. On over 18 instances, our college has found favour in the eyes of the courts and has retained its right to admit candidates of its own choice to fulfil its vision and mission, despite regulations passed by the state that could have denied us these rights.

But the year 2017 was different. We had started off on a good note: The regulation about common counselling, that gave the sole right of all medical seat allocation in the country to the government, based on NEET or National Entrance and Eligibility Test marks alone, had come out just before our PG admissions. Technically, our PG admissions last year should have been done through the state. However, as our interim application against common counselling was heard in the Supreme Court, even the senior lawyer of the Medical Council of India, our chief opponent in the case, acknowledged that CMC was an exceptional college that had the trust of the people. He himself submitted to the Judge that the admissions we had conducted should be permitted for that year. We were jubilant – we thanked God – we felt confident about going forward with our case – expecting a favourable outcome at all subsequent hearings.

But come July and August, the dates for the hearings on our interim applications for the MBBS and Super Specialty admissions kept getting postponed. Every time we went to court, we expected to hear a favourable order, but returned with no assurances. On the last hearing of our interim application, just before the deadline for admissions for the year 2017, we were told by the court to comply with common counselling through the government if we wanted to admit students.

The tough decision about what to do next had to be taken. We had had multiple discussions with the Faculty, Executive Committee, Council and lawyers and the painful decision to withhold admissions for both MBBS and Super Specialty courses for that year was taken. The words of Paul in 2 Corinthians 4:8-10 seemed so true.

"We are hard pressed on every side, but not crushed; perplexed, but not in despair...struck down, but not destroyed. We always carry around in our body the death of Jesus, so that the life of Jesus may also be revealed in our body."

The cost of standing for autonomy in admissions seemed terribly high. It was like a bereavement in many ways... Vellore was known for its seven wonders – river without water, temple without God, fort without king and so on. Now there was an eighth one – college without students!

We were facing the greatest existential crisis in medical education after the period in 1939-1941 when the LMP course we were running had been discontinued, and the institution had not been ready to start the MBBS course. This time, not admitting MBBS and Super Specialty candidates affected the morale of the college and community, and also had a great impact on the running of the Specialty departments. Patient care in the hospital was affected because of the shortage of junior postgraduates and the undue stress placed on senior postgraduates.

We hoped that the full hearing of the case scheduled for September would resolve the matter and actually permit us to admit students, but September turned to October and October turned to November. Hopes of admitting for the year had completely gone. Come December, our case was transferred to a new Bench. Our core team of lawyers warned us that this particular bench was a tough one. We tried to stay optimistic. After all, we had the prayer support of the whole CMC community, alumni and well-wishers across the country, and so many parts of the world.

But a visit to one of the senior lawyers of the Supreme Court, a previous attorney general of India, whom we were requesting to represent us in Court the next day, brought us face to face with reality. On hearing the particulars of the bench, we had been allocated to the next day, the senior lawyer refused to argue our case. Those of us from Vellore who were there, were shocked. We realized what a dire situation we were in. This time we actually felt crushed. The words of Psalm 143 seemed so true...

> "The enemy pursues us, he crushes us to the ground, He makes us dwell in darkness.
>
> So my spirit grows faint within me, my heart within me is dismayed.
>
> I spread out my hands to you; I thirst for you like a parched land
>
> Answer me Quickly, Lord; my spirit fails
>
> Do not hide your face from me
>
> Let the morning bring me word of your unfailing love".

O how much we wished that the morning would bring us good news, that the next day the judge would appreciate our high standards of health care, our subsidized education, and our contributions to the nation and give us autonomy in admissions as in the previous years. I could hardly sleep that night. I woke up at 4 o'clock and couldn't go back to sleep. So much was at stake. We just needed that favorable hearing so badly, but the chances looked so slim. We knew God could work miracles, but was he going to?

I opened the Bible: *"Ask and you will receive, seek and you will find, knock and the door will be opened to you"*. Matthew 7:7:

If God has promised that when we ask, we will be heard and when we seek, we will find and when we knock the door, it will be opened, I wondered again why our prayers were not being heard. Maybe we had not been asking for the right thing. So, I thought about what we actually wanted God to do for us. What was the core of our mission, our identity that needed absolute protection? That would surely be his will for us and what we should ask for.

Extensive discussions amongst our faculty, lawyers, the Executive Committee and council made it clear to us that what we needed the most was for every one of our MBBS, postgraduate and super specialty seats to be protected in the categories we have always had. Our sponsored seats had to be protected for our missions and our open seats for students from all parts of the country. Even under the most severe pressure, that was what we would have to preserve.

So, I realized that that was what we should be asking God for. Not telling him how our seats should be protected by an immediate order of the Supreme Court – but simply that they should be protected. We had to leave the methodology to God. And so, I asked God for the protection of every single one of our seats. That not one of them would go out of our control. And I believed that God was in control. That he would protect every single seat. He had to – because he had promised he would hear us. I had surrendered the problem to our God who can move mountains.

I felt at peace. It was 6 AM. The morning had brought word of his unending love for us. A love that assured us of his favour and protection. I knew that the outcome of our problem with admissions would not be decided by how well the lawyers argued our case or who the Judges were, who were going to hear our case. The outcome would be decided by our all-powerful God and when everything was in his control, we did not need to be afraid. And so….

We did not have to worry that morning when the best lawyer in the country was in a terrible mood before he argued our case …

When the Judges in the Supreme Court that day did not seem to have the least inclination to hear our case, and on the contrary set us back in the whole legal battle by asking us to go back and fight the original case against NEET, an almost hopeless battle, that had been put on hold about 5 years ago….

We did not have to despair when the next month a new set of Judges refused to hear our case and requested the Registrar of the court to find another suitable bench.

Nor when the Court was not able to find a suitable bench to hear our case for the next seven months, making it clear that we would have to comply with the common counselling regulation and admit candidates only through the government.

There were certainly moments of doubt, but we had a promise from God: a covenant he had made to protect us - every seat. I could not imagine how that could happen and did not even try to but knew that we would simply have to keep going in trust. And remain faithful to him.

Psalm 18:25 says *"To the faithful you show yourself faithful…."*Our responsibility was to remain faithful and leave the rest in God's hands.

We waited for the next hearing, but despite all attempts of our lawyers, we were not listed. We had to start making plans for admissions through the state. We knew the important aspects to our admission process were 3-fold:

The first, that candidates representing all the churches and Christian organisations that owned CMC had to be admitted and that at least a proportion of our postgraduate and super specialty seats needed to be reserved for such candidates.

The second aspect of our admission that had to be preserved was that our candidates had to have the right qualities and aptitude to become caring and competent physicians and surgeons, with a long-term commitment to serve their missions after completing their course. Candidates admitted for the PG and specialty courses had to be capable of providing the high-quality patient care expected of any team member at CMC.

The third aspect of our admissions that had to be preserved was an all-India distribution of candidates– potentially threatened by the new regulation that authorised the state government to conduct admissions.

The Registrar of the college and her team collected a lot of data that showed that in the past, our interviews and special tests had had a significant impact on our admission process and the choosing of the right candidates for training in CMC. So, it was decided that we had to try and preserve at least some sort of assessment of candidates through interviews and special tests before admission through the government.

But preliminary discussions with State Officials made it clear that this would not be permitted. We had to approach the problem differently.

Clinical experience had been a must for all candidates admitted to postgraduate courses in CMC, and now that our interviews and clinical tests were now not permitted, we realized that every candidate applying for courses involving patient care would simply have to have documented clinical experience for a minimum period of time. And experience in any clinical setup could not be recognized– it had to be in areas of need as we had always mandated in the past, to demonstrate a commitment to serve. This rule would have the added benefit of giving credit to those who had already worked in the missions or government PHCs or other needy areas. Our postgraduate seat matrix for admissions through the state therefore took both sponsorship and clinical experience into account. And we waited for the State officials to call us.

About 10 days before common counselling was due to start for the PG admissions, we were asked to surrender a proportion of our PG seats to the government quota. We were startled, because the courts had protected our seats as belonging entirely to the college without surrender to the government for the past 25 years. We humbly submitted to them that this was not possible. Several legal discussions later, we heaved a sigh of relief because the state acknowledged the freedom the courts had awarded us to reserve all seats for the college. We returned thinking all was well.

But 2 days before the date for counselling, we received a letter from the State that said that they would fill our seats with candidates from the state rank list. This meant 'No reservation' for sponsored candidates or those who had clinical experience in needy areas. Instead, admissions would simply be by NEET marks alone. The battle seemed to be turning against us.

This time we were stunned. The court was on vacation. Our students had given up seats in other good colleges trusting that we would have our admissions with sponsored seats. The departments were waiting for candidates with clinical experience to come in to work in their teams. Everything would be lost at this last moment.

I went back to the office and drew the blinds. I knew God was still in control. That he could still save us from this situation if it was his will. And if it was not, then we had to surrender to whatever outcome faced us.

We worked in the office till 2 AM on various options and then left for Chennai at 4 am.

We met the lawyers in the morning and found that trying to get a stay from the court was not an option. We seemed to have reached the end of the road. The sea lay ahead of us: literally and figuratively since the High court in Chennai faces the Bay of Bengal.

I called a respected teacher and previous administrator and asked for advice. He suggested us to go back and talk with the State officials. With prayers and great trepidation, we did so.

And this time, to our great wonder, they agreed to all our requests: Our sponsored category, our reservation of seats for those who have already got work experience and the need for a bond for the majority of candidates. In fact, the officials were pleased that we gave so much importance to service.

The Red Sea had parted for us. God had made a way for us to go ahead. He was showing us he cared for us and our service for him. Now we could be sure that he had heard the prayers of our community in CMC and our friends and well-wishers all over the world. It was a centenary miracle for CMC.

On the 26th of May we filled our PG seats with students exactly the way we had planned. The number of vacant seats at the end of the counselling process was even less than in the previous years. We returned to Vellore with immensely grateful hearts. I remembered God's promise in Psalm 126, *Those who go out weeping, carrying seed to sow, will return with songs of joy, carrying sheaves* **with them.**

The undergraduate admissions followed on similar lines. Our sponsored seats with reservation for all our churches were ultimately protected.

The Super Specialty admissions were next. This time the counselling process was through the Directorate General of Health Services. Prior discussions with the concerned officials had already warned us that we would not be able to reserve seats for sponsored candidates. We had had a quick round of discussions with faculty, the Executive Committee and Council and decided to have a mandatory bond for all candidates and a financial penalty for nonfulfillment of the bond.

The online counselling process for the Super specialty courses went off smoothly by God's grace. Amazingly, we had the exact same proportion of Christians we would have got if we had been permitted to have sponsored seats. God had worked it out yet again. And this time, with even less help from us.

Friends, as we face all these problems related to admission in the last two years, I often wonder whether the troubles we were facing had anything to do with our relationship with God, whether we had wandered away from his will, and were facing the consequences. Whether, his absolute favour had been withdrawn because we were wandering from his path. So many questions and doubts...

But now I know it is exactly the opposite. He loves us with an unfailing love. He is working behind the scenes to protect us and help us as we go about in our amateur and clumsy ways to serve him.

We need not worry about all the obstacles and problems that seem to threaten our identity and credibility as a Christian institution – only commit them to him whom we follow. And then be patient, faithful and responsibly follow the path he clears for us. And of course, be prepared for the miracles!

Towards a Renewal
in the Ministry of Healing

Valson Thampu

"Our age is without passion. Everyone knows a great deal, we all know which way we ought to go and all the different ways we can go, but nobody is really willing to move". -Soren Kierkegaard

C hristian Medical College, Vellore, began as an adventure in faith. Faith, says St. Paul, is foolishness to the Greeks. The professional and technical expertise that drive the routine work of the hospital and medical college is Greek, so to speak. This Greekness is sure to increase as years go by. It poses serious challenges that clamour for attention.

To the Greeks, what mattered most was objective, reflective knowledge. The basic problem was ignorance -or the lack of knowledge- which generated evil and suffering. The foremost good was the maximum expansion of knowledge and skills. This left very little margin for faith in professional activity. The mysteries of spirit could not be accommodated within the tightly and rationally organized fabric of Hellenic intellectual resources.

Faith, however, is a key determinant of the stature and scope of a human being. Faith is man's link with God, with whom all things are possible. With faith a little as a mustard seed one can move mountains.

Faith links the unmanifest and the manifest (Heb. 11:1). It represents a different order of possibilities, compared to reason, vis-a-vis resources and needs. Faith quickens the uniquely human and individual potencies in individuals by connecting them to what is beyond the physical and the natural.

Two things are of paramount importance to a patient -the person of the healer and the ambience of the sanctuary of healing. Both are influenced substantially by faith. There exists an unresolved, and profitless, tension between faith and science. This tension is bypassed via compartmentalization, with scientific-technical resources deemed solely relevant to a professional practice of medicine. That this model of medicine -the bio-medical model- is too narrow to accommodate the complexities of the healing process which has been recognized for decades. Even so, its enlargement to accommodate spiritual resources in the practice of the ministry of healing has seldom been addressed to the extent it deserves to be. As a result, the ministry of healing -as against the pursuit of medicine as a profession with exponentially increasing scientific-technical know-how- is languishing. There is an urgent need to revive and renew the 'ministry' aspect of the healing vocation. Upon this issue hinges the triad embedded in our present theme.

The problem, when it comes to spiritual matters, is that we take almost everything for granted. The current practice of medical education, and the practice of medicine that ensues it, turn a blind eye to the spiritual aspect of holistic healing. Even when medical education is administered through Christian medical colleges, the spiritual elements remain, at best, somewhere on the sidelines as institutional extras. They do not play an effective role in the academic formation of would-be health personnel. Consider an illustrative instance.

How would, a doctor trained in the present system of medical education, respond to the patient beside the pool of Bethesda (Jn.5)? Which diagnostic technology -which model of psychiatric practice-will enable him to deal with the situation as Jesus did? Which line of management, as per current pharmacopeia, will enable a present-day doctor to bridge the chasm between 'wishing' and 'willing' -the invalid wished to be healed (else, he would not have waited for 38 years) but was not willing to be healed (else, he would not have had to stay all of 38 years)- in such cases, which are not uncommon today?

The spotlight in this episode is, clearly, on the persons -the invalid and the healer. They are situated in a subjective sanctuary of truth. What existed till then was a sphere of objectivity. A stirring happens out there. Someone or the other helps this patient to get into the pool first. The plight of the patient was viewed objectively. Seen from the outside, this man is an invalid. The problem is only physical. Yet, it was anything but physical. It was spiritual. It is instructive to recall the testimony of Karl Jung that nearly 80% of the patients who sought his help needed no medicines at all. What they needed was forgiveness. I doubt if there is a doctor today who will have Jung's courage in acknowledging it.

It is not my purpose here to advocate a dilution or compromise in the level of our scientific-technological expertise. I am only pleading for an enlargement of the medical paradigm, not its dilution. Even as a society goes farther afield in the scientific-technological culture, argued Nicolai Berdyaev, it needs to send its spiritual roots deeper and deeper. He advocated the evolution of a new spiritual genre commensurate with the emerging genius of science. What we find, on the contrary, is a growing gulf, resulting from the stagnation of the spiritual, and the ever-burgeoning wares of the scientific-technological. This breed, and seemingly legitimizes, a prejudice against the spiritual as anachronistic -a sort of irrelevant baggage that needs to be either discarded altogether or, at best, accommodated in sterile zones, avoiding any integration between the spiritual and the scientific.

There is a problem with 'faith', which needs to be addressed as pertinent to our theme. An element of the 'absurd,' -as Soren Kierkegaard pointed out- inheres in faith. The 'absurd' -or the paradoxical- is what cannot be dealt adequately with the resources of intelligence. The absurd indwells the divine-human space, or the realm of faith. He uses the illustration of the intended sacrifice of Isaac. How is rationality to bridge the terrifying chasm between the promise that Abraham will be father of nations and the call to him to sacrifice the only son of promise? 'Offence' bristles in this space. There is no intellectual or academic resource relevant to mediating this offence which is of the essence of faith. It is this that makes faith a stumbling block to the Jews and foolishness to the Gentiles (I Cor. 1:23).

The offence of faith is, therefore, likely to aggravate even as we are more and more conditioned in the culture and worldview of modernity driven by science and technology. This poses serious challenges to the ministry of healing, which are, regrettably, taken for granted. As a result, Christian institutions slip into schizophrenia: harbouring a vertical split between their professional and faith dimensions.

This precipitates a crucial spiritual issue; especially in light of the teachings of Jesus Christ. You shall know a tree, he said, by its fruit. Almost four centuries before Jesus, Socrates in Athens said pretty much the same thing. He insisted that what is known only theoretically and is not acted upon does not exist at all. This insight has a crucial bearing on the 'identity' of CMC. If the resources and dynamism of faith are not expressed through the ministry of healing -as against merely being 'accommodated' in designated slots- how faithful are we as stewards of its Christian identity punctuated by the Ida Scudder legacy? Or, what is 'Christian' about the medical college and hospital we run? It is high time we do an objective and candid audit of this aspect of our identity.

Let me flag yet another issue germane to the present theme. We, in CMC, are increasingly inclined to be obsessed with quantity. In an overwhelming majority of the references to the identity of CMC I have heard over a quarter century, it is always size and scale that preponderate. We take pride, to take just one example, that the attendance at our OPDS exceeds 8000 patients per day. Surely, this is a significant index to the wider 'credibility' the institution commands. But the critical Christian factor is different from this. Jesus provides a measure for the spiritual stature of a Christian institution -the parable of the lost sheep. Quality, not quantity, is its defining feature. This is not to belittle quantity; for, after all, Jesus fed the five thousand. But even there, there is a little boy at the center of the picture. The seed of the miracle is not the crowd. It is the connectedness of the individual -the little boy- to Jesus, and, in turn, Jesus to his Father in heaven. The world may thrive on quantity and flaunt statistics, but spirituality is focused on the individual; whether it be a diminutive Zacchaeus, the rich young man, the woman of Samaria, or the lost sheep.

That is because spirituality is about being authentic persons, or the quality of being children of God. From a spiritual point of view, the ultimate healing resource is the person of the physician or surgeon, who has been quickened -or led into fullness of life- by Christ.

This raises yet another cluster of issues -critically important for the spiritual identity of CMC; all pertaining to 'workload' understood quantitatively. It is most pertinent to recall Jesus' words, "Come to me, all you who are weary and burdened, and I will give you rest." (Mtt. 11:28). The most explicit aspect of this invitation involves the core meaning of hospital -hospitality, or openness to all beyond discriminations on any basis whatsoever. What is significant is that this is not hamstrung by considerations of material resources; for the inviter is one who has nowhere to lay his head (Mtt. 8:20, Lk. 9:58). This takes away the familiar alibi -resource constraints. This is not a matter of mere posturing. Jesus, the inviter, is the exemplar of meekness and faith. "If you have faith of a mustard seed," Jesus said, "you can command mountains to move." Now, to move mountains, as Kierkegaard pointed out, you have to put yourself under the mountains, which is the logic of meekness at work. Meekness has extraordinary powers to mitigate weariness and burden, whereas sullenness and pride inflate and aggravate work-related weariness. It is meekness, not physical or intellectual strength, that empowers us to undertake responsibilities, refining them of the sense of burden and weariness that overhangs it.

'Faith-healing' is often referred to with a magical aura about it. Jesus uses 'faith' -as we should- in a logical-yet-paradoxical sense. Faith is not a license to trade and traffic in mysterious powers, as in faith-healing in a popular sense. Faith is the empowerment, via meekness, to make ourselves available to meeting human needs without looking for alibis. This, if done in the right spirit -or, in partnership with Jesus- caters continually to our personal growth and professional enhancement which mitigates 'burden and weariness'. Even a moment's reflection will convince us that 'burden and weariness' pertain to will power, or the lack of it. If we are deficient in will, even trivial things make us weary. That was the problem with the paralytic (Mk. 2:1ff). He had it in him to carry the bed in which he used to be carried; except that his will was paralyzed. It is a problem more ubiquitous than we care to reckon.

The second issue of critical importance for CMC's ministry of healing is how its employees relate to the institution, or what they perceive as its essence. Jesus addresses this issue, with astounding clarity, profundity and textual economy, in the parable of the Good Samaritan (Lk. 10:25-37). The counterpart of CMC in that parable is the road 'from Jerusalem to Jericho'. That road means different things to different characters in the parable. To the traveler it is a road, plain and simple -a geographical stretch, facilitating mobility from one place to another. To the thieves, it is the road of brutal self-interest. To the priest and the Levite, it is the road of indifference. To the Samaritan, it is the road of mercy, compassion and service; the road, if you like it, is the road of the ministry of healing.

There is nothing fixed about the significance of the 'road to Jericho'. What matters is not who is injured (the victim has no name) but how -or with what spiritual culture- it is walked. The attitude to the traveler -a universal type, for life is a journey- depends on who one is. Accordingly, the identity of the road will be defined. No institution can be 'Christian' in a fixed and guaranteed fashion, except in a nominal sense. Nominal Christianity is anything but Christianity. An institution is in continual need of becoming Christian until thy kingdom come. Heeding what this involves and facilitating its optimum realisation is a crucial aspect of stewarding CMC.

In the days ahead, this would be the decisive issue for CMC for the reason that it is going through inter-generational changes and its human resource component is in flux. The task of enabling every employee, at all levels, to stay connected to the spiritual essence, or 'is-ness', of CMC must be accorded top priority. All the more so now, as CMC is poised for a major phase of growth and geo-physical expansion.

Identity, Credibility, Accountability

Identity

Defining 'identity' is at once political and problematic. Yet it is a crucial and necessary issue in spirituality. Who we are, matters to God; as is evident from the teachings of Jesus. Our spiritual identity is a domain of silent and relentless contestation; the world trying to shape us as its own homogenized children. All cultures work in terms of coercive conformity. The pressure to conform (Rom. 12:2) comes loaded with paradigms of legitimacy. This is powerfully at work in all domains of science and technology, including medical sciences. The dogmatism of 'scientism' is at least as coercive and fundamentalist as religious dogmatism of the most primitive and zealous kind. It is because of this that Christian doctors find it increasingly difficult to draw from their spiritual culture or harness spiritual resources to their professional work. The Christian identity of a health professional is already anemic. There is an incremental loss of nerve in yoking the two together. This has significant consequences for the institution.

Identity is, in itself, an abstraction. It needs to be measured against something else. If there were no non-Christians there would have been no Christians, and vice versa. So, it is important at the individual and institutional levels to be clear about how our identity is defined and measured. A shepherd derives his identity from sheep. If his sheep are faring well, he is a good shepherd. A thief derives his identity from the house he burgles. When we were children, we derived our identity from our parents. Then our identities changed. We became 'the educated', 'the employed', 'the retired', and so on.

The measure of our Christian identity is Jesus Christ. That should be the case, irrespective of who you are, if you are indeed Christian. The problem is that the more distinguished a person feels himself to be -the higher one's professional ego- the more embarrassed he or she becomes about this. If our identity is that of a patient in a 'precarious' state, however, we would not have such a problem. That is why Jesus said, "it is easier for a camel to go through the eye of a needle than it is for a rich man to enter the Kingdom of God." (Mtt. 19:24). The more scientifically/professionally distinguished an institution becomes, the more complex and apologetic becomes the expression and consolidation of its Christian identity. There is a distinct danger that, over a period of time, Jesus ceases to be the 'measure' by which its identity is established. This was the problem that the Ephesian church faced: lost its first love (Rev. 2:4). Jesus ceased to be the 'measure' of its identity.

The Christian identity of CMC has implications, at least, for three important stakeholders: the healing community, the health personnel, and the patients. How an employee serves -or, to revert to the metaphors in the parable of the Good Samaritan, how the road to Jericho is traveled- depends on his awareness of the identity of CMC and his own faith identity and how the two harmonise. It is impossible to exaggerate the importance of this. For decades, the ready identification of employees with the spiritual culture of the institution has been the core strength of CMC. It uplifted them beyond considerations of pay and perks, and the niggling sense of under-privilege that comparisons with their counterparts in other institutions could have provoked. This also means that if and when the Christian identity of CMC gets diluted, a host of issues that remain hypodermic would erupt.

How the faith-identity of CMC may be understood as evolved over time, how it may be strategized today to be enunciated, accentuated and rendered intelligible to the healing community it is -indeed, the society at large- are issues beyond the limited canvas of this paper; and are, hence, merely flagged.

A word needs to be said, though, about the faith-identity of individual employees; especially with reference to strategizing, as mentioned above, a way of stewarding the identity of the institution itself.

A person is Christian, needless to say, on account of his faith. The 'faith' dimension of our identity stems from the fact, as Jesus said, that we are spirit. In his conversation with the woman of Samaria (Jn.4), Jesus reveals that "God is Spirit". We are created in the image and likeness of God (Gen. 1:27). So, we are, in essence, spirit. But the problem is that this awareness remains hidden in a forest of the material, the professional and the technological preoccupations. On account of our mis-formed Christian nurture we are 'spirit' only for an hour or two per week, on Sundays. The rest of the weak we are a different entity and have a different identity. We fool ourselves, if we assume that we can have 'faith' without also being quickened as spirit. For most of the time -especially in the professional domain- we are anything but spirit. We live staggering under a load of daily chores, the 'work-load' that makes us 'weary and heavy-laden'. The burdensomeness of our plight is largely due to the simmering tension between who we are inwardly and what we are obliged to be professionally. Every human being long to be an integrated individual. But professional work, as it has come to be organized even in the best of institutions, is hardly conducive to this need. Alienation smolders in all institutions. Since 'Christian' is the defining aspect of Christian institutions, this also breeds resentment towards Christianity even in Christians.

A major reason for this is the false teaching on Christianity, with an emphasis on its magical aspect. Spirituality is projected as a naive sphere of effortless existence, free from struggle and suffering. The biblical faith is infinitely more complex and realistic, as even a perfunctory glance at the life and teachings of Jesus Christ will prove beyond dispute. In an effort to render Christianity appealing to everyone, its faith-core is caricatured. So, even the educated and well-meaning Christians entertain vague and pagan notions about what it means to be Christian. Overlooking all this, we expect them to be, somehow, perfect Christian professionals just because they happen to be in CMC. This will not do. It is positively unwise, especially now, to take the 'faith' of employees for granted. CMC has an Associate Director for Human Resource Development. Even more importantly, it needs a passionately committed Associate Director for Faith Resource Development. Alternately, the Chaplaincy Department should address this challenge with due preparation and earnestness.

One thing is certain, in the Christian practice of 'healing' -as against the secular practice of curing- the person of the physician is a decisively important part of the healing resources. Spiritually, what we do -or the fruitfulness of what we do- is shaped by who we are. Our efforts will bear fruit, Jesus said, if we abide in him, and he in us (Jn. 15:4). Almighty efforts, superhuman skills and matchless expertise are all to be valued; but they may not guarantee fruitfulness in the healing ministry or in personal life. Today the spotlight is on how much a doctor knows and what skills he holds. Spiritually the spotlight should be on where he stands, and how far he has grown in all-round stature through the work he has done. Only such a doctor can be a healer. A healer, unlike a medical professional, abides with the patient as an aspect of abiding in the Lord. This doesn't mean that he stands at the bedside of his patients all the time. It means that who he is lingers with the patient as a healing influence all the way through. This mitigates the 'burden' of being a healer. 'Burdens' are, by the way, more subjective than is realized. It has a reference to who we are and how we are disposed. What seems burdensome in moods of sullenness seems light and enjoyable in cheerful moods. Also, a healthy adult walk lightly with what would be a crushing burden to an infant. Those who complain about their work-load often do not realize that they are talking more about themselves than about the quantum of the work they do.

Physicians, Jesus said, should heal themselves. Healing, irrespective of whether it takes place in the Christian or secular contexts, involves an element of faith. There will be no medical practice, if patents can't have faith in doctors and hospitals. Medicines and surgical procedures cannot have the desired beneficial effect, if patients are apprehensive and mistrustful. It is, hence, a contradiction in terms to have Christian doctors who have no faith! A century and a half ago, Kierkegaard condemned the Danish Lutheran Church for its 'formalism', by which he meant, nurturing armies of 'unbelieving believers'. He held the Pharisaism of the clergy responsible for it: "the hypocrisy of the clergy who neglect the Christianity they are hired to preach."

The crucial thing, in the end is this: what is our true identity, or our identity before God? Fishers of fish, or fishers of men? (Mk. 1:16-18) Technical means and professional skills will suffice to be fishers of fish. As for being fishers of me, as well, that's a different thing altogether.

Credibility

To me the profoundest formulation of the ingredients of credibility is Jesus's words, "I am the way, the truth and the life" (Jn. 14:6). Here's why-

Truth is the crux of credibility. Truth is experiential, not abstract. The truth of an institution is a matter of how it is experienced by those who relate to it. The truth of CMC will differ from person to person, depending on how its employees or patients relate to it. So, any genuine concern for the credibility of the institution will prioritize the quality and dynamics of connectedness.

The core strength of CMC from its inception has been its community life. CMC's is a healing community which is, itself, in good health. A practically important aspect of this strength is that it offers a stimulating and conducive environment for the professional and spiritual formation of its members. Indeed, the hallmark of a good institution is that it is a place of growth for all who belong to it. In the case of CMC, 'growth' needs to be understood also in a spiritual sense. Individual members of the healing community are enabled, in a variety of ways and through an assortment of experiences, to grow into the CMC-tradition of the healing ministry. This is a great strength, and it should not suffer dilution.

There is a dialogic relationship between the individual and the institution. The individual needs a matrix for his or her professional

and spiritual formation. The essence of the institution, at the same time, needs to be embodied and expressed through its members. The ideal condition for the credibility of an institution is one in which this dialogic process proceeds reciprocally and smoothly. Dissonance between the two -or stakeholders of the healing ministry pulling in contrary directions and all together tangentially to the core vision of the institution- will devastate its credibility.

There is a need, therefore, to enable all stakeholders of CMC to appropriate its institutional heritage. In fact, facilitating this process must be deemed the foremost responsibility of institutional leadership. Even as CMC grows in size and scope, and the cohesion of its community comes under stress as a result, efforts in this direction need to multiply and intensify. There is no substitute for the internal coherence and inviolability of the institution when it comes to maintaining its credibility.

This issue merits a closer look. Individual patients know the institution largely through individual health workers, who serve as the medium through which it is experienced. It is unrealistic to assume that every member of the CMC community is, for the accident of being located within it, a distortion-free medium for the patients and their relatives to experience the institution in its Christian authenticity. Minute and purposive attention needs to be paid to the dynamics that play in this zone all the time.

This is not to argue for creating a Big-Brother-is-watching-you sort of ambience of surveillance. I only wish to underline the fact that administrative intervention can be minimized if individual employees are nurtured adequately in the essence of the institution. There are, in the main, two ways by which individuals make choices, carry our work and conduct themselves. The first is with reference primarily to one's own tastes, interests and conveniences. The second is with reference to the genius of the institution. Today the cultural norm -especially for the elite sections of the society- is that of the autonomous individual. Personal liberty is on a high premium. When stretched beyond a point, this outlook legitimizes the inclination of employees to see the workplace as a place for earning a livelihood, seen more in terms of entitlements and less in terms of responsibilities. The essence of the institution is merely incidental to it. So, commitment to professional excellence and resentment of the Christian character of the institution can co-exist for a while. To such an outlook, the credibility of the institution takes a second place to personal advantages and inclinations.

Truth, in Jesus' perspective, is inseparable from 'the way'. That is to say, it is not an abstraction. It is a continually unfolding reality; or, a reality continually in the making. How you walk the way is more important from the perspective of truth than which segment of the way you walk. A class IV employee who endeavours to embody and honour the spirit of CMC is a greater asset than a professionally top-grade doctor who is too puffed up with pride to let the heritage of CMC culture to influence him. The truth of the institution will remain an abstraction, but for 'the way'. CMC has a distinctive way, of which we should never be apologetic. Rather, we must make every possible effort to ensure that that 'way' is walked with inner motivation and individual conviction by the CMC community as a whole.

'Life' is the lighthouse for truth and way becoming one, which is the secret of the morale of an institution. A hospital, more than any other institution, is a servant of life. The ministry of healing is, seen Christianly, not essentially a domain of technological wizardry or professional glamour. It is the theatre where the battle is joined on behalf of life. But, for that to happen all sections and limbs of the institution must be oriented to life. This life-orientation is, according to Jesus, the quintessence of spirituality or godliness. Christianity dogmatically believes that human nature can stay oriented to life only if it is oriented to God through Jesus, the light of life. Life is essentially spiritual. Considerations of profit and loss, popularity or unpopularity, control and contumacy, are alien to it. Ida Scudder heard the call of life. She left all she had, like one who came upon a pearl of great price for which it was well worth to give up all. This is what life-orientation is – a state of infinite passion for serving, defending, preserving and respecting life. Such an individual sees every patient as a neighbour who deserves to be loved as he loves himself (Lk. 10:27).

In a worldly sense, 'credibility' resides in how one fares in the eyes of men. Spiritually, it rests on how we are seen in the eyes of God. Only such credibility -credibility founded on the eternal- endures.

I have left out on purpose issues pertaining to professional competence, technological assets, and so on; for I believe that all that will not avail CMC -important though they are- if the institution does not exercise wise and vigilant stewardship over its morale, integrity and cohesion. Ultimately, it is the spirit that matters. And institutions, not less than individuals, are spiritual entities.

Contrast facilitates clarity of understanding. I would, therefore, conclude this section by counterpointing 'credibility' with 'comedy,' invoking Socrates, besides Jesus, for the purpose, and returning to the issue of 'truth' with which we began this section. Socrates found hypocrisy comic. A man stands up. He professes his faith. He is keen to appear that he understands his faith. And then goes out and does exactly the opposite, showing that he has understood nothing. Is that not comic, asks Socrates. It is healthier, in comparison, to profess and practice evil. That way, one is, at least, consistent. And consistency is basic to credibility. The Socratic dictum is, "to understand and to understand are two different things." That is to say, we do not really understand until we begin to 'understand' or stand under, what we profess. Or, as Jesus said, only one who does what he knows -via hearing the Word- understands it. He alone is wise (Mtt. 7:24-28).

A secular Christian professional understands Christianity but does not 'understand' it Socratically. He 'understands' -or, as Paul says, conforms to, the 'pattern' of the world, instead (Rom. 12:2). I would flag this as a serious issue vis-à-vis the credibility of CMC.

Accountability

Accountability inheres in faith. This insight underlies the parable of the talents. To live as a free agent of action is to be responsible. In the spiritual paradigm, life and freedom are inseparable; and freedom brings accountability in its wake. But the natural man -the autonomous individual, the one who thinks his life is his freehold- does not want to be accountable to anyone, even to God. As Dostoevsky said, such a person is tormented by freedom because he does not want to hold himself accountable. He is, as Kierkegaard would say, in despair. To be in despair is to will before God either to be not oneself, or to will before God to be oneself. To despair in the first sense of the term is to refuse to become what one ought to be. It is to be stone deaf to the call of God, calling you to be what you need to be. To despair in the second sense is to be obstinate that one will stay, in spite of thunder, just as one is. It slams the door shut against repentance.

In both states, freedom is a casualty. Freedom implies a state of becoming in which one is able to graduate towards life in all its fullness. It is meant to facilitate the realization of who we ought to be. Freedom in that sense is the motive-spring of identity. The Gospel narratives illustrate, time after time, that a human being can be truly himself or herself only through encountering God in Jesus. Jesus is the way. He is also the liberator of captives (Lk. 4:18). If we were to ask William Wordsworth, he would insist that the 'shades of the prison-house' play on all human beings.

Spiritual accountability is primarily a matter of how we steward our life. It is correlated, as Jesus taught, to the extent of our endowments and talents. To be entrusted with much is to be commensurately accountable. So, CMC, which legitimately prides itself on a great tradition, an over-abundance of God's blessings and mercies, is supremely accountable to God.

But there is a factor that undermines accountability. Accountability is shaped and sustained by coherence and inward integrity. An institution which is like the 'valley of dry bones' (Ezk. 37:1-14) -a disjointed aggregation of discrete employees and departments- cannot be in a state of accountability. Accountability is an 'individual' phenomenon. That is to say, only individuals are accountable. Accountability is alien to a crowd. That is why people prefer to do what is unlawful in crowds. They hide behind the impersonality and anonymity of crowds.

Large institutions, such as CMC is, are parallel to crowds. The problem becomes all the more acute when size is complicated with proliferation of specialisations that exist as vertical silos. Consider, as Tolstoy did, the legal delivery system to understand this. The policeman arrests a criminal and produces him before the judge. The judge listens to arguments by lawyers who, as experts, work according to the peculiarity of their discipline, by which law is more important than truth or justice. The judge condemns the criminal, say, to capital punishment. The executioner takes over. A life is snuffed out. Along this chain of processes, no individual agency -the policeman, the lawyer, the judge, the executioner- is accountable for what he does. He simply does -as Rudolf Eichmann said when he was tried in Jerusalem - carries out his duty. In contrast, a potter is responsible for the pots he fashions; for he is involved in a whole, integrated activity. Moderns systems are designed, willy-nilly, to obscure accountability.

In a spiritual sense, accountability applies, first and foremost, at the individual level. In the parable of the talents, each servant is called in an individual. He has to settle the account for himself, not for anyone else. The matter is not dealt with en masse. In a large institution with thousands of employees it is next to impossible to implement accountability of this kind. The Director of CMC, for example, cannot watch over every single employee and hold him or her to account. (He should not do it, even if he can.) The feasible thing to do is to make each person a judge of his own doings. The conventional term for this is 'conscience'. Conscience is the bridge between the individual and something larger than himself -God. (Or, if you like, as per the secular dogma, the mores of the society.) The autonomous, self-accentuating individual deems himself exempt from the duty to be accountable to any authority beyond himself for who he is and what he does.

Also, accountability is linked to our growth as human beings. That is the point illustrated through the transformation of Zacchaeus. When he was a 'man small of stature' the notion of accountability was alien to him. His world was full of opportunities and entitlements. Zacchaeus gives a stern warning against the universal tendency to divorce entitlements (or rights) from accountability. The outcome immediate to his personal transformation through Jesus is that he is re-located in a world of accountability. To be accountable is to be able to see a world of needs in which we are placed. This is also, incidentally, the essence of being a neighbour, as Jesus teaches the expert in canon law (Lk. 10:25-37). Neighbour is -Kierkegaard writes while commenting specifically on this text- the one you discover while doing your duty. No duty, no neighbour: that is the spiritual formula. It can be re-phrased as -No neighbour, no accountability.

The seductiveness of pettiness is that the range of one's accountability remains comfortably small. (We call this our comfort-zone). Jesus held himself responsible for humankind as a whole because in him, as Paul says, the fullness of godhead dwelt richly. There is always the danger that individual pettiness is mistaken for being in personal liberty insofar as it is a state in which the individual is not constrained by accountability.

In light of the above, an institution that takes its 'accountability' quotient seriously will pay appropriate attention at least to two frontiers. First, it will cater, via institutional culture and ambience, to the holistic development of individual employees. Second, it will prioritize the inner cohesion and integrity -the 'purity'- of the institution. It is commonly observed that individual employees who do not wish to be accountable are eager to undermine the coherence of the institution.

The familiar strategy for dodging accountability is manufacturing excuses. This Jesus illustrates through the parable of the wedding banquet. The parable offers yet another crucial insight. To dodge responsibility is to consign oneself to irrelevance, condemnation and misery.

The triad of identity, credibility, and accountability can be distilled into the essence of being an authentic individual in whom love for God gets expressed as love for the neighbour (Lk. 1:27). In the mission context, the institution takes the place of the individual. I give below a skeletal account of what, in Kierkegaard's view, are the essential features of being an authentic -that is to say, a spiritually sound- individual. Such a person-

-stands before God in a state of God-awareness, undimmed by the haze of conjured up excuses. He renounces the luxury of hiding behind excuses, which enhances personal authenticity.

-is a unified, integrated self, guided by a single purpose, which is the essence of 'purity of heart. This was the strength of Ida Scudder. To be pure of heart, to Kierkegaard, is to 'will one thing' as against being double-minded and tossed about by every passing wind (James 1:7).

-is a responsible self, who in freedom gives account for one's decisions or failures to decide. One's spiritually authentic self is constituted by the choices and decisions one makes.

-exists as a unique self that possesses a dignity above the crowd. The individual stands over and against the collectivity. To be an individual is to resist the conformity-ideals of the crowd and its ideologies. It is far more important to emphasize this in our times, characterized by its coercive and invasive agenda of homogenization, which weakens all aspects of individuality; in particular, accountability.

Spiritual freedom of the individual has two facets: remorse and repentance. Remorse involves the backward glance, the spiritual freedom, to learn from mistakes. Repentance is the forward glance, the willingness to heed the call to enter a new heaven and a new earth. Remorse calls us back; repentance calls us forward. This is made possible only in a state of individual coherence. A human being who is no more than a succession of postures and pretensions can experience neither remorse nor repentance. An institution replicates on a mega scale the patterns operative at the individual level. Institutions too need to undergo remorse and repentance. There are no short-cuts to renewal. Clearly, CMC has reached a phase in his unfolding history when such an experience of institutional renewal is critical and urgent. It is a sign of the residual vitality of a Christian institution that it is willing to enter such a state. The alternative to repentance and regeneration is death. Hard-heartedness, as the book of Exodus illustrates through the instance of Pharaoh, betokens death-orientation.

CMC, as Ida Scudder said, is not a mere institution; it is an unveiling, in the sphere of health care, of the Kingdom of God. Life is the culture of that Kingdom. Hence it is that, prefiguring this pattern, Moses, having led Israel to the door-step of the Promised Land -the Old Testament trope for the Kingdom of God- exhorts them: "This day I place before you the way of life and the way of death. Choose life!"

Identity-Credibility-Accountability

Joyce Ponnaiya

The debate on whether education, health care and other types of services can or should be characterized as "Christian" is an old one. There is a strong argument in favour of separating religion and state, and for keeping health, education, charitable work in the secular domain. Equally strong is the argument that most of the major religions expect good works from their followers and there are explicit commands on how these are to be performed.

In the present day, there is an increasing polarization of societies based on religion, and some would see putting religious labels on education and health care as divisive. As Christian Medical College and Hospital, what is our understanding of "Christian" medical education and health care.

I do not want to dwell on identity, credibility and accountability of Christian individuals, because commitment to Christ is a very personal decision, and each of us finds different ways to express this commitment in our lives. More challenging is the Christian identity of organizations and institutions and what that means in terms of our collective witness, credibility and accountability.

Identity

Recently I have been involved in editing a book of daily devotions for and by Christian health professionals. The contributions came from over 130 individuals from 36 countries. When I received the first set of over 100 submissions, I found that about half were based on Jesus' teachings from the Sermon on the Mount and of these about half were based on the passage from **Matthew 5:13–15:** Being Salt and Light. So, I would like to look at Christian Identity as defined in this passage.

Salt: Salt was and still is a vital ingredient of our food. It is used in small quantities as seasoning when it acts by enhancing the flavours and taste of the other ingredients. If the salt is in excess and draws attention to itself, then the food is unpalatable. Salt is also used as a preservative. Before the days of refrigeration, it was used to preserve meat and vegetables as it retards putrefaction. Salt is also known for its use in medicine as an anti-inflammatory agent and disinfectant. Jesus describes the value of salt as being in its intrinsic "saltiness". When this is lost, it becomes worthless.

Light: In John 8:12 Jesus says, "I am the light of the world". When he asks us to be the light of the world, it is a call to reflect his light.

In all cultures and religions, darkness is symbolic of sin, sickness, ignorance, superstition, poverty, despair, oppression, inequality and exclusion. Being light means engaging in the war against all these types of darkness. Unlike salt which is most effective when it works quietly and unobtrusively, light is expected to declare itself. As followers of Christ, we need to ask for the wisdom to know when to speak up and when to let our work speak for itself.

Fragrance: St Paul uses another symbol of identity – incense (2 Corinthians 2:14). "But thanks be to God who always leads us in triumphal procession in Christ, and through us spreads everywhere the fragrance of the knowledge of him. For we are to God the aroma of Christ amongst those who are being saved and those who are perishing".

The image here is of incense which was carried in procession, separating the armies of the victorious Romans and the vanquished city. The fragrance of the incense was the same, but to the Romans was symbolic of power, success and celebration, while to the defeated army it signified defeat, humiliation and disgrace. We are called to be authentic. How we are perceived by others should not change the way we present ourselves.

In summary, Christian Identity should encompass the following:

I.   Commitment to Jesus Christ and obedience to his commands

II. Integrity: no mismatch between what we believe, profess, practice

III. Honesty: in speech and actions

IV. Compassion: a special focus on those who are less privileged and vulnerable in society as commanded by Jesus in his Great Commission.

V. Humility: ascribing glory to God for our achievements.

Credibility: is the quality of being trusted or believed. Establishing a good reputation for integrity, honesty and reliability makes for credibility. Going back to Matthew 5:16, "Let your light shine before men, that they may see your good deeds and praise your father in heaven."

> "A good name is more desirable than great riches; to be respected is better than silver or gold."
>
> Proverbs 22:1.

The good name of an institution is built up over many years of service. It is spread by word of mouth of satisfied clients rather than created by advertisement and hype. Credibility is fragile and it takes only a couple of missteps to lose trust that has been built up over the years. Depending on God's guidance while making decisions, creating a culture of honesty and integrity, and consciously passing down values to the next generation are important in maintaining credibility.

Accountability: Most of us would accept that in the final analysis we are accountable to God. Romans 4:12 "So then each of us will give an account of himself to God". However, in an organization, it is important also to be accountable to each other. Being accountable requires trust and the ability to relate to each other in a non-judgmental way.

Leadership is often isolating, and it is important for leaders to have a support system. Someone who is wise, with a reputation for integrity and with sound values should be consulted at times when difficult decisions need to be made. Praying with such a person often helps resolve issues.

Accountability also means recognizing and taking responsibility for mistakes and taking steps to set things right. Christian organizations and institutions have a great responsibility at this time to be seen as beacons of integrity, accountability and compassion. May God help us as we endeavour to be his witnesses.

Accountability and Christian Healthcare

Hugh Skeil

F ree will means that we have been entrusted with the ability and the necessity to take decisions. Decisions bring responsibility, and we are accountable for our decisions. We are capable of deciding between right and wrong, and responsible for our action. However, when a person steals something that belongs to other, then one is responsible and should be made accountable for that action.

"Very few healthy things in the Christian life happen in secret. If you cannot or will not tell your spouse, your peers, or your superiors about something, then accountability falters" (Chapell, p.138).

Jesus told his followers to pray and give alms privately, but even (perhaps especially) in these areas of our lives we remain accountable to God. We should not be ashamed if what we do in secret is shouted from the mountain tops. Our lives are becoming increasingly transparent, whether we like it or not, and the call for greater accountability in leaders, in government, in healthcare and charitable organizations is becoming deafening.

God's purpose for us is to be righteous. Not just to act righteously, but to live in a right relationship with him and with others. However, we have a choice in this. Because God has given us free will, we are able to take decisions. These decisions may take us towards or away from righteousness. When we take decisions, we are responsible and accountable for them and the outcome. Responsibility, and its close relations accountability and stewardship, are rooted in the Bible. Creation, the fall, atonement and judgement all speak of responsibility and accountability. God's omnipresence and omniscience and the doctrine of final judgement remind us that however much we succeed in trying to hide things now, all will be laid bare, and we will have to give an account before God of our stewardship of resources entrusted to us, our treatment of our neighbour and our obedience to his commands.

But is an organisation able to take decisions? Does it have responsibilities, and can it be made accountable? An organisation is capable of harming people and the environment. However, since an organisation isn't capable of taking decisions, the responsibility lies with the leadership and other decision makers – all of whom are accountable in various ways for the impact that the organisation has. Apart from the large scale strategic and operational decisions they take, the leadership is also responsible for ensuring that the employees and agents of the organisation do not cause harm to others both within and outside the organisation. Various advantages may accrue to an organisation from acting in a socially responsible way, but for a Christian individual or organisation these are a by-product but not the reason for responsible actions. We should do good because it is the right thing to do, not because it may benefit us. The minimum level of socially responsible behaviour is complying with legal and regulatory requirements. Various levels can be added culminating in loving God and loving your neighbour as yourself. Christian individuals and organisations are called to the very highest level.

What does all this mean for healthcare institutions, particularly those that identify themselves as Christian? Healthcare and health research are unique in the relationship needed between care provider and "customer" - detailed personal interaction, intimate physical contact, and extreme vulnerability as the patient submits to tests and procedures often while unconscious that all carry some level of risk and may have fatal consequences. This demands extraordinary levels of integrity and responsibility in the carer, and great trust in the patient. All these require accountability. However, despite having a long history of strong history of ethical principles, in many respects healthcare lags behind some other professions and business sectors in its accountability and transparency. Useful lessons can be learned from, for example the Code of Ethics for Professional Accountants. This article concludes by suggesting some practical steps for healthcare organisations to enhance accountability.

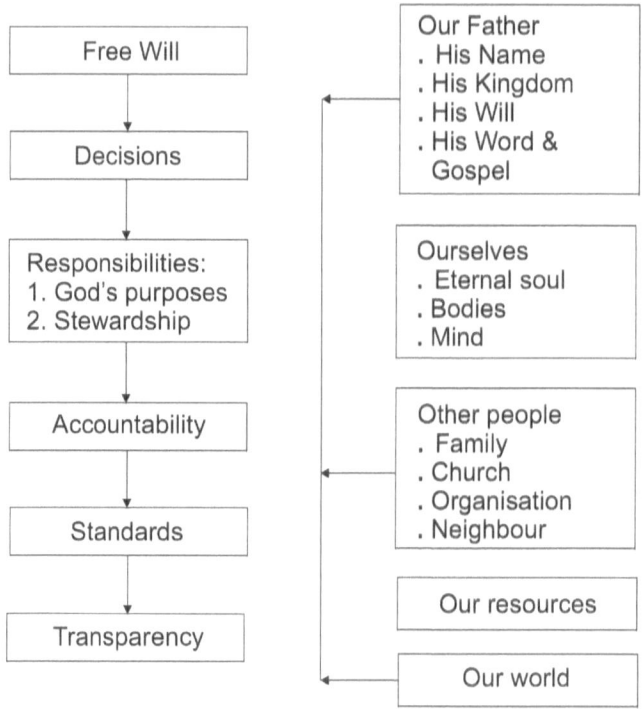

Theological basis of accountability

The Creation story tells us that God made human beings, both male and female in his image. This is the most important human identifier, and it is so important that it over-rides all petty distinctions we may choose to make according to gender, race, intelligence, or those based on human constructs such as caste, language or bank balance. It is the basis for the dignity of all human beings, and the foundation of equity.

Right in the very first chapter of Genesis (1:26-30) God gave mankind responsibility to care for the garden, and this charge is repeated in Genesis 2:15. Humans are given "dominion" but that does not mean "domination" but rather stewardship, in the words of John Stott, "Our dominion is a delegated and therefore a responsible dominion ... the earth belongs to us not because we made it or own it, but because the Maker has entrusted it to us ... we are not kings, ruling our own territory, but viceroys ruling it on the King's behalf ... we are accountable to him for our stewardship." (Stott, 1984: pp114f).

God gave human beings free will, the ability to make choices and decisions. This leads to responsibility and accountability. When Adam and Eve used their free will to disobey God, the first consequence was guilt, and they tried to hide from God, rather than face up to the evening progress review. Once exposed they tried to shift the blame on others. Trying to hide what we have done is the opposite of transparency and the enemy of accountability. Making excuses and passing the blame are examples of refusing to take responsibility for our actions.

After murdering his brother, Cain protests, "Am I my brother's keeper?" Gen. 4:9-10. Like him we want to offload responsibility and accountability for brother, neighbour, fellow human being. However, Cain is held accountable for his brother's blood. Later this was built into the Law, with capital punishment the sentence for murder, "Whoever sheds the blood of man, by man shall his blood be shed," Gen. 9:6. Even in the case of an unsolved murder, there was a sense that the collected community could be held responsible. A sacrifice and ritual were required with a prayer: "do not hold your people accountable for the bloodshed of an innocent person." (Deut. 21:8)

The Covenants established in the Old Testament between God on the one side and Noah, Abraham and the Children of Israel on the other, show God committing himself to his people. At the same time, he calls them to responsible, righteous living, and holds them accountable when they fail to comply. We should be especially careful of our words. For example, Deuteronomy 23:21 stresses the importance of keeping vows offered before God.

Personal decisions, responsibility and accountability for the outcome comprise a theme that runs throughout Scripture. In Judges and the historical books, the decisions taken by a leader or king affect the whole nation, and the leader is accountable to God for his conduct. In Ezekiel and Zechariah religious leaders are shepherds, responsible for caring for their sheep – and accountable for any that are harmed. The people as a whole choose to follow God, or to stray and have to live with the consequences. An individual sin, and the law holds him accountable, and even his grandchildren and great grandchildren may be affected. Even when, without any malicious intent, we are the cause of harm falling on another (for example if our bull escapes from its field and goes someone) we are accountable. People are accountable for the way they carry on their business and the way they treat their servants. Communities are accountable for the way they treat strangers, aliens and the destitute. The watchman posted on the walls is responsible for warning the people when danger approaches – if he fails to warn, peoples' blood will be on his hands (Eze. chapters 3 and 33). The prophets hold even foreign nations accountable before God for their unjust and cruel actions (for example Jeremiah 46-50).

But in the Old Testament there is a growing awareness that we cannot bear the weight of our own transgressions. The ancient Israelites had a kind of solution on the day of Atonement. While one goat was sacrificed, the other was chosen to be the scapegoat. Its job was to bear the sins of the community away into the wilderness.

On the cross Jesus cried out, "It is finished!" (John 19:30). The Greek word John uses for this is *tetelestai* – was also used to describe the complete repayment of a debt. In some mysterious way the atonement involves God taking responsibility for our failure to keep our side of the Covenant. "Surely, he took up our infirmities and carried our sorrows, yet we considered him stricken by God, smitten by him, and afflicted. But he was pierced for our transgressions, he was crushed for our iniquities; the punishment that brought us peace was upon him, and by his wounds we are healed." Is. 53: 4,5.

Much of the teaching and many of the parables of Jesus emphasise stewardship, personal responsibility and ultimate accountability. "But I tell you that every careless word that people speak, they shall give an accounting for it in the day of judgement". Matt 12:36. Tenants left to manage a vineyard, a steward placed in charge of the household while the master was away, three servants each entrusted with a sum of money to manage as they wish. All are accountable. When the Master returns, he audits their performance. Whatever is hidden will be brought to light and even shouted from the rooftops (Matt 10: 26,27). There is also a concept of hierarchy of responsibility: "From everyone who has been given much, much will be demanded; and from the one who has been entrusted with much, much more will be asked". Luke 12:48

Mathew 25 contains some very disturbing parables about the Parousia, the return of the King. The five foolish virgins failed to plan, but otherwise seem to do everything right. They ran out of oil, and rushed off to buy more – but were too late, and the door was closed.

Revelation 20:21 depicts judgement day, with books of account opened and the entire human race coming together to give an account of their stewardship. There is no escaping this final exposure. People will try to run and hide, terrified, like Adam. They will cry out to the rocks to hide them, but there will be nothing they can do to escape.

In John chapter 3, shortly after the famous verse 16, we read: "This is the verdict: Light has come into the world, but men loved darkness rather than light, because their deeds were evil. Everyone who does evil hates the light and will not come into the light for fear that their deeds will be exposed. But whoever lives by the truth comes into the light, so that it may be seen plainly that what he has done has been done through God." John 3:19-21. Our natural inclination is to hide away from the searchlight of God's presence. But it is only when we step into this light and allow the accounting to take place, that God's grace heals us.

Thus, the Bible calls us firstly to righteous, holy living. But knowing that we will fall encourages us not to try hide our failures and our guilt but bring it to the Cross of Christ. Transparency is the best policy that allows for forgiveness, while providing a good motivation to resist temptation.

Organisations and responsibility

> *No man is an island,*
>
> *Entire of itself,*
>
> *Every man is a piece of the continent,*
>
> *A part of the main.* (John Donne)

Individuals take decisions all the time and are responsible and accountable for their decisions.

The concept of the "Social Contract" was first posited by Plato and Socrates but in more modern times it was extensively developed by Hobbes. We surrender some of our rights and freedoms, in order to gain the security, peace and orderliness of living in a regulated community. It allows for a totally secular argument as to why we should pay taxes, obey the government rules, refrain from insisting on our rights, and help others around us. Once we have "signed up" to this contract we have to keep to its rules. However, the Social Contract is not a Christian concept, and it should not be the reason for conforming to Society's rules and norms.

People often blame "the company" or "the system" for cruel, unfeeling things that they have to do as employees or agents – for example the bailiff who repossesses someone's home on behalf of the bank because the mortgage is in arrears. However, we cannot blame the bank, anymore than we can blame the rain for causing a flood. Organisations, like inanimate objects and wild animals cannot be considered responsible or accountable for their actions.

Yet organisations can have a huge impact on individuals, communities, entire nations and even the globe. We cannot ignore them or say that there is no such thing as "corporate social responsibility". Individual people, not the company, are ultimately responsible for a Bhopal tragedy or the payment of slave labour rates to employees.

"In the actions of nations, such as war, there is a vast and solemn responsibility somewhere; but it is often extremely difficult to locate whether it is in the ruler, the ministry or the people. So interesting and perplexing are such problems often that a morality for bodies of people, as distinguished from individuals, is felt by many to be the great desideratum of ethics at the present time". (Stalker, 1915)

Organisations are tools that work on behalf of people, and it is people who take the decisions and who are ultimately responsible for the consequences. Everyone in an organisation makes decisions, but those at higher levels of authority who have higher responsibilities: their decisions tend to affect more people. This is one of the reasons why compensation levels rise with growing seniority. But the higher authority and greater power wielded by the leadership demands that they must be held accountable, and must be transparent, except where there are necessary commercial or legal reasons for keeping things hidden.

Apart from the large scale strategic and operational decisions they take, the leadership is also responsible for ensuring that the employees and agents of the organisation do not cause harm to others both within and outside the organisation.

- Who is accountable to whom?
- Individual to organisation and state & vice versa – social contract
- Organisational - stakeholder theory, legitimacy theory
- leaders to others
- individual responsibility towards each other – physical mental social and spiritual health

- towards Church and other partners
- towards God
- holding others accountable – particularly community leadership, medical establishment, government
- But is stakeholder theory a Christian concept? Or legitimacy theory? Is it all about enlightened self-interest – or is there a different compulsion at work for the Christian and Christian organisations?

Why should we act responsibly?

Why should an organisation act responsibly? Is it to comply with the "Social contract", or to enhance the brand? Some people talk of CSR as a risk reduction strategy – it avoids many of the problems associated with bad publicity. Another reason advanced for responsible behaviour by organisations is Legitimacy Theory. This suggests that are all good things that can flow out of acting responsibly and being accountable – enlightened self-interest.

Christians – righteousness, fostering right relationships with God and others. Doing right because it is right, rather than because it may be to our benefit. But does that mean that we can do without accountability? No, because we are flawed human beings and never hold to our ideals – even more so when bound together in an organisation which seems to take on a life and momentum and consciousness of its own, allowing us to say - "I hate to do this but it's the system". So we need accountability both for individuals and for the organisation. And accountability only operates when there is transparency.

Levels of social responsibility
- Duty of Care / Responsibility levels:
- Legal obligations – regulations, social contract
- Industry or professional standards

Non malfeasance:

The duty not to harm another – even unintentionally.

- Our general responsibility beyond this for other human beings, both present and future. The key legal case Donaghue vs. Stevenson [1932] set the precedence that a person could be held liable for harm suffered by another owing to their "negligence" - even though they had never intended any harm and had no prior knowledge of or contact with the person harmed. Later cases established that a surveyor can be held liable if a party with whom he had no contractual obligation relies on his negligently prepared report on a property. The duty of care extends to those who may reasonable expect to rely on an expert's statements.

- Other legal cases take this one step further. A property owner even owes a duty of care to a trespasser who comes onto their property – for example to warn them of hidden dangers. A building site may be attractive to children, and a simple warning or "danger" sign is unlikely to deter them, so the builder must take steps to prevent children entering the site, such as fencing it off.

- As a charity – looking after money that is not ours, we hold it in trust.

Beneficence – the duty to do our best to help others, where we have the power to do so. This is expounded best in the Sermon on the Mount (Matt 5-8). Jesus commands us to go the extra mile, and pray for those who persecute us.

- "Corporate Social Responsibility" - this term has now been taken by the government and made to refer to the obligations laid down in the Companies Act, 2013 under which larger companies are mandated to give 2% of their profits to carefully defined "charitable causes". This is more like a tax really than a gift since the government requires it.

- Going beyond the official "CSR", some companies give, but do so with some self-benefit in mind.

- True Social Responsibility.

- Healthcare & education – special case generally assumed to be automatically charitable (in British & Indian law). People are entrusting us with much more than just their money – their bodies, their futures, their very life.

- Christian calling – Love for neighbour, extends far beyond those we feel obligated to or connected with "Good Samaritan." Special concern for the marginalised and vulnerable.

Responsibility and accountability in healthcare

Turning now to Healthcare, it is striking to consider the uniqueness of this group of professions. Where else does the client or customer submit themselves so completely into the hands of another? Patients offer their very bodies to the most intimate scrutiny and probing. They answer personal questions regarding their background, choices and lifestyle. They allow themselves to be prodded and pricked with needles. Even the insides of their bodies are exposed through ultrasound, powerful magnetic fields or potentially harmful radiation. They may undergo the ultimate indignity and surrender of being rendered unconscious, cut open and their internal organs dissected. They willingly follow the physician's advice and ingest a variety of chemicals, all of which may have side-effects.

And when the doctor gets it wrong, the consequences may be far worse than in many other fields. When an investment adviser gives poor advice to a client, the client may lose precious money, but no lives or wellbeing are at stake. The only mitigating aspect is that, unlike an airline pilot or truck driver, the consequences of doctor failing in their duty of care is normally limited to just one individual and their dependants.

With another human being so vulnerable before them, the therapist, nurse and especially the doctor cannot be accountable merely to the level of a shop keeper, accountant or teacher. The level of accountability required in healthcare must be far above nearly any other activity one can imagine.

Doctors can boast of having the first ethical framework and set of behavioural standards of any profession, in the Hippocratic Oath. This sets out valuable guidelines and provisions.

Lessons from Accountancy profession

- Comparison to Ethical code for accountants (IESB)

- Principle based

- NOCLAR

- Practical steps towards accountability.

- Compliance with all legal and regulatory requirements. Decision not to cut corners 2 Tim 2, keep our promise even when it hurts Ps 15

- Industry/professional Standards

- benchmarking against Best practice – where this exists we should match or exceed – governance, policies, training, awareness, enforcement

- Leading the way Exceeding

- Balanced scorecard, Social accounting

- Social auditing http://www.csim.in/social-audit.php Social Audit Network SAN

- Credibility alliance

- Planning for positive impact

References

Chapell, Bryan. *Holiness by Grace.* Crossway: Wheaton, Illinois, 2001.

Stalker, James. *Definition for 'ACCOUNTABILITY',* in International Standard Bible Encyclopaedia, Ed Orr, James bible-history.com - ISBE; 1915.

Stott, John. *Issues Facing Christians Today.* London: Marshall, Morgan and Scott, 1984.

PART-5
Patient Perspectives about Healing

A Patient's Understanding of Healing

Usha Jesudason

The idea of healing to anyone who is a patient - is that we will be as we used to be before disease and sickness hit us. With no scars, no weakness, no tubes going in and out of us, no needles and all the paraphernalia that comes with being diseased. We come to hospital, not for treatment, but for healing, to be made whole and normal again. To be able to do the things we once used to do. To have energy, a desire for life, for food, for company for all the pleasures of life. What we expect from our healers is extreme compassion. For them to be able to understand our fears and ignorance and recognize our pain. I know that this is a very naïve and unrealistic outlook, but this **is** how a patient feels. And in this naïve way, this is what healing really means to a patient.

Taking naiveness out of the picture, what is healing, has been a question that has followed me most of my life. When I was just under two years, I fell ill with a fever which was later diagnosed as polio. My anguished mother and grandmother brought me to Vellore, to consult with Dr. Cochrane, and I believe a young Paul Brand. But there I was, almost lifeless - only able to move my neck. Not much could be done for me, so I was taken back to Madras. In the space of the next two years I was taken to just about every kind of healer and eventually, brought back to Katpadi to a local family who used a particular mixture of oils. And as you can see, I recovered. My grandmother swore it was the oils, massage and prayer that led to my being able to walk again – in their minds - this was the healing they all prayed for.

But in my child's mind – healing to me was something very different. Slowly over a period of two years, my limbs came to life again, but one leg was shorter than the other so just after my 6th birthday I was to have a stretching operation. I was told that I could run about and play just like anyone else after the operation. I would be healed, so the operation and the preparations were much looked forward to. Well, after the operation, I was left with a raw angry scar all down my leg, and although the limp was less, there was no healing of my leg according to my little mind. One night, two aunts came over, touched my leg and prayed 'That I would be healed completely.' They read me the stories of Jesus healing the blind and the lame and sick people. Then they told me 'it is not enough for only 23 of us to pray, you too must have faith that Jesus will heal you. So, you too must pray.' And I did, so fervently sure, that I would wake up healed with no scars and a perfectly good leg. I still remember the joy with which I woke up that morning. I lifted the sheet away from my legs slowly and then ……. the great shock and disappointment. There had been no healing. I still had that horrible scar. So, the idea of what is healing has been one that has followed me ever since. I was blessed to have grandparents and parents who at that tender age helped me to understand that healing isn't always physical and as miraculous as the Bible stories. In their own way, they helped me accept my disabilities and not hide behind them and pushed me to stretch my budding talents further than everyone else of that age. This I think was their way of preparing me for a healed life. Although I didn't realize it - from that time, till now as I was preparing for this talk, I have always been, in some corner of my mind, the shadowy woman who came looking for healing.

Here, I switch stories to my husband, who in his early forties was diagnosed with liver complications brought on by hepatitis B. Disease, hospitals, our relationships with doctors, pain and how to relieve it, alternatives to western medicine took over our family life for almost a decade. He of course went through all the phases I mentioned earlier. We very sadly realized that there would be no healing of his disease, that his life had a time limit. On what was probably the worst day of his life, when medicine could neither heal nor help, he decided that enough was enough, pulled out all his tubes and against all medical advice came home. The next day being Sunday, our priest and friend, Dr. Fritschi hearing about this, asked if we would like a communion service at home. So early that morning, there in our beautiful garden bright with flowers everywhere, birds chirping, our grave looking helpless children , our helpers, family and some friends, we held the service of Holy Communion. Dr. Fritschi, encouraged each one of us to lay our hands-on Kumar's head with anointed oil and pray for 'healing or release'. And so, we did, one by one, bound by love for this man. There we were Hindu, Muslim, Christian, atheist, - all accepting the body and blood of Christ, – praying for a miraculous healing.

As Kumar opened his eyes, the anger and frustration with his disease seemed to magically disappear, and he was 'healed', in his words. Not his tormented worn out body, but his anguished soul. He was smiling, friendly to his visitors, asked for breakfast and was a completely different person from the night before. It took some time to understand what this magical turn around healing was. For him, it was an acceptance that this life that he had was over. Accepting and being sure too that there was another life which this 'healing' moment had prepared him for. The next two weeks were times when we discussed 'what is healing if not cured?" and how exactly was he healed when the physical pain still persisted and there was no cure for his disease. And what did his healing mean to me his wife, to our children and to his doctors? And what if we had not gathered together in love that morning to participate in the act of Holy Communion and the laying on of hands? Would that inner healing have been withheld? Why was this inner healing so important - both to him and us his family and his friends and colleagues? We who knew him, saw healing as the restoration of a broken spirit.

Just as pain and suffering are mysteries, so too is healing. One that we are called to participate in, in mysterious ways. Most often as agents of healing in the form of loving acts. About two years after Kumar died, a friend whose wife was in a coma after an accident was distraught and the gathering of the families did not bring healing but more pain. So along with people close to him we gathered around her bed and did a similar kind of healing service. At some point, we held each other's hands - even the warring relatives – and at the end, there were tears and words asking for and giving forgiveness, words of love followed by hugs and tears. The healing in which we were participating was the healing of the wounds, memories and bitterness each one there had carried - some since the couple's wedding many years ago. Once again, love stepped in to heal. The healing of memories and inner wounds is as important as the healing of bodies.

The healing of loss and the memory of pain have never quite been healed in our family. My sons rarely spoke of their father, and moments by Kumar's graveside always left us in silent tears –even twenty years later. The painful shadow of grief did not unite us but separated us and followed us everywhere – through weddings, births, happy occasions –always silent and brooding. Although time is said to be a great healer, it really wasn't so for us. To my great surprise, my younger son, who was the most affected, and who has never spoken of his father, stood up at his father in law's retirement service a few months ago and said, "I lost my father 20 years ago, and have now found someone I can call father." I was shocked senseless, but there he stood calm, composed and as he looked at me, I realized that finally after all these years, the process of healing had begun – and once more the starting point was love. *Love that had come into his life and been the healing force.*

A door opened for me as a consultant and writer with the World Council of Churches on issues of healing. Along with my friend and co-author Gert Ruppell, I travelled wherever there was pain and suffering. Africa where AIDS was raging, Belfast recovering from decades of violence, Greece and parts of Turkey where young men just disappeared during the war, Romania recovering from years of Communist life. We collected stories of pain, from Rwanda's civil war, from apartheid South Africa, 36 years of violence in Guatemala, Argentina, Cambodia, Vietnam, Thailand, Sri Lanka. Then we looked at the issue of healing as well. How did these people who had suffered so much find healing? How did they rebuild their lives? And always, healing began with little acts of love and asking for and giving forgiveness. Each story was so personal.... Beatrice looked into the eyes of the boy who killed her sons and then gave him food and their clothes; 'he was just a lost boy without his mamma' she said. A small group in Corrymeela Northern Ireland formed from where healing and friendship could spread to both catholic and protestant communities. Memories of pain were spoken aloud and recognized so that healing could begin. An unforgettable conversation with Nobel Laureate for peace in 1980 - Peres Esquivel as he spoke of years of torture in an Argentinean jail, and how his quest for healing not only for himself, but for his country was through the arduous and painful path of peace and reconciliation peppered with daily acts of kindness and love. Thus, came about my vocation as a healer through the medium of writing.

I wrote the story of Kumar's illness and acceptance in a book called 'I Will Lie Down In Peace'. This book has travelled all over the world in a mysterious way, and it still surprises me when I get a letter from someone who has read it. As an author, it is humbling to get such letters, but once pain has been shared, it cannot be ignored, so relationships have grown.

Perhaps you are wondering how relevant all of this is to an institution like CMC. When meditating on issues of healing, should we not also include a wounded heart, a divided family, a family facing loss, a divorce, someone having difficult children or parents, someone tired of life and unable to see the silver lining? Which department do we go to for healing for all of this? Which doctor should we see? Where does healing for all of this come from? Don't we all carry some kind of deep wound that has never been spoken of, much less healed, and yet don't we carry on daily with our given lives?

I had learnt to live with loss, learnt to live with the disability of polio, had carved out a nice life for myself as a writer, when out of the blue I discovered that I had cancer of the breast. Another quest for healing began when I thought that I had some of the answers at least. This time, there was cure - an end. Scans and reports all said the same thing. My surgeon and oncologist said I could go home, I was cured. I should have been ecstatic at being cured, - but I wasn't. What I still wanted and needed was healing. 'Cured, but not healed' is a horrible curse. What a paradox! How was I to find healing from a disease that stripped me of things I held so dear? So, I found myself back on the long road...........looking for healing.

The need for healing, is so vast – touch me, and I will be healed.......... just say so and I will be healed......................let me just be in your presence and I will be healed.........or in great desperation, let me just touch the hem of your garment and I will be healed.

Healing, in my experience as a patient is **a daily affirmation of personal faith............ that life is good**.........that .... I can **live, and live well,** despite many limitations that come my way. I can still do good in very small ways. I can be the loving mother and grandmother, the kind friend, **I can be the balm that brings healing where there is strife. The process of healing within me always begins with counting my blessings and being grateful for them.**

My Journey from Brokenness towards Healing

Anthony Samy

M y name is Anthony Samy, my wife is Maria and we have two children. My daughter, Aruna Shanti did Medical Lab Technology, she is married and settled in Bengaluru and I have a grand-daughter. My son Francis did MBA and left for Australia 3 months ago to join his wife. I have HIV and have been living with it for 29 years.

In 1989, I paid money and got HIV. I was unaware of this till I donated blood in CMC in 1990, when I was informed that I have HIV. It was a confusing time and I had repeated blood tests and met doctors, social workers and counsellors. Sadly, the counsellor told me I would only live for 2 or 3 years and advised my wife to leave me or she would get HIV too. But my wife and I decided to stay as family and look after our children.

I was assured that my diagnosis would be kept confidential but soon in the Christian Institute that I worked in I was harassed, stigmatised, falsely accused of stealing, mentally tortured and forced me to resign. It was then that they informed that they knew I had HIV. I was also forced to leave the Institution accommodation immediately and moved into a car shed. I was not paid my month's salary, nor did they give me 3 month's salary for terminating me. I got my gratuity only after Dr. Jacob John, Virologist at CMC and Dr. Jayakaran Isaac, Principal of Voorhees College intervened. After forcing me to resign they mentioned in the Institute's monthly newsletter that as I was sick and unable to work, I had to leave my job and they requested the staff to pray for me. As the news spread about my illness, I was not able to get any other job. My ex-colleagues who visited me, made me feel very bad and told me I was accused of many bad things.

In Church they did not accept me, my brothers and sisters did not want to have anything to do with me or my family. Christians thought I was a sinner and thought they would get infected if they interacted with me and so they were scared of me. I was stigmatised at home and if I was called for a family function I was made to sleep outside their house. My wife and I started going to Churches where we were not known.

More than my illness, it was how people treated me that made me physically and mentally sick. Gradually I lost a lot of weight, lost hope and became depressed – I was a broken person and my wife, and I were considering committing suicide. We had food only for 1 more month and my wife and I cried so much that there were no tears in our eyes. It was then that I decided to go to Velankani to spend some time with God on my own. There I read Matthew 6:26, 27 – "Look at the birds of the air, they neither sow nor reap nor gather into barns, and yet your heavenly Father feeds them. Are you not of more value than they? And which of you by being anxious can add one cubit to his span of life". When I read John 8:3-7 - I asked for forgiveness from both God and my wife and I felt my heavy burden being lifted off of me.

I read the story about the prodigal son (Luke 15: 11-27) and identified myself with him and felt God waiting expectantly for me to come back to him. That Christmas of 1991, my family attended a church where no one knew us, we returned home to make rice and sambhar for our Christmas lunch. However, God comforted us by sending biriyani and cake through Mrs. Anna and Dr. Jacob John.

In January 1992 I was selected to work in the Saudi Naval Force. I went for medical screening and blood tests in Madras and Saudi and for some reason (a miracle for me) the tests were negative in both places. I worked in Saudi for 4 years and saved enough money to buy a plot and build a house. I returned to India in 1996.

In 1996, Dr. Santosh from the CMC Mental Health Centre taught me how to counsel people and I started to counsel other patients like me and later started counselling family members too. My own experience enabled me to easily and effectively reach out to HIV patients and families who were devastated like I was. At this time, I bought a car and provided taxi services to support my income. The CMC weekly Infectious Disease clinic was and is a big support to us. CMC also arranged people from various departments to teach our positive group on various issues related to health.

In 2006, Dr. Anand Zachariah, started the Ida Scudder support group for HIV positive people. He made me an important member of this group and later I became the leader of this group. Through CMC and other NGOs, once a month we counselled people, helped people with legal issues and helped to get training and jobs for HIV affected people. I was able to help 35 women get jobs as outreach workers. I have conducted HIV classes in the College of Nursing for 6 years and in various Government departments in Vellore District. In 2006 the Government started giving free ART and this benefitted many people. I started ART in October 10, 2007 and my viral load has been kept in check.

At this time, I did not have enough have enough money to support my daughter who had got into BSc Microbiology and as the ART had side effects, I could not drive my taxi and had to sell my car. God sent Suku and Romani to support my daughter's education till her MSc.

In 2008, God showed me a new way to make a living. I was called to United Evangelical Lutheran Church of India, Chennai where they gave me further training in counselling and vocational training. From the training choices they offered I chose to learn to make silk-cotton mattress and pillows, foam and rexin mattresses for hospital use and shoulder bags from waste cloth. This was the next blessing from God.

During an HIV awareness meeting in 2008, I met the District collector and he helped me get a contract with Co-Optex and as my business gradually grew, I was able to supply mattresses for the whole of Tamil Nadu. I was able to employ HIV positive people to do this work. At the same time my wife was allotted a stationery and photocopying shop in the Collectorate. Both these I believe were a major blessing and gift from God. With income from this I was able to get my daughter married in 2012. However, in 2015 due to corruption and requests for bribes I had to close down my business. In January 2018 my son got married and I can say that my major duties to my family are over.

Even though I was born in Christian family, I met God only through my brokenness after I contracted HIV. He has used me to help and counsel and provide hope to many others who are in similar situations. I have been able to spend about 5 lakhs of my own money to do this work for which I am very grateful. I have counselled about 4000 people since I started my new life and there are many people who have benefitted through my personal involvement. In a day I get about 10 phone calls from HIV affected people for help, counselling and advice. Through UELCI I have visited many places in India to provide training and counselling on HIV. I have also been invited to Germany and Thailand to share my life experience and how God has helped me on my Journey from Brokenness towards healing.

The lessons I have learned through this journey are:

I.   Forgiveness is very important.

II.   God has given me a better understanding of the Bible.

III.   Positive thinking is very important - now when people call me names, I use them as my "degrees."

IV.   I have learned to be satisfied and content with life.

V.   Money and power are not qualifiers, all people are equal in the eyes of God.

VI.   Doing and being are more important than talking.

VII. I do not worry about tomorrow.

VIII. I am ready to meet God at any time.

To people I am HIV + but I reverse this and say in front of God (+) I am a very important human.

From 'Take up your Bed and Walk' to 'My Grace is Sufficient for You'

Reema Samuel

Healing- different experiences

The Gospels record numerous accounts of Jesus healing people during his ministry. These are mostly instances of immediate, complete, apparently effortless cure of even congenital and chronic conditions. A word, a touch, or just contact with his robes was sufficient for the person to be completely cured. However, the clinical reality of a tertiary care hospital is that for many people, cure is often a time consuming, incomplete and laborious process. There are numerous conditions which can only be *controlled* and not *cured*, and yet other conditions where the state of the patient fluctuates through the illness course. There are conditions which leave people with residual limitations and those where nothing can be done for the patient but ensure a dignified death. There are sudden, unanticipated accidents or traumas which lead to long term suffering.

This lived experience of most patients with chronic conditions are more reminiscent of Apostle Paul's 'thorn in the flesh' than of Jesus' commanding the paralysed man to 'take up your bed and walk'. The Bible tells us that Paul thrice asked God to heal him, was refused, being told that it was in his weakness that God's strength is manifested

(2 Corinthians 12:8,9). This example is all the more relevant in today's health care scenario where many people cannot be realistically expected to be completely healed as in a return to premorbid status.

The mismatch between the high expectations of patients coming to a Christian institution expecting to recover completely and the ground reality of their ongoing conditions can lead to disillusionment. It can also lead to health care providers feeling pressurized to meet unrealistic goals, leading to burnout in extreme cases. This is all the truer for India, where the onus of care and thereby accountability lies disproportionately with the health care providers as opposed to western cultures where the relationship is more collaborative. The situation is also complicated by cultural beliefs of India where suffering and disease are often thought to be resultant from sin, thus adding guilt and shame to patient's negative experience of the condition.

Healing- different definitions

The recovery models of care which have gained prominence over the last few decades bring into contrast the dichotomy in understanding of recovery between health care providers and patients (Piat, 2009). Health care providers tend to focus on *clinical recovery*, implying absence of any pathology and approximation to cure – in other words, recovery *from* an illness. On the other hand, patients advocate for *personal recovery* or recovery *in* the illness- a process that re builds self-identity in order to find empowerment and life satisfaction within and around the lived experience of the illness. Recovery from the patient's perspective is much more than a onetime cure; it is more a journey with many stops, detours and backtrackings than a destination. This journey cannot be undertaken alone, but with the support necessary from family, society and the health care systems. If the goal of recovery is to be attained, there has to be inclusion of patients and their families in a more collaborative decision-making process and commitment from health care providers to offer hope and continued support in addition to symptomatic treatment. It necessitates looking beyond readily visible superficial pathology and striving for a deeper, broader view of the person as a whole. It is looking beyond the diagnosis, the set of demographic data and seeing the person behind.

Patricia Deegan, one of the pioneers of the recovery centered models, likens the person who goes through a chronic illness to a seed that is under the dark earth, waiting for the soil to soften and the rains to come (Deegan, 1988). The responsibility of health care professionals is to create environments which nurture and bring out the plant in the growing seed. This needs to be done at the patient's pace, without preconceived notions based on clinical decision making of who can and who can't get better. This analogy is reminiscent of Jesus' parable of the sower scattering his seeds on various terrains (Matthew 13:1-8, 18-23). Although he used the parable to describe how various people respond to the word of God, the same can be used to see how recovery of a patient can depend on the surrounding environment- whether in fields, on rocky ground, among thorn bushes, or in good soil.

The importance of moving beyond physical pathology has also been resonated elsewhere. The WHO defines health as 'a state of complete physical, mental and social wellbeing and *not merely the absence* of disease or infirmity'. The ICIDH (International Classification of Impairments, Disabilities and Handicaps), with its focus on consequences of disease mostly at an individual level, was succeeded by the ICF (International Classification of Functioning) which highlighted that while physical and psychological difficulties require attention; in the long run it is the *social* and *productivity* factors that warrant special focus (WHO, 2001). Amartya Sen, in his Capabilities Approach (CA) has gone forward and views *capability* as the presence of all essential resources (education, income, wealth, housing, water, sanitation, energy, employment, transport) and absence of all barriers to functioning (poverty, stigma, discrimination) (Bickenbach, 2014).

However, these changes will continue to be an exercise in semantics if at the ground level, health care professionals are unable to focus on optimising the physical and social environments surrounding people. This is all the truer for India where people with chronic illnesses have a double disability- first which is caused by the illness, second which is complicated by poverty, unemployment, illiteracy, gender inequality and stigma. Add to this the cultural concept of sin/ karma/ inauspiciousness of those with an illness, and there begins a process where non- health factors continue to impair functioning even after health factors have been addressed (World Bank Group, 2018).

Healing- strength amidst weakness

There are many biblical references to the need to holistically fulfil people's needs. Jesus feeding the five thousand men was precipitated by the realisation that while he was providing food for the soul, he was not providing food for the body (Matthew 14: 14-21). In the story of the Good Samaritan, he not only bandages the wounds of the attacked man, but also provides for shelter, food and money (Luke 10: 30-35). The Book of James states that if there are poor and needy around us, it is necessary to fulfil those needs before we pass benediction on them (James 2:14-17).

Professing to be a witness in the healing ministry of Christ therefore calls us to be aware of our patient's social, cultural and economic contexts and to minimise the limitations imposed by them in order to promote healing. It also requires health care professionals to acknowledge that healing being an intensely personal experience; needs to be viewed from the person's point of view. Even when complete recovery from the illness is not possible, what makes a difference might be just a listening ear, a smiling face, the autonomy to make decisions regarding their lives or to feel empowered. This might be a challenge considering the ever-increasing caseloads and complex conditions CMC encounters, but that is where his grace works in our lives. Undeserved, unmerited grace, which reminds us that we are but reservoirs and channels for the Great Healer; that all that we have are but gifts from above and not our own to boast about. When we can't provide all the answers that our patients need, that is when we are also forced to acknowledge like Apostle Paul that his power is made perfect in our weaknesses.

References

Bickenbach, J. 'Reconciling the capability approach and the ICF', *European Journal of Disability Research*, 8, 2014 10-23.

Deegan, P. 'Recovery: The lived experience of rehabilitation', *Psychosocial Rehabilitation Journal*, XI (4), 1988 11-19.

Piat, M., Sabetti, J. 'The Development of a Recovery-Oriented Mental Health System in Canada: What the Experience of Commonwealth Countries Tells Us', *Canadian Journal of Community Mental Health*,28(2), 2009 17–33.

World Health Organization. *International Classification of Functioning, Disability and Health: ICF*. Geneva: World Health Organization, 2001.

www.who.int/about/mission/en.

www.worldbank.org/INDIAEXTN/Resources/295583/Chapter02.pdf.

The Care-Giver's Cross

Bibhudutta Sahu

bibhuduttasahu@instagram

Welcome to my state of mind, as my world came crashing around me at 22:30 on the 25th of May 2013, two hours shy of our 12th Wedding Anniversary when my wife succumbed to lung cancer. Coming back to the place where the journey of the biggest loss and lesson of my life began may very well be a part of the process of gaining closure and healing. It set in motion, a cascading motion of events that I could not have predicted in my wildest dreams. But those are a series of stories for another day and may not be suitable for all ears.

A Care-Giver's Cross is both a blessing and a burden for the bearer. To be able to dedicate an entire portion of your life to the well-being of your loved one, amidst the finality of the situation, is the struggle of heroes but also the abode of spiritual peace. A cross, by virtue of the word, signifies a sacrifice and the weight of the world on one's shoulders. At the same time, in the context of Christ, it conveys a stronger message of love intertwined inextricably with liberation so beautifully, that it is hard to argue otherwise. We have all been called upon to make innumerable sacrifices and faced many losses, but none can compare with the loss of a loved one who has been under one's care for a period of time. This is the common narrative of many a mother, father, sister, brother, husband, wife, daughter and son and the conflicting world of choices and consequences while convincing oneself that it was carried out with a clean conscience. It is the world that echoes back at you when you see the vacant spaces in the eyes of her loved ones. It is the cyclic reverberations of the faintest wish that she would return for one final encounter and those sleepless nights when the emotions well up and flow over the tipping point.

With the passage of time, the sequence of events gets a little foggy but the stark reality is that my wife and I landed in CMC Vellore with no idea of the world that was about to unfold in front of our eyes. Within a span of 2 weeks, our world went spiralling from that of a twisted nerve in the shoulder to full blown lung cancer. I recall very vividly the restless pacing up and down the corridors of the 4th floor of the 'A'

Block hoping for the best and preparing for the worst. We had left our daughters back to Shillong, Meghalaya with their grandparents and the extended family. This was going to be the first of many sojourns back and forth in the bleak hope of a miracle.

My wife, Natashia D. Kharkongor, was diagnosed with Stage 4 Adenocarcinoma (lung cancer) and as the diagnosis suggests, the cancer had spread to multiple locations in the body with no practical recourse to combat the disease. My wife was a picture of health for all the years of our marriage, she did not smoke, ate well and was tenacious in her fight against any minor illnesses the family members went through. It is a frightening scenario to encounter, an abyss of sorts, given the positive disposition of both of the patient and the care-giver. It is a death sentence without any appeal for mercy.

Entering the campus of CMC Vellore, one is confronted with the magnitude of malaise in the world and the faith of the multitudes in the CMC medical fraternity. At the same time, to the uninitiated, the world of CMC Vellore can be a labyrinth of procedures and confluence of communities and possibly confusion. It is unlike any other private medical institution in India with a sea of humanity pouring in through the gates of CMC Vellore. At this point, it is pertinent to applaud and appreciate the institution for the services rendered to the patients over the years even when the ground reality is that they are expected to cater to far more than they can handle. The system has to deal with the barrage of languages, cultures and expectation.

The concept of time and space takes on new dimensions within the campus as does the harsh reality of one's own mortality. Time slows down with every step of appointments, moving from test to test, the interminable waits in between and the confrontation of one's own thoughts. It is the perfect ground for the collision of hopes and dreams, researching the internet for news/ views / contradictions and snatching at snippets of succour. It is the time to value the beauty of companionship and upholding each other in those moments of uncertainty and the myriad emotions that follow. I can recall the distinct memories of taking the stairs to the 4th Floor to gather my thoughts and check my emotions, impossible as that was at the time. An experience in CMC Vellore demands your patience and mindfulness. For most of the time, we are sitting, sitting and a little more sitting. We sit in the OPD, in the doctor's chambers, while eating, waiting for the medicines, in the lodge etc. And during the period of sitting together waiting for the next round of consultations, chemotherapy, scans etc., there develops a bond borne out of the crucible of conversations, choices and consequences. People talk about mindfulness and meditation, but it is in the melee of the medical madness that self-awareness is not an option but forced onto the patient and the care-giver.

One is grateful for the level of engagement in completing the tasks as though one is in a rush against time. These tasks keep the mind occupied and even give the care-giver a false sense of achievement. The care-giver may be, as I was, drawn into a warped world of thinking wherein the successful completion of the simple tasks converts into blessings which in turn lead to miracle.

The environment within the A-Block can be summed up in one word – HOPE! The doctors and the staff have an ever-present smile on their faces that is both reassuring and hopeful. Their actions and words reflect a deep ingrained philosophy of faith and hope that communicates itself in the corridors of the medical institution. The level of patience and commitment to service is unparalleled in the medical fraternity. I have often heard words of encouragement ranging from "I'll be praying for you" to "Don't worry, have faith and trust God". During the most trying of times, these few words can provide a layer of comfort for the hurt and healing. Their attention to detail from the cleanliness of the bed sheets, pain threshold of the patient, lighting, meal timings and just popping in to smile and just engage in small talk. Being far away from home, CMC Vellore can become a lonely place with the whole world buzzing around and visitors few and far in between, these interactions become a lifeline to the world outside and break the temptation to dive into a rabbit hole of despair.

The most striking fact of CMC Vellore is the attention to detail with the number of tests and reports. No stone is left unturned to ascertain the cause of the illness. Painstaking as it may be for the Patient and Care-Giver, I applaud the doctors and staff for their dedication to conduct a comprehensive analysis of the course of treatment based on the reports. Each step was clearly defined within the limitations of the facts that were presented to us. The doctors are dealing with decisions of life and death incessantly and need all the available facts before doing so. Fortunately, the hospital still abide by Dr. Ida Scudder's legacy of ensuring medical treatment that is affordable for the public and therefore providing much needed quality treatment at economical rates. Ergo, the beeline for CMC Vellore has not abated till today.

As a care-giver, I was faced with the challenge of instilling hope and confidence while battling my own apprehensions. There have been many times that I have gazed out at the twin hillocks and imagined the outline of a cross as the sign of delivery from this on-going struggle. I have paced the passageways of the A-Block (a FitBit might have been a great help at that time) fervently talking with God and looking back on my life to identify the decisions I could have made to avoid this prevailing predicament. The self-flagellation combined with the passionate requests for swapping places with my wife because I knew in my heart and head, that she would have made a much better single parent than I, in raising our two beautiful daughters. The rude interruptions in my conversations with God would jolt me back to the physical world and there would be a need for my services to turn the lever to raise the bed, call the nurse, check the drip, listen attentively to the doctor as he came on his rounds etc. While battling my own emotions, I would have to play the role of the ever-hopeful and look at the sunny side of life. And even for a predominantly positive person like me, that was an uphill task when faced with the facts that nobody had ever recovered from 4th stage lung cancer in known history.

And this is where I pause for a moment and draw my attention to the world of the doctors and the weight of responsibility that can get the better of them in their honest attempts to provide hope. My wife and I were still awaiting the results of the tests and whiling away our time in the calm comfort of the private rooms in the A Block. The door opens slowly and in walks our doctor whose opening remarks remain etched in my memory forever. His comforting statement at the time, "there is no reason why you can't live to the age of 90" haunt me till today. My wife passed away at the age of 40, two years after the diagnosis. It does not take a rocket scientist that we fell way short of the mark of 90. There is a thin line between hope which provides an added boost to the human spirit and hype which draws you in but in the end deflates the spirit of any fighting endeavour. The doctor's statement was well intentioned but as patients, we hold on to every word of the medical fraternity in times of crisis. Our conditioning as laymen places the medical fraternity as godmen and any ray of hope, if not converted into reality, can destroy the will to carry on. I guess it is a cross that the doctors have to carry. Throw us the ropes of reality and help us climb them. Every subsequent chemotherapy, every medication, every meal saw the gradual deterioration and the slow dissipation of the assurance.

At times, I wish I was not born in the era of the internet as the flood of information on 4th stage lung cancer can suck the life out of you with the breakdown in mortality rates and the various treatments available (hoax or genuine). The renewed search for alternatives bordered on desperation where I was left clutching at strands of hope in any form. With the free time available, we pictured ourselves as victors over the disease in the near future and emerging as beacons of hope for cancer fighters. Ignorance is bliss when you are dependant solely on the reports and advice of the doctor. But the human mind is curious enough to compare and compile information that would provide greater understanding on the current condition. We surf from website to website with an obsession to discover the cure through the permutation and combination of practices. Self-preservation has the power of giving birth to almost magical abilities to extend the inevitable and it is even greater when all around you are egging you on to eclipse the benchmark of mortality. This constant exercise of encouraging my wife to change her diet, enjoy her life, cherish the moments with her daughters and family and much more becomes a habit to achieve the unattainable which many would describe as a fool's paradise. There was a time when we both believed that I had the power to relieve her pain by placing my right hand above the pain points and praying for her.

The institution radiates with the glow of the Christian culture and message of miracles, hope and blessings. The surrounding community plays a great role in nurturing a desire to live and survive. They provide additional support to the primary care-givers during the intervals, and though they are never planned, they are always welcome. I would like to proffer a study in contrast from our time in Bhubaneswar and Shillong / Vellore. Once the news of the cancer had become common knowledge in Bhubaneswar, it almost felt like a pall of gloom had descended and it felt like a death warrant. This form of understanding pre-dates to the old cycle of karma and overall view that disease and death are reward for the lives we have led. The fire to fight back was extinguished in the eyes of most of the visitors and that in itself can be quite a downer. Contrast this to the environment in Shillong and Vellore and one will notice the upbeat approach to tackling the beast of cancer. There are prayer meetings, regular visitors, words of encouragement, and stories of life changing experiences that provide food for the soul. These nuggets of spiritual upliftment work wonders for the patient as well as the care-giver. It must be understood that the patient and the care-giver are almost inseparable and share a bond that familiarizes them to each other to the extent of becoming predictable. They depend on each other for physical, emotional and spiritual sustenance.

Standing at the gate in quiet contemplation, one notices an edifice that provides solace to all who enter the premises. You can witness a beeline for the shrine located outside the main administrative building with a plateful of prayers. Multi-coloured candles, some carefully located and others strewn across, adorn the shrine and people laying their hands on the shrine, kneeling on the ground and drawing additional support from the spiritual world. Religion is irrelevant but faith is. The chapel itself is located in the heart of the building and is the place where my wife and I would visit to regain our strength for the coming week. The hymns and the contributions from the various departments would satiate our emotional well-being even though uncertainty prevailed. This chapel and the chaplains provided a means of selfless service for the masses and personal relief for all the weary souls. It was a cross religious phenomena and you got a sense that this was a family of care-givers, each playing their roles in earnest. The pastors wouldn't confine themselves to the chapel but would drop in regularly in the wards to offer a prayer or two.

An aspect that was missing was the active role of counsellors for the patients and the care-givers. The mind of the patient contains a million thoughts and feelings without being able to express themselves until the platform is provided. In many cases, the patients cannot approach the counsellor at their chambers and therefore visits to the wards would be an added benefit. This is equally important for the care-giver too.

A little splash of colour can do wonders for the patients, care-givers and staff of C.M.C Vellore as it is proven that colour therapy plays its part in creating a cheerful and positive environment. We must move away from the dual tone buildings and ensure that the corridors, open spaces provide much needed relief for those traversing the campus of C.M.C Vellore.

While the world is slowly waking up to the needs of the people with disability, our medical institutions must gradually transact towards making the premises and the facilities accessible for people. Accessibility audits are becoming the norm for the institutions and there is funding available from the government for such initiatives. Ramps are only part of the progression to accessibility. The benefits of accessibility go beyond the world of persons with disability but extend to children and senior citizens.

We are well aware of the limitations of allopathic treatments within the dominant medical fraternity and that the other forms of medical treatment have never been explored in CMC. Complementary and holistic approach to the treatment of the patient would definitely benefit the patient. A unit can be created to explore the marriage of allopathic treatment with the other forms of treatment available for the patient. Nature has a lot of answers that we are not listening to just yet. If God created the world and everything within it, the remedies to a lot of the problems lie in nature. Maybe it is time for us to pay attention to God through mother nature keeping in mind that they are not entirely exclusive entities. This could include lifestyle changes especially in the region of natural food, stress management, homeopathic, ayurvedic treatments etc.

A care-givers cross weighs heavily on the shoulders of the bearer at the end of the journey and it is a burden that raises a million questions of what if's and but's. My wife had fought such a weary battle throughout that I truly believe that she fought just to stay alive because we wanted her to. She would be embattled with thoughts concerning the well-being of her daughters. I think, that somewhere in the back of her mind, she didn't harbour much hope in my parenting skills. And being very honest, I would have had to agree with her... at the time. On the evening of her passing away, I had gone to the local market to purchase a few clothes as my current lot were worn out. It was one of my very rare days off hospital duty. During my shopping visits, I received a call from a very close friend of mine who had visited Natashia that afternoon and suggested that I give my wife permission to move on. It was a bitter pill to swallow but the pain and her unresponsive nature must have been unbearable for her as much as her loved ones. She was fighting for each breath and every day. I might have laughed off the idea at the time, but the idea played on and on in my mind causing a sense of uneasiness and a clash of priorities. Unless God himself performed a miracle that night, I might have been tempted to stave off the notion of letting her go. But it is no wonder that God didn't rise up to the challenge of saving my wife that night. At 22:00 hrs, as we prayed over her, I silently and reluctantly released her from her earthly obligations and submitted her to the life beyond. It was within 30 mins that she breathed her last after a protracted battle to stay alive amidst the pipes being thrust down her throat and drops of blood that were emerging from the suction pipe. What if I hadn't taken let her go and/or I hadn't allowed the nurse to insert the pipe? The care giver is always struggling with the ramifications of his decisions which can take a lifetime to resolve.

Care-giving is a collective effort wherein the primary care-giver takes on the role of the constant physical and emotional support while the others provide the support services for the patient and care-giver to focus on the well-being. It is in this context that I recall the time and sacrifices of our families in the environs of a single room guest house on the outskirts of Vellore, trudging as a team to the OPD, cooking, chatting, praying and taking walks that became routine for all concerned. This ecosystem of support is critical to ensure the well-being of the patient towards extending the lifespan or ensuring full recovery.

On a lighter note, my daughter and I were reminiscing on our times in CMC Vellore and we both agreed that there were very few to compete against the Chocolate and Coffee on offer at the vendors stall within the campus.

My humble submission to my daughters:

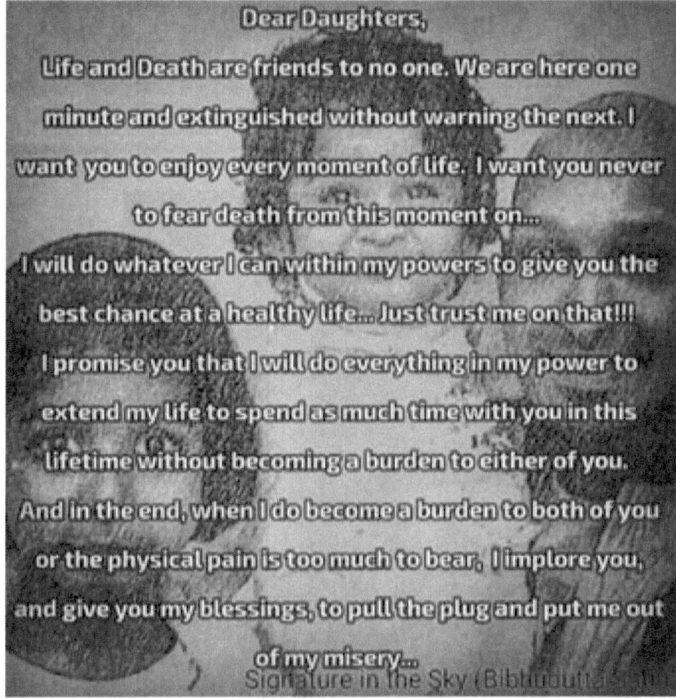

Dear Daughters,

Life and Death are friends to no one. We are here one minute and extinguished without warning the next. I want you to enjoy every moment of life. I want you never to fear death from this moment on...

I will do whatever I can within my powers to give you the best chance at a healthy life... Just trust me on that!!!

I promise you that I will do everything in my power to extend my life to spend as much time with you in this lifetime without becoming a burden to either of you. And in the end, when I do become a burden to both of you or the physical pain is too much to bear, I implore you, and give you my blessings, to pull the plug and put me out of my misery...

Signature in the Sky (Bibhudutta Sahu)

bibhuduttasahu@instagram

Last but not least, I dream of the day when I shall sit and watch the sunset one last time and in that gentle breeze, I shall feel her presence guide me as I slip away to the other side. For, as her Care-giver, I bear that badge with pride and would do it again and again.

PART-6
Pastoral Care
and Healing Ministry

Biblical Interpretation in Healing Ministry

Arul Dhas T

ible is a book used both by believers and scholars on a serious manner. I would like to highlight the need for dynamism, over against the static in the way we interpret the Bible.[1] Biblical interpretation cannot be a static one. The interpretation which was done in twelfth century in Europe need not be and cannot be the same when the same unchanging text is interpreted in Indonesia in twenty first century. Every time someone gets involved in interpretation, the meaning of a text gets transferred into a new context, new time and by new people.

Classically, we are familiar with allegorical interpretation, typological interpretation and Midrashic interpretation. Later on, higher criticism developed based on literary forms, cultural backgrounds, social rhetoric, etc. We are also familiar with further developments of interpretation from the liberation perspectives, feminist perspectives, Dalit perspectives and other specific perspectives developed in specific situations.

One aspect of Biblical interpretation is Biblical translation. Bible translation is an important activity – a dynamic one - which happens in every linguistic group and in every time. It involves significant amount of contextualization of the language, meaning and experience of the community. We are grateful to the committed Bible translators all over the world who take all efforts to bring the Scriptural texts alive in the translations we see today.

I would like to quote what Bishop Lesslie Newbigin told about interpretation. He highlighted the centrality of the experience of the congregation and the way the congregation lives as the critical evidence of Biblical interpretation:

> "How can this strange story of God made flesh, of a crucified Savior, of resurrection and new creation become credible for those whose entire mental training has conditioned them to believe that the real world is the world which can be satisfactorily explained and managed without the hypothesis of God? I know of only one clue to the answering of that question, only one real hermeneutic of the gospel: a congregation which believes it."[2] - Lesslie Newbigin.

It is true that our interpretation gains its authenticity in our lives, community lives. In a community of faith, in a community of healing the scripture finds expression and interpretation which is relevant and authentic.

Examples of biblical interpretation

Scriptural interpretation and making safe space seminar

The Theological College of Lanka, Sri Lanka which brought people from two different ethnic backgrounds together for a seminar between 2010 and 2012. It was a time when there were inner wounds, hurt, painful memories, suspicion and non-acceptance between Tamils and Sinhalese in Sri Lanka. In fact, one of the students of theology narrated how eight of her family members were killed on a single day. The whole exercise was developed basically as a Christian initiative. Biblical narratives, passages were expounded to help in the process. Lessons and mandates were drawn from the specific teachings of Jesus and writings of Paul. The Christian communities saw that there is a need to come together in peace to witness to Christ's love.

Non-judgmental space was provided to the participants to share their painful stories regarding the armed conflict which recently ended and at the same time an ambience of listening was created by different activities and nuances. Faithful ones from both groups were able to see and experience each other's pain. It unmistakably brought people together in some measure of peace.

The focus here is how Bible is interpreted to bring forth peace among people. During the whole process the validity and authority of the Bible was maintained. Jesus' Sermon on the Mount carries one statement "Blessed are the peacemakers, for they shall be called the children of God." Textual faithfulness, historical underpinnings, cultural sensitivities, contextual need and the spiritual inspiration were honored and upheld. Biblical scholars, elders of the congregations and the believers were involved in the whole process. I believe this is one of the valid and authentic examples of Biblical interpretation in action.

Hermeneutics and grief counseling training

The second example is from Christian Medical College, Vellore, India. Maybe it is an experience of many or all who do such training all over the world. However, I draw some insights from this training programme to understand dynamic biblical interpretation. James 1:19 reads "Let everyone be quick to listen, slow to speak, slow to anger." In a fast moving world, many faithful ones do not pay attention to this biblical mandate. One reason for the situation is that people think that they know so many things and their main responsibility is to speak - Speak emphatically, loudly and clearly so that others will follow.

Grief is one context in which many would like to speak even though they don't know what to speak. But this is one situation where as faithful community and as spiritual leaders we are called and expected to minister. We have witnessed in our pastoral ministry how some well-meaning persons feel so urged to say something and they end up making foolish statements – uncaring and unbiblical.

In this programme, the scriptural base is taken as something which guards and guides us in our ministry. The participants are trained in the skills of listening. The hindrances of listening – both internal and external are elaborated highlighted so that they will identify and avoid them. Many who undergo this fifteen-module session are able to obey

James 1:19 in a dynamic way in their day to day life and ministry. Along with this the need for silence in appropriate places is also highlighted. Becoming sensitive to other's need and one's own need are focused. Programmes like this are the outcome of the dynamic interpretation the church and the believers are able to make in their own context as an expression of their discipleship.

Biblical interpretation in bioethical discussions

The third illustration is about the way healthcare professionals make interpretations of the scripture. I am sure all the Christian healthcare professionals are familiar with the strong ethical traditions they uphold in their practice. They want to be faithful to the scripture since they see their profession as a Christian calling.

As a discipline, it is not an exaggeration to say that the bioethical principles like beneficence, non-malfeasance, autonomy and justice emerged as an articulation of Christian faith expression. Beneficence and non-malfeasance are expressions which came from Jesus' command "to do unto others as you want others do unto you". Autonomy is a combination of respect for human beings and value each human has in the sight of God (for example, Psalm 139). Justice is a response both prophets and Lord Jesus demands from the disciples. This comes out so powerfully in the Kingdom parables of Jesus.

Followers of Jesus who are healthcare professionals take their situations like beginning of life, end of life, allocating scarce resources, technological advancements in the light of value of life, eugenics and so on and see how they could live out their faith in Christ like manner. Therefore, the whole discipline of Bioethics is a practical application of biblical hermeneutics. One reason why there are developments and new issues coming in this discipline also is due to this dynamic nature of biblical interpretation. Different examples could be expounded to help theological students in their hermeneutical journey.

Interpretation and healing of relationships

In a healthcare setting, we come across people who suffer due to different relationship issues and stresses. These issues show forth in the form of physical expressions. When the followers of Christ want to be true disciples of Christ, they want to follow his commandments. One nursing professional refused to recommend a patient for discharge since he had some relationship issues to be addressed. All the other medical needs were met and the patient was introduced to the chaplain to address the spiritual and emotional hurts he was going through. The nurse understood that the healing of relationship is part of the calling mandated by the healing ministry.

Understanding Christ as the Lord of healing demands the healthcare ministers to be part of it uncompromisingly. The founder of CMC, Dr. Ida S Scudder understood that she was not building a medical school, but God's kingdom. This kind of contextual interpretation has made the life of CMC meaningful and relevant.

Some principles for dynamic hermeneutics

The task of biblical interpretation is not for biblical scholars alone, the whole community of faith. It is happening in different fields and arena of life. It is so heart-warming to see that our lives are expressions of our faith. Here we will delineate some common principles we could follow in different contexts, different times and different issues to make this interpretation meaningful, close to the original burden and relevant to the community of believers today.

Applications of hermeneutics

We see this dynamic of hermeneutics operating in every authentic ministry – preaching, teaching, pastoral care, healing ministry, spiritual formation and others. In our drawing of principles, it is good to look at various dimensions of our life and ministry as individuals and as congregations of faith.

Mind the gap

We are familiar with the warning "Mind the gap" as we travel through some structures. I believe, as those who are keenly interested to interpret the scriptures, we need to mind the gap – gap of different kinds. What is recorded in the scripture is removed by time significantly from that of ours. That brings some carefulness, thoughtfulness and insight. We cannot understand that text with no relevance to the time difference.

Cultural and religious gap is another dimension we should be aware of. What emerged as a Palestinian phenomenon cannot encompass the sensitivities and burdens of India. We need to learn carefully the culture and religion in which the Bible is translated and interpreted. Even the words and expressions, analogies and language should be handled with this understanding of gaps.

Historical context

The words that were used 2000 years ago may mean something different in today's context. Therefore, as responsible stewards of the word, we need to look at the appropriate interpretation "then and there", as well as "here and now." The biblical genre we are trying to interpret should be very well understood and learnt by the interpreter.

Bias, objectivity, awareness, sensitivity

As the church of a place and time, we have a goal of interpretation. This can be very well influenced by the interpreter and his philosophical leanings. Just as we focus on what is interpreted, we need to focus on who is interpreting. The personal bias, experience, sensitivity and awareness are directly interconnected with how the interpretation is done. The complete objectivity in biblical interpretation will be something unachievable from human point of view. It is true that whatever hermeneutical approach we follow there is a connection between our interpretations and our philosophical underpinnings.

Divine guidance

Whatever plurality of interpretation we may end up with, since the scripture and its interpretation has a divine dimension, we can rest over the fact that there is a divine control about the variation. Holy Spirit has a control over the interpretation and we as interpreters should submit our will and enthusiasm to God's spirit.

Sensitivity about the contextual issues

As faithful followers of Christ and responsible stewards of our expertise, we need to keep the contextual issues in front of us as we undertake hermeneutics. As ministers of the word and as preachers we are called to hold the scripture on one hand and the newspaper on the other hand. That will make our interpretation relevant, vibrant and dynamic.

Hermeneutics is not just an academic discipline. It is part of Christian discipleship. As we read, meditate, critically study the Bible, the contextual issues and experiences come in front of us. Therefore, we are called to constantly interpret the signs of time and the sourcebook of eternity which God has graciously given us. It is not enough to do this activity as individuals. We are called to undertake this exercise as a community along with divine guidance.

Endnotes

[1] An earlier version of this article was given as a presentation on 4th July 2018 in The Association of Theological Schools in Indonesia, Ambon, Indonesia.

[2] Top 25 Quotes from Lesslie Newbegin, https://www.azquotes.com/author/45909-Lesslie_Newbigin, accessed on 22nd March 2019.

"To Serve:
A Counter Pedagogy of 'To Be Served'"

Deepak Gnana Prakash

The greatness of the Christian Gospel is about the transformation which takes place within oneself. This gospel is challenging in nature through the medium of Christ's love. It embraces suffering in the society and stands tall against evil. The Gospel of Christ urges its believers to enhance and embrace the activity of Christ's ethics and morality. Thanks to the early church for narrating her story of *persecution*, of her *fall and rise*, of her *loyalty*, of her *vision* and of her zeal *to serve*. This gospel enriched the Indian soil with fresh aroma of love, justice and peace. This gospel has been the reason for the emergence of many Indian Christocentric movements but there is a lack in reaching the unreached. For many decades, these movements have been successful in following their vision in varied ways according to one's calling. In this context, Christocentric Indian medical mission movements played a vital role in healing the society by reaching the unreached and touching the untouched by fulfilling their vision. In contemporary times, it is also evident that the existence of mission hospitals in India are being challenged by external and internal forces on theological misconceptions, relishing on past glories and socio-political stress. Healing ministry is not a bed of roses, as it is often bound to face challenges, temptations and trials. The mission bodies are forced to encage their vision and mission due to such challenges. Therefore, it is necessary to reflect on the meaning of "to serve" theologically, contextually and hermeneutically.

'To serve': A theological understanding

Understanding the covenantal relationship of God with us is more important to understand God's mission. The *covenants* which God initiated and made in the beginning with human kind; and the *New covenant* that Christ instituted with his followers in the upper room are summarized at the top of the mountain in *the Great Commission, "Therefore go and make disciples of all nations, baptizing them in the name of the Father, and of the Son and of the Holy Spirit, and teaching them to obey everything I have commanded you. And surely I am with you always to the very end of the age"* . In human made covenants or agreements, usually, the parties are regarded to be equal & are expected to retain their promises; but in the divine covenant the equation is different, it is between the infinite God and the finite human. God's initiation of the covenants are to be regarded as a privilege for humans because through the intervention of Christ Jesus, we've become a part in God's salvific plan. This covenant is unconditional and filled with grace, but we are *'commissioned'* to fulfil the gospel of the (new) covenantal relationship of God with us.

Understanding the mission of God is the primary principle to carry out the gospel. *Missio Dei* (God's mission), that is, God's self-revelation as the One who loves the world, God's involvement in and with the world, the nature and activity of God, which embraces both the church and the world, and in which the church is privileged to participate; *Missio Dei* enunciates the good news that God is a God-for-people. On the contrary, God's nature, mission and purposes are subdued and polluted by the laws which came out of flesh. God's mission and its objective should emerge from the suffering as a service to the suffering. It involves denying oneself and carrying the cross (Math. 16:24) in order to participate in God's mission. It's an ongoing mission of God where we who are the participants in it, have to commit and inherit the deeper purpose to it just like Jesus Christ who understood, pronounced his purpose and committed himself for the mission of God (*the Nazareth Manifesto*, Luke 4:18,19). Kudos to the mission pioneers for they have proclaimed God's favour by bringing peace, harmony and hope among the suffering. God's mission is for the sick, unloved, uncared, unnoticed, untouched, and for all those who are in need of comfort, consolation and justice.

Understanding the salvation of God: The revelation of God in his mission is always for the sake of the salvation of human being. The purpose of the mission is salvation and it requires a (w)holistic approach to define salvation in God's term. There's a lack of careful thought about the (w)holistic approach towards salvation. It has been demeaned as a onetime event in life and salvation has been mostly termed with targets and achievements. This holistic understanding does not deny the supernatural experience of God in one's life when one accepts Christ into his life but stresses on the Christian life that follows that is, being a disciple. Salvation of God should not be subjugated and framed as a short term based mission instead it should be prioritized like apostle Paul as an ongoing mission of God in a person's life *("…because of your partnership in the gospel from the first day until now, being confident of this, that he will carry it on to completion until the day of Christ Jesus. Philippians 1:5-6).*

Understanding the vision of the missions is a challenging part for the participants who are involved in the mission of God. According to one's calling, there may be diversity in vision but it is very important to have a Christocentric vision rather than a vision based on one's own benefit. There are chances for missions to standby in attaining their vision due to external and internal pressure and persecution; drifting away from the vision for which it was established. Many a time the failure to hold on to the vision is being unaccounted for. It is a bitter fact to accept and ponder that missions are called to be persecuted for the sake of Christ; the great commission is a call to come out of our comfort zone and sustain in God's covenantal relationship. If we carry Christ's new life and everlasting love to the desperate world then the healing of our society is God's mission rather than ours. Jesus Christ illustrates his vision with an affirmation to accomplish it in the context of mumbling, rejection and persecution. *"No prophet is accepted in his hometown"*, is a promise, an encouraging and prophetical statement that the vision of the missions will be tested and challenged by the evils in and around us.

"To be served…" Understanding the context

Once upon a time…: This phrase is familiar for most of us especially for those who celebrate the beginning of the healthcare mission and terribly miss the past zeal, commitment, vision and mission atmosphere. In today's context, why do we lack the past zeal? What did they have? Did they have a better understanding of 'to serve' or 'not to be served'? Why do we sing their glory? Is it not in their sacrificial ministry that we take pride in? Is it not the persecution which they've faced that we testify to? To whom were they accountable? To whom were they sent? What made them compassionate towards the sick and the suffering? Because of the fear of disputes, disharmony and insecurities, most often these questions are usually left undiscussed and less pondered.

The urgency: The voice of the martyred is still alive and is motivating us not to drift away from our commitment to serve. In today's context, how do we take a stand in defining, what is 'to be served'? We are compelled to re-read the passage of the request placed by the sons of Zebedee, James and John. The expression 'to sit, one at your right hand and one at your left' is ironic. In the mouth of James and John 'right and left' (verse37) refers to positions of power beside Jesus. But for Jesus, and for the perceptive reader, 'right and left' refer to a very different kind of positions beside Jesus, they are not positions of privilege but places of suffering. Jerry Camery-Hoggatt has suggested that the use of 'right and left' in Mark 10.35-40 should be linked to the usage in 15.27 as part of an ironic construction. The only place in the Gospel of Mark where people actually appear on the right and left sides of Jesus is in 15.27: the two bandits crucified with Jesus. These requested privileges were not rejected but it was challenged by Christ Jesus under the statement

"For the Son of Man did not come to be served, but to serve, and to give his life as a ransom for many." 'To be served' means,

- To ask for privileges
- To attain positions
- Choose to be followers than disciples
- Short term-based visions and objectives for personal benefits
- Living in the past glory
- Not realizing the otherness in others
- Misusing and misunderstanding the ministry of Christ
- Favoritism, etc.

To be served in the context of healthcare missions

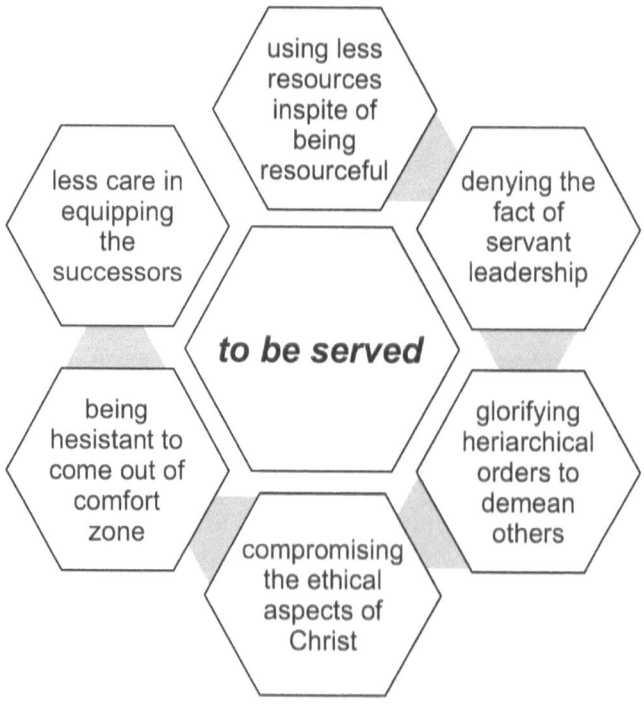

In the process of growth, the healthcare missions need to introspect about being *served*. This introspection should lead us to bring a change in the growth rather just being aware of it. Being 'served' shouldn't be our choice to be in the comfort zone or for survival of our missions. To build a better community and a humane society, Christ's advice for us is to become a ransom for many than to be served. Are we being served?

"To serve: A counter pedagogy of 'to be served'"

The logic: In the midst of an autocratic society and systems filled with loop holes, Jesus' ethics of suffering may sound fishy or even not contextual. Mark 10:32-45 narrates the actual administration of any mission agency of Christ. The sons of Zebedee ask for positions of privilege beside Jesus' glory. Jesus, however, identifies these positions with the places at his right and left beside his cross. In doing so, Jesus presents his glory as the glory of the cross in radical contrast with the glory of the rulers. "…to serve" serves as a counter pedagogy to the glory driven by the world - "to be served". It glorifies the cross alone.

The challenge: What is 'to serve'? What does it mean in the context of healing? There's a fear deep inside the healthcare missions to adopt and to sustain in the 'to serve' module of Christ. Many have compromised but very few are standing firm. The healthcare missions which adopt the 'to serve' module of Christ are consistently being challenged by the feudalists, religious fanatics, commercialists and other external forces; and internal forces such as, disunity, power and position tensions, identity crisis, corruptions, etc.

'To serve: an administrative motif': Ad-ministration (to minister or to serve) is associated with the Greek word ('diakonia, service). The very motif of administration is being in the service with objectives and vision. The principle of Christ's administration always stands against the world orders. Therefore, missions should not be surprised of being cornered or demeaned by external forces. Missions should take privilege in taking shelter under God's *charis* (grace). 'To serve' doesn't mean to be submissive but being persuasive in advocating the society with

positive attitude and facilitating the suffering to experience God. The rapid decline in the (w)holistic approach towards healing ministry are due to the disputes in understanding the vision and mission of an administration. Healthcare missions should be mindful of being effective instruments of God's salvific plan.

'*To serve: a proposal*': The mission of God is an on-going process. We have been invited to take part in the table of Christ's suffering and the glory of the cross. Christ proposed the concept of 'to serve' in an optimistic way to ensure that God's kingdom be built for the suffering community. Are we ready 'to serve'? The challenge is placed in front of us to ponder and respond. Having known the significance of 'to serve', are we still being passive? 'To serve' is a proposal to the present generation to choose or deny; but remarkably it is the only option for Christ's mission to build God's kingdom. One cannot decorate (build) God's kingdom without being empathetic in vision and objective. 'To serve' means 'how much we have lost rather than how much we have earned?' May the triune God help us to serve and not to be served.

Spiritual Care Through Healing Communities

Finney Alexander

A healing community functions as the arm of the Church in the healing ministry of Christ. Mission hospitals and other healthcare organizations who adhere to the call of God to be a witness in the healing ministry of Christ form healing communities. They provide medical, social, emotional, mental and spiritual care to those who suffer with various kinds of diseases. Trend for specialization and scientific approach to medicine may negate seeing a patient with spiritual needs. Christ's summary of the commandments gives us clarity to care for a person spiritually. He said, "Love the Lord your God with all your heart, with all your soul and with all your mind. And love your neighbour as yourself." The reference to heart, mind and soul provides an integral and wholistic approach to a person. We worship God engaging our heart, mind and soul and we serve others recognising the fact that people whom we serve have got needs of the heart, mind and soul. Loving God and loving our neighbour is not optional. It is an obligation. Even when the Indian church faces opposition to its witness at various levels, we need to provide the message of healing, love and hope to so many. No force can overpower the Christ's message of love, because it is self-giving and sacrificial. The relevance of spiritual care through healing communities has a greater relevance for healing communities in the present time.

Health, spirituality and spiritual care through healing communities

Judith Allen Shelly makes a meaningful description of health: "Health is being able to live as God created us to be – as an integrated whole, living in loving relationship with God, self and others."[1]

The origin of Christian Medical College, Vellore and other mission hospitals in India are founded in the vision to meet the health needs of the community by partnering in the healing ministry of Christ. It involves providing competent and compassionate care to the patient in the spirit of Christ. Here, the patient is also seen as a Spiritual being. A spiritual being has got spiritual needs. A health care professional who primarily takes care of the body of a person should also be aware of the spiritual needs of a person. The definition of health goes beyond how it is defined by the World Health Organization or some medical dictionaries. Dorland's illustrated medical dictionary defines health as: "a state of optimal physical, mental and social wellbeing and not merely the absence of disease and infirmity."[2] It has failed to add the spiritual dimension to the physical, mental and social wellbeing of a person. This fourth dimension called the "spiritual" dimension of health is very integral in the practice of medicine. Rosaline Hudson argues that "Spirituality is not an optional extra in a healthcare system."[3] Daniel P Sulmasy gives a valid explanation to this. He says, "Illness is a spiritual event. Illness grasps persons by the soul as well as by the body and disturbs both. Illness raises troubling questions of a transcendent nature – questions about meaning, value, and relationship. These questions are spiritual."[4] He argues that attending to the spiritual needs of a patient is a moral obligation. Thus, the call upon healing communities is to attend to the needs of a person as whole – including their spiritual needs.[5] Considering health should be considering the needs of the complete person as created by God.

Dictionary of Pastoral care and counselling defines Spirituality as "a person's life and activity in relationship with God, and to oneself, other people, and all things in reference to God."[6] Spiritual Care is defined as "the activities and ways of being that bring spiritual quality of life, wellbeing and function – all of which are dimensions of health to clients."[7] As we talk about wholistic care, I acknowledge the fact that there are misconceptions about understanding the role of spirituality in the healing process. Studies done in this area have found out positive outcomes between spirituality and healing. This brings a focused attention on incorporating spirituality and spiritual care practices in health care practice. I did a small study among 20 patient relatives to understand and assess the perception Spiritual Care by patient's relatives who bring their loved one for treatment in Christian Medical College, Vellore.[8] The methodology used for this assessment was through self-administered questionnaire and interviews.

Perception of spiritual care from a patient's point of view

The analysis of my study reveals that patients and their relatives esteem highly the spiritual care provided by Chaplaincy in Christian Medical College, Vellore. The most valued response was the prayer at the bedside and prayer and worship services conducted in the chapel. Patients and their relatives expressed their gratitude for:

a. Recognition of the presence of God in the campus. Patients and their relatives say that they feel the presence of God in a powerful way as they step into the hospital campus. These patients are not necessarily Christians. Most of them are non-Christians. They have a special regard for the hospital and its facilities. They believe that God is in this palace and they go through a divine experience.

b. Visit of a chaplain in the ward. As a chaplain I get so many opportunities to be a witness for Christ. When I visit patients in the ward, they are generally open for prayer and receiving Bible literature. I use this opportunity to share tracts, New Testaments. I have witnessed how Christ transforms people in their ties of need. We have a practice of taking the choir to the ward and song for patients. Many patients tell that it is very comforting for them. For many this is a first-time experience.

c.   Excellent medical treatment offered to them. They said the medical treatment happening in CMC is par excellence. The hospital has got good facilities for diagnosis and for treatment.

d.   Trustworthy doctors and medical staff. The patients and their relatives are able to trust doctors wholeheartedly.

This brief analysis of the patient's perspective of Spiritual care encourages us to do more through the work of healing communities. Antonia M. van Loon provides a health ministry model for healing communities through the example of Faith Community Nursing. The model represents healing ministry as a life-giving tree that brings forth healing transformation, health and life for individuals and community. The tree is grounded and rooted in love for God and love for others. Here, the healing community is called by God to offer one's gifts and talents to promote health, transformation, and healing and the compassionate care of people.[9]

Compassionate care: face of a healing community

We want our patients to experience the compassionate care of Christ through our service. When Jesus looked at the crowd, he had compassion on them. We want the patients and their relatives to know that they are not like sheep without a shepherd. Let them know that there are people who care for them. CMC believes in sharing the trust and love of God to everyone in need. We don't hope to advertise for our services. Rather we would like it to happen through the *word of mouth*. We want our nation to know what Christ can do in every patient's life. We would like to be a 'counter culture' in this world of 'business culture'. We don't want to be known as a hospital making money out of somebody's sickness.

Physical: Compassionate care speaks volumes on physical wellbeing of a person. The word 'Compassion' means 'with those who suffer'. Compassion tells about the number of physical activities a person does towards the physical health of individuals and communities.

Social: A society is built by people who treat each other with love and compassion. The healing ministry of Christ is fueled by the compassion and mercy of Christ. Those in need are able to recognize this value more and pass it on to others. No one can negate the power of compassion. Any one in need and their dear ones are so satisfied when someone deals with them in a compassionate way.

Spiritual: Compassion is a spiritual value. Bible says, "When Jesus saw the crowd, he felt compassion for them because they were like sheep without a shepherd". We understand the character and nature of God through his compassion. As the Word of God reminds us, his compassion never fails. (Lamentations 3:22)

Intellectual: The compassionate care provides opportunities to heal the mind and the heart. Because it is a godly virtue, it affects the functioning of the brain, mind and heart in a positive and healthy way.

Economic: CMC wants to identify with the marginalised and the poor. But as an institution we also want to treat the rich. We provide good facilities for the rich while they are admitted. Most of the rich people would be having Insurance Medical Coverage. CMC charges on these patients are according to the 'market rates. But the idea behind this charging is to get a share of the income treating the rich people is given for charity fund. Those who are genuinely poor will get concession for their treatment. Much money is given for charity through CMC. CMC never advertise all this. It is a work done quietly like a yeast, to be the salt and light of the society.

Thus, the compassionate care of Christ is extended through staff and students to the patients who come to our hospital. Christ centered compassionate care is being provided to integrating medicine and faith. It reflects the display of being the counter culture by becoming the salt and light. It is very encouraging to see that this core value of our institution is incremental and transformative, as staff and students are able to catch on the vision to a greater extent.

A temple of healing

Rev Dr Valsan Thampu in his book "Be Thou my vision" comments about the verse, "My house shall be called a house of prayer for all nations". He highlights the integration of worship and acts of healing in the temple – the place of worship. "To pray in the name of Jesus is also to be willing to intervene in the affairs of the world in obedience to His call".[10] While chasing the money lenders and the traders from Jerusalem temple, Jesus reinstated the purpose for prayer and worship. Jesus was happy to heal the sick and the suffering who came to the temple. He healed them (Mathew 21:14).

Understanding the model – prayer and medicine

Jesus' three-fold model of ministry of preaching, teaching and healing. It is the model for healing communities too.

Matthew 4:23 underlines this. "Jesus went around Galilee, teaching in their synagogues, preaching the good news of the Kingdom and healing every disease and sickness among the people." As Jesus was sending his disciples for ministry, he send them with this instruction: "As you go, proclaim this message: 'the kingdom of heaven has come near. Heal those are ill, raise the dead, cleanse those who have leprosy, drive out demons. Freely you have received, freely give." (Matthew 10:7,8). Jesus gave the same pattern to the disciples to follow and to us today to continue the same. Looking at the context of CMC Vellore, I would like to mention two patterns of ministry done by the Bible women and Drs Paul and Margaret Brand.

Bible women

CMC's 118 years of witness to the healing ministry of Christ is a living example of God's faithfulness and blessing when we as a body of Christ becomes faithful to his call. When Ida Scudder started her medical practice, she invited a group of Women to work with her as Bible women. When Ida Scudder went into the community to see patients, these Bible Women would accompany her. As Ida Scudder treated the physical ailments, these Bible Women spoke from the Word of God. They read the healing narratives of Jesus and shared the love and compassion of Christ with people. This resulted in the healing of the body and soul of the individuals and communities, thus Bible and Medicine was given together. Faith and Science went hand – in hand. There was no separation of the body, mind and soul. It was a wholistic care.

The ministry of the Bible women eventually became the work of Chaplaincy. We continue to share from the Bible about the love, forgiveness and healing Christ provides to patients and their families in the wards and in the chapel services. Patients who had never heard about Jesus gets an opportunity to hear about Jesus, read the Bible and experience the healing and salvation Christ provides. Once a 70 year old gentleman came to me and said: Your God (Jesus) is a powerful God. Please pray to him, I want to come out of my smoking habit. It was a good opportunity for me to share the gospel and pray for him.

Dr. Paul Brand and Dr. Margaret Brand

Later the work of transformation was expanded in many forms. Dr. Paul Brand pioneered the work among the Leprosy patients. It was a time when the leprosy patients were looked upon as 'Untouchables' of the society. Dr. Paul Brand through his research found that the bacteria led infection causing damage to the limbs and other body parts cause the loss of pain. Hence, they were prone to more injury causing more wounds. Dr. Brand invented the 'Tendon Muscle' reconstructive surgery to make the limbs work. It was a success. The care and compassion seen in the doctor and the innovative medical approach won the hearts of many 'untouchable'. They were really touched by Dr. Paul. Later he established a rehabilitation campus for them to stay with their families. Thus, so many families who lost identity and meaning in life regained it by the work of Dr. Paul Brand and his wife Dr. Margaret Brand.

It is interesting to note that Dr. Paul Brand's vision to build communities of healing had a spark through his divine exposures. We need to thank God and the parents of Paul who instilled this vision in him. He was sent to their home called 'Nethania' in England for formal education. 'Nethania' means 'gift of God'. He understood life as a gift of God and all life is of God. He came to regard all of God's creation as of immense value. This understanding motivated him to 'see God in everyone and 'God's love in everything'. He worked for a world where individuals and communities received healing in the face of suffering and despair through the power of the love of Christ. He saw pain as the 'gift' nobody wants.

Faithful to the call as a healing community

A trend that can hinder the community transformation through our institutions is the trend to go in the 'Corporate Style'. Our institutions are called to be on the side of the marginalised and the poor. We should be relevant to the needs of the common person. Our development should not be at the cost of the poor. As we have new campuses, buildings and other infrastructure, let the poor and marginalised feel at home in our campus. Our developments should not keep away those in real need and in poverty.

When Ida Scudder started her work in Vellore in 1900, she used to go to the villages in her cart to see patients. There was no concept of a hospital then. When people did not come to her establishment, she went to them. This is a very 'inside out' approach. Afterwards patients began to come to the hospital. We see in the approach of Ida Scudder the ability to bridge gap. We need to continue this approach despite all 'developments. I strongly believe that as Jesus was available to the common man and woman – on the streets and in the margins. Healing communities should continue to identify ourselves with the 'least and the lost'. In this way we fulfil the commandments of Christ – 'loving God and loving our neighbour'. A transformed community would look like "individuals and communities being a witness to the love of Christ as we offer the care of Christ"

Go and do likewise – the wider impact of healing communities

Christ's work of transformation is the reason for our witness. When the Samaritan woman received a personal encounter with Jesus Christ, it evolved a transformation in her life. Jesus addressed her physical, social, emotional and spiritual needs. The healing that Christ brought in her life empowered her to go to her community and tell everyone about what Christ did to her. We see that people believed in what she told them. They were challenged to come and see Jesus. So, the Samaritan woman led her community to witness Christ. They said: "We no longer believe just because of what you said: now we have heard for ourselves, and we know that this man really is the Saviour of the world" (John 4:42).

Take the case of Zacchaeus. Zacchaeus' personal encounter with Christ led him to stand before his people to say; "look Lord! here and now I give half of my possession to the poor, and if I have cheated anybody out of anything, I will pay back four times the amount" (Luke 19:8). Through the parable of the Good Samaritan, Jesus teaches us that we need to continue to do the ministry of the Samaritan. At the end of the parable Jesus asked the expert of the law: "Which of these three do you think was a neighbour to the man who fell into the hands of robbers?" The expert in the law replied, "The one who had mercy on him." Jesus told him, "Go and do likewise."

As a Christian institution, we have the mandate from Christ to "Go and do likewise" so that individuals and communities experience the transforming power of Christ to heal and to be 'made whole.' Ministering as Christ would minister calls us for an effective partnership. A culture of caring based on the compassionate presence of Christ will have ripple effects in our communities. The people are waiting to see the physical demonstration of the work of the Kingdom of God through the witness of the church. Our call is to enhance the building of God's Kingdom in the vision of abundance of life for all as offered by Jesus Christ in the Gospel of John 10:10. It is so encouraging to see that Christ calls ordinary people like us to accomplish extra ordinary things for him. As healing communities, we need to renew this call and continue in the work of his Kingdom till the ends of the world. This is our privilege and our purpose.

References

Hudson, Rosaline. "Personhood", *Oxford Textbook of Spirituality in Healthcare*, eds., Mark Cobb, Puchalski, Christina M. Bruce Rumbold. Oxford: Oxford University Press, 2012.

Sulmasy, Daniel P. *The Rebirth of the Clinic*. Washington: Georgetown University Press, 2006.

Shelly, Judith Allen. "Nursing: Remaining Faithful in an Era if Change." in *The Changing Face of Healthcare* edited by John F. Kilner, Robert D Orr, and Judith Allen Shelly. Grand Rapids: William B Eerdmans, 1998.

Dorland's Illustrated Medical Dictionary, 28th edition.Philadelphia: W.B. Saunders Company, 1994.

Ministry to the Dying

Samson Varghese

Das was admitted with a cancerous tumour in his gall bladder. Lying in the hospital bed, tears were rolling down his cheeks as he watched his wife also in tears. He was ventilating his feelings to the Pastoral caregiver who had come to meet him.

Jayalakshmi was diagnosed with breast cancer. She underwent chemotherapy, but knew that her days were numbered. Her children were taking care of her. She displayed lot of strength and courage as her treatment progressed. After few months she became very sick and one morning she passed away.

Raghu was watching his cancer affected wife lying in the bed partly unconscious. Different thoughts were coming to his mind, thoughts about the future, her chances of survival, the treatment, children, thoughts about God etc.

These are a few instances of people facing the reality of death. Sometimes in our life we may go through such experiences or maybe called to care for the dying and their family members. Sometimes 'death' happens in a sudden unexpected way. At such moments, the family members are left in a state of 'shock'. But at other instances, if there is enough time, the dying and the loved ones can be helped to come to a state of acceptance.

Thomas C. Oden defines 'death' as, "a point of separation from the known to the unknown, from being to non-being. It is to lose vital power, to become breathless, inanimate and devoid of motion." As we live in a society, which has a death-denying culture, there is all the possibility for the dying and their loved ones to either postpone or not discuss the topic of 'death' at all.

Do we accept the ministry to the dying as part of the healing ministry? Can 'death' mean healing in a person or is death a threat to healing?

Let us see in brief the Christian understanding of death.

Christian understanding of death

In the raising of Lazarus (John 11:11-16) and the daughter of Jairus (Mark 5:39 42), Jesus refers to death as 'sleep'. By doing this, Jesus distinguishes between physical death and ultimate death. St. Paul tells about 'death' as a daily occurrence (Romans 6: 3-11). The physical death and resurrection of Jesus is something we need to relate to daily, so that death and resurrection becomes a daily experience for us.

In Luke 12: 16-21, Jesus teaches about our approach to death: that we need to be ready at any time for our death or our loved ones. In John 17:1-5 as well as in 2 Timothy 4:6–8, we see Jesus as well as St. Paul, telling about their death with enthusiasm. The Apostle Paul to some level was able to conquer death, for he was able to say, "for me to die is gain" and "O death, where is thy sting, O grave, where is thy victory?" (1 Corinthians 15:55).

The caregiver's role

Therefore caregivers have a challenging role to play in preparing the dying and their loved ones come to terms with death and face it with courage and hope. Following the example of Jesus who 'healed all kinds of sickness' (Matthew 9:35), the Church has from the beginning shown concern for the care of the dying. This process can be painful and complex for the dying, their family as well as for the caregivers. Feelings such as fear, anger, self-blame, helplessness, frustration, loneliness and guilt may arise as one encounters death or as the family cares for the dying.

The caregiver should give the dying the freedom to express their feelings, fears, faith and hopes. It requires time, energy and help in going through this delicate process. The caregiver should also be aware of his/her own view of death so that it can be a personal reference point in ministering to the dying.

Jesus cared for the whole person. He cared before he cured. The caregiver embodies someone with whom they can hope and journey with. As sickness and suffering brings out the individuality of each person, with their strengths and weaknesses, the caregiver has a task in identifying with the individuality of each person. It was this personalized caring that made Jesus attractive to the sick ones. The dying are at ease if they know that those caring for them are concerned for their comfort and respect them as individuals.

The greatest pain of the dying is often the pain of loneliness, rejection and isolation. Therefore the caregiver needs to establish a relationship with them. He is one who is alongside the dying, at the same time being fully human and a witness to Christ.

The caregiver needs to go along with the pace of the dying and their loved ones; and during this process they place their trust in him/her. The caregiver can be transparent in admitting his/her inadequacy and powerlessness in understanding the mysteries of death. This can be binding force in their relationship. When the bond gets strengthened, feelings of anger, loneliness, isolation, guilt and fears come to the surface.

The caregiver also has a great role in 'listening' to the dying. It is not what to tell the dying, but of what we will let him tell us. They should be given the opportunity to express and ventilate their feelings. They should be given the freedom even to throw their accusations at God. The caregiver through his interactions shows that God is great enough, not only to accept our faults, but also our accusations. While listening the caregiver also understands whether they are ready to face the fact or not.

The family plays a significant role during the illness and their reactions affect the dying's response to his/her illness. For the loved ones, it is a struggle between being forced by circumstances to surrender the person to death and being compelled by emotional ties to "hold on" to them. Therefore the caregiver needs to be aware and sensitive to the many feelings of insecurities that the family may be going through like child-rearing, finance, loneliness etc. He accompanies them in their impending bereavement. Often family members hide their feelings from the dying and try to keep a smiling face. Involved listening to the family's concerns, wishes and needs, sincere participation and acceptance of tears and brokenness contribute to healing.

The caregiver should encourage the dying and their loved ones to discuss openly their thoughts, feelings and questions about death. It is a positive way of dealing with life's most universal truth. The caregivers can relieve the family of some of the tasks, cook an occasional meal or take the children to play. When the dying person is bed-ridden or limited in their functioning, there may be a sense of loss. The family needs will vary as the illness progresses and moves towards death. The caregiver can contribute in helping the family to maintain a balance between serving the dying and respecting their own needs.

The dying may have various worries about unfinished jobs. They can be helped in this. They can also be reassured by stressing what they did achieve and what his life has stood for.

The presence of a stable reliable caregiver can bring the dying a great sense of safety. They may experience a great relief from being able to unburden themselves of fears, grief, guilt, failure, loneliness and frustration. But the caregiver has to be prepared to be disturbed by their uncomfortable feelings.

The caregiver can help the dying discover a meaning in his/her sufferings and thereby keep him/her away from depression. Through these stages, the dying swings between being dependent and self-sufficient. Regular and frequent visits should be given to the dying to show that interest is still being taken in them.

Pastoral caregivers can be called to administer sacraments like Holy Eucharist or Anointing. This brings the presence of Christ very real to them. Though the physical strength is disintegrating, the spirit is elevated through the sacraments.

Caregivers who see many people die should remind themselves that what is familiar for them maybe the biggest adventure for the dying. Such care provides a sense of purpose, self- esteem and dignity to the dying.

Being involved in the intimate moments of one's death is a privilege and a challenge. The care of the caregiver helps the dying and their loved ones face up to the mystery of death and have a positive approach towards death. The visible presence of the caregiver helps them to understand the invisible God. A 'divine encounter' takes place at the bedside and strengthens the dying to go through the valley of the shadow of death.

Being and Becoming
a Community of God's People

Sunny Philip

The early Disciples of Jesus Christ saw themselves as a called out, set apart and sent out community.[1] **To be set apart**, in the vocabulary of Christ, did not mean isolation or separation from the world. The called-out community was also **a send out community.**[2] The relevance of the community is evidenced in its *going out* – their mission. The way of the Kingdom must therefore become a life-style.[3] "The kingdom of God is not only a new place to go but a new way to get there."[4] It is expected that the way God's people live will, by its very nature, affect the lives of those they live with.[5] A person or an institution is credible when they know who they are and conduct their lives in congruence with that knowledge.

Coming together of a community

Once Jesus told a story about a man who had an unexpected visitor, at the most inconvenient time.[6] The visitor was hungry and needed to be fed. The unprepared host had nothing to put before his famished visitor. It wouldn't have been a major problem if the visitor had not arrived in the middle of the night. The shops were already shut and people in the neighbourhood were asleep. Being duty bound to feed his hungry guest, he walked over to his next-door neighbour and knocked at his door. At first his neighbour refused to get up and help him. *"Please leave me alone. I am already in bed and I don't want to wake up the children who are asleep with me."* But he persisted. A little later the reluctant man invited his friend to his store room and let him help himself to whatever he needed.

Jesus shared this story to encourage his hearers to invite God into the affairs of their lives, to include him in their daily deliberations and not to give up, even if it might initially appear to be a lost cause. One man's untimely visit showed up another man's emptiness, which initially revealed the third person's reluctance to help because he was inconvenienced. In the end there was togetherness and happiness. This is how a group of people become a community. This parable, though, initially intended to illustrate the importance of prayer, holds many lessons about the coming together of the Christian community. The identity, credibility and accountability of a community is evidenced in the way they choose to live in the context of their call and mission.

Emptiness

Even a casual reader of this story is drawn towards the man who is woken up in the middle of the night to be greeted by a hungry friend. With a bit of imagination, we can listen to the conversation between him and his wife. We feel their shame and embarrassment in having nothing to set before the hungry traveler. Then we move with the host as he goes to his next-door neighbour. We wait with him outside the door. We listen to the embarrassing conversation. So far the story is all about emptiness. But the story also teaches us that we have no need to be afraid of our emptiness. If we hide our emptiness our guests will remain hungry. When there is plenty next door, there is no need for my guest to go to bed hungry.

From a sociological point of view, Jesus' little story captures the predicament of the world today. There are people with resources who refuse to get out of bed because all they can think of is their personal peace and affluence. On the other side, there are those who are at the mercy of others whose dishonesty, arrogance and complacency keep them in spiritual and physical poverty. Then there are those who pretend that they have no need for anything though they are empty and have nothing to offer to anyone.

From a spiritual point of view, Jesus wanted his hearers to understand that we don't have to be afraid of being empty, provided our emptiness:

1. Does not stop us from doing what God wants us to do- keeping our eyes open to the world around us; and

2. Drives us closer to God so that we can get to know him better – keeping our eyes open to see God as he truly is.

Sometimes we feel intimidated by the thought of emptiness. But this parable is not about our emptiness or the needs of the people around us. It is about the heart of God. Having narrated this parable, Jesus drew the attention of his disciples to the importance of prayer (vv.9, 10). Then he told them why we should pray. We pray not because we have a great need, but because we have a great God. Need is the occasion not the reason for our prayer. What motivates us to pray is the heart of God.

The man who had nothing to give to his friend, went to his neighbour because of his relationship with him. He persisted because he knew his heart. We go to God in our emptiness and come away with God himself. We may go to him for bread, but we come away with his embrace. Emptiness is for filling. Even better, emptiness *is* filling.

Sharing

We sometimes falsely assume that equality is the key to community. In the story of the three friends narrated above, Jesus did not advocate equality. The opposite was the reality. The three people in the parable represent three diverse sections of every community. First, there is the hungry and homeless man. He is far away from home- helpless and dependent on others' kindness and goodness. The second man is neither hungry nor homeless. He ate his dinner with his family and now he is in his own bed sound asleep. But he has nothing to spare. Nothing left over for the next day. The third man has sufficient supplies for his needs and has surplus. This is community then and now. This is us, in spite our sophisticated technology and social development. In a couple sentences Jesus painted a picture that no discerning person can ignore. No. We are not all equal. We have never been equal, and we will never be equal. And inequality is not the problem of the human race. Our problem is our unwillingness to share.

The chain that binds us is the fear that if we share we will not have enough for tomorrow. From a sociological point of view, the hungry, homeless man fuels my fear of becoming like him if I am not *careful*. And carefulness becomes apathy which may even lead to cruelty. Social, ethnic and religious prejudice, discrimination, oppression and even slavery are the visible expressions of the doctrine of self-preservation. Those who succumb to the self-preservation ethic eventually form island communities. They find their identity in their homogeneity instead of their diversity. They feel safer in their cages.

From a spiritual point of view, in the name of orthodoxy we have made God sterile and static. We prefer to preserve God for future generations rather than experience His presence with us. We have become petrified of anyone who is different from us because we believe that we have the only way to connect with God.

Sharing unchains us from the fear of insecurity and creates a new chain that connects. It is a different kind of binding where our individuality finds expression in the context of the community. And our freedom comes from the assurance of knowing that we belong. The chain that connects is the opposite of the chain of bondage. It is the cord of harmony.

Christians are called to live as the people of God in the world of God. They are a community within a community- part of it, but different from it. It includes all kinds of people- the people who have been caught in the very act of *adultery* and the people who are itching to stone those who are caught (John 8:2-11), and those who don't care about how others live. Every community is made up of people who lack identity: people who destroy others' dignity, and also those who don't care about others. The Christian community exist within this wider community, as prototype rather than a monotype. We are a sign of things yet to come rather than the perfection of it.

If community is a place of belonging, then sharing is the key to it. And this sharing must happen not only among those within my immediate community but also those outside that community. Or else the belonging simply leads to exclusivity and selfishness. We must take care to protect the otherness within the togetherness. That which gives me identity and solidarity can result in hostility and discord. That which gives me security can lead to insecurity. Sharing is the mission of the community, as it reaches out to others and becomes an agent of transformation and renewal.

Inner vulnerability

The idea of sharing might give us the impression that we are by nature wired to share. In fact, we are not by nature geared to share. The raw human impulse is self-preservation. The human race, alienated from God and ignorant of God's design for life, cannot overnight become a sharing community. For this we need the grace of God. Living in Grace is different from living for grace. (We have not time to elaborate on this. Experiencing inner vulnerability is the antidote to spiritual dishonesty, which is a form of self-deception).

The problem with evangelical Christianity, as I see it, is that we have made it rather sterile. We are very happy to talk about all the bad things we did before Christ. In fact, we think, the worse it was, the better it is. So we even embellish them. But how about all the bits after the great discovery of Jesus? We seem to suffer from selective amnesia!!

We seem to give the impression that we are super humans now that we have Jesus. It is far easier to write about pre-conversion sins, of sins we have repented of, than of those with which we still struggle on a daily basis. Inner vulnerability is acknowledging our struggle with the persistent sins of our lives to which there is no easy or immediate solution. The Bible is a good starting point for our education in this area. This collected work of sinful saints is a record of the experiences of highs and lows and everything in between.

Spiritually speaking, inner vulnerability is allowing God's grace to work silently on our troubled and restless lives. Vulnerability is not the same as victim-mentality. The victim, in this case, is our own defeated self, the self that rebels against God. Christian ministry is not only the ministry **to** the weak and vulnerable, but it is the ministry **of** the weak and vulnerable- the "bruised reed." The "Servant of the Lord" who was sent to minister to the "bruised reed" (Isaiah 42:1-4) was himself "smitten," "crushed," and "wounded" (Isaiah 53:1-10).

Sociologically speaking, when inner vulnerability is accepted as a way of life, power becomes a matter of self-limitation rather than self-exaltation. Jesus cautioned those who wished to follow him, "if any man would come after me, let him deny himself and take up his cross daily and follow me." This is the voluntary abdication of the right to power. We are empowered by what we let go of rather than what we hold on to. Recognition must come to us rather than us wasting a lifetime searching for it. We get to places of importance by invitation. Our significance must come from what we let go of rather than what we hold on to.

Life of a wounded soul with a healing spirit

Why does a soul become wounded? Is it because of what has happened, or due to its inability to respond to what has happened in a Godly manner? It is easier to manipulate and control people than to love them. Love is best expressed in the context of healthy, intimate relationships, while manipulative power is exercised in the absence of such relationships. The Bible does not tell us about a manipulating God who takes advantage of the gullibility of his creation, but of one who is prepared to stay with them, however painful that may be, not only with a view to redeem them but also because he cares for them and wants to experience their pain. The central theme of the Bible is that of the God who understands and stays with his people in their suffering (Genesis 21:15-21; Exodus 3:5-10; Luke 2:25-32; Rev 21:3,4). The biblical history is a suffering-sensitive story. Jesus refused to live by the self-protective ideology adopted by the leaders of his time (Matthew 6:8,16-18; 7:15-20). For him, leadership that was devoid of suffering was to be abandoned at all cost (Matthew 5:11-12; 8:20; Luke 9:23-26; 12:4, 22; 18:31-33). And he did so at the cost of his life.

This is the essence of the grain of wheat falling on the ground and dying, or the same grain falling between two stones and being crushed and later on baked in a hot oven to be made into life-sustaining bread. It is broken for a purpose: for the nourishing of others. It is not good enough for the soul to be wounded. It must, in its woundedness, become a conduit of the spirit of healing.

Living an antithetical life

Jesus challenged the world by what he did, or even better, the way he did what he did. Jesus also challenged the world by what he did not do, refused to do, and the reasons for not doing it. We are pretty good at NOT doing things that are bad, evil, ungodly, etc. But how good are we at NOT doing things that are good, needful and relevant. It seems Jesus practiced both. There is a time to turn water into wine and to feed thousands with a few loaves of bread. There is also a time to refrain from turning stones into bread, though there is nothing wrong with that. Why didn't Jesus make poverty history? It may be a good idea to look at all the things Jesus could have done but did not do, even at the cost of being misunderstood.

"Am I prepared to be misunderstood for what I believe I should not do?" is a question worth asking. In this regard, a healthy theology of failure is important for every Christian leader. We must walk away from two temptations: 1. Refuse to turn stones into bread if it is for the wrong reason, 2. Stop pretending that stones are bread.

Our spirituality shapes our principles and our principles shape our actions. Then, the way we live becomes a matter of priorities: What is important? Unless we have a proper relationship with God on a daily basis our priorities will become contaminated and controlled by our needs and wants. Then we will become self-centered and irrelevant even to us.

As a community of God's people, we need to ask the question "Am I prepared to walk away?" or, even more importantly, "What am I prepared to walk away from?"We are constantly instructed to walk away from sin. We are even good at defining sin. But are we equally good at defining what is ungodly. What is ungodly are those of our thoughts and actions that dishonor God though they may not be bad in itself. Just because there is a need and just because I can, I don't have to do it. Not every need is my responsibility. I don't have to do everything I can do.

Living in grace

Living *in* grace is not the same as living *for* grace. Those who live in grace demonstrate grace and extend it even to the most undeserving. After all, that is the very essence of grace – unmerited favour given to the most underserving person. But those who live for grace feel that they have nothing to contribute. Often the good they do ends up being selfish because they crave and demand others' approval for what they do.

Growing by learning

A living community is also a learning community. We learn from our past experiences, success and failures. We also learn from others like us and unlike us. A truly godly community hears what God says to them, interprets what they hear and then acts on that understanding. We do not *hear* God's word just on Sunday in the church. We hear it every day in God's world. That is where we learn from God. Learning happens when we are prepared to put "our story" next to the stories of the people around us who may or may not be like us. Island communities cannot become learning communities.

United by forgiving

We cannot understand forgiveness unless we understand the character of God. When God forgives me, what I should focus on is not the personal benefit of that forgiveness, but the character of God manifested through that forgiveness. Forgiveness is not just the cancellation of the past. It has implications for the future: creating new transformed relationships. This is what John the Baptist demanded from those who came to receive his baptism. He said, bear the fruit that befits repentance. This is **discipleship**. I forgive because I am forgiven. Forgiveness is proclaiming the character of God: his goodness, love and grace. This is our **witness** to the unrepentant community around us.

The community of Jesus Christ is not just a group of likeminded people coming together for a purpose. He expects them to be a learning, growing, giving, forgiving organism. Their credibility is not that they do everything right but that they aim to do the right things and are not afraid to acknowledge it when they are wrong. They are not afraid to make mistakes and are prepared to take risks in the name and spirit of Jesus Christ. Ultimately, they demonstrate the character of their Lord and Master.

The Christian community finds its identity in the very nature and purpose of its existence as a called out, set apart and send out people. This paper explores certain basic principles that defines and distinguishes it from many other communities. Sharing from emptiness, caring in vulnerability, healing and forgiving when wounded, growing by learning and living in grace are some of the hallmarks of the people of God. This community exists as an organic, dynamic humanity, ever changing, moving towards a climax. Its aim is not just to exist or to perpetuate itself from generation to generation but to influence and transform cultures and communities. The methods it adopts must be consistent with the life and teachings of its master who was not afraid to give his life so that we may find life. The Christian community is not a perfect specimen but a prototype of what it eventually becomes. It must constantly evaluate what it is becoming rather than being preoccupied with their current accomplishments or past glory.

Endnotes

[1] Mark 3:13,14; Acts 1:7,8; Matthew 28:19; 1 Peter 2:9,10). George Forell describes the church as "a colony of heaven" with the "double function" of "opposing and permeating' the world "simultaneously like leaven and salt." *Christian Social Teachings* (Minneapolis: Augsburg Publishing House, 1966), 13.

[2] Mathew 28:18-20; 1 Peter 2:9,10.

[3] Gordon Preece, a theologian and a professor in social ethics, captures this idea in the colourful title of an article he wrote for the Zadok Paper- *'The Republic of God is a Great Outdoor Restaurant,'* (S 91, Summer, 1998), 3-8. In this essay he argues, "If politics is about everyday life, even more so is theology.", 5.

[4] John Stoner and Lois Barrett, *Letters to American Christians* (Scottdale, Pennsylvania: Herald Press, 1989), 78.

[5] Matthew 5:14,16; 1 Peter 3:1-2, 16.

[6] Luke 11:5-8.

Inclusive Hospitality of God's Kingdom

Joseph Devaraj D

T he word 'health' is mainly understood as the wellbeing of the physical body. If anyone doesn't have any ill health, according to the above mentioned understanding, she or he may be the person with good health. The same way, the term 'healing' is also widely misunderstood with the connotation of 'curing'. Therefore, we should have a correct understanding of both 'health' and 'healing'. However, this article would try to bring out the right meaning of health and healing, and also this would try to bring out how health and healing has a vital relationship with the entity of the Kingdom of God. Also, this article would enhance the readers to understand that health and healing in the Christian sense, means healing of the whole person. The World Health Organization (WHO) emphatically defines the term health "is a state of complete physical, mental and social well-being and not merely the absence of disease or infirmity."[1] It would also be beneficial to include the spirituality and faith aspect of a person to see a person as a whole. Eng Hoe, the author of the book, *The Gospel of the Kingdom*, opines that, "the Gospel is not only a message of good news to get us into heaven, but also good news that we can be part of God's Kingdom on earth which involves living whole and fulfilling lives here on earth. God is concerned for the whole person, not just his spirit and soul, not just his eternal salvation but also his whole being here on earth…"[2]

Theology of health and healing

As we are working among the sick and suffering community, every day we see their pain and pathos, that compels us to understand God intended health and healing at the context of pain, suffering, death and various other constrains of the humanity. When we talk about health and healing in the context of divine involvement, it should have a strong theological foundation. As we have seen in the introduction about the meaning of health and healing that envisage the wellbeing of a whole person can be taken as an act of restoring the broken relationship of human being with their Creator God, Yahweh. God created man and woman in their absolute nature contains the Imago Dei (Image of God or in its original meaning the essence of God). Because of the sin of disobedience to God's instruction about the fruit in the forbidden tree at the Garden of Eden, the Imago Dei in the human being become distorted and fallen short of God's glory. This distortion caused damage to the whole person that includes body, mind and soul. However, the triune God, because of his grace and love, he initiated the act of restoration of the broken relationship happened with his created humanity through the his salvation plan, so that, the distorted nature of human being can be made well with his or her wholeness; when a person experiencing this salvific act of the triune God in his or her life, they can experience health and healing in every realm as a whole person. The supernatural event took place at the Valley full of dry bones, mentioned in the prophetic book of prophet Ezekiel 37: 1-14 not only focuses on the eschatological wholeness of humanity, but also illustrates the healing power of the Spirit of God brings in our lives in the situation of sickness and suffering. God is not just able to heal us; he is willing to heal us. This isn't something God has yet to decide, he has already done it when Jesus bore our sins and our sicknesses and carried our pain at the Cross (1 Pet. 2:24; Isa. 53:4-5). Healing in the Kingdom lays a foundation from God's word on his will to heal the whole person in spirit, mind and body.

Jesus Christ proclaims that, as the Son of God, he came to this world to give life, the life in its fullness (John 10:10). Therefore, the

theology of health and healing would be nothing but the restoring act
of the triune God, which can be shared with everyone (Romans 14:17),
especially with the community enduring pain and suffering because of
various distorted reasons. As we are involving in the healing ministry of
our Lord and Saviour Jesus Christ, we strive hard to impart the whole
of Christ's redemptive love to the whole of a person's being. Our Lord's
work of salvation was to free humanity from the total effect of sin, evil
and ignorance. When Jesus healed the blind man at Jericho, He said,
"Receive your sight, your faith has saved you'/ made you whole' (Lk.
18:42). This was reflected in the Nazareth manifesto of Jesus through
the words of prophet Isaiah:

> *"The Spirit of the Lord is upon me, because He has anointed me to preach
> good news to the poor, He sent me to proclaim release to the captive and
> recovery of sight to the blind, to set at liberty those who are oppressed, to
> proclaim the acceptable year of the Lord."*(Luke 4:18 – 19)

Messianic implications in health and healing

Health and healing is an essential part of the Kingdom of God, which
includes its messianic implications. Messiah means the 'anointed one.'
Jesus proclaims through his Mission manifesto in his native town
Nazareth that …He has been anointed by the Spirit of the Lord to preach
the good news to the poor…to release to the captive ….recovery of sight
to the blind….set at liberty those are oppressed…and to announce the
year of the Lord's favour. Is it not something noteworthy to mention?
When Jesus talked to the Samaritan woman and set her free from her
distorted life, and restored her back to the wonderful relationship of
God the Father to drink the 'living water', The woman said to Jesus,
"I know that Messiah is coming" (who is called Christ), (John 4:25); at
once, she ran to her village and proclaimed "Come and see a man who
told me everything I have ever done! *He cannot be the Messiah,can he?"*
(John 4:29).

It would be appropriate to note here about Jesus' answer to the
doubtful question about Messiah, raised by John the Baptist, asked
through his disciples- *"John's two disciples found Jesus and said to him,*

"John the Baptist sent us to ask, 'Are you the Messiah we've been expecting, or should we keep looking for someone else? At that very time Jesus cured many who had diseases, sicknesses and evil spirits, and gave sight to many who were blind. So he replied to the messengers, "Go back and report to John what you have seen and heard: The blind receive sight, the lame walk, those who have leprosy are cleansed, the deaf hear, the dead are raised, and the good news is proclaimed to the poor. Blessed is anyone who does not stumble on account of me" (Luke 7:20–23). Through these passages, we clearly understood that the health and healing is absolutely has the Messianic implications.

Inclusive hospitality of God's kingdom

Health and healing cannot be envisaged by leaving out the thought on the message of the Kingdom of God. If we try to sum up the Mission and Message of Jesus during the time of his earthly ministry, in to one essential phrase that would certainly be the 'Kingdom of God.' As we all know from the four canonical gospel literatures that the Kingdom of God is not a geo-political entity; unfortunately this was wrongly understood by many, including the disciples who were with Jesus, in spite of the vivid teachings of Jesus at many occasions that the Kingdom of God would absolutely be the experiential Kingdom by God's children. Jesus went on to demonstrate the inclusiveness of the healing ministry by preaching, teaching, casting out demons and healing the sick (Lk. 4: 31-41). Such a comprehensive ministry can be viewed as the **"Inclusive Hospitality of God's Kingdom."** Gospel writer Matthew was able to envisage in Jesus' earthly ministry - "That evening they brought to him (Jesus) many that were possessed with demons; and he cast out the spirits with a word and healed all who were sick. This was to fulfill what was spoken by the prophet Isaiah, 'He took our infirmities and bore our diseases'" (Mt. 8:16 & 17).

Therefore, this still can be viewed as the inclusive nature of the Kingdom of God. Because, when Jesus was preaching about the nature of the Kingdom of God, he emphatically stated that the Kingdom of God cannot be an established political kingdom, rather it can be the empirically experienced Kingdom – the Kingdom values can be experienced by all/everyone. No one is excluded for this nature of inclusive Hospitality. Every kind of people with physical, spiritual, mental needs being brought to Jesus. Jesus welcomed them without any reluctance. Thus, Jesus exhibited hospitality of inclusiveness as a part of the Kingdom of God.

Healing the sick and casting out of demons were the clear outward demonstrations of the Kingdom of God, manifested to the humanity by our Lord Jesus Christ. Jesus said, *If I cast out demons by the Spirit of God, surely the **Kingdom** of God has come **upon you**" (Matt. 12:28). "Then Jesus went about all the cities and villages, teaching in their synagogues, preaching the gospel of the Kingdom, and healing every sickness and every disease among the people" (Matt. 9:35). After Jesus resurrected the apostles reaffirm the message of the Kingdom of God, by saying "You know of Jesus of Nazareth, how God anointed Him with the Holy Spirit and with power, and how He went about doing good and healing all who were oppressed by the devil, for God was with Him" (Acts 10:38).*

Jesus teaches that the Kingdom of God would always welcome everyone who believes that they are part of this experiential Kingdom. Also, the Kingdom of God essentially ensures the wellbeing and harmony of all created by God (Matthew 9:35 & Isaiah 11:1-10). The Greek word for the Kingdom of God is *Basilea,* which means "the reign of God' or the "Lordship of God." God reign over all the earth, hence, he takes care of the wellbeing of his children who are created by him; he gives his grace and shows his mercy to everyone with his inclusive generosity. Therefore, the theology of health and healing would be nothing but the inclusive hospitality of the Kingdom of the triune God, who envisages and ensures the abundant life of his children.

The theology of healing articulated by the Christian Medical College, Vellore for the past 118 years in its Hospital service and 100 years in its Medical education must be having this foundation of inclusive hospitality when the founder Dr. Ida Sophia Scudder stated that, she is not interested on building a medical school/college, but on building the kingdom of God. Indeed, Christ obligated his body, i.e. his church has to be actively involved in healing ministry. Though his body is wounded and weary, since the day of Pentecost, Christ empowers his body with his life and power to manifest his healing to the wounded and weary.

Lord Jesus Christ, the Master Healer has commissioned his Church to act in enhancing his abundance of life which he promised in Jn. 10:10 under his authority. Therefore, Christian Medical College, Vellore as a part of Christ's body would still continue this ministry of healing as the inclusive hospitality, because our Lord gave a Vision and a Mission through his servant Dr. Ida Sophia Scudder, and it's a mandate for all of us who are part of this vision to faithfully carryout the legacy of the inclusiveness of the Kingdom of God through the great resource of healthcare.

Endnotes

[1] https://en.wikipedia.org/wiki/Health.

[2] Eng Hoe, Lim, "The Gospel of the Kingdom – Revealing the Heart of God", 2nd Edition, Published in India in April 2012, 21.

PART-7
Conversation

Conversation

The Colloquium was a conversation with multiple voices, multiple stories and multiple perspectives. It was just the 'beginning of a beginning'. The common desire was to continue the conversation but 'how, when and where' is left unanswered. The multiple voices were to locate 'health and healing' in context, taking into consideration the paradigm of the presence of God in health and healing process. The unequivocal voice was to follow the model of Jesus of Nazareth- ministry of teaching-preaching- healing through his birth, death and resurrection. One significant focal point that emerged was to revisit the patient care in doing theology of health & healing. The testimonies of those who went through the painful process of pain and suffering but healed were the climax of the whole Colloquium. It is the spirit of hospitality that needs to be addressed, interpreted and practiced. Does a patient feel welcome and cared for when they enter CMC? The striking part of testimony was **'Cured-not healed' vis a vis 'Not cured -but healed'.**

The keynote address tried to bring and locate in a wider but meaningful perspective of 'Waiting on God'. The categories of stewards of the past, stewards of the present and trustees of the future are paramount in the life of an Institution. The future conversation should be as trustees of the future. But the challenge is the 'mission drift' which must be taken into consideration in any institution. The premier institutions do deviate from their founding vision and mission.

The parochial identities in medical mission - Baptist mission, Lutheran mission, Orthodox mission and not least only to serve in the sponsored institution are obsolete. What is the healthcare of Indian church? What should be our medical mission? What is the paradigm of medical mission? It has been referred that the struggle of admission issue continues in the Supreme Court. We have been knocking the door of the court but time has come to take a call. How many years more we can go on doing this and not address the issue. There ought to be a forum to discuss the issue as a priority by the stakeholders. It was beautifully put as the 'conspiracy of silence'. The management should bring the multiple stake holders of CMC together, talk together, think together and plan together. Any future Colloquium must have equal representation from different constituencies of the larger family of CMC for a meaningful conversation that was the missing point of the Colloquium 2018.

Highlights of Conversation

Dr. Ravi Tiwari: The context of the colloquium is the CMC Centenary celebration. I am not talking to the theological community. We think that the theological community has the right to do theology. Here I see the development of a counter theology taking place. That is a welcome sign. It is developed by those who are in the context. Therefore, the term 'hospitality' which was used by Bishop D.K. Sahu and others may be repulsive to the theological thinkers but here something new and groundbreaking is attempted by the community in Colloquium. What should be the paradigm of the theology of health and healing?

Dr. John Oommen: We have come with a lot of expectations to this colloquium. For some, it is a side issue. For us in the mission network in central India it is a life and death issue. If we do not pursue this conversation, I don't think we have a reason for existence, and I don't see a future for Christian Healthcare in central India. In South, you have got a momentum of your own because of numbers.

I am very grateful to the various talks and I like Bishop D.K. Sahu's statement, "it is a 'beginning of beginning". The purpose is a living conversation that goes on. One part of our thinking has been about CMC, the relevance of this in the centenary year today being Ida Scudder's birthday and the relevance of the history. A concentration of goodness in one place which one rarely sees and yet that is also our single biggest weakness or danger.

I think listening the testimony of Usha, Edward and Antony was what we needed. We needed to ground conversation to locate it in the realities of the people and not in an abstract philosophy. It was very moving for all of us but it also helps us to focus the conversation. We need the humility of the willingness to accept that there is much scope for improvement. I am looking for meaning and understanding in what we do. I was searching for understanding across the mission hospital network and I found the cupboard is bare, we are settling for very simplistic, three points to salvation kind of approaches because there is no depth of thinking in the Christian Healthcare Network.

The church in India as a Christian community is in a crisis in the last six months. We have been in the news for all the wrong reasons. You can blame the media in part but the primary blame is with us. We are two to three percent of this country, the perception of the remaining 97 percent about us has degraded heavily in the last few months and we are to blame. This is not to blame anybody else.

"Should healthcare be in the church? Should church be in healthcare?" I think both of us have lost because of the separation between church and health care. To make our hospitals more efficient, we tried to ban the bishops. We tried to draw lines between us. The other way around as well. Both have lost. For the church to stay rooted in the pain of the people health care and involvement in the pain of health is actually a huge opportunity. And for hospitals that refuse to have this conversation going constantly returning to the conversation, we are becoming sterile and just the pursuit of numbers, the pursuit of sustainability has become our mission.

We have exchanged Paul for Jesus. I find that we don't want Jesus, we want Paul. We want Paul as a role charismatic charismatic model.

We do not want Jesus crucified at 33, I'm over 23 years post expiry date. I'm seeing this across the mission circles that Jesus is not our role model anymore. We are extremely Paul centered. Similarly, we have exchanged the church for the Kingdom of God.

Can we move towards the defining of a center and focus less on the boundaries? So much of our mission work, our church work is around defining who's in and who's out, who's going to heaven and who's not going to heaven. We are not the Visa office. Can we say that Jesus Christ is the center and let the boundaries be blurred, undefined. That's why the hospital chapel in CMC is so beautiful where people would come and worship in the way they understood best, somebody would prostrate themselves in the middle of the chapel. Somebody would light candles allowing that expression to be different because there is no one expression but there is one center. Can we be more center focused? Eucharistic centre, rather than defining the boundaries of who's in and who's out.

My plea is can we work towards an Indian Christian theology of health, healing, wholeness, that is rooted in the reality of our people. Our patients live in one world and we live in another world. Counseling - so much of what is taught as counseling is actually foreign to our ground unless we correct it and re-align it to our people.

Dr. MJ Paul: I think Rev. Valson Thampu is the one who really challenged me, not to be too complacent and face the challenges of an institution.

There is a paradigm change in the way we talk to people with cancer. I am very upset when I hear stories of doctors telling their patients that they have six months or three months to live. I would say that is complete nonsense. I do not know if I am going to live tomorrow even if I do not have the disease. So, who am I to say whether you have three or six months? So, we must shift the focus on life now and think how healing comes in. The patients who come in with a survivor stories are amazing. They say, "thank God for my cancer because it changed my whole attitude to life. I was just a normal guy thinking I couldn't do anything but once I had the cancer and got healing through the cancer, it opened up my eyes to the possibilities that I could do myself." So, this transformative aspect of disease, like pain, is something that we need to stress upon. Many of us have gone through that in our own lives and perhaps that is a focus that we need to teach the medical profession as well.

Dr. Edison Samraj: I was wondering whether CMC Vellore can initiate a process where it can take music as a model for healing. Music can be a stimulating factor in enhancing and making healing faster. There was a girl from Agartala who was traveling by flight from Calcutta to Bangalore. She was head neck down paralyzed. She was a national gold medalist in swimming, but she dived into shallow waters and broke her neck, where she was admitted in the hospital there in Bangalore and NIMHANS could not treat her. I had one of my friends, neurosurgeons in Bangalore and he tried for a month, could not succeed. So, I took a small iPod filled with classical western music and gave it to her to listen for 10 days. I just got a message this morning from the girl. She is now discharged. She is able to lift her hand.

I suggest integrating alternative therapies which are scientifically validated into holistic healing. CMC Vellore should consider seeing what is best within our own cultural milieu and absorb that into our methods of healing as well. I am part of the Global Innovation Partnership Club in India and so many people who are working towards industrial innovation follow this techniques. I think that same platform should be even in the medical field so that that platform exists on a platform like this.

Dr. Stanley Macaden: Hospitals should have a very strong palliative care department because sixty percent of all deaths need palliative care. After birth the very definite thing is death. So, I think it's very important that this facility should be looked at seriously and it is not high tech. It is the low cost and high touch and so it's easy for any mission hospital to do it and in places like Vellore and all should be at the forefront of this in the country.

Dr. BJ Prashantham: The presentations and conversations so far, I find them much thought provoking inviting everybody to think of fresh. I am reminded at this point of a press conference in which a psychologist by the name is Dr. Seligman who championed the cause of looking at the potentialities of people. He said that after 100 hundred years of modern psychology, it was pathology that has been emphasized but his studies show that people all over the world face their challenges by using a God given potentialities. So, he was bringing a corrective balance to this without ignoring problems and pathology. He said, "look at the potentialities, just like in mental health now they are saying mental illness or mental well-being the positive side." There was a press conference in which Dr. Seligman was asked 'can you say in one word what has been the state of psychology in hundred years or after 100 years. If you ask me to say in one word it is "good". They were not satisfied. So, they persisted and said, "all right use two words and say what has happened after 100 years and how do you evaluate?" He said, "not good". They were disappointed with that answer and they said to him, "last time now three words." He said only three words, he said "not good enough".

I am seeing some such struggle going on here which is normal, natural, good and for growth. Sometimes, some of the developments in the secular world also can stimulate some good thinking for anyone in the Christian institutions also. One such is a book I came across recently from a Harvard University professor called Marshall Goldsmith. He wrote this book for very senior leaders like general managers, managing directors, Chairman Director, sub boards, so they consider him as a guru of some kind of executive coaching, Marshall Goldsmith and the title of his book is 'What got you here will not get you there'. So, there is a need for continuous thinking and conversation.

Patients are not just recipients of some all-knowing wisdom of any set of health providers. But they are equal partners. More than never before with the kind of technology that the present generation has, it reduces humans to some objects. They are subjects of the dialogue. It calls for a reorientation in the model of healthcare or care giving. There is a huge merit on what is just said, and this has to be pondered and better understood.

Dr. Atul Aghamkar: I'm not a medical professional but urban missiologist, an urban trainer. I thought it to be really good for me to know what is happening here. And let me tell you, I was deeply touched by what I heard here. I'm a layperson amongst you probably and therefore my reflections would be nonmedical. Several of you have put your hearts and I think the passion and the fire that has just come out of the room and is just contagious. I can see the passion there and I think I'm very deeply touched by some of those passionate, words and presentations that have been made here.. One of the major questions, Dr Oommen has raised was, "why are we needed in India when we have so much happening in medical world today with so many new, medical facilities and emerging specializations. Why are we needed there?" And I believe that there is a resounding 'yes' for the Christian medical services in India. We must not forget the fact that we are unique. We are called to serve and the services that CMC has given to the world in India are extraordinary. Taking that further is not a challenge, but also a privilege to make a difference as Christians who are called to make a difference in this world.

One of the uniqueness in CMC is, you do it because you love your God. You're a partner with God. God has already called us to be involved in healing and wholeness. There is much to be done in India. There are so much medical services that are needed, and you probably have something unique to offer. CMC has been considered as one of the leading medical institutions. You are path breakers. People are looking up to you, but you have the potential. You have the rich experience and you have expertise that probably not very many in India have. The struggles are immense, the challenges numerous, and yet the opportunities are tremendous.

Dr. Sushil John: Johnny talked about how CMC was able to inform global understanding of a healing ministry and about the Tubingen meetings. I think he said you wish or you hope that CMC should do more to be involved in shaping the understanding at the national level and global level of the theology of health and healing. So, my question is, do we have any practical ideas of how we do that? And he alluded to that saying that the book is side product. So that is something for us to think about.

We keep on thinking of health from a disease perspective, but there is disease in our relationships with each other, there's disease in our relationship with our environment and nature and that is also something we need to think about. Anthony's story and some of the other comments that I heard from others reminded me and brought home to me the fact that we as healthcare providers can actually contribute to making it worse, create disease and brokenness. And so that is something that we need to think about.

Dr. Vijay Aruldas: There is a larger issue when we try to understand the theology of health and healing in a different context. The issue of social acceptance has not entered our understanding and our discussions here because I think as medicos, we tend to look at the individual interaction and build our theology of health and healing out of that. Whereas if you look at society's acceptance, taking on from where Stanley Macaden mentioned, I have always felt that, perhaps the reason why Jesus called the woman back was not to heal her but to heal others because everyone would have known she was not well and she could not go around proving that she had been healed. This was not only an affirmation that she was healed. It was an affirmation of her faith and so she could go, it was really an affirmation in many different ways and an acceptance that it was okay for a person who was bleeding to touch him and so therefore it was a stigma being removed.

We are the signposts to God and not the destination for healthcare. And I think for CMC as we celebrate the fact that we are high up on the rankings, we need to remember that it is a goalpost and a sign post to health, not a goalpost for healthcare, so to speak. What we need to do, is the role of institutions because Christian institutions are that expression and when we individualize it, it becomes what we individually experience. I will be happy if somewhere down the line we can also understand how institutions discover, rediscover, and develop their understanding of the theology on health and healing. And not just what it means as an individual, otherwise we will always be struggling.

Rev. Robin Phipon: One person from West Bengal came to my office some years ago and told me that his brother died after a heart operation in this institution many years ago and he was there. When the body was being released from the present silver gate area, his brother's treating doctor also had come there. He stood by while they were doing all the procedure to receive the dead body. And he suddenly noticed that the doctor was holding hand like this and shedding tears. He did not do anything. Then I realized how much the doctor loved my brother. Life and death are in God's hands. So even though I lost my only brother after treatment, I love the respect and hope for the care, love and treatment. I told other friends from my place and also some of them asked me to help them to come here. Another person said that CMC is not like before; he was talking how technology between doctor and the patients are helping to nominal thing and how the personal touch is losing.

Rev. Joseph Devaraj: This conversation should be ongoing. One possibility could be to form a core group to work on the theology time and again with the problems and the issues and the context in which we are in. Theology is always a movement; it is not static. We can have online discussions back and forth. We can send our ideas online and discuss since it is not practical to come together often physically.

Dr. K.S. Jacob: We often see that people have diseases and no illness and suffering; people have illness and suffering, but no diseases. People are cured of their diseases but continue to suffer and are not healed; people are healed but not actually are cured of their diseases. I have been studying the role of black magic in mental illness for the past thirty years. We have been asking people "Tell us your belief about your diseases". What we found is that if you have an acute condition and you do well, then people say that it is the problem of the body. Even nowadays, if you cannot get down with fever, they will tell you "what sort of doctor are you? Give me an injection and get it down". They know that fever is not black magic. But when you have chronic conditions which donor respond to medications, then people are struggling to cope with this reality. Maybe it is a belief – it is God's will, God's plan, karma, black magic, diseases of brain, disease of the body. What we have found is that people hold multiple beliefs especially when things are not going too well particularly in the long run. So, the challenge for us is when we cannot cure, how do we heal? As a clinician I spent lot of time with people who do not respond with the treatment. There are lots of conditions like spinal cord injury, malignancy which cannot be cured, even diabetes which cannot be cured and only controlled.

We are not grappling with the complex issues that our patients face. There are various dichotomies which we need to look at. Disease verses distress and illness, Cure which we want and healing, their subjective emotions with our search for objective science and clinical phenomena. Our looking at the mind body dualism, the differences and distances between patient and physician perspectives, the contrastic models we use, we look for naturalistic explanations and patients are searching for personalistic meanings. The distinctive foci: their focus on suffering, our focus on science, tests and treatment. Dissimilarity of the logic: for us the universal trumps the local, we are looking for single logical explanations, while our patients hold multiple and contradictory beliefs and coping strategies. The dissimilar paradigms: disease versus their disability approaches. The dispirit cultures: our paternalistic cultures - we know the solution to their problem.

The question is how we get them to re-engage with life despite the problems we face. I sometimes feel that maybe we come down from abstract to some practical points. Otherwise we are saying lot of things which from a practitioner point of view we need to translate these abstract questions when we are trying to heal the people whom we cannot cure. We live in different realities. Our worlds - patient's world and the world that we inhabit are actually incommensurable, I feel that we are a part perception of their problem, If we offer simple and single approaches as many have been suggesting, I feel we will get it wrong. We need to look at patient centered care. What is healing for us may not be necessarily healing for our patients. I really feel that we are approaching this very simplistically by talking about our mental health and our healing. We really have to step back and ask ourselves whether there are patients going through such complex life situations, with very difficult choices they have to make and with very difficult futures. We should pause and ask them. Maybe they are in a better position to find meaning, maybe they are in a better position to find their own solutions.

Dr. Jayakumar Christian: In every suffering, every situation of poverty and marginalization, there is a natural tendency for people to ascribe meaning. It is embedded in their worldview. And what you are pointing is in the direction for a need for us to address that worldview with the sense that my worldview is in no way superlative to theirs. At some point it is important for us to have that meaningful conversation. I am hoping that this would be the competence of every health professional, not just simply do the spitting on the ground, taking clay, applying it on the eye and sending them to the pool of Siloam for wash. There is a meaning that needs to be challenged. Very often it is that meaning that tends to hold back people from being proactive.

Every anonymous patient is the opportunity to transform. 1.3 billion people of our nation is the opportunity you need to work at. As kingdom people Ida scudder says, 'do not err on the side of being small'. We are on the business of establishing the kingdom. As the Tamil song says, 'my dream is that I would see the heaven filled with Indians'. I am hoping that will be our dream too. Remember that passion is always contagious, professionalism is rarely contagious. If you and I are in the business of transforming lives, we need to invest life. This is our opportunity. As Dr. Ravi Tiwari said, this is the time; the practioners construct theology not the theologians and get the hands dirty. We have too many insulated theologies, too clean for human consumption. We need theology from practioners who live in the midst of suffering like all of you.

Rev. Dr. Valson Thampu: I had been suffering from cervical spondylosis from 1981. That had aggravated in 1989, I was admitted here in Neuro 2 and then I was discharged. I went back to Delhi. But in 1992 I was paralyzed. My head wouldn't move, I completely lost my left hand. I was on continuous traction for three months, 24/7. Then I was taken to the UK because I was advised a surgery. My Neuro Surgeon in the UK told me that he had never done it three level spine surgeries. He wasn't sure about doing it and he told me that I had only a maximum of 10 years left. In five years' time I would lose both my hands. That was his words of encouragement. And he also told me that I had cold compression that I should never travel at all.

I was brought back; I was in bed. And I remember one night something breaking within me and I started crying and tears would not stop. After long hours of lonely, struggle with it, a kind of unearthly peace descended on me, it continued for few more days. Then one day it occurred to me to try and lift my head and I could. From there I made a remarkable recovery. It took me another six months to get my left hand back. As a patient, it struck me like a bolt when the doctor said you will never walk again. With what certainty? With what assurance? On what basis? On what evidence? I experienced a lot of a benign callousness. Nobody was cruel to me, nobody wanted to hurt me, nobody wanted to discourage me, but that is the voice of a profession speaking.

I believe every member of the medical team must remember that faith is the freedom to see the other side of the question. The medical profession works somewhat entirely through stereotypes like, " If this is a symptom, this is a consequence. If this is a finding, this is the medicine. You must eat this medicine; you must eat that medicine. Otherwise you're finished". There is another side to all these issues which we are not daring to look at. I was admitted to CMC last year and for eight days I was here. I had reached a level of complete saturation with medicine which was affecting my concentration. I decided to do hard manual labor. Today I'm a proud farmer from 10:30 am till 12 noon; I work in my land. I do the hardest physical. Today I do not take a single tablet, not one. And I feel so much better. My memory has improved. My balance has improved to quality of life which cannot be described. Now is there any room in the present paradigm and practice of medicine to accommodate this kind of possibility? We are a Christian institution, where is the faith element?

A Centenary Thanksgiving Sermon

Nicholas John Wood[1]

Text: Luke 1:46-55, Luke 22:24-27

Theme: "I am among you as one who serves" (Luke 22:27)

The motto of the Christian Medical College in Vellore is "not to be ministered unto but to minister", or as more recent translations put it, "not to be served but to serve" (Mark 10:45). This mark of Christian service has been a hallmark of this now great institution from its humble beginnings a century ago. It was characteristic of its Founder, Dr Ida Scudder, and from what I have heard, and from what I have seen in my brief stay here, it remains typical of its ministry to the present day – not to be served, but to serve.

But perhaps because it is so typical and so familiar, we may be in danger of overlooking its very radical implications – for a life of service, whether in the time of Jesus, or in today's world.. In the time of Jesus to be a servant all too often meant to be a slave. One of the most frequent New Testament terms (*doulos*) is often translated as 'servant' when it might better be translated as 'slave'. As Jesus points out in one of his all too frequent conversations with his disciples on this topic, to be a servant or slave is to be at the beck and call of others – "for who is the greater," asks Jesus, " the one who sits at table of the one who waits upon him?" (Luke 22:27). The self-evident answer, at least for the disciples, was clearly that the greater person was the one sitting at the table. Clearly such a one is in the position of power and authority. The person at the head of the table has the respect of all – whether fellow-guests, or those who wait upon them.

The servant, by contrast, is hardly noticed. In fact, it is the characteristic of a good servant to be unobtrusive, not to draw attention to themselves; not to be the centre of attention. The good servant hovers around the edges, waiting patiently to attend to the needs of 'the great and the good'. The servant is at the mercy of others and at the mercy of events – in other words they are not in control. The characteristic of those in power is that they are at the centre of things – they make the decisions; they are in control. But to be a servant is to be out of control, to cede power and authority to others, to wait upon them for their decisions.

But Jesus said, "I am among you as one who serves."

A servant ministry was at the heart of Jesus' identity, which raises the question, where did this come from? One of the most frequently given answers is to see the roots of Jesus' servant ministry in the Old Testament, especially in the writings of the Prophets, and in particular in the so-called 'servant-songs' of the Prophet Isaiah. Especially in the central section of Isaiah's work, chapters 40-55, we see the emergence of a key figure in the outworking of God's purpose in salvation – and the key description of that person is that of a servant:

But you, Israel, my servant,

Jacob, whom I have chosen,

the offspring of Abraham, my friend;

[9] you whom I took from the ends of the earth,

and called from its farthest corners,

saying to you, 'You are my servant,

I have chosen you and not cast you off';

Isaiah 41:8-9 (NRSV)

Repeatedly in these chapters God identifies a servant, a chosen one, literally a 'Messiah', who will fulfil God's purposes for the redemption of the world:

> Here is my servant, whom I uphold,
> my chosen, in whom my soul delights;
> I have put my spirit upon him;
> he will bring forth justice to the nations.
> ² He will not cry or lift up his voice,
> or make it heard in the street;
> ³ a bruised reed he will not break,
> and a dimly burning wick he will not quench;
> he will faithfully bring forth justice.
> ⁴ He will not grow faint or be crushed
> until he has established justice in the earth;
> and the coastlands wait for his teaching.
>
> Isaiah 42:1-4

As the beautiful poetry of the Servant Songs unfolds in these key chapters of the prophet's work, it becomes ever clearer that the role of God's servant is a demanding role. A constant refrain during these chapters is "Be not afraid", and you can be very sure that if this is God's repeated message to the servant, then there must have been much to be afraid of, at least in human terms!

It is a demanding task because of its scope. The range of God's salvation is nothing short of global in its vision:

> 'It is too light a thing that you should be my servant
> to raise up the tribes of Jacob
> and to restore the survivors of Israel;
> I will give you as a light to the nations,
> that my salvation may reach to the end of the earth.'
>
> Isaiah 49.6

No wonder this is a daunting task! The servant is called to be God's instrument of salvation which reaches to the very ends of the earth. Just like Dr Ida Scudder, when we are caught up in the purposes of God, we must appreciate that, although we are always people of our own time and place, we are, nevertheless, part of a much greater story which is unfolding in all times and in all places. The great story of God's purposes in creation and redemption for the whole earth and all its peoples; in fact, God's purpose is nothing less than the redemption of the universe. This is cosmic!

But then we learn something else about the daunting nature of the servant task – and that is its cost. To be a servant is always a demanding role; it demands much of us in terms of time, and energy, and skill. But more than this, to be God's servant requires that we give nothing less than ourselves. Most scholars believe that at the heart of Jesus vision for his servant ministry is the poignant song we find in Isaiah chapters 52-3, which is headed in my Bible 'The Suffering Servant'.

See, my servant shall prosper;

he shall be exalted and lifted up,

and shall be very high.

14 Just as there were many who were astonished at him

—so marred was his appearance, beyond human semblance,

and his form beyond that of mortals—

15 so he shall startle many nations;

kings shall shut their mouths because of him;

for that which had not been told them they shall see,

and that which they had not heard they shall contemplate.

53 Who has believed what we have heard?

And to whom has the arm of the LORD BEEN REVEALED?

2 For he grew up before him like a young plant,

and like a root out of dry ground;

he had no form or majesty that we should look at him,

nothing in his appearance that we should desire him.

3 He was despised and rejected by others;

a man of suffering and acquainted with infirmity;

and as one from whom others hide their faces

he was despised, and we held him of no account.

4 Surely, he has borne our infirmities

and carried our diseases;

yet we accounted him stricken,

struck down by God, and afflicted.

(Isaiah 52:13-53:4)

I am sure that Jesus learnt all this and more through his knowledge of Isaiah and indeed so much else from the Hebrew Scriptures. But I am also convinced that he also learned this, and what it really meant, from his earliest days in the family home as he watched his mother Mary. As she cradled him from the manger in Bethlehem; as she nurtured him through his growing years in Nazareth; as she accompanied him on his final journey to Jerusalem, when with those other faithful women she stood at the foot of the cross, and watched his final act of sacrificial service; though all this and much more, Jesus learnt the meaning of love and sacrifice through Mary.

Through these days of Advent, we relive the events of the nativity of Jesus, and earlier we listened again to Luke's retelling of the infancy narratives of Jesus and his cousin John the Baptist. The Magnificat, that great song of praise which features so strongly in our worship, is attributed by Luke to Mary in her encounter with John's mother Elizabeth. Listen again to that familiar opening line:

'My soul magnifies the Lord,

47 and my spirit rejoices in God my Saviour,

48 for he has looked with favour on the lowliness of his servant.

(Luke 1:47-8)

Who is Mary, and how does she understand herself? She is a humble servant. This is how she had responded to the message of Gabriel, God's messenger, who tells her of the key role for which God has chosen her: 'Here am I, the servant of the Lord; let it be with me according to your word.' (Luke 1:38) Mary had replied. And in her wonderful song, that great outpouring of praise to the Saviour God, Mary celebrates the great reversal of fortunes which the coming of God's Kingdom must entail:

> 52 He has brought down the powerful from their thrones, and lifted up the lowly;
>
> 53 he has filled the hungry with good things, and sent the rich away empty.
>
> 54 He has helped his servant Israel, in remembrance of his mercy,
>
> (Luke 1:52-54)

God's great kingdom comes through the mission of God's servant Israel, through the obedience of God's humble handmaiden Mary, and above all through the mission of Jesus, who says to us again this Advent: "I am among you as one who serves."

But as I mentioned at the start, this is a hard lesson for us to learn. It was not easy for Jesus' first followers to understand. The motto here at CMC Vellore comes from an episode in Mark's Gospel where James and John are bidding for power and glory. They want to be those who sit at Christ's left and right hand when he comes to power; the place of prestige and honour. Not surprisingly the rest of the disciples are upset, but Jesus rebukes them and says: "whoever wishes to be first among you must be slave of all. For the Son of Man came not to be served but to serve, and to give his life a ransom for many." (Mark 10:44-45)

But the argument is a recurring one amongst Jesus' followers. Earlier in the previous chapter of Mark Jesus had already taken a small child and set it before them as an example – "whoever wants to be first must be last and a servant to all" (Mark 9:35). Even then the lesson had not been learnt, and according to Luke, at the Last Supper itself they were still arguing about the same things. It is this argument which elicits from Jesus the words of our text today: "I am among you as one who serves".

According to John's Gospel it is at this same final meal that Jesus washes their feet as a servant in a dramatic attempt to drive the lesson home.

But it is only as Jesus suffers and dies upon the cross that the full extent of his servanthood is revealed. Now it becomes clear just how radical Jesus' demand has been. In the face of all worldly authorities, in the face of the power struggles in all communities and groups, Jesus offers himself in humble service, a life and death of sacrificial commitment, for his friends and enemies alike. If we at CMC are serious about our motto, as we celebrate a centenary of servant ministry in this place, we must be clear that this is what our service of Christ entails. Such demanding service can only be sustained as we come again to the Table of the Lord, to receive his grace and mercy. Here Jesus again takes the role of the servant; here at this table he puts himself once again at our disposal. Here in bread and wine he gives himself again to us – that we may give ourselves in service to Christ and to the world he came to save.

As always, he is among us as one who serves. Amen.

Endnotes

[1] The Sermon was preached on 9th December 2018 in Ida Scudder Auditorium.

Contributors

Rev. Dr. Nicholas John Wood is the Dean, Fellow in Religion and Culture and Director of the Oxford Centre for Christianity and Culture at Regent's Park College, Oxford. He is also a minister in the Baptist Union of Great Britain, member of the Faculty of Theology and Religion, University of Oxford, Vice-Moderator of the Baptist World Alliance Commission on Inter-Faith Relations.

Dr. Joseph George is Professor in the Department of Christian Ministry with specialization in Pastoral Counseling, a pastoral counselor in Bangalore and is the Dean of Doctoral Studies at United Theological College, Bangalore.

Bishop Dr. D.K.Sahu was the bishop of the Church of North India in the Diocese of Eastern Himalaya, Vice-Principal of Serampore College, General Secretary of the National Council of Churches in India and at present he is the Dean of the Faculty of Theology, SHUATS, Allahabad.

Rev. Dr. Samuel Richmond Saxena is the University Chaplain & the Head, Department of Advanced Theological Studies, Faculty of Theology, SHUATS, Allahabad. He is also an associate member of the International Society of Science and Religion, associated with Theological Commission of World Evangelical Alliance.

Rev. Dr. Ravi Tiwari was the Registrar of Senate of Serampore, Vice-Principal of Serampore College, Principal of John Robert Theological Seminary, Shillong and Professor of Religion & Philosophy.

Dr. Jayakumar Christian is the former National Director of World Vision India and Partnership Leader for Faith & Development with World Vision International.

Dr. Joshua Kalapati is the Associate Professor and Head, Department of Philosophy, Madras Christian College.

Dr. John Oommen is the Medical Superintendent of the Christian Hospital, Bissamcuttack and Vice-chairman of the Council, CMC Vellore Association.

Dr. Sunil Chandy is the Professor of Cardiology & former Director, CMC, Vellore.

Dr. Selva Titus Chacko is the Professor of Nursing and the former Dean of the College of Nursing, CMC, Vellore.

Dr. Sarah Bhattacharji is the former Professor of the Community Health and the former Head of Low-Cost Effective Care Unit, CMC, Vellore.

Mr. Ruby Nakka is the Director of the 'Hope House', Vellore.

Mrs. Hima JB is an Occupational Therapist, Department of Neonatology, CMC, Vellore.

Dr. B. J. Prashantham is the Professor of Counseling Psychology and Director, Christian Counseling Centre, Vellore

Dr. Stanley C. Macaden is the Honorary Palliative Care Consultant, Bangalore Baptist Hospital and the National Coordinator of the Palliative Care Programme of the Christian Medical Association of India.

Rev. Dr. Richard Howell is Principal of Caleb Institute in Gurugram; Executive Secretary of EFI Council of Churches and member of the International Committee of the Global Christian Forum.

Rev. Dr. John Swinton is the Chair in Divinity and Religious Studies, the School of Divinity, History and Philosophy, University of Aberdeen, Aberdeen.

Dr. M.J.Paul is the Professor of Endocrine Surgery, Christian Medical College, Vellore.

Dr. Edison Samraj is the Director, Health Ministries Department, Southern Asia Division of SDA and serves as the Peace Ambassador for United Nations.

Dr. Reena George is the Professor and Head, Palliative Care Unit, Christian Medical College, Vellore.

Rev. R. Christopher Rajkumar is an ordained minister of the Church of South India and former Executive Secretary for the Mission, Ecumenism and Diakonia in NCCI.

Dr. Anna B Pulimood is the Principal of Christian Medical College and Hospital, Vellore.

Dr. Valson Thampu is the former Principal of St Stephen's College, Delhi.

Dr. Joyce Ponnaiya is the former Director of Christian Medical College & Hospital, Vellore and a Professor of Pathology.

Mr. Hugh Skeil is the manager of the Development office, CMC, Vellore.

Mrs. Usha Jesudasan is a journalist and a writer from Vellore.

Mr. Anthony Samy is a Counsellor and Resource person for HIV, Vellore

Mrs. Reema Samuel is the Tutor of Occupational Therapy, Mental Health Centre, CMC, Vellore.

Mr. Bibhudutta Sahu is engaged in the RAISE North East project on inclusive education as the Project Director and the Managing Trustee (voluntary) of Barefoot Trust.

Rev. Dr. Arul Dhas is an ordained minister of CSI, Senior Chaplain of the CMC, Vellore and teaches New Testament, Pastoral Counseling and Bioethics.

Rev. Deepak Gnana Prakash is an Ordained Minister of the CNI and a Chaplain at the Christian Medical College, Vellore.

Rev. Dr. Finney Alexander is a Chaplain at the Christian Medical College, Vellore.

Mr. Samson Varghese is a Chaplain at the Christian Medical College, Vellore.

Dr. Sunny Philip is a former chaplain at CMC, Vellore and now directs a training program: *Transform4Life.*

Rev. Joseph Devaraj D is a Chaplain at Christian Medical College, Vellore.

Participants of Colloquium on Theology of Health and Healing,
Christian Medical College, Vellore, 8th and 9th December 2018

www.ingramcontent.com/pod-product-compliance
Lightning Source LLC
Chambersburg PA
CBHW031144050726
47495CB00018B/515